As an author, Chris Bradford employs a technique he terms 'method writing'. For his award-winning Young Samurai series, he trained in samurai swordsmanship, karate, ninjutsu and earned his black belt in Zen Kyu Shin Taijutsu.

For his new BODYGUARD series, Chris embarked on an intensive close-protection course to become a qualified professional bodyguard. During his training, he acquired skills in unarmed combat, defensive driving, tactical firearms, threat assessments, surveillance, and even anti-ambush exercises.

His bestselling books are published in over twenty languages and have garnered more than twenty-five children's book award nominations.

Before becoming a full-time author, he was a professional musician (who once performed for HRH Queen Elizabeth II), songwriter and music teacher.

Chris lives in England with his wife and two sons.

Discover more about Chris at *www.chrisbradford.co.uk*

Books by Chris Bradford

The Bodyguard series (in reading order)
HOSTAGE
RANSOM

The Young Samurai series (in reading order)
THE WAY OF THE WARRIOR
THE WAY OF THE SWORD
THE WAY OF THE DRAGON
THE RING OF EARTH
THE RING OF WATER
THE RING OF FIRE
THE RING OF WIND
THE RING OF SKY

Available as ebook
THE WAY OF FIRE

CHRIS
BRADFORD

PUFFIN

Warning: Do not attempt any of the techniques described within the book without the supervision of a qualified martial arts instructor. These can be highly dangerous moves and result in fatal injuries. The author and publisher take no responsibility for any injuries resulting from attempting these techniques.

PUFFIN BOOKS

Published by the Penguin Group
Penguin Books Ltd, 80 Strand, London WC2R ORL, England
Penguin Group (USA) Inc., 375 Hudson Street, New York, New York 10014, USA
Penguin Group (Canada), 90 Eglinton Avenue East, Suite 700, Toronto, Ontario,
Canada M4P 2Y3 (a division of Pearson Penguin Canada Inc.)
Penguin Ireland, 25 St Stephen's Green, Dublin 2, Ireland
(a division of Penguin Books Ltd)
Penguin Group (Australia), 707 Collins Street, Melbourne, Victoria 3008, Australia
(a division of Pearson Australia Group Pty Ltd)
Penguin Books India Pvt Ltd, 11 Community Centre, Panchsheel Park,
New Delhi – 110 017, India
Penguin Group (NZ), 67 Apollo Drive, Rosedale, Auckland 0632, New Zealand
(a division of Pearson New Zealand Ltd)
Penguin Books (South Africa) (Pty) Ltd, Block D, Rosebank Office Park,
181 Jan Smuts Avenue, Parktown North, Gauteng 2193, South Africa

Penguin Books Ltd, Registered Offices: 80 Strand, London WC2R ORL, England

puffinbooks.com

First published 2014
001

Text copyright © Chris Bradford, 2014
Map by Mandy Norman
Yacht diagram by David Atkinson
All rights reserved

The moral right of the author and illustrators has been asserted

Set in 10.5/15.5 pt Sabon by Palimpsest Book Production Limited, Falkirk, Stirlingshire
Printed and bound in Great Britain by Clays Ltd, St Ives plc

British Library Cataloguing in Publication Data
A CIP catalogue record for this book is available from the British Library

ISBN: 978-0-141-34006-7

www.greenpenguin.co.uk

MIX
Paper from
responsible sources
FSC
www.fsc.org   FSC™ C018179

Penguin Books is committed to a sustainable
future for our business, our readers and our planet.
This book is made from Forest Stewardship
Council™ certified paper.

For my godparents, Ann and Andrew,
Thanks for looking out for me all my life

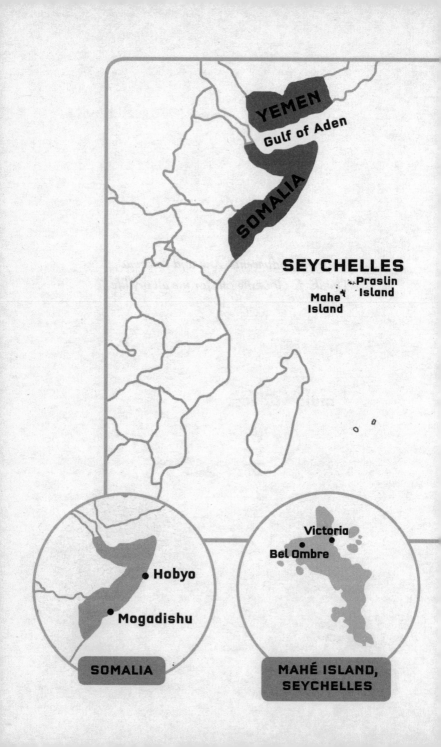

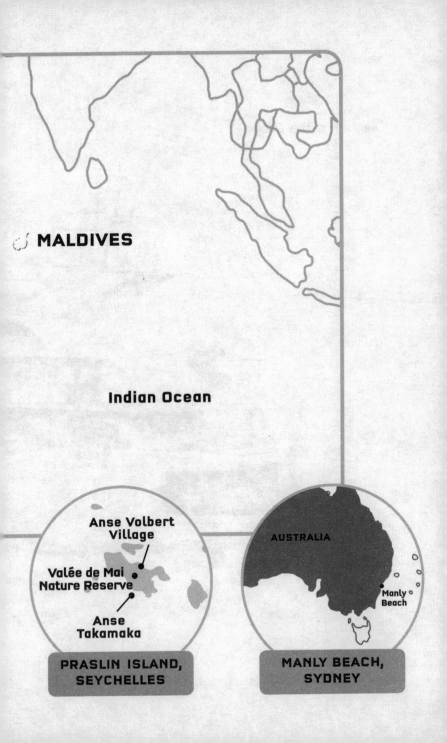

MALDIVES

Indian Ocean

Anse Volbert Village

AUSTRALIA

Valée de Mai Nature Reserve

Anse Takamaka

Manly Beach

PRASLIN ISLAND, SEYCHELLES

MANLY BEACH, SYDNEY

Diagram of the *Orchid*

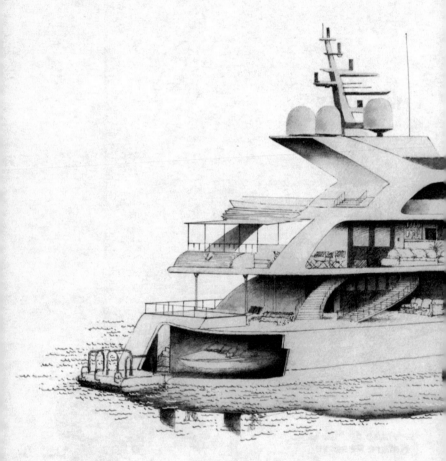

'The best bodyguard is the one nobody notices.'

With the rise of teen stars, the intense media focus
on celebrity families and a new wave of millionaires
and billionaires, adults are no longer the only target
for hostage-taking, blackmail and assassination –
kids are too.

That's why they need specialized protection . . .

BUDDYGUARD

BUDDYGUARD is a secret close-protection
organization that differs from all other security outfits
by training and supplying only young bodyguards.

Known as 'buddyguards', these highly skilled
teenagers are more effective than the typical adult
bodyguard, who can easily draw unwanted attention.
Operating invisibly as a child's constant companion, a
buddyguard provides the greatest possible protection
for any high-profile or vulnerable young person.

In a life-threatening situation, a buddyguard
is the **final** ring of defence . . .

The girl felt the cold hard barrel of a gun thrust against the back of her head.

'Kneel,' ordered the man, his voice as dry and cruel as the desert wind.

With no choice but to obey, the girl blindly sought the floor. The dusty rag round her eyes let in only glimpses of light, its fraying cloth reeking of stale sweat. She winced as the dirt floor grazed her bare knees and drew blood. Then, hearing the ominous *click* of a round entering the gun's chamber, her body instinctively stiffened.

Her captor leant in close. His breath, a bitter mix of coffee and nicotine, was warm and familiar in her ear. 'Farewell, my little sparrow.'

So this is it, she thought with a numbness born out of exhaustion. After weeks of uncertainty and too many sleepless nights to count, she was beyond caring. Beyond even fear. In truth, her heart almost welcomed the end to her ordeal.

But, as she waited for the inevitable bullet, a small voice of fury rose within her.

Why have I been abandoned like this? Why hasn't the ransom been paid? What's gone wrong?

Despite all the promises and hopes she'd clung to, she was going to die. A bullet through the head. Her body dumped in the desert.

Will anyone find me? Will they recognize who I am after a few days in the blistering sun? And will they even care?

'Get it over with,' she muttered, willing her executioner to pull the trigger and end her suffering.

Silence.

No click. No bang. Not even a reply. Only the buzz of flies circling in the stifling heat.

What's taking him so long? Is this another one of his mind games?

A bead of sweat rolled from beneath her blindfold and down her grime-covered cheek.

'Lost your nerve, have you?' she croaked, her voice quavering as her impatience turned to frustrated anger. Still no answer.

With a trembling hand, she removed the rag. Blinking away the dust, she discovered she was *alone* . . . abandoned in the centre of a single-roomed mud-brick building. A makeshift wooden door barred the only entrance through which beams of sunlight speared the darkness.

Should I try to escape? But she had no idea what lay beyond the doorway. Her captor? The barrel of a gun? Most likely miles of unbroken desert –

Suddenly the door burst open and she was dazzled by the glaring African sun. A shadow passed across her face as a huge man filled the doorway. Dressed in khaki army fatigues and his finger primed on the trigger of an assault rifle, he swiftly scanned the room for threats before his gaze targeted her.

'Emily Sterling?' the soldier grunted.

Her throat too dry to reply, Emily managed a weak nod.

The soldier thumbed his radio mic. 'Yankee Four to X-ray, hostage found alive, I repeat, ALIVE.'

Scooping Emily up in his arms like a fragile doll, the soldier carried her to the door.

As the realization of her rescue hit her, Emily began to sob uncontrollably.

'It's over,' promised the soldier. 'You're safe now.'

No, thought Emily as her tears dripped on to the man's shirt. *I'll never be safe again.*

CHAPTER 1

'Keep your head down!' Connor shouted as a barrage of bullets raked the brick wall.

His Principal had gone into shock and kept trying to bolt from their hiding place. But that was the worst possible reaction the boy could have. A casual stroll down the street had turned into a bodyguard's nightmare and now they were pinned down in a well-planned ambush.

Connor knew his next move would be crucial. In his head, he ran through the A-C-E procedure . . .

Assess the threat. Two shooters. One in an alley. Another behind a tree. Intention to kill, not capture.

Counter the danger. His first priority was to find cover and secure the Principal. But the low brick wall they had hidden behind provided only temporary protection. As soon as the shooters repositioned themselves, he and his Principal would be exposed again.

Escape the kill zone. Easier said than done!

Connor tapped his mic. 'Alpha One to Control. Request Emergency EVAC.'

His earpiece burst into life and he heard Charley, Alpha

team's operations leader, respond, '*Alpha One, this is Control. Back-up on its way. Three minutes out.*'

Three minutes? thought Connor. They'd be dead meat in that time. And, without any firepower of their own, they were defenceless. Connor needed an exit strategy . . . and fast.

Covering the Principal with his body, Connor peeked over the wall and scanned the immediate area. A clump of bushes off to their right gave some visual cover for an escape, but no physical protection from gunfire. A car parked further down the street provided little hope either; he was fourteen years old and had no idea how to drive, let alone how to hot-wire a car! He looked at the building behind them – a small warehouse with offices attached. The back entrance was only ten metres away, but it was across open ground. Checking on the enemy's progress, Connor saw that the shooter behind the tree was advancing to get a clear shot. He had no choice but to risk it.

'Move!' he growled, seizing his Principal by the arm and sprinting towards the warehouse.

Keeping his body close, Connor shielded the boy as the enemy opened fire. Bullets whizzed past. One almost clipped his ear. Their feet pounded across the tarmac and, whether through speed or pure luck, they made it to the entrance unharmed.

Connor yanked on the handle.

'NO!' he cried, tugging furiously at the locked doors.

He spun round. They were now sitting ducks. Connor shoved his Principal into the shelter of a large wheeled refuse bin. The boy tried to run on, crying, 'I don't want to die!'

'Stay down,' Connor ordered, forcibly pushing him to the ground. Then through clenched teeth he added, 'Amir, you're not making this any easier for me.'

'Sorry,' replied his friend, offering a flash of a grin from behind his safety goggles. 'But I'm supposed to be a panicking Principal.'

'Well, panic *less*,' Connor pleaded as several bullets thudded into the metal bin.

Amir flinched and covered his head with his arms. 'A bit difficult under the circumstances, don't you think?'

Richie, who was playing the part of the first shooter in the training scenario, had left his position in the alley and was unleashing a hail of paintballs from his assault rifle. So too was Ling, the other shooter, who by now had reached the far end of the low wall. If either of them managed to hit Amir with even a single paintball, Connor would instantly fail the exercise.

Ever since his successful assignment protecting the American President's daughter the month before, the rest of Alpha team had been impressed but also a little envious of his newly acquired status. The only other person on the team to have earned a gold Buddyguard badge was Charley – and she truly deserved it – whereas he was just a first-time rookie.

That's why certain fellow buddyguards had made it their mission to test him to the limit – in Ling's words, 'to make sure Connor doesn't get too big for his boots'. While

Connor had no problem with a bit of good-natured ribbing, deep down he questioned whether his first assignment had just been beginner's luck. It was true his father had been in the SAS and one of the best bodyguards on the circuit. But that didn't mean Connor was made of the same stuff. For his own peace of mind, he needed to prove himself . . . beyond a doubt.

Connor clicked his mic again. 'Alpha One to Control. Where's my pickup?'

'*Alpha One. Thirty seconds out. Maintain position.*'

As more paintballs thudded into the bin and splattered the paving at their feet, Connor wondered, *Do I have any other choice?*

Richie closed in, setting his sights on Amir. Connor pressed Amir further down behind the wheelie bin. Paintballs rattled off it like hailstones. A black 4x4 Range Rover roared down the road, its tyres screeching as the driver braked hard and spun the armoured vehicle to form a shield against Richie's attack. The paintballs now pinged harmlessly off the bodywork.

But that still left Ling as a threat. With fifteen metres of open ground between them, she *couldn't* miss her target. Connor realized he was in a no-win situation. Whether they ran or stayed put, one or both of them would be shot down.

Then Connor had an idea. Kicking off the bin's brakes, he grabbed Amir and shoved the huge container with his shoulder.

'What on earth are you doing?' cried Amir as the

wheeled bin began rolling down the path towards the Range Rover and Connor pushed him ahead in order to stay covered.

'Getting rid of the garbage,' replied Connor with a grin as the bin resounded with the furious impact of Ling's paintballs. The bin was picking up speed now and Connor and Amir had to sprint alongside it to stay shielded from Ling's assault. Then the bin struck the wall and came to a dead stop. Having lost their only cover, the two of them made a final mad dash for the Range Rover.

Paintballs peppered the bonnet and windscreen as Connor wrenched the back door open and shoved Amir inside. Connor dived in after, landing on top of him in the footwell.

'GO! GO! GO!' he screamed at the driver.

Flooring the accelerator, the driver sped away from the kill zone.

CHAPTER 2

Connor allowed himself a quiet smile of satisfaction. Against all the odds, he'd done it. He'd saved his Principal. Then Amir turned to him and the smile was wiped from his face. Planted squarely in the right eye of Amir's goggles was the red *splat* of an exploded paintball.

'How come you got hit?' Connor exclaimed, clambering into the passenger seat and thumping the armrest in frustration. 'I had you covered on all sides.'

Amir tenderly peeled off his safety goggles and rubbed the bridge of his nose. Originally from Delhi, Amir was a slender boy with an angular face, bright eyes and a slick of black hair. 'I wish you *had* protected me. That really hurt.'

The driver brought the Range Rover to a halt and glanced over her shoulder at them. Jody, a former SO14 Royal Protection Officer, was one of their instructors at the Buddyguard Training Headquarters in Wales. Kitted out in a black-and-red tracksuit, her dark brown hair bunched in a ponytail, she looked more like a personal fitness trainer than a bodyguard. But that was the point. Few people ever suspected women to be part of a close protection team and that gave them the edge.

'Exercise over, Connor – your Principal's definitely dead,' she said, arching a slim eyebrow in amusement at Amir's paint-splattered face. Then her expression hardened. 'If that had been a soft-nosed sniper bullet, Amir would be headless now.'

'That wouldn't be such a bad thing,' remarked Charley, who sat in the front passenger seat. 'He doesn't use it much anyway,' she added in her sun-soaked Californian tones, shooting him a wink.

Amir's mouth fell open in exaggerated offence. 'Hey! *You* can be the Principal next time.'

Staring out of the passenger window, Charley sighed to herself. 'If only . . .'

As Jody spun the Range Rover round, Connor caught sight of Charley's reflection in the glass. Her sky-blue eyes had lost their sparkle and her usual confidence appeared to have faltered for a moment.

'Nothing to stop you being the shooter next time,' Connor suggested.

In the window, he saw Charley brush aside a loose strand of blonde hair and her smile return.

'That would be unfair,' she replied, her reflected eyes meeting his and narrowing in challenge. 'You wouldn't last ten seconds.'

Connor laughed. He didn't doubt it. Despite the difficulties she faced, Charley was a girl of many talents: a former Quiksilver Junior Surfing Champion, she was also a skilful martial artist, as well as fluent in Mandarin. For all Connor knew she was probably an elite markswoman too!

Jody parked in front of the disused warehouse and ordered Connor and Amir out, as the other members of Alpha team gathered for the training debrief. Marc, a lean boy with bleached blond hair who'd been filming the training exercise for class assessment, patted Connor sympathetically on the back. '*Quelle malchance!* You were almost home free.'

Opening the door for Charley, Connor shrugged at his French friend. 'Yep, almost.'

'*Almost* is no good for a bodyguard,' Ling pointed out, hefting a gun that looked huge against her tiny sleek figure. Her oval face was framed by a bob of jet-black hair and a silver piercing glinted on one side of her elfin nose.

'Yeah,' Richie agreed in his thick Irish accent. 'It's like *almost* jumping out of the way of a train. You still get hit.' He fired off a couple of paintballs at the abandoned bin for effect.

'*Cease fire!*' scolded Jody, as she brought out Charley's wheelchair from the Range Rover's boot. 'Not everyone's wearing safety goggles.'

'Sorry, Miss,' Richie replied. He offered an apologetic grin, his braces catching the sunlight like a diamond-toothed rapper. 'Just celebrating our victory.'

Charley slid nimbly into her chair and joined the rest of them. But Connor noticed there was still one person missing from the team.

'BULLSEYE!' shouted Jason, suddenly dropping down from the fire escape of the building opposite. He strode

12

over with his paintball gun slung across his shoulder like Rambo. Muscular for his age, with a thickset jaw and tousled dark hair, Connor wouldn't be surprised if his Aussie teammate actually thought he *was* Rambo.

'I should change sides and become an assassin,' said Jason, high-fiving Richie and Ling.

'You kill me,' cooed Ling, her half-moon eyes twinkling mischievously as she dead-punched him on the arm in return. 'Or at least . . . you could try!'

'You were on the *roof*?' challenged Connor. 'I thought there were only two shooters in this exercise.'

Jason shrugged. 'Sorry to disappoint you.'

'But that's unfair,' said Connor, turning to Jody for an explanation. 'Everyone else just had two.'

'As a bodyguard, you can't presume anything,' she replied. 'Threats can come from all directions and can be any number. That's why you need to have eyes in the back of your head.'

She addressed the rest of Alpha team. 'Under the stress of a combat situation, your body floods with adrenalin and stress hormones. While this benefits your strength and ability to react, one of the negative effects is "tunnel vision". You lose your peripheral sight and only focus on the danger in front of you. As Connor's just experienced, that can lead to fatal mistakes.'

Connor gave a dismayed sigh. He hadn't looked up once during the exercise. This was his *fourth* failed test in a row. Given his poor performance, he was seriously beginning to question his abilities as a bodyguard.

'Don't look so glum,' said Marc. 'The refuse bin was a clever idea. I got it all on video. It was hilarious!'

'And effective,' Ling admitted begrudgingly. 'I wasted all my ammo trying to hit you.'

'But the bin wouldn't have protected them from real bullets,' Jason was quick to point out.

'An unseen target is harder to hit,' countered Charley. 'It was a good distraction.'

Jody nodded in agreement. 'That's very true. Connor's tactic would have increased their chances of survival. However –' she pointed to the paint-smeared Range Rover – 'since he didn't protect his Principal, it's his job to clean the car.'

'Mr Gibb! Mr Gibb! Are these accusations true?'

'No comment,' mumbled the Australian Minister for Resources and Energy, as he fought his way through the pack of reporters. A camera was thrust in his haggard face, its flash half-blinding him. He pushed it angrily away.

'Do you intend to resign?' shouted another reporter.

'How much money did you make from the deal?'

'No comment,' spat Harry Gibb, reaching the glass doors and squeezing through to the air-conditioned safety of the Canberra governmental building. The security guards kept the press pack at bay as Harry scuttled across the polished marble floor towards the lift. He jabbed a podgy finger at the Call button and a moment later a *ping* signalled the doors sliding open.

'Harry!' called a familiar voice from behind him.

The senator's tone was sharp. But Harry, pretending not to have heard his colleague, entered the lift and thumbed the Close-doors button. The senator increased his pace but was a second too late and the metal doors clanged shut in his face.

As the elevator rose steadily, Harry took the brief moment of peace to slick down his thinning windswept hair and adjust his tie. He was breathless and could feel patches of sweat seeping through his shirt. At the fifth floor he exited. A potbellied man, whose suits always failed to fit him, Harry strode through the open-plan office with as much dignity and authority as he could muster. He knew everyone would have heard the news by now. He was a marked man. But he refused to show it.

As he approached his own office, his secretary rose to greet him. She sheepishly offered him that day's correspondence, but he dismissed it with an irritated wave of his hand.

'Later,' he muttered, conscious of the uncomfortable silence that had descended over the workplace.

Shutting his office door behind him, he dropped his briefcase and slumped into his high-backed leather chair. Rubbing his bloodshot eyes, he let out a troubled sigh. For a moment, he allowed himself to believe that he'd escaped the political storm threatening to engulf him. Then, on opening his eyes, he was confronted by an edition of the *Australian Daily* on his desk. His hangdog face was plastered across the front page. The headline ran: MINISTER FOR MINES LINES HIS OWN POCKETS WITH GOLD.

Harry glared at the offending words, a vein throbbing in his temple.

His phone rang, demanding his attention. He ignored it.

As he stared at the accusing newspaper, Harry suddenly felt his chest tighten. He scrambled in his jacket pocket for his heart pills. At the same time, he wrenched open his desk drawer and pulled out a slim silver hip flask 'kept for emergencies'. Shaking several of his beta-blocker heart pills into his open palm, Harry washed them down with a stiff measure of whisky. He coughed at the harsh kick of alcohol. His doctor had warned him to stay off the booze. But today he didn't care.

Leaning back in his chair, Harry waited for his chest pain to pass. As the angina slowly subsided, his anger began to rise again.

'*Damn that interfering snake!*' he snarled, slamming his palm on the mahogany desk and sending the newspaper flying across the floor.

His mind swirled with furious thoughts. Just because Sterling owned the *Australian Daily* and virtually every other national newspaper, that didn't give him the right to meddle in his affairs. It wasn't as if the media magnate's hands were squeaky clean. How many times had that slippery fish managed to escape prosecution for tax avoidance, illegal takeovers and business scandals? Sterling was at least as corrupt as he was, if not more so!

Harry took another swig of whisky. He was a *victim* of Sterling's need for scandalous headlines. The target of an overzealous smear campaign simply to sell more newspapers. But Harry Gibb hadn't got this far in political office without knowing how to protect his own interests. And he certainly wouldn't roll over and die without a fight.

He was a survivor. He would do *whatever* it took to save himself.

CHAPTER 4

The sun shone brightly. The crowd cheered. American flags and pennants fluttered wildly. Connor stood at the edge of the podium scanning the joyous crowd as the US President delivered his speech. 'I prayed for a miracle and one was delivered . . .'

The western end of the National Mall was overflowing with the smiling faces of men, women and children, all gathered to celebrate the President's daughter's safe return.

But Connor wasn't celebrating. He was looking for a face. The face of a killer.

It was like searching for a hornet in a hive of bees. The assassin would blend in, become the grey person in the crowd. And that made everyone a potential suspect . . . Then Connor's eyes honed in on the barrel of a gun, protruding between a boy and his younger sister. The President beckoned for his daughter, Alicia, to join him. The gun sights tracked her as she stepped on to the stage. The siblings continued to flourish their flags, oblivious to the lethal weapon between them. Connor screamed at the Secret Service agents stationed by the barrier. But none heard him above the roar of the crowd.

In desperation Connor rushed on to the stage. But gravity seemed to weigh him down. The harder he ran, the slower he went. He cried out a warning. Turning, Alicia gave him a bemused look.

A noise as loud as a thunder-crack punctured the cheers. Connor thought he could see the actual bullet emerge from the gun barrel. He dived into its line of fire. But the deadly bullet whizzed past, missing him by a fraction. He landed in a useless heap on the stage as Alicia gazed down in shock at the blood-red stain blossoming over her crisp white dress.

'NO!' cried Connor, watching her crumple slowly to the ground . . .

'Connor! Connor! Are you all right?'

Shaken by the shoulder, Connor blinked, for a moment disorientated. The room was swallowed in darkness, just a rectangle of muted light spilling across his bedroom floor from the open doorway.

'You were crying out,' said Charley, who sat beside his bed in her wheelchair, her face half in shadow. She took away her hand from his shoulder. 'I hope you didn't mind me checking on you.'

Connor sat up and rubbed his eyes. 'No . . . not at all . . . I was just dreaming.'

'Sounded more like a nightmare to me.'

Connor hesitated, unsure whether admitting his inner doubts would be regarded as weakness for a buddyguard. Then he realized, of all the members of Alpha team, Charley would be the one to understand most.

'I keep reliving Alicia's assassination attempt.'

'Near-death experiences can do that to you.' A haunted look entered her eyes but was gone so quickly that Connor could have been mistaken.

'But in my dream I'm always *too late*,' he explained.

'It was a close call. You got shot. So such anxiety is understandable. But you *did* save her.'

'I know, but what if that was just beginner's luck? I mean, I've not passed a *single* Buddyguard training exercise this last week.'

'Training is where you're supposed to make your mistakes,' she reminded him. 'Besides, the tests are designed to be tough so that we're at the top of our game when we're on an assignment.'

Connor let out a weary sigh. He felt the mounting pressure of his forthcoming mission. The responsibility of protecting another person was overwhelming. 'But what if next time I don't react quickly enough?'

Charley gave him a chastening look. 'You mustn't allow yourself to think like that. You *did* protect the President's daughter when the time came. That should be proof enough you're up to the job.'

'Exactly my point. Everyone thinks I'm this hotshot bodyguard. But I'm not. A second later and . . .' He faded into silence at the terrible thought.

Charley glanced towards his bedside table where a plastic key fob was propped up against his alarm clock. 'Listen, it's in your blood, remember?' she said softly, directing his gaze to the key fob.

Connor studied the faded photo beneath its scratched surface. His late father, Justin Reeves, stared back at him. Tanned, tough and with the piercing green-blue eyes that Connor had inherited, his father looked every inch the soldier – a man who could be relied upon in even the most dangerous situations.

Connor felt a weight even heavier than responsibility upon his shoulders. 'I'm *not* my father,' he admitted quietly. 'As much as Colonel Black believes I am, I can't live up to his name. Dad was Special Forces, I'm Special *Nothing*.'

Charley's eyes met his with a fierce intensity. 'That's negative thinking. Of course you're going to fail if that's your attitude! Listen to me. You can't measure yourself against a memory.'

Connor was taken aback by her sudden fire. 'I know. You're right. It's just –'

A door creaked open somewhere down the hallway. They weren't supposed to be in each other's rooms after ten o'clock at night. Charley eased herself back towards the door. At the threshold, she paused and looked at him.

'Don't doubt yourself, Connor. Whenever I question my own abilities, I remember the saying: *Whether you think you can, or think you can't – you're probably right.*'

She shut the door and Connor lay in the darkness, thinking about what she had said. About the power of self-belief. As he closed his eyes, he pictured his father's face willing him on, like he always had when he was alive.

CHAPTER 5

'Operation Gemini commences in two weeks,' announced Colonel Black. 'I trust you've all done your homework.'

The colonel stood, arms behind his back, at the front of Alpha team's briefing room. His broad shoulders, chiselled jaw and silver-grey crew cut were highlighted by the glow of the projector screen. As founder and commander of the Buddyguard organization, the ex-SAS soldier took a personal interest in every assignment and made certain he attended every operational briefing. On the screen behind him, spinning in 3D, was Buddyguard's official logo: a silver winged shield.

Connor swiped a finger across his new tablet computer and prepared to take notes. The next few hours would be an onslaught of information from each Alpha team member regarding different aspects of the operation: Principal profile, location intel, threat assessments, security requirements, 'actions on' procedures, role assignment and logistical support, to name but a few. Each element was crucial to the success of the mission and all team members were required to have a working knowledge in case of role swaps or last-minute replacements.

Colonel Black stepped aside to allow Charley to the front. As Alpha team's operations leader and most experienced buddyguard, she always led the briefing.

'On this assignment, there are *two* Principals needing our protection,' she explained, clicking the projector's handheld remote. A photograph of two young girls, virtually identical in looks, flashed up on the screen. 'These are the twin daughters of Mr Maddox Sterling, the Australian media mogul and billionaire.'

'They look like the Valley Sisters,' cracked Richie with an approving grin, referring to the famous teenage TV pop duo.

'Got all their albums, have you?' teased Ling.

'No! Of course not. I have musical taste . . . unlike you. I mean, Black Sabbath. Talk about morbid.'

Ling narrowed her eyes at him. 'You haven't *lived* until you've listened to *Paranoid*.'

Tuning out his teammates' bickering, Connor carefully studied the photograph. The twins had matching straw-blonde hair, sea-green eyes and well-defined cheekbones. They could very easily pass as pop stars – and equally as one another. It would be hard to tell them apart.

Pointing to the girl on the right, Charley continued with the Principal profile. 'Chloe is the eldest by twelve minutes. Aged fifteen, she's outgoing, sociable and intelligent; though, word has it, she can be a bit of a princess.' Charley shrugged her shoulders as if to imply that came with being the daughter of a billionaire. 'Emily, on the other hand, is quieter and more introvert. She favours reading, nature and walking in contrast to Chloe's love of netball, sunbathing and partying. But that isn't surprising. Last year she was the victim of a kidnapping.'

'Sounds like they hired us too late,' quipped Amir, looking round at the others to join in his joke.

However, a stern glance from the colonel's flint-grey eyes swiftly ended Amir's attempt at humour. 'Tragically, that's often the case. Hindsight brings wisdom.'

On the screen, Charley flicked to a composite image of various newspaper clippings. The headlines bullet-pointed the distressing progress of the kidnap: STERLING GIRL MISSING . . . HAVE YOU SEEN EMILY? . . . MEDIA MOGUL'S MULTIMILLION DOLLAR RANSOM DEMAND . . . HOSTAGE GIRL NEGOTIATIONS STALL . . . IS EMILY DEAD? . . . STERLING SISTER RELEASED.

'Emily was snatched while on a family vacation in the Côte d'Azur,' Charley explained. 'The Corsican Mafia was the suspected organization behind the kidnapping, although this wasn't proven. She was held in the Algerian desert for several months, before eventually being released following lengthy negotiations over the ransom payment.'

Ling held up a hand to ask a question. 'If the father's so wealthy, what took so long?'

Colonel Black replied, 'Ransom negotiations are rarely straightforward. There's a great deal of bluff and counter-bluff, rejected offers and impossible demands. The most important thing is that the hostage was released, unharmed.'

'So, how's Emily doing now?' asked Connor.

'Surprisingly well,' Charley revealed, pulling a medical report from her file. 'Physically she is fit and healthy, no lasting after-effects. Her psychological report indicates the occasional mood swing, withdrawal and a fear of the dark and confined spaces. Emily's been prescribed medication to help her cope with the anxiety attacks – but it can have side effects of drowsiness, confusion and impaired thinking. However, that's all to be expected considering her ordeal. Alpha team's task is to ensure that such a tragedy doesn't happen again.'

Clicking her remote, Charley pulled up a map of the Indian Ocean. 'We're to provide low-profile protection for the Sterling sisters during their forthcoming holiday in the Seychelles and the Maldives.' She indicated the two tiny clusters of tropical islands amid the vast blue swathe of ocean separating Africa and India. 'The operation will last a month and be based on Mr Sterling's yacht.'

A sleek fifty-metre, multidecked super-yacht filled the display.

'Wow!' exclaimed Amir, his coffee-brown eyes widening in amazement. 'That's *some* boat.'

'That's no boat; it's a floating palace,' Marc corrected, as he squinted at the yacht's top deck. 'It's even got a *jacuzzi*.'

Jason shot Connor an envious glance. 'You've landed a cushy assignment,' he said. 'Must be your reward for saving the President's daughter.'

'You think so?' replied Connor, recalling the difficulties he'd faced protecting just one Principal. 'I reckon twins mean twice the trouble.'

CHAPTER 6

'You have to be careful with female Principals, don't you, Connor?' said Charley, glancing meaningfully in his direction.

Her comment went over the heads of the others, but Connor knew Charley was referring to the time she'd caught him and Alicia kissing. As a buddyguard that was a line never to be crossed – although strictly speaking he'd no longer been protecting Alicia at that intimate moment. But Charley clearly wasn't going to let him forget it.

'And for that reason,' Charley continued, ignoring the team's bemused expressions, 'Colonel Black has decided there'll be *two* buddyguards on this operation.'

The room went quiet as this new information sank in. No one had anticipated the need for a *second* operative. Yet, with two Principals to look after, a dual protection unit was logical for effective security.

All eyes turned to the colonel. Jason straightened himself in expectation. Marc, in inverse proportion to his eagerness, leant casually back in his chair. Ling tensely bit her lower lip, while Amir was so on the edge of his seat that he was in danger of falling off. Richie simply chewed on a fingernail, aware that he was out of the running having only just returned from an assignment. As much as Connor respected the others on his team, he hoped that the colonel would select Amir. He knew his friend was desperate to go on his first assignment and earn his winged badge.

Colonel Black only held them in suspense for a few seconds. 'Ling, you'll be buddyguard 2 i/c.'

'Yes!' said Ling, clenching her fist in delight.

Jason bumped fists with Ling in respect. 'Congratulations, captain, best get your bikini ready.'

'Oh, and I thought I could borrow *yours*,' she said, winking at him playfully.

Meanwhile, Amir quietly deflated like a punctured balloon.

Connor offered his friend an encouraging smile. 'Don't worry, there's always next time,' he whispered.

Amir gave a half-hearted nod by way of reply.

But as the colonel's exact words registered with Ling her delight turned to a frown. '2 i/c? *Second*-in-charge?'

The colonel raised an eyebrow. 'You've a problem with that?'

'Of course not,' said Ling, offering an amiable smile at Connor. 'It's just that this being my third mission, I thought –'

'You'll both have *equal* responsibilities when it comes to protecting your Principals,' cut in the colonel. 'But there must always be a clear chain of command on the ground. Now, Amir, brief the team on the threat situation . . . Amir?'

Amir looked up. Rousing himself from his disheartened daze, he headed over to the lectern and busied himself connecting his tablet PC to the projector, taking a little longer than necessary in an attempt to hide his disappointment. Clearing his throat, he began to read direct from his notes, barely glancing up.

'I'll start with the Principals' father: Maddox Sterling. Fifty years old, he's the founder and chairman of Fourth Estate Corporation, Australia's largest media company.'

A suave silver-haired man in a well-cut suit appeared on the screen.

'The corporation's interests include newspaper and magazine publishing, internet, Pay TV, and film and television production. Fourth Estate essentially owns and controls Australia's national media.'

Amir clicked through a series of images showing various newspapers, movie posters and television channels.

'Because of this, Mr Sterling has many powerful allies in both government and industry. Equally he has made many enemies – either as a result of his aggressive business tactics, or due to his newspapers' controversial style of investigative journalism. For example –' a slide of a slim dark-haired lady popped up – 'the former government opposition leader Kelly Brocker was forced to resign last year following revelations about her private life.'

Amir switched to an image of a tanned middle-aged man with auburn hair.

'This is Joseph Ward, the former CEO of Ward Enterprises, who was jailed for ten years for corporate fraud. The financial scandal was exposed by *Insider*, a current affairs programme on one of Mr Sterling's TV networks. As a result, Mr Ward, a business rival of Mr Sterling, was declared bankrupt and the media arm of his company was absorbed by none other than Fourth Estate.' Amir raised his eyebrows at the significance of this coincidence. 'At the time of his arrest, Mr Ward publicly vowed revenge on Mr Sterling. Although presently Mr Ward remains in jail.

'Then the most recent case is the exposure of a high-level Australian politician, Harry Gibb, who has been accused of financial mis-dealings over the country's mining rights.'

A front page from the *Australian Daily* flashed up, the headline declaring 'GREEDY GIBB MUST GO!' This statement was supported by an unflattering photo of a portly gentleman with thinning hair and a ruddy complexion, caught at the moment he was stuffing a large burger into his mouth.

'While none of these people are a direct threat to our two Principals,' explained Amir, 'any enemy of the father must be considered a potential enemy of the daughters. So I've included full background intel on each of them in your operation folders.'

'What about their mother?' asked Ling. 'What's her story?'

'Sadly,' said Amir, 'the mother died in a car crash when the girls were only eight years old.'

Connor felt his throat tighten at the news. Having lost his father around the same age, he felt an immediate empathy with the girls.

'Recently, however, their father became engaged.' Amir pressed the remote a few times to bring up a picture of the new fiancée: a glamorous and unexpectedly youthful woman in a figure-hugging red dress. 'Amanda Ryder is a twenty-nine-year-old swimsuit model, who is a regular on the Sydney socialite circuit. As a future member of the family, she'll be joining you on the yacht.'

'Should make for an *entertaining* holiday,' said Marc, with a sly grin at Connor. 'At least the views will be good.'

Connor stifled a snigger at his friend's remark.

'Get your minds out of the gutter and focus on the mission!' snapped Colonel Black.

His stern tone wiped the smiles off both their faces in an instant.

Amir quickly resumed his report. 'In terms of threat level, Ms Ryder appears to have more admirers than enemies. It's really Mr Sterling's immense wealth – estimated at one and a half billion dollars – that makes him and his family a vulnerable target. Emily's kidnapping has already proved that the daughters are a tempting prize for any criminal organization. And, while the Corsican Mafia shouldn't be on the radar in the Indian Ocean, a secondary kidnapping attempt by extreme terrorists like the Seven Sabres of Somalia or an international crime syndicate, such as the Russian Bratva or the Chinese Triads, is a definite risk to consider.'

'Any other potential threats?' asked Connor, very much aware that the colonel's frosty glare was still on him and Marc.

Amir nodded. 'Like any tourist resort, robbery and theft

are common in the Seychelles and the Maldives, especially around the harbours. Such crime tends to be opportunistic, so you'll have to stay alert. There's also the chance of harassment: the Sterling sisters are well recognized by the paparazzi, even more so since the kidnapping. But, surprisingly, Mr Sterling's request for privacy has been honoured. So far.'

Amir paused in his threat report and finally looked up.

'Of course, there is one obvious danger when sailing the Indian Ocean.' He brought up a photo of the skull-and-crossbones. 'Pirates.'

CHAPTER 7

'You mean, like Captain Jack Sparrow?' said Jason, trying hard to suppress a grin.

'No, he means *real* pirates,' replied Colonel Black. 'Somali pirates, to be exact. And they're no joke. Forget your image of Johnny Depp with an eye patch and a parrot on his shoulder. Today's modern pirates use high-powered motorboats and are armed to the teeth with AK47s and RPGs – rocket-propelled grenade launchers.'

To prove the colonel's point, Amir played a jerky video clip of a narrow white-and-blue skiff cutting through the waves at high speed. Crouched on board were seven young African men wielding automatic rifles. The *crack* of gunfire could be heard above the furious roar of the skiff's outboard motor. A pirate in the bow held a rocket launcher trained on an unseen target. Connor and the others watched in stunned silence as the RPG scorched through the sky towards the cameraman. The picture juddered as the cameraman ducked in panic, but somehow he still managed to track the RPG's trajectory as it rocketed past the bridge of the ship.

The clip abruptly ended.

No one said a word, their image of the roguish yet lovable pirate from Hollywood movies shattered by this violent reality.

'Fortunately, a warship was within range and came to the cargo ship's rescue,' the colonel revealed to everyone's relief. 'But all too often these pirates do succeed in hijacking a vessel and holding it – and its crew – for ransom.'

A graphics chart appeared on the screen with columns of coloured blocks rapidly increasing in height like an ever-steepening staircase before plummeting in the last period.

'As you can see,' said Amir, pointing to the screen, 'the annual number of pirate attacks has soared in the last six years, from fifty-five to almost three hundred at its peak. Ransom demands have also risen. Five years ago the asking price was three hundred thousand dollars. Now it's as much as twenty *million* dollars and beyond.'

Richie whistled through his teeth. 'We're obviously in the wrong job.'

'The problem is,' said Amir, 'success breeds success. Pirate gangs have become more organized and turned piracy into a full-blown business. Already this year there have been forty-two attempted hijackings and six ships taken hostage. A decrease on last year, but still worrying.'

'If that's the case,' questioned Ling, 'why are we sailing in this area *at all*?'

'A fair point,' agreed the colonel. 'But, while the dangers are apparent, the risks are relatively low, as Amir will now explain.'

Amir brought up Charley's map of the Indian Ocean again. 'Although attacks have occurred up to a thousand nautical miles from the Somalian coast, the majority are concentrated along the International Recommended Transit Corridor in the Gulf of Aden.' He pointed to a wide passage of water separating Somalia in the south from Yemen to the north. Then, indicating a stretch of ocean far to the south-east, he continued, 'The planned route for Mr Sterling's yacht won't go anywhere near the danger zone.'

'But wasn't an elderly British couple taken hostage near the Seychelles some years back?' asked Connor, vaguely recalling the media coverage of their ordeal.

'You mean the Chandlers,' answered Colonel Black. 'They were *very* unlucky . . . wrong place, wrong time. Since then there have been marked improvements in security. For example, NATO's counter-piracy mission, Operation Ocean Shield, and the setting up of a Regional Anti-Piracy Coordination Centre in the Seychelles itself. These measures have curbed pirate activities significantly. Furthermore, it's relatively rare for the pirates to target a private yacht. The Somalis see the big money in the commercial vessels as they have ransom insurance.'

Amir nodded in agreement with the colonel. 'It's true. Out of twenty thousand ships that pass through the Transit Corridor each year, only three hundred are ever attacked – and less than a quarter of those are captured. Of this number, just a handful have ever been private yachts. I worked out the actual odds.' Amir scanned through his notes. 'You've less than a one in ten thousand chance of being hijacked.'

'Care to bet on it?' challenged Ling.

Amir gave a shrug. 'Why not?'

CHAPTER 8

'How can we trust you?'

Harry Gibb sat alone in the booth of the darkened restaurant. The disembodied voice was ominously threatening and he daren't look in the adjacent booth for fear of the consequences.

'My enemy's enemy is my friend,' he stated with conviction. 'I want this as much as you.'

'And you're willing to do whatever it takes?'

'Yes, yes. I want Sterling's life ruined. Just like he's destroying mine!' Harry ground his teeth and clenched a fist in fury at the thought of his collapsing career.

'Then we must hit him where it hurts: his family.'

Harry felt a chill run through him. He stared at his fist and slowly unclenched it. 'R-really?' he questioned, his voice quavering slightly. This was something he hadn't considered. 'You're not expecting *me* to do anything, are you? I'm not that sort of person.'

'Oh, Harry. It isn't as if you're an angel. I'm sure you've trampled over many innocent people on your way up the political ladder.'

'Yes . . . but this is different.'

The voice gave a hollow laugh. 'No, Harry, this is no different. Politics is just as ruthless as revenge. It's just with politics you inflict harm *before* someone has done you an injury. With revenge, at least it's after the act – a lot more honourable.'

'I'm not sure I'm a hundred per cent comfortable with this,' Harry admitted, feeling the situation slipping out of his control. He only wanted to wreck Sterling's credibility and distract him from the campaign against him.

'Too late, Harry, you're up to your neck now. And I can assure you, Mr Sterling has no qualms about crushing you. But don't you worry – my men will do the dirty work. The question is: do you have the means to make it happen?'

'Y . . . yes,' Harry replied, reaching into his jacket pocket and taking out a thick brown envelope, stuffed with five hundred crisp $100 notes.

A waiter eerily emerged from the shadows – or at least the man carried a waiter's tray. With a prominent tattoo and gorilla-like hands more suited to brutal work than simply serving food, the shadowy figure wasn't an obvious choice for a high-class establishment. Harry laid the envelope on the tray and the 'waiter' departed without a word.

'When will the "campaign" begin?' he asked.

The adjacent booth was silent.

'I said, when will you make a start?'

Still Harry got no answer. Warily, he rose from his seat and peeked over the divide. The booth was empty, except for a wireless loudspeaker on the table. His contact had never even been in the room with him.

Making his way past the cloakroom, Harry headed for the rear exit where a bald-headed bouncer in wrap-around shades opened the fire door for him. Sunlight burst into the darkened corridor, dazzling Harry as if a police spotlight had caught him in the act. His heart racing, he scuttled out of the building and into the alleyway. The door clanged shut behind him with a booming finality that signalled there was no going back.

CHAPTER 9

Connor snatched for every breath as he sprinted headlong down the indoor track. His heart pounded in his chest and his muscles burned. Jason was neck-and-neck with him. Elsa from Bravo team was close on their tail, as was Sean from Delta. The other recruits followed up behind, some already struggling with the intense circuit.

'Come on, AMIR! Don't be the first to quit; a bodyguard needs to be fit!' bellowed Steve as he ran alongside them with apparent ease.

A towering slab of honed muscle, his limbs seemingly hewn from black marble, the ex-British Special Forces soldier was their unarmed combat instructor and fitness coach. He'd summoned the three Buddyguard teams – Alpha, Bravo and Delta – to the sports hall for one of his infamous circuit training sessions. To ensure their full commitment, he'd pitted them against one another and, with group pride at stake, no team wanted to be last.

'No pain, no gain,' called out Steve, offering questionable incentive to the stragglers.

Connor reached the end of the shuttle sprint and

dropped to the floor for fifty knuckle press-ups. Beside him, Jason pumped away like a jackhammer, clicking off reps every second. More students joined them, racing to catch up. Connor felt the burn in his triceps. But compared with the mental overload of an operational briefing the physical exercise was a relief.

Amir dropped down next to him, the last of Alpha team. 'I think . . . I might . . . die,' he gasped in between press-ups.

'That's the spirit,' said Steve, grinning a bright white smile at his student's torment. 'It means you're putting in one hundred per cent effort.'

He stood sentry over the teams, ensuring no one skipped a rep.

'An unfit bodyguard is a liability,' he told them. 'Not only to himself but also to other members of the team, and most of all to the Principal.'

Jason was first to finish his press-ups and went straight into the next exercise – fifty stomach crunches.

'In an emergency, you'll need such strength to get you and your Principal out of the danger zone,' continued their instructor as his students sweated and groaned on the floor. 'Fatigue, on the other hand, will hamper your ability to make quick decisions and choose the right course of action.'

'But we did a . . . ten-mile run . . . only yesterday!' panted Luciana, a dark-haired Brazilian girl from Delta team.

'Your fitness isn't about yesterday; it's about *today*,' Steve lectured. 'You must treat your fitness like a tyre with a slow puncture – you have to keep topping it up.'

He strode over to a boy in Bravo team who'd given up halfway through his press-ups.

'Would you trust your security to an overweight slob?'

Too out of breath to reply, the boy shook his head.

'Nor would I. Now let's see what you're made of. Keep going!'

His arms trembling with the effort, the boy resumed his exercise. Meanwhile, his teammate Elsa had completed her stomach crunches and was running to beat Jason to the chin-up bars. Connor was only a few paces behind. Charley, who'd used a vertical chest press and played catch with a medicine ball in place of press-ups and stomach crunches, powered her adapted sportschair over to a lowered chin-up bar. She fired off twenty reps before anyone else had even managed ten. Then, dropping back into her chair, she sped off along the track for another shuttle run – now the leader in the race.

As soon as she reached the end of the track, Steve announced, 'Piggyback sprint.'

This was met with groans of disbelief from the weary teams. But everyone dug in for what they prayed would be the final exercise. In Alpha team, Connor partnered Amir, Jason ran with Richie, while Charley pulled herself up on to Ling's shoulders.

The teams raced in relay down the hall. Ling managed to hold Alpha's lead, then Jason extended it. But Richie staggered under the weight of his brawny teammate.

'This is murder!' Richie moaned, gritting his teeth as Delta team swiftly passed him by.

'Winners train, losers complain,' Steve growled. 'When things go wrong and you need to run for cover while carrying your Principal, you'll be thankful for this exercise.'

'I'll be thankful when it stops!' he gasped.

By the time it was Connor and Amir's turn, Alpha team had fallen into last place. Amir did his best to catch up, but had nothing left to give. It was a miracle he even managed to carry Connor over the line. Now they were almost ten seconds behind the leaders.

'It's all down to you,' said Marc as a burnt-out Amir clambered on to Connor's back.

Naturally fit from six years of martial arts training, Connor summoned up hidden reserves of energy and raced after the two rival teams. They quickly passed Bravo team as Elsa stumbled and went sprawling with her partner. But Delta still had the lead. And with only thirty metres left in the race, Connor had to dig deep.

'*Go! Go! Go!*' cried Amir, geeing him on as if he was a racehorse.

Connor could see that Luciana, with Sean on her back, was fading fast. He pumped his legs and charged after them.

'*Come on!*' Amir urged.

They began to draw level. With victory almost in sight, Connor raced for the finish line.

Suddenly aware she was about to be passed, Luciana leant forward like a jockey in the final few paces . . . and beat Alpha team by a nose.

Delta team cheered and high-fived Luciana in celebration

of their slimmest of victories. Gutted at their loss, Connor collapsed to his hands and knees in an exhausted heap, Amir rolling off him on to the floor.

'Good job, everyone,' said Steve. 'Take a break. I'll be back in ten minutes for combat practice.'

As Steve passed Connor, he clapped a meaty hand on his shoulder. 'You may have lost out this time, but that's what I call fighting fit.'

Connor managed a weak smile. 'Well, I'm fit for nothing now!'

CHAPTER 10

Connor slumped on the bench and reached inside his training bag for his water bottle. Popping the cap, he almost drained it in one slug. Amir lay at his side, breathing hard, a weary arm draped across his forehead.

'I shouldn't have . . . made that joke . . . about hiring us too late,' panted Amir.

Connor looked over at his friend, unable to believe Amir had the energy to dwell on the buddyguard assignment after such a gruelling circuit session. 'The colonel's choice had nothing to do with your joke. He'd have made up his mind before the briefing.'

Amir propped himself up on one elbow, sweat dripping from his brow. 'Then why didn't he choose me? I'm the only one in Alpha team who hasn't yet been on an assignment.'

'Must be because you're so good with the tech stuff,' said Marc, chucking Amir a towel. Amir wiped the sweat from his face but his dejected expression remained.

Connor nodded encouragingly. 'That's it! The colonel's playing to your strengths. During the mission, you'll be needed in HQ to maintain comms and run the IT. Remember last time, it was *you* and Bugsy who figured out the Cell-Finity bug.'

'Great,' said Amir without much enthusiasm. 'So while you're off sunning yourself in the Seychelles with "Miss Swimsuit", I get stuck in wet Wales doing circuits!'

'Look, Amir,' said Connor, trying one last time to console his friend. 'Ling was the most obvious choice.'

'Why?'

'Because she's a girl.'

'*Just* because I'm a girl!' remarked Ling, shooting daggers at Connor as she leant against the ropes of the sports hall boxing ring.

'No . . . I didn't mean it like that,' Connor stammered.

'Whatever, *Boss*,' she replied, her tone laced with sarcasm.

Connor sighed. This didn't bode well for their forthcoming assignment. 'Let me explain –'

'Be my guest,' she said, lifting the ropes of the boxing ring and inviting him to join her.

'But we've just done circuits!' exclaimed Connor.

'Is that your excuse?' Ling gave him a withering look, somehow still appearing as fresh as a daisy herself. 'Or is it because I'm a *girl* you don't want to fight?'

Connor shook his head, wondering how he was going to avoid the sparring challenge. Although he was a black belt in jujitsu and kickboxing, that didn't mean he took a match with Ling lightly. At their very first encounter, she'd demonstrated she was a supremely tough combatant. In Amir's words, 'Ling *always* wins her fights.'

45

It was as if she had something to prove. And Ling wasn't to be dissuaded now. She bounced nimbly on her feet and pulled on the sparring gloves Jason offered.

'I don't think Connor's up for it,' Jason remarked, handing Ling her gumshield while eyeballing Connor. 'I hope he's not going to be a liability on your mission.'

Members of Bravo and Delta teams were soon drawn to the ring by the excitement of a challenge fight.

'I thought you were Battle of Britain Kickboxing Champion,' remarked Luciana, still gloating over her victory. 'Let's see you prove it.'

'Go on, Connor,' urged Sean. 'You know how "Lightning Ling" only sees sense in the ring!'

Connor looked to Amir for a way out. But his friend just shrugged his shoulders. 'You don't seem to have much choice,' he said. 'You'll have to play to *your* strengths.'

Despite his exhausted state, Connor ducked under the rope, entered the ring, put on a pair of sparring gloves and turned to face his opponent –

An explosive jab almost took his head off. Only blind instinct enabled him to spin away in time. A right hook came flying in and Connor had to weave sharply aside again. Ling certainly wasn't waiting around to start the fight officially.

'So the colonel's choice,' said Ling, launching a roundhouse kick to his thigh, 'has nothing to do with my previous experience?'

'Of course it does!' Connor grunted, blocking the kick with his shin and countering with a front-kick.

Ling skipped out of range, then came back in with a body hook punch to his ribs. 'Or my surveillance skills –?'

Connor grimaced as the strike hit home. Ling might be small, but she was *lightning* fast.

'Or my fighting ability?' she demanded.

Like a whirling dervish, Ling came at him with a flurry of kicks and punches. Connor fought hard to defend himself. He ducked her spinning backfist, blocked her cross and evaded her crescent kick. As he retreated from Ling's relentless onslaught, Luciana goaded him from the ringside, 'Some champion you are, Connor!'

Needled by the taunt and wanting to get a word in edgeways with Ling, Connor now went on the attack.

'Ling, I meant you got the job,' he replied with a blistering combination of jab, cross and upper cut, 'because . . . our two Principals . . . are girls. It therefore makes sense –' he almost floored Ling with a back fist – 'to have a *female* buddyguard.'

Ling was driven into the corner by a pounding side-kick to the chest. She tried to fight her way out, but Connor kept her trapped with a series of punishing body blows.

'You can go places I can't,' he said. Ling, taking the hits, fought hard to escape, but Connor maintained the pressure. He still had more to say. 'And their protection is supposed to be low profile, so a *girl* bodyguard will be even less noticeable than a boy.'

Connor grunted as Ling thrust a front-kick into his gut, forcing him backwards.

'Is that low profile enough for you?' grinned Ling, relishing the buzz of the fight.

Connor ignored her and retaliated with a front-kick of his own that propelled Ling back into the ring's corner pad.

'So, apart from your core skills, being a *girl* makes you the obvious choice,' explained Connor, moving to finish her off with a couple of head shots.

But Ling displayed some nifty footwork and escaped the corner. 'Fair enough,' she said, with a disarming smile. 'My mistake, please accept my apology.'

She backed off from the fight and Connor dropped his guard. *Finally* he'd got through to Ling. 'Of course I do. We're teammates. I didn't mean any offence –'

Ling spun on her heel, shot out a leg and caught him bang on the jaw with a spinning hook-kick. 'There's my apology.'

Connor went down like a sack of potatoes, his last conscious thought: *Ling* always *wins her fights*.

CHAPTER 11

Harry Gibb hurried through the deserted government office. He knew even his most eager civil servants wouldn't show their faces until at least 8 a.m. That gave him two hours of solitude. Still, he glanced nervously around before unlocking the main archive room and ducking inside.

Flicking on the switch, he waited for the fluorescent strip lights to cast their stark white glare over the rows and rows of grey filing cabinets. Each one was a carbon copy of the next, impossible to tell apart, but Harry knew exactly what he was looking for. Heading straight over to the sixth cabinet in the third row, he pulled out a thick binder of documents marked MINING RIGHTS, GOLDFIELDS, WA.

Despite everything being stored digitally nowadays, there was *always* a paper trail in government. While he'd been careful to remove any evidence from his computer, these damning documents were the remaining crumbs that could lead to him and his under-the-table dealings.

Yet he *wouldn't* destroy the files. The contents of this folder, detailing his co-conspirators, were his insurance policy. Harry Gibb knew that those who had profited from the shady deals also had a vested interest in protecting his reputation. If he went down, so would they.

Smiling to himself, Harry closed the filing cabinet, switched off the light and locked the archive room. Clutching the files to his chest, he scurried across to his office and bolted inside. Only when he'd secured the door behind him did he feel safe in his domain.

Turning to his desk, Harry almost jumped out of his skin when he discovered a man in a grey suit sitting in his chair.

'M-my secretary didn't mention any meetings this morning,' he blustered.

'She doesn't know of *this* meeting,' replied the man. 'No one does.'

The uninvited guest did not get up or introduce himself. He just studied Harry with unblinking eyes that seemed chiselled from ice.

'Who are you?' Harry demanded, gathering his wits and now becoming angry. 'Are you a reporter? Get out of my chair!'

The man was indifferent to Harry's outrage. 'I represent a certain investor.'

'And who might that be?' Harry challenged.

'Your primary investor.'

'I don't know what you're talking about,' said Harry. He felt himself becoming flustered. There was something deeply unsettling about this man. Like a spider crawling across his skin, Harry wanted him gone. 'If you don't leave right now, I'll call security.'

'I'd advise against that.'

'Are you threatening me?'

The man sat as still as a block of stone, his silence more unnerving than any reply. Then he said, 'Equilibrium.'

'What?' snapped Harry, frowning in disbelief.

'You heard me.'

'Ahh,' said Harry, relaxing slightly. This man *had* to be from his key investor. There could be no other way he'd have known of the organization's name. It had taken Harry weeks to discover it for himself – Equilibrium, the parent investor behind all those false 'shell' companies who'd invested in the mining rights.

Feeling once more in charge of the situation, Harry strode over and dropped the thick binder on to his desk.

'I'm dealing with the problem,' he said, waving a dismissive hand in the man's direction. 'Equilibrium need not be concerned. Neither their existence nor their involvement will be revealed. Plans are in place to handle Mr Sterling and his prying newspaper.'

'But *you're* familiar with Equilibrium.'

'Of course,' said Harry. 'I was *thorough* in selecting my investors.'

'And are they fully protected from the current crisis?'

'Oh yes,' Harry assured. 'I've erased all evidence from my computer records.'

'So have I,' said the man, pulling a tiny USB drive from the back of Harry's computer. 'A malware virus has just wiped your hard drive.'

'You can't do that!' exclaimed Harry.

'And what about those files there?' asked the man, ignoring Harry's protest and nodding at the thick wad of documents on his desk.

'These? They're just an insurance policy.'

'Hmm, that's the problem,' said the man, adjusting the crisp white cuffs of his shirt. 'Not only do you know Equilibrium's name but you possess evidence of its existence.'

'I . . . I'm not going to expose Equilibrium's involvement in this. The file is just for my own protection from the other parties. They know nothing about Equilibrium,' said Harry, suddenly feeling a chill run down his spine from the man's sinister casualness. 'Trust me. I'm a man of my word.'

'You're a politician,' the other corrected sharply, his ice-pick eyes fixing him with a contemptuous look. 'But I'll take your word . . . for what it's worth.'

Without further discussion, the man stood and left. Once the door closed on him, the room seemed to breathe again.

Harry opened his desk drawer and pulled out his silver hip flask. With an unsteady hand, he removed the stopper and took a swig to calm himself. As the whisky delivered its familiar warming kick, the burn continued down his throat, into his stomach . . . and kept spreading.

His chest began to tighten, his throat constricted, his breath became short and pained.

Harry hunted for his tablets. He fumbled with the lid, scattering beta blockers across the desk as his heart was seized in a vice-like grip. Harry rolled from his chair on to the floor, his lips foaming with spittle. He clutched at the little white tablets strewn around him. But his body was racked with pain, fire raging through his veins.

'H . . . h . . . *help!*' he moaned. '*Heeelp . . .*'

The man in the grey suit re-entered the room.

'*P . . . p . . . please*,' Harry begged, clawing at the tablets.

But the man merely observed Harry writhe on the carpet with an almost inhuman detachment. Harry's eyes bulged, unable to comprehend the man's indifference. A sharp pain speared his chest. He shuddered once more then lay still.

The man in the grey suit checked Harry Gibb's body for signs of life. Satisfied, he picked up the documents from the desk and the poisoned hip flask from the floor. Quietly closing the office door behind him, he headed for the emergency exit, the first phase of his mission accomplished.

'Enter,' barked Colonel Black.

Taking a deep breath, Connor stepped inside the colonel's office. An old-fashioned wood-panelled affair with high-back red leather chairs and a heavy mahogany desk the size of a small boat, it reminded Connor of M's office in the old Bond movies. Yet, despite the room's antique appearance, it was equipped with the most advanced state-of-the-art technology. Built within the desk was a discreet multi-core computer, its slim glass monitor retractable into a hidden recess. A super-thin LED display hung on the wall, broadcasting international news feeds and up-to-the-minute security intel. There was a high-definition video-conferencing system enabling the colonel to govern Buddyguard operations worldwide, while hidden CCTV cameras provided total security for the room.

As Connor approached the desk, the colonel lowered his monitor and raised an enquiring eyebrow.

'That's an impressive black eye,' he remarked.

Connor managed a pained smile. 'An *apology* from Ling during combat training.'

The colonel grunted in amusement. 'Glad to see you're getting along so well. Let's hope the bruise has faded by the time of your assignment. It wouldn't be professional to turn up looking like some street brawler.'

Connor nodded. 'I'm putting ice on it. But it wasn't exactly my fault. I don't think Ling likes me.'

The colonel looked surprised. 'Whatever makes you say that?'

'She's . . .' Connor wasn't sure how to phrase it and didn't want to sound like he was whining, 'she's *waspish* with me. Has been since my return from America.'

'Ling can be like that,' replied the colonel, brushing away Connor's concerns with a wave of his hand. 'I'm aware her social skills require a touch more finesse. But she comes from a tough background.'

Connor frowned. 'What do you mean?'

Colonel Black sucked his teeth and shook his head. 'Not my place to say. But don't concern yourself over whether Ling likes you or not. I'm confident she respects you. And that's what counts on a mission.'

'How can you be so sure?' asked Connor.

The colonel offered a wry grin. 'She wouldn't want to fight you if she didn't respect you.'

He indicated for Connor to take a seat. 'Now, why did you want to see me? I'm sure it's not just to show me your black eye.'

Perching on one of the red leather chairs, Connor summoned up the courage to talk. Unable to meet Colonel Black's piercing gaze, he admitted, 'I . . . don't think I'm ready for this assignment.'

'Nonsense,' snorted the colonel. 'I've just been reviewing your progress. That video of you and the refuse bin was inspirational. I'm even considering showing it to the other teams.'

'But I *failed* to protect my Principal.'

'No,' he instantly corrected Connor, 'you learnt what you should do next time to *prevent* that happening. Failure is the key to success; each mistake teaches us something. So when you're out in the field all that training comes together and you avoid such mistakes.'

'But I feel like I'm rushing too fast into my next assignment,' Connor argued. 'I've only just got over my injury –' he rubbed his thigh where the assassin's bullet had struck – 'and I've hardly had any advanced training.'

'Don't worry. You'll get more training once you're out there,' assured Colonel Black. 'The Ship Security Officer on board Mr Sterling's yacht is a former member of the Australian SAS. I've checked his background. Brad Harding is a good man. He'll back you up and he's agreed to teach you and Ling the necessary maritime security skills.'

'But . . .' Connor stopped. He realized he was losing this line of argument, so went straight to the heart of the matter. 'But I'm worried my first assignment was just a fluke. Beginner's luck.'

The colonel fixed Connor with an incredulous stare. 'If

that's the case, you have the luck of the gods, since you protected your Principal on *three* separate occasions. Listen, Operation Hidden Shield was a challenging assignment for any bodyguard. *Don't doubt your abilities.* You've proven your reactions are second to none. Without question, you're a chip off your father's block.'

'But I'm *not* my father,' said Connor firmly. 'I bet he never doubted himself like this.'

Colonel Black leant back in his chair, steepled his fingers and gazed thoughtfully at Connor. 'I'll tell you a story about your father.'

Connor's ears suddenly perked up. This was one of the reasons he'd joined Buddyguard in the first place. To learn more about his dad and the secret life he'd led as an SAS operative. Colonel Black, having been in his father's squadron, was the key to much of his hidden past.

'We were based in Afghanistan at the time, when two SAS troopers were seized by the Taliban who had infiltrated the Afghan police,' began the colonel. 'Our commander immediately initiated a rescue operation. We knew that the hostages were still being held in the police station, but that they could be spirited away at any moment. Our unit was all ready to go in, when we got word from Operation Command that permission for the rescue *hadn't* been granted by the MoD. There were apparently more important matters at stake than the lives of two soldiers . . . *diplomatic* reasons.'

Colonel Black's face grew thunderous at the memory of such political betrayal.

'The men were furious, none more so than your father,

Justin. He lived by the decree that "no man is left behind on the battlefield". So, as the unit's captain, he decided to launch the rescue mission anyway.'

'He disobeyed a *direct* order?' said Connor, shocked.

The colonel nodded. 'I know Justin harboured doubts as to whether he should go ahead with it. After all, his actions were tantamount to mutiny. Failure would result in catastrophic consequences, not just militarily but diplomatically. But his priority was the captured soldiers.'

Connor nodded and smiled. 'That sounds like my father. My mother often said he always put others first.'

'And that he did. Your father and the rest of his unit blasted their way into the police station. The soldiers fanned out, firing stun grenades and clearing each of the rooms in turn. As your father entered the last cell, he was confronted by a Taliban militant slicing a knife across one of the hostage's throats.'

Connor swallowed, instinctively putting a hand to his own throat at the gruesome image.

'Your father's reactions were second to none. He dispatched the militant with a single shot to the head.'

'What about the hostage?' asked Connor, breathless.

Colonel Black reached up and pulled his shirt collar down to reveal the long white scar that circled his neck.

'He survived,' the colonel said with a smile. 'That's why I have such faith in you, Connor, to protect others – just like your father did.'

CHAPTER 13

Connor pulled on his board shorts and stuffed his belongings into the locker. Stifling a yawn, he made his way through the empty changing room to the pool. Never in his life had he got up so early to go swimming. In fact, he'd rather do an early morning run than a swim any day – and on a Sunday a lie-in was preferable to both. But, with his forthcoming operation being at sea, Connor figured that he needed to work on his swimming skills.

As he stepped from the changing rooms, he caught sight of an abandoned wheelchair lying up-ended by the side of the pool. He glanced around, but nobody was to be seen.

'Charley?' he called, his voice bouncing off the white tiled walls and echoing his concern.

No one answered. Then he spotted her body at the bottom of the pool. Connor tossed aside his towel and dived in, the chill water shocking his system. Opening his eyes, the underwater scene was a blur of blue shadows and refracted sunlight from the pool's glass ceiling. He spied her black swimsuit against the white tiles and swam hard toward her. Grabbing hold of an outstretched arm, he kicked upwards with all his strength.

Charley's head bobbed to the surface at the same time as his.

'Hey!' she spluttered. 'What're you doing?'

Connor blinked away the water from his eyes and stared at her. 'You're OK?'

'Of course I am,' she replied, floating easily at his side. 'I was practising holding my breath. Useful if you're pinned down by a wave while surfing.'

'B-but I thought . . . you'd drowned.'

Charley crinkled her nose in puzzlement. 'Why on earth would you think that?'

'Because . . .' Connor glanced towards her wheelchair.

Charley immediately gave him *that* look. The one that said, *Don't judge me by my chair.*

'Sorry,' Connor mumbled, treading water. 'My mistake . . . I haven't had breakfast yet, not thinking straight,' he added by way of a lame excuse.

'Forget it,' she replied with half a smile. 'It's kinda sweet that you dived to my rescue, though. A true bodyguard reaction. The chair tipped over as I got in the water. I must have forgotten to apply the brake. But I can handle myself in the water.'

'Of course you can,' he said, annoyed at himself for forgetting that she'd once been a surfing champion. 'Still, isn't it a bit dangerous to be swimming on your own?'

'I could say the same about you,' she countered, a steely flash in her eyes. 'Since I've been in a wheelchair, I've had countless people tell me what I can and can't do. They see my disability as inability. But I soon realized the only person who can place restrictions on me is *me*.'

'You're right,' Connor replied, holding up a hand in apology. 'I was just . . . worried about you.'

Her expression softened slightly. 'What are you doing here anyway? You're never in the pool, not at this time at least.'

'I'm trying to prepare myself for Operation Gemini. And you?'

'Swimming, of course!' she said, laughing, her mood lightening as she lay back in the water. She splashed, twirling effortlessly with a single stroke of her arm. 'This is the one place where I can forget about my disability. All day long I'm like a prisoner in that chair. So this pool offers me the most freedom I can experience since losing the use of my legs.'

Connor didn't know what to say to this. He still had no idea what had happened to Charley on that fateful assignment the previous year. But he didn't press her for details. No doubt Charley would tell him in her own time, if she ever wanted to.

'I virtually grew up in the sea,' she continued. 'For me, swimming is second nature. Now it's the one thing I can do free of my chair. Yet –' Charley spun to look directly at Connor and he saw the fierce burn of determination in her gaze – 'my real dream is to surf again.'

She grinned at the impossibility of the challenge she'd set herself. 'And when that day comes I intend to be ready for it.'

Ducking her head beneath the water, she swam off down the length of the pool. Connor watched her speed away with the grace of a dolphin and could only admire her resolve. He realized Charley was the sort of person who, when faced with a barrier, wouldn't stop and turn round; she'd just smash through it. Inspired by her spirit, Connor questioned how he could doubt his own abilities, when Charley with her disability wouldn't even let doubt enter her mind.

With a new resolve, Connor put his head down and swam after her.

But after only eight lengths he found himself completely out of breath and his pulse racing. Gasping for air, he splashed the last few metres and clung on to the lip of the pool to recover.

'It's your breathing technique that's the problem,' said Charley as she towelled herself off on the poolside.

Connor glanced over. Blessed with slender limbs, tanned golden skin and beach-blonde hair, Charley looked the quintessential Californian beach girl. Legs dangling in the pool, it was hard to imagine that she had a disability at all.

'Your stroke is basically fine,' she continued, 'but you're trying to inhale *and* exhale when your head's above the water. Exhale *under* the water, then when you go to breathe you only have to inhale.'

'OK,' said Connor, nodding his appreciation.

Charley put down her towel and pulled herself into her chair. 'Next time I'll teach you how to breathe *bilaterally*. That'll make a massive difference to your swimming technique. You'll be able to cut through the water like an arrow.'

Wondering whether he'd heard right, Connor tried to clear his ears. 'Next time?'

'Yes,' beamed Charley, flipping the towel over her shoulder and wheeling away. 'I can't leave a job half-finished. Meet me in the pool tomorrow.'

'What time?' called Connor as she disappeared into the girls' changing room.

'Same time,' her voice echoed back.

Grateful as he was for her training offer, Connor groaned at the thought of another early morning start. *Why couldn't my assignment have been on dry land?*

CHAPTER 14

Dust swirled in the hot dry air as a white-and-chrome Land Cruiser bumped its way down Hobyo's unpaved street. In the furnace of mid-afternoon, the Somalian harbour town was largely deserted, except for a few scrawny children kicking a football made of plastic bags.

Sharif, a pot-bellied Somali with a thin moustache, gazed through his vehicle's blacked-out windows at the crumbling concrete buildings beyond. Some were whitewashed, others matched the dull brown of the road. All were topped with green corrugated tin roofs that had warped under the glare of the African sun.

The driver honked his horn and a goat, bleating indignantly, trotted out of the path of the oncoming 4x4. Turning a corner, the Land Cruiser entered the central square where, unexpectedly, the town was bustling with life. A throng of people crowded outside a two-storey building with flaking yellow walls, pockmarked by bullet holes.

The Land Cruiser ground to a halt beside three other 4x4s that were haphazardly parked in the middle of the road, their stereos blaring reggae-inspired tunes. Several young men in T-shirts and loose wrap-around *ma'awis* sarongs were slumped beneath a tree, chewing green khat leaves, AK47 machine guns cradled in their laps. They eyed the Land Cruiser with mild suspicion but made no move to investigate.

Sharif clambered out of the air-conditioned cocoon of the vehicle, his blue cotton shirt instantly sticking to him in the sapping heat as he strode over to the gathered mob.

'*Ii warran?*' he asked a woman wearing a black headscarf.

The young woman, her face dark and smooth as ebony, grinned at him. 'A ransom payout!' she replied in Somali and held up a slip of paper. 'I'm waiting to collect my share. I invested my ex-husband's rocket-propelled grenade in the company.'

Other fortunate investors, who'd gambled their money, weapons or belongings with the successful pirate gang, pushed and jostled their way forward to make their claims. But not everyone was jubilant. An elderly woman in a long blue *jilbaab* squatted in the dirt, her eyes red raw with tears.

'Has . . . anyone news . . . of my son?' she sobbed, raising her hands to the heavens.

Another woman crouched at her side, trying to offer comfort. 'I'm sure he's still at sea –'

Ignoring the old woman's sorrow, Sharif shouldered his way through the crowd into the former mayor's office that now housed the pirates' 'stock exchange', a facility for raising funds for hijack operations. Six brokers were dealing with the numerous claims of the town's investors, as well as welcoming new investments.

Sharif approached a round-faced man wearing gold-rimmed glasses. Sitting at a rickety wooden desk, the broker welcomed him with a gap-toothed grin.

'*Soo dhowow!*' he said in greeting. 'Cousin, please sit down.' He gestured to a battered plastic chair. 'How can I help you?'

Sharif immediately got down to business. 'I represent a client who wishes to invest in a pirate gang.'

'You mean "maritime company",' corrected the broker with a knowing wink.

'Ah . . . yes, of course,' Sharif agreed amiably, although both men knew what they were really talking about. 'And he only wants the best, the most reliable.'

The broker didn't even pause before replying. 'That'll be Oracle and his men.'

Flipping to a fresh page in his battered ledger, the broker licked the tip of his pencil, wrote the date and scored a line down one side. He glanced up at Sharif. 'What does your client have to invest? Weapons? Supplies? Cash?'

'Cash. And moreover he wants to be the *sole* investor in an operation.'

The broker's eyes widened, gleaming like silver coins in his black moon-face. 'I trust your client has deep pockets . . . start-up costs are a minimum of thirty thousand dollars.'

Sharif nodded and placed a blue sports bag on the table. 'There's fifty thousand. My client wishes to ensure the "maritime company" has the best resources for the job.'

The broker unzipped the bag and licked his lips at the sight of five large bundles of crisp $100 notes.

'I'll contact Oracle straight away,' he said, re-zipping the bag. But as he went to take it Sharif grabbed his wrist and locked eyes with the broker.

'My client *expects* results.'

The broker gave Sharif a regretful smile. 'Of course I respect such a request, but in this business, as you well know, we can offer no guarantees. Hijacking a ship is a risky business.'

'Then this should reduce the risk,' said Sharif, handing the broker a large brown envelope.

The broker went to open it.

'No,' said Sharif. 'For Oracle's eyes only.'

The broker held up his hand in apology. 'I only wished to note its contents. The return on a successful hijack-and-ransom is usually ten times the amount invested.' Placing the unopened envelope in the bag, he then carefully wrote down the items in his ledger. 'Who shall I name as the official investor? Yourself, Sharif?'

'No, I'm merely the middleman. No name. Just date it,' instructed Sharif.

The broker raised an eyebrow at this, but nonetheless did as instructed. He glanced up as he wrote. 'Is your client trustworthy?'

Sharif shrugged. 'He's rich. And pays cash in advance.'

'Then who needs trust?' laughed the broker. He tore a strip of paper from the bottom of his ledger. 'Your receipt.'

Sharif took the scrap of paper. 'Thank you, cousin. *Nabadeey*,' he said, bidding his farewell.

67

Leaving the bustling 'stock exchange', Sharif crossed the dusty square and clambered back into the Land Cruiser.

'It's done,' he said in English, handing his client the receipt.

The man in the back pocketed the paper slip without a word.

CHAPTER 15

'*Mayday, Mayday, Mayday! This is motor yacht* Athena, Athena, Athena. *Mayday* Athena. *My position is South 3° 52' 23", East 55° 34' 42", approximately five miles south-west of Denis Island. We have hit submerged object and are sinking. I have four persons on board. We require immediate assistance. Abandoning to life raft. Over.*'

The VHF radio crackled loudly with static.

No one responded to the distress call. Nor was a response expected.

Ling, who'd sent the message, sat safe and sound in Alpha team's classroom at Buddyguard Headquarters, miles from any sinking ship. She turned to Bugsy, radio mic in hand. 'Why does everything have to be repeated three times?'

Their surveillance and communications tutor, a bald-headed man with the stocky build of a wrestler, held up two stubby fingers. 'First, to ensure that the message is heard accurately. And, second, to distinguish it from other radio chatter.'

He lowered the radio's volume and faced the rest of the team.

'Knowing how to make a Mayday call is a vital skill for any crew member aboard a boat. It can mean the difference between life and death at sea.' His sharp beady eyes flicked across to Connor. 'Summarize the Mayday procedure for me.'

Connor glanced at his notes.

'Turn on VHF radio, check power, press and hold the red Distress button for five seconds –'

'Good. Now, Amir, what does this action do?' interjected Bugsy.

Amir was quick to respond. 'It broadcasts a digital alert to all DSC-equipped craft as well as the local coastguard. This will include your MMSI – the unique number identifying your craft – along with your position and the time.'

Bugsy gave his student a big thumbs up and Amir beamed. 'Jason, what if there's no response within fifteen seconds?'

'Err . . . repeat the distress call.'

'That's right. But this time by voice, just as Ling did.' Bugsy turned to Richie, who was gazing out of the window with a blank expression. 'Richie, what VHF channel should you transmit on?'

Richie fumbled for an answer. 'Umm . . . ten?'

'No, Channel Sixteen!' snapped Bugsy, tapping the dial on the radio that clearly indicated this. 'Pay attention. Just because you're not going on this mission, Richie, doesn't mean you won't need this knowledge in the future. All distress, urgency and safety signals are transmitted by international agreement on VHF Channel Sixteen. Make a note of this.'

With a begrudging effort, Richie opened his laptop and typed the information down.

Bugsy tutted at his student then resumed his questioning. 'So, Marc, what must you check before sending a verbal Mayday?'

Marc rubbed at his temple, trying to jog his memory. Then he clicked his fingers as he remembered. 'That the radio is switched to *high power* to transmit.'

Bugsy nodded. 'Connor, what is the official format of the Mayday call?'

Connor didn't need to check his notes this time. 'Repeat Mayday and the name of the vessel three times, then give your position, nature of the emergency, the number of people on board, what assistance you need, and finish by saying "over".'

Bugsy fired more questions around the room, allowing *no one* the opportunity to switch off from his lesson again. Once satisfied that Alpha team knew the protocol inside out, he announced, 'One important proviso about VHF radios – they have a limited "line-of-sight" range. In real terms, that's about forty miles from a coastal station, but only ten miles between two yachts. So, considering the size of the oceans, this is by no means a foolproof distress system.'

'How about using a mobile phone instead?' Amir suggested.

Ling laughed. 'You're at sea, stupid! Where will you get a signal?'

'In actual fact, mobiles can be used for requesting help,'

said Bugsy. 'In areas of little or seemingly no signal, a text might still stand a good chance of getting through.'

Amir gave Ling a triumphant look and waved his mobile in her face. 'See! It would work.'

'Teacher's pet,' she muttered, her eyes narrowing.

'Loser,' shot back Amir.

Ling made a grab for his mobile. 'Watch it or I'll stick that phone where there's *definitely* no signal!'

'Settle down, you two,' said Bugsy, wagging a finger at their childish squabbling. 'Ling's got a point, though. The signal range is limited to the coastal areas. Also, only one person hears your call and a mobile can't be homed in on as easily as a VHF transmission.'

Ling stuck her tongue out at Amir in smug victory.

Bugsy frowned at her behaviour but continued with his lecture. 'That's why most boats are equipped with satellite systems featuring voice, data, fax and GMDSS capabilities.'

'What's GMDSS?' asked Jason, struggling to make notes fast enough.

'Global Maritime Distress and Safety System. It's a highly sophisticated worldwide distress system that delivers emergency, safety and other communications, such as weather warnings and search-and-rescue messages –'

The class bell rang for lunch and, like all schoolkids, Alpha team began to pack away with impatient urgency.

'Just one more thing,' said Bugsy, holding up a bright yellow plastic cylinder with a light and short aerial at one end. 'This is an emergency position-indicating radio beacon. It transmits a distress signal to satellites and relays the information to a rescue coordination centre. EPIRBs are pretty cool gadgets, since they automatically activate upon immersion in water and have a float-free bracket if the vessel sinks.'

Bugsy placed the EPIRB on the desk for the class to examine. Then he stowed away his laptop, popped a piece of chewing gum into his mouth and headed out of the door.

Alpha team gathered their belongings and filed past the EPIRB, giving it the once-over.

Jason picked it up and regarded Connor. 'Let's pray there aren't any Maydays on your mission.'

'I'm with you there,' said Connor. Then he caught the odd expression on Jason's face. 'Hey, what do you mean by that?'

'Well, you got shot last time, didn't you?'

Nettled by the implied criticism, Connor held his rival's gaze. 'And I heard on your Caribbean assignment you got second-degree sunburn!'

A moment of tension hung between them. Then Jason's mouth broke into a wide grin.

'Fair point,' he chuckled, putting down the EPIRB and clapping a meaty arm round Connor's shoulders. 'That was rather stupid of me, wasn't it?' He glanced in Ling's direction as she left the classroom with Amir, the two of them now laughing together. 'Look, just watch Ling's back for me. That's all I'm asking.'

'I think she can look after herself,' replied Connor, indicating the faded shadow of his black eye from the previous week.

'Sure, she can,' agreed Jason, 'but if something goes wrong . . . you've only got each other to depend on.' His earth-brown eyes searched Connor's face as if looking for a chink in his armour. Then, with a final encouraging squeeze of his arm, he let go and shouldered his bag. 'I hear you and Ling are flying out to Oz to meet the girls before the holiday?'

Connor nodded. 'Yes, by request of Mr Sterling.'

'Well, enjoy my home turf,' he said with genuine warmth, heading for lunch. He paused a moment in the doorway as if remembering something. 'But watch out for dropbears.'

'Dropbears?' queried Connor.

'Yeah, vicious little creatures. Like koalas, only with teeth. My uncle was savaged by one last summer,' Jason explained. 'They hang in treetops and attack their prey by dropping on to their heads from above. Just be careful is all I'm saying.'

'Thanks for the heads up,' said Connor.

'No worries,' replied Jason, smiling.

CHAPTER 16

Connor and Ling entered the logistic supply room to find Amir already there. He stood behind the desk with an eager look on his face as if Christmas had come early.

'I've been waiting all morning to hand over your Go-bags,' he said.

Unable to contain his excitement any longer, Amir produced two black and fluorescent-yellow backpacks and laid them with due ceremony on the table. 'I've customized them specifically for Operation Gemini.'

'Well, no one's going to lose these in a hurry!' remarked Ling, eyeing the lurid yellow dubiously.

'That's the point,' said Amir. 'Ultra-reflective strips on the front and shoulder straps for maximum visibility at sea. A high-powered LED beacon for emergencies.' Amir indicated a tiny plastic dome beside the top grab handle. 'And these bags even have a mini-SART sewn into the lining!'

Amir looked up expectantly, waiting for them to share in his enthusiasm. Connor and Ling exchanged bemused glances. Amir rolled his eyes.

'Don't you two know anything? SART? Search-and-rescue transponder.' He pointed to a slightly fatter right-hand seam with an activation tag. 'The slim tube inside contains a small, battery-powered receiver and transmitter that operates on the 9-GHz frequency.'

'You've still lost us, I'm afraid,' admitted Connor.

'That frequency, 9 GHz, is the frequency . . . of X-band radar . . . on a ship,' Amir said slowly, as if explaining to two nursery kids. 'If you get into difficulties at sea, the transponder sends out a locating signal. Usually these gizmos are on life rafts and about the size of a two-litre water bottle. Bugsy, however, has managed to miniaturize it. The downside is the battery only has an eight-hour lifespan and its range is less than five nautical miles. Still, it could make all the difference in a search-and-rescue operation.'

Amir unclipped the top section of the backpack and began to unroll the opening.

'No zips mean no leakage,' he said, justifying the unusual roll-top design. 'This means the Go-bags are one hundred per cent waterproof and fully submersible. As long as you aren't carrying rocks, they'll even float!'

Amir patted the Go-bags proudly as if they were his favoured pets.

'Do they have a foldout liquid body-armour panel like before?' Connor asked.

Amir's expression fell a little. 'Unfortunately not,' he admitted. 'We couldn't fit an additional panel inside. But the back section itself *is* bulletproof.'

'That's good,' said Connor. He didn't wish to dampen Amir's spirits, but the foldout panel had been a key factor in saving his and his Principal's life during his first mission. A single panel, while still useful, would barely cover him, let alone his Principal.

Amir reached into the bags and produced a pair of mobile phones enclosed in bright orange neoprene covers.

'Your smartphones, upgraded to the newest operating system and virus-protection software.' He arched an eyebrow in Connor's direction. 'No danger of Cell-Finity bugs this time.'

'Glad to hear it,' said Connor as he weighed the phone in his hand and examined the unusual cover. 'A bit bulky, isn't it?'

'It was a trade-off,' said Amir, shrugging apologetically. 'We've waterproofed the phone with a spray-on microlayer, but to produce a buoyant cover we had to compromise on size.'

'I suppose it's better than losing it at the bottom of the sea,' said Ling cheerily.

Connor pressed his thumb to the screen, triggering the fingerprint security system. He examined the display of apps: *Advanced Mapping, Tracker, Face Recognition, Mission Status, Threat Level, SOS* . . . 'I'm glad to see your SOS app is still on here.'

'Of course,' Amir beamed. 'Version two. Improved battery life. Also, it allows for short message transfer as well as location data.'

Amir dug out the rest of the Go-bag's contents.

'You'll have all your usual gear: med-kits, earpieces with built-in mic for covert communication with one another, prepaid credit cards –'

'Now that's more like it,' grinned Ling, snatching up a card. 'Shopping time!'

'You'll need expert surveillance skills to find a shop in the middle of the Indian Ocean,' laughed Amir.

'You forget airport duty-free,' Ling replied with a devious wink, nudging Connor with her elbow.

Amir handed them a pile of clothes each. 'Here's your Buddyguard-issue gear: baseball cap, shorts, T-shirts, polo-shirt . . . all fire-retardant, stab-proof and, of course, bulletproof,' he said, looking up at Connor.

'Don't worry, I'll definitely be wearing these,' said Connor, holding up and inspecting the pocketed blue polo-shirt. It still amazed him that such soft thin fabric could stop a bullet from a handgun or the sharpened steel point of a knife.

'Is there a bulletproof bikini for me?' asked Ling.

Amir searched through her pile of clothes. 'Err, no, sorry.'

A smirk appeared on Ling's lips. 'I was only joking.'

Amir reddened as it dawned on him how ridiculous such an item would be. 'Oh, very funny.' He pulled a slim black torch from the Go-bag. 'By the way, Bugsy's supplied you with a new torch.'

Amir depressed the button and a glaringly bright green laser strobe flashed out.

'Hey, watch it!' exclaimed Ling, shielding her eyes. 'You almost blinded me.'

'That's kinda the aim of it,' said Amir, grinning like a Cheshire cat at his retaliation. 'It's a Dazzler.'

'A what?'

'A non-lethal weapon that temporarily blinds or disorientates your enemy.'

'Seems pretty lethal to me,' said Ling as she blinked away tears.

'Well, it won't kill anyone, and it works as a standard torch too,' Amir explained, putting the Dazzler back in the bag. 'Anyway, at the other end of the spectrum, so to speak, are your sunglasses.'

'It's all right, I still have mine from the last mission,' said Connor.

'Not like these you don't,' replied Amir, excitedly handing them each a pair. 'Put them on.'

As Connor and Ling slipped on the shades, Amir closed the blinds and switched off the room's light, plunging them into darkness.

'Hey, I can't see a thing!' Ling exclaimed.

'Flick the switch on the right edge of the frame.'

Finding the tiny switch with his fingernail, Connor gasped in awe as Amir and Ling reappeared before his eyes in a shimmering silver light. 'Now these are cool!'

'Night-vision sunglasses,' explained Amir, enjoying the looks of astonishment on his friends' faces. 'Cutting-edge nanotechnology in the lens allows you to see in the dark as if there's a full moon. There's a smart layer of nano-photonic film that converts infrared light to visible. Unlike standard night-vision goggles that only amplify visible light, these have the advantage of not being vulnerable to flaring when confronted with a bright light.'

Amir switched on the main light to prove his point. Connor could still see perfectly well, even if the room before him appeared over-exposed. He flicked off the night-vision mode and everything returned to normal.

'What else is in your bag of tricks?' asked Ling, now caught up in the thrill of such advanced gadgets at their disposal.

'Well, there's this,' said Amir, handing Ling a large white bottle.

'What is it?' she asked eagerly. 'A miniature life raft? A smoke grenade?'

'No, but it will protect you from the greatest danger you face on your mission.'

Ling looked expectantly at him. 'So, what is it?'

Amir was barely able to suppress his grin. 'It's sunscreen.'

CHAPTER 17

'What's going on in maths? You've got Bs and Cs in your other subjects, but an *E* for maths.'

Connor groaned down the phone. '*Mum* . . . I've had a few other things on my mind recently.'

'Like what?'

Connor didn't know how to answer that. His mum had no idea he was training and operating as a professional bodyguard. She'd been told that he was attending a boarding school for gifted and talented sports students, the cost sponsored by a special government scholarship scheme. That's why his mum only received a report card for the standard subjects. His appraisals in the other topics, ranging from world affairs to unarmed combat to anti-ambush training, went direct to Colonel Black.

'It's difficult to explain,' he admitted.

'Oh . . .' she said, a knowing tone entering her voice. 'You mean, a girl?'

Connor shifted awkwardly from one foot to the other and felt a flush fire his cheeks at his mum's line of questioning. 'No, nothing like that,' he protested.

'Listen, you can't let girls distract you from your work,' said his mum, ignoring his protest and thinking she knew better. 'They'll cause you enough trouble when you're older.'

Connor could think of two girls – Emily and Chloe – who *might* cause him trouble a lot sooner than that.

'Can we talk about something else?' he urged. 'Like you. How are you doing, Mum?'

'Oh, really well, thanks,' she replied cheerily. 'Improving day by day with Sally's help.'

Connor listened as his mum told him how her live-in carer had encouraged her to take vitamin D and do some light yoga exercises. This, along with a recent course of acupuncture, had really helped to ease her symptoms. However, all the while his mum talked, Connor could tell from the strain in her voice that she was putting on a brave front. As a sufferer of multiple sclerosis, his mum had difficulty with coordination and balance, was easily fatigued, and was often struck with numbness or grinding pain.

Her condition, along with his ageing gran's needs, had been the primary reason for Connor agreeing to join Buddyguard. In return for his service, Colonel Black had offered a complete care package for his mum and gran. Such health support was way beyond the financial reach of an unemployed army widow like his mother. And, at the time of the offer, his family was already struggling with basic day-to-day living costs. The colonel's deal was a virtual godsend. But as part of the deal Connor couldn't reveal to her his true role. The highly secretive Buddyguard organization relied on the fact that few people knew of its existence, allowing teenagers like Connor to act as invisible defence shields for vulnerable and high-profile targets. Besides, his mother would probably be furious if she discovered he was following in his father's footsteps – a path that might easily lead him to an early grave too. He didn't like deceiving her about it one bit, but he *did* like seeing her cared for properly. It was a trade-off and one worth making.

'I'm really glad to hear things are improving,' said Connor, despite his deeper concerns for her. 'Listen, I'm calling to let you know that I'll be away on a sailing trip next month, so I might be out of contact for a bit.'

During term time, Connor religiously rang home every week to check on his mum and gran, and he knew they both eagerly awaited his calls.

'A *sailing* trip! You certainly lead an exciting life at this new school of yours,' remarked his mum. Connor heard her relay the news to his gran and Sally before returning to the phone. 'One thing, son, please take extra care. I don't want you injuring yourself like last time.'

'I will,' said Connor, hoping the same himself. His mum had been led to believe that he'd hurt his leg falling off a mountain bike, the pretence necessary to keep his involvement in Buddyguard confidential.

'Hold on, love, Sally's calling me, but your gran wants a word. Speak again when you get back.'

There was a clatter as the phone changed hands. 'How's my big man?'

'Fine, Gran. And you?'

'As fit as a fiddle and as right as rain,' she replied brightly.

Connor laughed; that was what she always said.

His gran lowered her voice. 'I know she won't have told you, but your mum may have to go into a wheelchair soon.'

'What?' said Connor, stunned. 'She said she was getting better.'

'In some respects she is, and she doesn't want to worry you. Sally has just recommended that your mum uses one when she goes out. She's not as steady on her feet as she was.'

'But Mum was fine when I saw you both last month.'

His gran sighed. 'She had a relapse last weekend.'

Connor fell silent. This cruel disease was slowly stripping his mum of her quality of life. Every time he called or visited, it seemed like another little piece of her had been taken away. And there was nothing he, or anyone else, could do about it. He balled his hand into a fist and screwed his eyes shut, holding back the tears that threatened to come.

'As you would expect, she's not particularly happy about the idea,' continued his gran, 'but Sally says your "scholarship scheme" will cover the cost of the chair.'

Connor managed a sad smile. He might not be able to stop his mother's deterioration, but at least he could provide the necessary care for her – as well as for his gran. His work as a buddyguard meant they would be in safe hands, even if he was putting himself in harm's way and spending a lot less time with them both. He now understood his father's dilemma when he'd been alive.

'Are *you* all right, my dear?' asked his gran gently.

'Yeah,' he replied, wiping a sleeve across his reddened eyes.

'I hear you're going on a sailing trip,' she asked, switching topics. 'Anywhere nice?'

Connor realized her question was loaded. 'The Seychelles.'

'Ooh, lovely,' she cooed. 'Anything else you can tell me about your "trip"?'

'Not really . . .' replied Connor, aware that he was breaking security protocol just by telling her his destination.

Charley appeared round the corner and gave him the nod.

'Sorry, Gran, I have to go,' said Connor. 'Give Mum my love and I'll see you both soon.'

'Is that a promise?'

Connor momentarily hesitated. His gran's question was no mere platitude but a wish for a binding agreement. 'Of course, Gran.'

'Good. Then stay safe, my dear . . . stay safe.'

Connor could hear the anxious crack in his gran's voice as she ended the call.

He hated putting his gran through such worry and often wondered whether he should ever have told her about Buddyguard in the first place. But his gran would have seen through his half-truths like a priest in a confessional. She was too sharp and had lived too long to be fooled by anyone, let alone her grandson. Besides, Connor trusted her and needed her. She was his rock and, when life got tough, the one person he could always turn to for advice.

'Everything OK at home?' asked Charley.

Connor looked up, suddenly aware he'd been staring off into space. 'Yeah . . . my gran's fine. But my mum may have to go into a wheelchair. She isn't looking forward to it.'

'I know the feeling,' said Charley, patting the armrest of her chair. 'If your mum ever needs someone to talk to, then I'd be happy to give her a call.'

Connor smiled warmly at Charley's kindness. 'Thanks, I'll let her know.'

'Come on,' said Charley, pivoting on the spot. 'The car's waiting to take you to the airport.'

Connor followed Charley out to the black Range Rover parked on the long sweeping drive of Buddyguard Headquarters. The rest of Alpha team had assembled on the steps to see him and Ling off. Jody was in the driver's seat, checking the satnav for traffic, while Ling sat in the back, seat belt on, ready to go.

'Hurry up, partner!' she shouted, slapping the seat next to her. 'Let's get this show on the road.'

As Connor flung his bags into the boot, Amir shouted, 'Careful! That's my Go-bag you're chucking about.'

'It's mine now,' replied Connor with a grin. 'But I promise to look after it.'

'You'd better,' warned Amir, shaking his head in despair at the mishandling of his precious equipment.

'Good luck,' called Marc, waving. Beside him, Richie offered a mock salute.

'Don't let Connor take all the glory, Ling,' said Jason as Connor clambered in beside her.

Ling blew him a kiss. 'Don't worry. He's carrying my bags!'

With a final thumbs up to his teammates, Connor went to close the door, but Charley reached in and touched his arm.

'Try not to catch any bullets this time,' she said.

Connor gave her a quizzical look. 'Surely that's the point of a bodyguard?'

Charley locked eyes with him. '*Only* if all else fails.'

CHAPTER 18

'*Wake up, you lazy fish-eaters!*'

The stern order in Somali barely roused the loose band of pirates who lay sprawled, like dozing lions, beneath the shade of the courtyard's single acacia tree. The blazing sun had baked the earth bone-dry and the glaring white walls reflected the heat like mirrors. It was too hot even for the flies that buzzed listlessly in the still air.

'I said, GET UP! Oracle wants to see us,' growled the towering man who strode over from the main building of the walled compound. With broad shoulders and rippling muscles, forged from a hard and brutal life, the man moved through the shimmering heat like a charging black rhino. Over his shoulder was slung a battle-worn AK47.

'Hey, Spearhead, relax, man,' said one of the pirates, chewing languidly on some khat leaves.

Spearhead ground his ivory white teeth into a snarl and kicked the man in the ribs.

'Oww!' yelled the pirate, rolling away from the abuse.

'When I say move, Big Mouth, MOVE!'

The other men quickly got to their feet. Picking up their

rifles, they begrudgingly followed Spearhead across the blistering hot yard towards the main house. As they entered a dim wide hallway, the harsh sun was left behind and the air became cool and welcoming. Leaving their weapons by the door, the pirate gang trudged barefoot into a spacious living room. An ornate crimson rug took centre stage, framed by a slender beige divan. Thick maroon drapes blocked the persistent sunlight that tried to force its way through the barred windows behind. Each man instinctively salivated as their nostrils filled with the mouthwatering aroma of stewed goat's meat.

Oracle reclined on the rug against a gold-tasselled bolster, a wooden bowl of spiced ribs in one hand. In the other, he held a thin bone, which he gnawed at for the last vestiges of meat. Dressed in an olive shirt, with a red shawl slung over his right shoulder, and a black diamond-pattern *ma'awis* around his hips, Oracle cut a princely figure compared to the unkempt appearance of his pirates. A pair of silver-mirrored aviator sunglasses were perched high on his closely shaved head. Behind him on the divan, within arm's reach, lay a loaded Browning semi-automatic pistol.

'Sit,' said Oracle, picking with a fingernail at a bit of meat stuck between his teeth.

The pirates each found their spot on the luxurious rug and, squatting, waited mutely for their boss to finish his meal.

Eventually putting aside his empty bowl, Oracle licked his fingers then wiped them on a square of white cotton cloth. 'You'll be going to sea again within the week,' he announced.

The pirates all looked at one another with a mix of excitement and trepidation.

'You've had another vision?' asked a rake-thin man with jug ears.

Oracle smiled enigmatically. 'Well, let's say . . . I foresaw fortune headed our way.' He patted the blue sports bag cradled at his side. 'We have a new investor.'

'So what's happening with the cargo ship we've already got?' asked Spearhead.

'That'll take a few more months of negotiation,' replied Oracle. 'Red Claw and his men can handle the babysitting. I need *you* for the serious work.'

'But what about boats?' asked Big Mouth. 'We lost two skiffs in the last hijack.'

'It's all in hand,' reassured Oracle. 'Four brand-new twin three-fifty horsepower outboards are on their way from Dubai.'

'Can I pilot one?' beamed a skinny buck-toothed young pirate.

'When you can grow a beard you can!' laughed Spearhead.

As other pirates joined in the laughter, a mobile phone chirped loudly.

'It's not mine,' said Big Mouth quickly, knowing how much their boss frowned on having his meetings interrupted.

The ring persisted and now every pirate checked his phone, each one praying it wasn't his. Gradually all eyes turned to the innocuous sports bag.

Oracle's brow furrowed slightly. Then he nodded to

Spearhead to investigate. The great man bent down, unzipped the bag and removed a brown envelope. Its contents rang and vibrated. Ripping the envelope open, he pulled out a slim mobile phone.

Oracle indicated with a jut of his chin for Spearhead to answer.

'*Iska warran?*' Spearhead listened for a moment, then said, 'It's for you, boss,' offering the handset.

Oracle warily studied the intruding phone, then put it to his ear.

'*Haa* . . . Yes, I speak English . . .' he said, switching languages fluidly. 'Not at all, I was just having lunch . . . It's always a pleasure to hear from an investor.' However, his cordial words did not match his stony expression. 'Yes, I've received the full amount . . .'

The other pirates looked on, bemused by the foreign conversation. Only Spearhead among the pirate gang had a working command of English, and he listened with growing curiosity.

'Your request is highly unusual . . . What do you mean it *isn't* a request?' Oracle's expression darkened at the caller's unheard response. 'I answer to *no one*!' he snapped. 'No . . . I have not yet looked in the envelope.'

Oracle waved an impatient hand at Spearhead to pass it over. Turning out the contents, several typed sheets of paper and a large photo print of a yacht landed on the carpet. 'Yes, I can see the target you propose. But why would you want *that* when I could get you an oil tanker?'

Oracle listened to his investor's reply and his eyes took on a diamond-like sheen. '*How much* did you say?'

As the figure was reconfirmed, a greasy smile slid across Oracle's lips. 'Then we are in my business, my friend. I'll let you know as soon as my men are ready.'

Oracle flipped shut the mobile and laid it beside his handgun.

'Get Mr WiFi,' he ordered.

Spearhead jerked his bald head at Big Mouth, who left the room and returned a moment later accompanied by a bespectacled young man. With a neatly trimmed goatee, Bermuda shorts and a blue New York Yankees T-shirt, Mr WiFi looked more like a university student than a hardened pirate. Under his arm he carried a battered laptop.

'We have a hijacking to plan,' announced Oracle.

'About time,' smiled Mr WiFi, opening his laptop and angling the screen so Oracle could see the live satellite image of the Gulf of Aden. 'I'm tracking several high-value vessels as we speak.'

'Forget about them,' Oracle said, causing Mr WiFi's smile to vanish in dismay. He handed him the photo along with one of the info sheets. '*This* is our target.'

Perching on the edge of the divan, Mr WiFi hunched over his whirring laptop. The pirates ostrich-necked to try and see what he was doing as his fingers rapidly danced across the keyboard. In the search window of a hacked Marine Intelligence Unit website, Mr WiFi typed: *motor yacht Orchid* . . .

CHAPTER 19

Maddox Sterling's office was a glass wonder. A capsule of 360-degree views, its four walls were constructed from electro-chromatic smart windows. The special glass, stretching from the floor to ceiling, automatically altered its transparency according to the sun's strength and position in the sky. Being mid-morning, the eastern wall had darkened amber-brown against the golden light streaming over Sydney's Central Business District.

Maddox Sterling, his back to the shaded sun, stood as Colonel Black, Ling and Connor were ushered in by his PA. Entering the office was almost disconcerting. For Connor, it felt as if he could step right off the edge of the towering skyscraper and plummet fifty floors to the pavement below.

The office's interior design was as minimalist as the walls themselves. There was no furniture beyond a slim glass desk and four chrome and black leather chairs. For a man in charge of a billion-dollar corporation, the see-through desk was strangely uncluttered. No paperwork, no computer monitor, no ornaments, not even a picture of his daughters – just an ultra-thin aluminium laptop and a cordless phone.

'Welcome to Sydney,' said Maddox Sterling, greeting each of them with a firm handshake and a slick smile, then gesturing for them to take a seat.

'Thank you, Mr Sterling,' said Colonel Black, settling into one of the designer chairs, Ling and Connor taking their places either side of him.

From behind his desk, Maddox Sterling swivelled towards an unbroken view of one of Sydney's most iconic landmarks. With a broad sweep of his hand as if he owned it, he declared, 'Without doubt, the finest natural harbour in the world, made even more magnificent by our stunning opera house and the Sydney Harbour Bridge. Truly a sight to behold.'

Connor stared out of the window – first, at the sparkling waters of the harbour, then at the overlapping shell roof of the opera house, and finally at the dramatic latticework of arching girders that spanned the waterway. It certainly was an impressive sight.

'They call the bridge the Coathanger because of its arch-based design,' Mr Sterling explained, a hint of disapproval noticeable in his tone. 'But that does it a great disservice. Up close, it's truly majestic. The arch soars so high a ten-storey building could pass beneath. And the weight of the bridge is monstrous. Over three hundred and fifty thousand tons of steel and six million rivets went into its construction.'

He glanced sideways at Connor and Ling, checking to see they were suitably impressed.

'The bridge has a surface area larger than sixty football pitches, which means it needs a fifty-man team working three hundred and sixty-five days of the year just to clean and repaint it. Obviously such maintenance is incredibly dangerous work. That's why they've recently employed two autonomous robots for the more hazardous sections. An appropriate reduction of risk.'

Mr Sterling pivoted back to face them. His cobalt-blue eyes fixed first on Ling, then on Connor, with an intensity that seemed to cut right through them both.

'Similarly, I've employed *you two* to reduce the risk in my family's life.'

Connor wasn't sure how he felt about being compared to a mindless robot, but Mr Sterling didn't seem to consider this an insult and carried on regardless.

'I already have a personal protection officer, who will be accompanying me on the holiday. My yacht has a ship security officer and there are other safeguards in place here and at home. But, as you know, that wasn't enough. I have two beautiful daughters who are very precious to me. And God forbid that I have a repeat of last year.'

'You can rest assured, Mr Sterling, that my buddyguards will protect your daughters,' said Colonel Black. 'Since this is a family vacation, their presence will appear to be relaxed and low profile. But I can guarantee they'll be on constant alert to any threat and avert any danger.'

'Your organization comes highly recommended, Colonel Black, so I expect nothing less.'

Colonel Black didn't flinch under Maddox's steely gaze.

And he gave no answer, none being required when his belief in his recruits was absolute.

Mr Sterling wagged a finger in Connor's direction. 'Is this the lad that saved the President's daughter's life?'

Colonel Black nodded.

'Then I want *him* protecting Emily.'

Connor glanced over at Ling. Her lips had tightened, clearly taking the role assignment as an affront to her abilities. But she stayed silent.

'Not a problem,' agreed the colonel. 'Now I understand that you –'

A knock at the door disturbed them and the PA appeared. 'Sorry to interrupt, but the editor-in-chief says this can't wait.'

Mr Sterling nodded his assent and a red-headed woman in a tailored pinstripe jacket-and-skirt suit entered.

'What is it, Ruth?'

She shot a doubtful glance at the colonel and two young teenagers in his office. 'This might be better in private.'

'My apologies, Colonel Black,' said Mr Sterling with a regretful smile, 'but the world rarely stops in my line of business.'

'We understand,' said Colonel Black, rising to his feet. 'I can communicate any outstanding queries via your PA.'

'Then I'll bid you farewell and look forward to seeing these two in the Seychelles,' said Mr Sterling, offering both Ling and Connor a courteous nod. 'But before then I've arranged for you to meet my daughters for lunch at one of my restaurants. My PA has the details.'

Ruth stepped aside to allow them out through the glass door. As the door slowly closed behind them, Connor overheard a familiar name.

'There's more to Harry Gibb's heart attack than meets the eye . . .' the editor-in-chief began. '. . . Speculation he was murdered.'

'What evidence do you have?' asked Mr Sterling.

'Nothing conclusive at the moment. But I may have a source.'

'OK, look into it. If true, it'll take the flak off the *Daily* for allegedly causing that idiot's death through stress. As well as help sell a bucketload more papers –'

Then the glass door slid shut.

CHAPTER 20

'Is this a *joke*?' said Emily, putting down her glass of lemonade hard enough to make the ice tinkle. She stared at Connor and Ling as if waiting for the punchline.

Sitting in a rooftop restaurant overlooking the golden-sanded curve of Manly Beach, Connor removed his sunglasses and shook his head in response. 'Not at all. We've been assigned as your buddyguards.'

He looked from Emily to Chloe, a mirror image of her sister, with what he hoped was a convincing and reassuring smile. Both the girls wore pale-yellow summer dresses and matching designer sunglasses, flipped back on their heads to keep their straw-blonde hair out of their eyes. The twins had ordered the same tuna salad and tall iced lemonades.

Chloe maintained her composure, while Emily gave an incredulous snort. '*Buddy*-guards?' she laughed.

When her sister didn't join in her laughter, Emily spun on her, eyes narrowing with suspicion. 'Did you know about this?'

Chloe went to open her mouth, but Emily had already read her expression. 'Typical!' she cried, picking up her fork and waving it at her sister. 'Our father tells you everything.'

Chloe sighed. 'He didn't want you to flip out, thinking that he was being overprotective.'

'*Overprotective?* When has he been around us long enough to even *be* protective!' Emily stabbed at her tuna salad with the fork. 'Well, it's blindingly obvious just how much Daddy values our lives if he isn't even hiring a proper bodyguard.'

Chloe offered a rueful smile to Connor and Ling. 'Sorry,' she said, then mouthed, *Not a good day*, and raised an eyebrow meaningfully. Connor, recalling the psychological report detailing Emily's mood swings, nodded in understanding.

'But I do have to agree with my sister,' continued Chloe, her tone hardening. 'You're not what I expected. You don't really look like bodyguards.'

'We're not supposed to,' said Connor. 'We act as low-profile, invisible protection. This makes you less of a target when we're out and about.'

Chloe gave Ling the once-over, clearly unimpressed. 'You aren't exactly very big or strong. How on earth can you protect us?'

'I'm a black belt in martial arts,' Ling replied coolly. 'So is Connor.'

'*Really?*' said Emily, her tone dripping with sarcasm. 'Can you catch a fly with a pair of chopsticks like Karate Kid?'

Connor noticed Ling's fingers clench round her glass of

iced tea as she struggled to control her rising irritation with the girl. He shot her a silent warning to chill out. Taking a deep breath, Ling managed a strained smile. 'No, but I do know how to bring down a fully grown man by kicking him in the –'

'They get the point,' Connor interrupted, holding up a hand and wishing now that Colonel Black hadn't gone back to the hotel. He turned to the sisters. 'Look, I realize that we're not your stereotypical bodyguards. But we *are* fully trained in unarmed combat, surveillance and threat assessments.'

'I feel safer already!' muttered Emily.

'And we have experience in protecting people like you,' Connor persisted.

Chloe raised a dubious eyebrow. 'Like who?'

Connor replied with a regretful shrug. 'Unfortunately, we can't tell you. It would break client confidentiality.'

'So . . .' said Chloe after a moment's serious thought, 'you're asking us to trust *you* with our lives.'

'Absolutely,' Connor replied with as much confidence as he could convey.

'I *don't* think so,' said Emily, wielding her fork at them like it was a weapon. 'The last time I trusted someone I didn't know, I ended up in a hell hole!'

CHAPTER 21

An uncomfortable silence hung over the table, Chloe trying to make eye contact with her sister while Ling and Connor fidgeted with their drinks. Connor wanted to offer his sympathy, but there was little that could be said in response to Emily's outburst without sounding trite or insensitive.

After a few minutes of pushing their salads round their plates, Chloe sighed and piped up, 'Listen, Emily, our father's made his decision. They'll be with us on the yacht whether we like it or not, so we might as well try to get along. And why not take advantage of their supposed protection? Let's go down to the beach. We haven't been allowed that much freedom in months!'

Emily pushed her plate away and put aside her napkin. 'Fine,' she said, offering Connor and Ling a civil smile. 'At least my father will have someone to blame this time when things go wrong.'

Connor tried not to react to Emily's cynicism. Instead, he returned her smile and replied good-naturedly, 'With us on board, it should all be plain sailing.'

'Ha ha,' said Emily without humour as she picked up her Gucci handbag and strode off.

Shouldering a matching leather handbag, Chloe joined her sister and headed for the stairs.

'Well, that was a pleasant lunch,' said Ling, turning to Connor with a forced smile. 'Can't wait for the holiday!'

Connor sighed at the thought. 'They just need time to get used to the idea.'

'Well, I'm sure glad Emily's *your* responsibility,' said Ling, rising from her chair.

'So much for team spirit!'

'Hey, you're the hotshot bodyguard,' she replied, punching him playfully on the arm. 'You can handle her.'

Connor just hoped he could. An uncooperative Principal made the task of being an effective bodyguard almost impossible. 'Then we'll just have to convince them both we can do the job.'

Catching up with the twins at the restaurant entrance, Connor quickened his pace to reach the glass double doors first. Stepping outside and holding the door, he did a quick scan up and down the road. Although Operation Gemini hadn't officially started, he nonetheless took up his bodyguard role. So too did Ling, who hung back inside the cafe to cover their backs.

In his split-second surveillance sweep, Connor observed a couple of cars heading in their direction and a battered white pickup truck parked on the opposite side. Further along the street a lady was pushing a stroller with a screaming baby inside, while nearby a young couple was entering a clothes store. Satisfied none of these presented a viable threat, Connor stepped aside to allow Emily and Chloe out.

'Thank you,' said Chloe, taking Connor's door-holding as a gesture of politeness rather than security.

'Just checking the coast was clear,' Connor explained.

She glanced over the road at the turquoise sea and white-crested waves peeling along the shoreline. 'Of course it is!' She laughed, donning her sunglasses. 'It's a glorious day.'

'You misunderstand,' said Ling. 'Connor was performing a security sweep before you left the restaurant.'

Chloe raised an eyebrow. 'Manly Beach is *hardly* a war zone.'

'You'd be surprised,' said Connor as they crossed the road to the wide treelined promenade that hugged the golden stretch of beach. Passing by a bench, Connor noticed the eyes of four teenage surfers keenly following their progress. But he wasn't overly concerned. Emily and Chloe's twin looks naturally attracted attention – though Connor realized at some point they were bound to draw *unwanted* attention.

'There may not be guns or bombs going off around here,' he explained, 'but you're still at risk.'

'From what?' asked Chloe, gesturing with her hand at the idyllic scene – the path thronged with laughing teenagers, sun worshippers, red-faced tourists and bronzed surfers, their boards tucked under their arms. A leisurely stream of bikes glided by on the cycle lane, while inline skaters weaved in and out at high speed.

'You're not only at risk from known threats, such as enemies of your father or professional kidnappers,' Ling replied, glancing meaningfully at Emily, 'but also from anything that might happen on the street – muggings, pickpocketing, car accidents, trip hazards, fights –'

'You're beginning to sound like our father. We're only going for a *walk* along the beach,' said Chloe, sighing in exasperation.

'That's when a Principal is most vulnerable,' stated Connor. 'See that woman over there.' He pointed to a lady in a red bikini spread out on a beach towel, chatting on her phone and gazing at the surf. 'She's in Code White.'

'Code *what*?' asked Emily, showing her first sign of interest in the conversation.

'Code White. It refers to a person's mental state when they're switched off to their environment, lost in their own bubble. Most people live their lives like this: oblivious to the potential dangers surrounding them. Even from here I can see her bag contains her wallet, car keys and an iPad. Someone could rob her before she's even aware her belongings are gone.'

'Aren't you being a bit paranoid?' Chloe suggested.

'No, just hyper-vigilant,' replied Ling. 'As your buddyguards, we can't afford to switch off like that. We need to be in Code Yellow – relaxed awareness – the default mindset of a trained bodyguard.'

'So you're constantly on edge?' said Emily, her curiosity overcoming her mood.

'Not exactly,' replied Connor. 'We're just aware of the

people around us, the environment we're walking through and any potential dangers. For example, did either of you notice the white pickup truck parked on the other side of the road earlier?

'No,' said Chloe, looking back over her shoulder.

'Then you wouldn't have seen the two guys in the front cab.'

Chloe and Emily turned to stare.

'So what?' said Chloe. 'They're just hanging out.'

'If that's the case, why do they have a pair of high-powered binoculars on the dashboard?' Connor challenged.

Chloe shrugged. 'Maybe they're checking out the waves?'

'Or they're bird spotters,' suggested Emily, nodding up towards the branches of the pine trees where a couple of white cockatoos squawked loudly.

'With bandanas and shades, they don't strike me as the type to watch that sort of birdlife. And, with no boards in the back, they aren't here to surf.'

'So what *are* they doing?' asked Chloe, an edge of excitement entering her voice.

'I've no proof they're a threat,' said Connor. 'They could be undercover police officers on surveillance. Or simply workmen on their lunch break. I only *suspect* they might be bag thieves. But since I'm alert to their presence they can't take me by surprise, like they would that woman.'

'Wow! I didn't realize there was so much to this bodyguard business,' said Chloe, studying Connor and Ling in a new light.

'That's barely scratching the surface of what we do,' replied Ling, shooting Connor a sly wink that at least Chloe was beginning to appreciate their worth. 'But, if people were more aware, they'd be less likely to get into trouble. Who knows, if either of you or your father had been more switched-on last year, the kidnapping might not even have happened!'

Connor winced at Ling's tactlessness.

'Well, it did,' said Chloe, glaring at Ling as Emily's expression darkened and she once more fell into tight-lipped silence. 'Anyway, you don't know what happened, so you have no right to pass judgement.'

'I'm only saying . . . that it won't happen this time because you've got *us* to watch out for you,' blurted Ling, trying to rescue the situation.

Chloe's phone rang, a chirpy pop tune interrupting the tense moment. Chloe pulled out a slim white mobile and answered. 'Hi, Josie . . . Yeah, OK . . . Just down on Manly . . . I know, first time in ages . . . Yeah, I'd love to, but you know what my father's like . . . You could come over to ours . . .'

As Chloe chatted with her friend, she slowed to a stop by the sea wall. But Emily kept going – splitting the group up. Ling hung behind, giving Chloe the space to talk, while Connor stuck with his Principal, purposefully manoeuvring himself to her right-hand side. During close-protection 'walking drills', he'd learnt that this position was best for a right-handed bodyguard. In an attack, he could pull the Principal away with his left hand, while at the same time using his stronger right arm to fend off the attacker or draw a weapon.

As they wandered away, Ling held open her palms in a sign of sheepish apology to Connor. But he just waved the problem aside. Mistakes happened.

Now he was on his own with Emily, Connor decided it was an opportunity to try and bond with her. 'Sorry about what Ling said back there,' he began. 'She can be quite . . . *blunt* at times.'

'Hmm,' said Emily, barely acknowledging him, her mind seeming to be elsewhere.

'Perhaps it would help if you told me what did happen?'

'I'd prefer not to talk about it.'

'Sure,' said Connor.

After a couple more attempts at conversation, both of which resulted in monosyllabic replies, he decided the best strategy would be to walk in silence. No point in annoying Emily further. Besides, it wasn't his job to be her friend. He was there to protect her.

Connor maintained a sharp watch on his surroundings. A couple of inline skaters were speeding along on the path ahead. A pair of rainbow lorikeets screeched in the branches above. A blond surfer with his board tucked under his arm strutted past. He gave Emily the eye until he noticed Connor staring at him.

As they strolled along the shaded avenue of towering pine trees, Emily studied Connor out of the corner of her eye.

'Why do you keep looking up?' she asked eventually.

Connor, who hadn't realized he was being so obvious, replied, 'Dropbears.'

Emily did a double take, then let out a short burst of laughter – her first genuine expression of good humour.

Connor furrowed his brow. 'What's so funny?'

'You are,' she replied. 'Dropbears of all things!'

'But my Aussie friend Jason said they were really vicious.'

Emily searched Connor's face and saw only genuine concern, which made her laugh even harder. 'You actually think they're *real*. It's just a joke Aussies tell tourists to scare or confuse them. You Poms are so gullible!'

Connor felt his face flush. He'd been suckered by Jason's dropbear story. And now he looked like a fool in front of his Principal. This was not a good start to the operation. Emily would think him a total idiot –

But he was snapped out of his thoughts when Emily's laughter suddenly turned to a scream.

The attack happened so fast – and so unexpectedly – that for a split second Connor failed to react . . .

Then his bodyguard training took over. Seizing Emily's shoulder with his left hand, he wrenched her away from the threat and stepped forward to shield her with his body.

The inline skater was a blur as he barrelled into Connor. The man grabbed Emily's Gucci bag and attempted to rip it from her shoulder. His forward momentum spun Connor and Emily round, almost pulling them off their feet.

In an effort to break the skater's fierce grip, Connor drove his knuckled fist into the tendons of the man's wrist. The skater, a bare-chested brute with a roaring lion tattoo on his bicep, grunted in pain but hung on tenaciously. Spinning them round again, he caught Connor across the jaw with his elbow. Connor's head rocked back and he tasted blood. The skater yanked at the bag and the strap snapped. Emily tumbled to the ground, Connor sprawling on top of her.

'Are you . . . all right?' Connor gasped as he watched the mugger skate away, his loot in tow.

She nodded, then stuttered, 'M-my bag . . .'

But the high-speed thief didn't get far.

Ling, who'd witnessed the attack from a distance, snatched a board from a passing surfer and swung it hard at the escaping thief. The edge slammed with full force into the man's gut. A pained exhalation burst from his lungs and he lost his grip on the bag. Nosediving into the concrete, the skater careered across the path and into a nearby tree trunk.

But no sooner had Ling dealt with this attacker than a second skater charged in Chloe's direction.

'Watch out!' Connor bawled at the top of his lungs. But Chloe just stood there, wide-eyed, like a rabbit caught in the headlights.

The skater, a dome-headed black man with wrap-around shades, sped towards her with the force of a battering ram. With only seconds to react, Ling discarded the surfboard and launched herself into his path. Small as she was, she collided hard enough to knock him off course. They both struck the concrete sea wall and toppled over the side. Pile-driving into the sand below and crushing a child's sandcastle, Ling and the skater fought to disentangle themselves.

Meanwhile, Connor rushed over with Emily to her sister in readiness to protect them *both* if he had to.

'Stay close to me,' he ordered the girls, as Ling and the skater battled it out on the beach.

Wrestling in his grip, Ling flipped her head back, catching the skater under the chin. His teeth rattled in his skull and he roared in fury. Shoving a large hand into Ling's face, he pushed her away, rolled on top and used his weight to crush her. Ling was pinned but Connor couldn't go to her rescue.

If he did, he'd be leaving both their Principals unprotected.

He needn't have worried, though. As the man attempted to subdue her, Ling reached down and pinched a nerve point in the middle of his inner thigh. He yelped like a kicked dog and leapt off Ling as if he'd been electrocuted.

'Leave me alone, you wild cat!' he shouted, shocked by her combat abilities.

As Ling flipped to her feet and advanced on him, he snatched in desperation at a handful of sand and threw it into Ling's face. Too close to avoid the attack, Ling staggered away, half-blinded. By the time she'd wiped the grit from her eyes, the skater had stumbled along the beach and up the steps to the boulevard.

Stunned beachgoers stared at the four teenagers, trying to make sense of what had just happened.

'Are you OK?' Connor called to Ling.

'Yes,' she replied, still spitting sand. 'Are the twins safe?'

Still buzzing with adrenalin, Connor scanned the area for further threats. Just because they'd fended off this attack didn't mean the danger was over.

'Yes, it seems all clear.'

The lifeguard was sprinting over, calling the police on his walkie-talkie. A group of beach bums were applauding Ling's fighting skills as she made her way up the steps. The blond surfer near Chloe was kneeling beside his board, checking it for damage.

But the two skaters had vanished.

So too had the white pickup truck.

'That was no random mugging,' said Connor, nursing his lip with a bag of ice from the hotel's minibar. Having called Mr Sterling's chauffeur, they'd escorted the girls back to their home, a gated mansion on Point Piper. Then the two of them had been dropped off at their hotel in Circular Quay.

'Thieves often work in pairs,' Ling observed as she settled back on her bed and flicked through the TV channels.

'Don't you think it's a little suspicious that *both* the girls were attacked?'

Ling shrugged. 'Not really. They were carrying expensive designer handbags. That made them a target. Hey, cool, a Bruce Lee movie!' She tossed aside the remote.

Connor set down his bag of ice. 'How can you be so relaxed about all of this?'

'We stopped them. Job done,' said Ling, folding her arms behind her head and focusing on the TV screen. 'Now stop worrying and watch the film.'

'I disagree. There's *everything* to be worried about. It can't be coincidence. The attack had to be planned. What about those men in the pickup truck? Perhaps my instinct was right. Maybe they were carrying out surveillance on us?'

Ling glanced over. 'For what purpose?'

'To test our skills.'

Ling sat up and muted the TV. 'Are you suggesting that Mr Sterling would have his own daughters *mugged*?'

Connor nodded. 'Either that, or someone else has a personal grudge against the girls. If it's the latter, then we have a real problem on our hands.'

There was a knock at the door. Connor got up, checked the peephole, then unlocked the latch.

Colonel Black strode in and switched off the TV. 'I've just come off the phone with Mr Sterling.'

Connor braced himself for the fallout. Although they'd protected the girls, he knew he'd been slow to react. That stupid dropbear prank of Jason's had distracted him at the crucial moment. If he'd been switched on and in Code Yellow, he would have noticed the skater's approach, questioned his diversion from the cycle track and taken action to remove Emily from the danger zone *before* the attack. Only Ling's speedy intervention had stopped the skater escaping with her bag.

'So what did he say?' Ling prompted.

Colonel Black offered one of his rare smiles. 'He was delighted with your reactions today.'

Relieved, Connor slammed a fist into his palm. 'I told you!'

The colonel's brow knotted with puzzlement. 'What are you talking about?'

Connor explained his suspicions regarding the mugging being a set-up job.

Colonel Black glanced out of the hotel window at the opera house and rubbed his chin. 'You've no firm proof. And, judging by my conversation with Mr Sterling, I'd be surprised. So we must assume a hostile party is involved. Could you identify the men?'

'The two skaters, yes. Mine had a distinctive lion tattoo on his arm,' replied Connor.

'And I won't easily forget how bad my guy's breath smelt!' said Ling, waving a hand in front of her pinched nose.

'But the men in the truck, no,' Connor admitted. 'Their bandanas and shades covered most of their faces.'

'Then this is our wake-up call,' said Colonel Black, fixing them with his flint-grey eyes. 'Operation Gemini has to be watertight. In the Seychelles, you'll be surrounded by sunscreen and bikinis, but you must remain focused on the job. Remember, you are *not* on holiday.'

CHAPTER 24

Mr WiFi whistled in admiration as he examined the *Orchid*'s specifications online. 'This is one fine yacht: fifty metres of pure French style and craftsmanship.'

He scrolled down the page, his small rounded eyes sucking in the information.

'Four decks, six guest cabins, a range of four thousand nautical miles, cruising speed of *twenty-four knots*.' He glanced over the rim of his glasses at the mighty bulk of Spearhead. 'That's fast for its size! Carbon-reinforced hull and superstructure, jacuzzi, sauna, gymnasium, speedboat, jet skis –'

'Just give me the weaknesses,' ordered the pirate, who sat cross-legged beside the computer whizz in Oracle's makeshift operations room. No more than a whitewashed concrete box, the airless room had a red tiled floor, two barred windows and a bare electric light bulb that hung from the cracked ceiling like a withered fruit. The bulb flickered, a slave to the fluctuating output of the compound's generator, and its pale yellow light dimmed over the two plotting men.

Mr WiFi sucked his teeth thoughtfully. 'Well, her top speed is twenty-eight knots. That means your boats will be hard pushed to outrun her. So you'll need to sneak up in the blind spot of their radar –' he indicated the rear of the vessel on the laptop screen – 'to have any hope of getting the jump on them.'

'Leave the battle tactics to me,' grunted Spearhead. 'What's the height to the deck?'

Checking the boat's dimensions, Mr WiFi frowned. 'The freeboard is quite high for a yacht, over five metres. That might cause some probl–'

'Pah!' Spearhead dismissed, swatting at a mosquito on his neck. 'I've scaled far higher. No problem.'

'Still, I'd advise taking the *Orchid* from the stern,' said Mr WiFi, angling the screen for the pirate to get a better view of the yacht. 'See where the hull slopes over the tender garage. That's her weakest point.'

Spearhead nodded, his marble-smooth brow shining in the glow of the buzzing light bulb. 'How many crew?'

'Ten,' replied Mr WiFi, pulling up an internal layout of the boat. 'Their quarters are located in the bow on the lower deck. The bridge is on the upper deck. This plan doesn't show a citadel, but I'm guessing the best location for a safe room will be either the crew's quarters here –' he pointed to an area in the bow – 'or the master cabin on the main deck. The yacht's equipped with a satellite Global Maritime Distress and Safety System, DSC radio and EPIRB, so you'll have to ensure all these are disabled as soon as you board.'

Spearhead snorted. 'Shame we can't sabotage them beforehand. So, what about defences?'

Mr WiFi laughed. 'It's a *pleasure* boat, Spearhead. No razor wire or water cannon. You won't be impressing us with your war stories this time.'

'Where's the challenge then?' he said with a sly grin, his teeth appearing like a crescent moon in the twilight.

Mr WiFi peered over his glasses and replied, 'There isn't any. Compared to a cargo ship, the *Orchid*'s a sitting duck.'

As Connor and Ling stepped from the gangplank on to the main deck of the super-yacht, a portly gentleman in a crisp white short-sleeved shirt with gold insignia, navy-blue trousers and a peaked white cap greeted them.

'Welcome aboard the *Orchid*. I'm Captain Thomas Locke,' he said, tipping his cap respectfully at Ling. 'This here is my chief officer, Danny Fielding.'

A large bearded sailor with a tanned face, wrinkled by sun and saltwater, saluted in greeting. 'A pleasure to meet you,' he said in a deep gravelly tone.

The captain gestured towards the third man who completed the welcoming party on deck. 'And this is Brad Harding, our ship security officer.'

Tall with a sharp crew cut, Brad appeared every inch the textbook security officer. He possessed a well-honed physique that threatened to split the seams of his white polo-shirt. With his anvil-like jaw, he looked as if he could chew through steel. When he offered a calloused hand to shake, Connor all too easily felt the iron strength in the man's grip.

'I've never worked with nippers before,' said Brad, his Australian twang prominent as he beamed a lopsided smile, 'but I expect we'll get on famously.'

Connor and Ling smiled back, a little in awe of the sheer physical presence of the man. 'I'm sure we will,' said Ling.

'You'll be reporting to Brad while on board,' Captain Locke explained. 'He's fully briefed me as to your "purpose" on my ship.' His tone hardened slightly. 'But as captain I have *ultimate* authority over all matters of safety and security. If you see something suspicious or there is a security breach of any sort, you're to report it immediately to either Brad or myself. I do *not* want you operating on your own. Do you understand?'

Connor exchanged a glance with Ling, both aware they'd need to report any such incidents to Colonel Black and Alpha team too.

'Yes, Captain,' he replied, the correct form of address seeming to allay Captain Locke's concern.

'Good. Then I expect Mr Sterling's vacation to go smoothly,' he said with a satisfied nod. 'The rest of the crew, who you'll meet tomorrow, aren't aware of your credentials. They've been told you're special guests of Mr Sterling. I think this is best to maintain your cover and your security function.'

'That's how we prefer to operate,' said Ling.

Captain Locke tipped his cap again. 'Then I'll leave you in Brad's capable hands.'

The captain and his chief officer strode off towards a flight of steps leading to the bridge.

'I guess you must have had a long flight,' said Brad, nodding at their crumpled clothes and washed-out faces.

'Twenty-seven hours and three flight changes, to be exact,' replied Ling wearily. Dark shadows ringed her eyes, not surprising given the fact she'd chain-watched movies and only catnapped. Connor had barely slept either, the mysterious double mugging still preying on his mind.

'Well, I'll just give you a brief tour of the yacht before showing you to your quarters.'

Picking up their bags, Connor and Ling followed Brad across the expansive aft deck. He opened a set of bay doors and they exchanged the balmy warmth of the tropics for the cool interior of a large salon.

'This is the main living area,' explained Brad as Connor and Ling stared open-mouthed at the luxurious decor. White leather couches with lemon-zest scatter cushions took centre stage round a low-slung coffee table. At the far end, a white oak dining table was complemented by a mirrored cocktail bar. Floor-to-ceiling windows on either side let in reams of natural light, while offering unbroken views of the Indian Ocean to port and, to starboard, the leisurely comings and goings of the island's main harbour.

'That's some view!' gushed Ling, peering through the window at the mist-shrouded peaks of Mahé's mountains, their lush forested slopes seeming to tumble into the glassy waters of the bay.

'But isn't this lounge a little *exposed*?' Connor observed, his bodyguard brain noting the security flaw.

Brad arched a wiry eyebrow at him. 'Not bad observation

skills, nipper, considering your jet lag. But these are smart windows. Mr Sterling has a thing for them. Flick of a switch and they become obscure.'

Reaching over to a wall panel, Brad pressed a button and the windows instantly turned white.

'Cool,' said Ling.

Brad ushered Connor and Ling into a large hallway with a curving staircase, one flight leading up, another heading down.

'On this main deck, we also have a galley, study, cabin for Mr Sterling's personal bodyguard and, up front –' Brad opened a sleek wooden door – 'Mr Sterling's personal master suite.'

He stepped aside to allow them a peek into a spacious leather-upholstered bedroom. A wide panoramic window offered a captain's-eye view of the ocean from the comfort of a kingsize bed. As Connor and Ling tried to take in the sheer opulence of the room, Brad continued his tour talk, 'On the upper deck is the sky lounge, a VIP guest room, the captain's cabin and the bridge. Above that is the sun deck with another bar, sunloungers and a jacuzzi.'

'It's like a five-star hotel!' Ling gasped, unable to believe her eyes or ears.

'For Mr Sterling and his guests, it certainly is,' Brad replied, winking at her. 'But it's a little more cramped in the crew's quarters.'

'And that's where we're staying?' asked Connor.

Brad laughed. 'No, you lucky gits! For security reasons I've kept you close to the girls.' He directed them down the curving staircase to the lower deck. 'Emily and Chloe's rooms are just down the corridor from you. These are your cabins.'

He opened a pair of adjacent doors, revealing two well-appointed rooms with low futon-style beds. One was decorated in shades of olive green, the other kitted out in a rich chocolate-brown decor.

'Now unpack, freshen up and get some shut-eye,' instructed Brad. 'We'll start your MARSEC training in the morning.'

'MARSEC?' queried Connor.

'Maritime Security. Meet me on the upper deck at 0700 hours.'

He gave them a cheery nod of his head, then bounded back up the staircase.

'Bagsy this room,' said Ling, tossing her pack on to the neatly pressed olive linen of her chosen bed. She explored the en suite shower room, a gleaming cubicle of mirror and glass, then on inspecting the designer built-in wardrobes, was delighted to discover a concealed TV screen behind one panel. Throwing herself on the bed, she gazed out of the large porthole window. Through the glass, the topaz tropical waters rippled in the golden sunlight and the fronds of palm trees could be seen swaying along a pure white beach.

'This is paradise,' she cooed, glancing over her shoulder at Connor. 'I know what the colonel said, but how can this assignment be anything *but* a holiday?'

CHAPTER 26

'When it comes to maritime security matters, this isn't just the same as land that's blue,' said Brad, indicating the turquoise sea lapping around them. 'You need to acquire specialist skills and adopt a completely different mindset.'

Connor and Ling listened as they ate their breakfast in the sky lounge. The chef, a jolly man with a reassuringly large belly, had prepared them a delicious platter of watermelon, pineapple, kiwi and strawberries, along with honeyed Greek yogurt, granola and freshly squeezed orange juice.

The morning sun, shimmering in a cloudless sky, was wonderfully warming on Connor's back and he felt more at ease than he had for a long while. Perhaps it was the combination of a good night's sleep, the idyllic surroundings and Brad's easy confidence that reassured him the operation would go smoothly.

Ling appeared even more laid-back and at one with the yachting lifestyle. Kitted out in her shades, a bikini top and shorts, she looked ready for a day of sunbathing on the beach. But any sense of holiday spirit was soon quashed by the training itinerary laid out by Brad on the table.

'We've only a week before Mr Sterling's arrival. So we've a lot to cover in very little time,' he explained, pointing to the first day of the schedule. 'You need to be able to handle the powerboat, read radar, understand charts, learn open-water survival techniques, be familiar with the ship security plan, operate the VHF radio –'

'We know how to do that already,' said Ling, popping a fresh strawberry into her mouth.

'Stellar!' he grinned. 'Then *you* can show me later, Lightning Ling.'

Ling sat up. 'How do you know my nickname?'

Brad tapped his nose confidentially with his index finger. 'I do my research. Now finish your brekkie and follow me.'

Leading them up to the sun deck, he stood by the gleaming rail and with a wide sweep of his arm gestured at the almost 360-degree outlook. Connor was once again struck by the majestic beauty of the island: all lush forested slopes, coconut palms and colourful tropical birds, their gleeful chatter filling the scented air. And, judging by the number of other yachts and sailboats moored in the harbour, this slice of Eden attracted the super-rich like bees to a honeypot.

'Vigilance is the key to protection on board a boat,' Brad explained. 'A constant watch is needed, both at sea and in anchorage. Don't rely on the crew to do any security detail; they're fully engaged in their normal crew duties.'

Leaning against the rail, he pointed down at one of the deckhands, a lanky South African called Jordan, who was mopping the main deck while listening to music on his headphones.

'When in safe harbour, the crew are generally relaxed and unobservant, but *we* can't afford to be.' He jerked his chin in the direction of a rubber dinghy buzzing by. 'Small craft like that tender are scooting round all the time, so the approach of a suspect boat can go unnoticed. In a popular harbour like this, anyone with criminal intent has lots of useful cover, and it's even harder to spot them at night. That's why gangplanks should be raised whenever possible.'

He glanced down at the *Orchid*'s lowered gangway and clicked his tongue in irritation.

'In practical terms, the need for shore access means this only happens late at night. The problem is that harbour areas attract thieves and other low life. So suspect *anyone* approaching our yacht, even officials in uniform. Don't be afraid to question them. Deception is a common tactic of the criminal. I've known ruses from people masquerading as pier-side pizza delivery boys, to parading a pretty girl in a bikini as a distraction. Not that I've fallen for that one, of course.'

He shot Connor a sly wink, then beckoned them both to follow him back down the stairs and along a short corridor. Brad knocked on an open bulkhead door.

'Request permission to come on the bridge, Captain.'

'Request granted,' replied Captain Locke.

As they entered, Captain Locke nodded a brief greeting in their direction, then returned to the ship's systems check with Chief Officer Fielding.

The bridge wasn't anything like Connor had envisioned. Gone were the traditional wooden wheel for the helmsman, the brass compass tower and table overspilling with paper charts. Instead, this super-yacht's bridge was decked out with computer monitors, dynamic positioning systems, integrated communication units, electronic radar displays, and a sports car-style steering wheel and throttle, complete with leather-upholstered captain's chair.

'It's like the Starship *Enterprise*,' remarked Connor.

The chief officer grunted a laugh. 'That's why you need a master's degree in computing just to pilot her.'

'You don't say,' said Ling as she stared perplexed at a screen of concentric circles, bearings and electronic waves and blips.

'That's the radar display,' explained Brad. 'Later I'll take you through the basics on how to read it, but the radar's main function is to detect land or other vessels. From a security point of view, it's the vessels we're interested in. If tuned correctly, the radar can give us early warning of a possible attack. See that blip there.' Brad indicated a green dot, then pointed out of the window. 'It's that fishing boat coming into harbour.'

Connor and Ling looked out to sea and spotted the trawler approaching. Another smaller dinghy with an outboard was crossing its path.

'Where's that boat on the radar?' asked Connor, checking the display.

'Ah, that's the problem with radar. It has limitations,' replied Brad. 'Small craft like that are often missed or appear as haphazard blips. If the sea is choppy, then this degrades the radar's operation further. And if the pilot of the boat steers in a zigzag pattern they become even more difficult to detect. On top of all that, you've got the radar's infamous blind spot directly to the stern of this yacht. For those reasons, when at sea, there must be someone on watch 24/7.'

Brad looked at them both. 'Remember, when it comes to detecting a threat at sea –' he pulled at his lower eyelid with a fingertip – 'the Mark One eyeball is always the best defence.'

CHAPTER 27

The *Orchid*'s tender, a seven-metre luxury launch with 260-horsepower stern drive, powered across the bay leaving a foaming wake in its trail. As Ling opened up the throttle, the wind whipped through Connor's tousled brown hair and he had to grip the armrest for balance.

'Steady as she goes,' said Brad, keeping a careful watch for other craft in their vicinity. 'She's not a racing car.'

But, judging by the grin plastered across Ling's face, she clearly thought it was. Connor had already received full instruction on how to start, steer and dock the tender. Now it was Ling's turn to get some practice. As she swung the boat round for another run, she hit an unexpected wave and Connor was bounced out of his seat so hard that he tumbled over the side.

'MAN OVERBOARD!' Brad shouted as Connor hit the water, skipped once across its surface, then plunged beneath.

The sea, warm as it was, still shocked Connor's system and the rushing thunder of water in his ears and eyes momentarily disorientated him. Brad had warned them both that any man-overboard situation was potentially fatal. Drowning, exposure, hypothermia and impact injury were all very real risks, especially if the person wasn't wearing a life jacket. Fortunately, Connor was and he rapidly floated back to the surface. By the time his head cleared the water, Ling had cut back on the throttle and was starting to make a controlled turn towards him.

As the tender approached, Ling tried to keep a fix on his location. He'd already drifted further out to sea with the current and it would be easy to lose sight of a head bobbing in the water, even in a little swell.

'Slow down,' Brad warned Ling. 'You're approaching too fast.'

Ling cut back on the throttle but it was too little too late.

'Careful!' said Brad. 'You're going to run over him.'

Ling tried to correct the tender's direction, but without enough power the rudder responded too slowly. The fibreglass hull cut through the water on a direct collision course with Connor's head.

'Go astern,' Brad ordered as Connor, unable to dive due to the life jacket, held up his arms to shield himself.

'Astern? What's astern?' cried Ling, her voice rising in pitch as the tender ploughed towards Connor.

'*Reverse!*'

Connor could no longer see what was happening, but he heard a crunch of gears. When it came to piloting a boat, Ling was clearly more adept at speed than steering. The tender's engine roared and the hull stopped within a fraction of Connor's head.

'Switch off the engine,' shouted Brad, 'before the propellor chops him to sushi.'

He leant over the bow rail and offered Connor a broad grin. 'That was a close shave in more ways than one, wasn't it?'

By the time Ling appeared to help pull him aboard, the boat had drifted and Connor was once again beyond reach.

'You'll have to make another pass,' said Brad.

Ling let out an exasperated sigh. She returned to the helm, started the engine and put it into reverse.

'No,' said Brad. 'If you go astern, you're in danger of butchering him.'

'Why can't he just swim to us?' said Ling, her jaw set with frustration.

There was another crunch of gears. Brad raised his eyes to heaven and Ling caught him in the act.

'Don't you dare say anything about lady drivers,' she muttered, hammering at the gears.

'Heaven forbid!' replied Brad with his most guileless expression. 'You girls are capable of running over just about anything. That takes some skill.'

After three further attempts, Ling finally managed to pull alongside Connor and safely haul him aboard single-handedly.

'Well, we got there in the end,' said Brad, patting a seething Ling on the shoulder. 'But I think we need a bit more practice at the man-overboard drill, don't you?'

He raised an eyebrow at Connor, who stood dripping wet on the deck.

'Are you willing to throw yourself over for another drill?'

'Sure,' said Connor. 'But only if Ling promises not to try to run me over again.'

Ling narrowed her eyes at him. 'Well, hotshot, perhaps next time I'll leave you to the sharks!'

CHAPTER 28

'Pirates always hold the high cards,' explained Brad, leaning forward and resting his elbows on the table in the sky lounge. 'As the hunter, theirs is the choice of time and place. And, of course, they know that a yacht like this is virtually defenceless.'

'But what about NATO's counter-piracy operation?' asked Connor.

'Yeah,' said Ling, through a mouthful of tuna salad. 'They've got warships that can protect us.'

Brad laughed, a deep booming sound as loud as a foghorn. 'That naval task force is pretty much useless! It's not their fault, mind. With just one small fleet in an ocean this size, it's like a single police car trying to patrol the whole of France. An impossible task. Therefore, at sea we're on our own. And we must be prepared to defend ourselves.'

The week of intensive MARSEC training had flown by. The two of them were now proficient in reading radar, interpreting charts and using the yacht's comms equipment. Brad had also shown them how to tackle on-board fires, deploy a life raft, fire a flare gun, and what the emergency procedure was for abandoning ship. Now, over lunch, their mentor was briefing them on the ship's security plan in the event of a pirate attack.

'Our defence strategy is to Detect, Deter, Destroy,' he said, thumping the table top to emphasize each stage. 'As you already know, the key to thwarting pirates is to detect any possible attack *before* they can get alongside and board us. Once they know they've been spotted, they lose their element of surprise. From my experience, many will back off to wait for a less observant crew to sail past. So, to help us with that, we'll use the radar, binoculars, night-vision goggles and a twenty-four-hour watch shift.'

'Will *we* be on lookout duty?' asked Connor.

Brad shook his head. 'No, the crew might question your involvement. Between myself, the chief officer, Mr Sterling's bodyguard and one of the deckhands, we'll cover that. But both of you still need to keep a sharp lookout. The more eyeballs, the better.'

Brad took a sip of iced water and a chunk of sandwich.

'If we do run into pirates, our next step is to deter them,' he continued, wiping his mouth with a serviette. 'On a commercial ship, we would use razor wire, electrified fencing and water hoses. But I don't think Mr Sterling would appreciate his fifty-million-dollar holiday yacht being turned into a battleship.' Brad raised his eyebrows at his own suggestion. 'So initially we'll have to rely on Captain Locke outrunning them and performing evasive manoeuvres. Meanwhile, we'll try to attract attention with distress flares, searchlights, sirens and of course the radio.'

Ling set aside her empty plate. 'I hate to say this, but we've seen a video clip of a pirate attack. Their skiffs are pretty fast. And they have *rocket launchers*. I don't think a few flares and a bit of fancy sailing is going to dissuade them.'

'Fair point,' admitted Brad. 'But most pirates prefer an easy target, so such a strategy can and often does work. Although you're right, some can be more determined. If that's the case, then we destroy them.'

'So what weapons do we have?' Ling asked eagerly.

Brad offered an awkward smile. 'That's a tricky issue. At sea, international law allows merchantmen to possess and use firearms for self-defence. But in most ports it's illegal to carry guns. So it's a bit of a catch-22 situation.'

'Then what are we going to use?' asked Connor.

Brad raised his hands, palms up. 'Pretty much anything goes. Although the *Orchid* is his pride and joy, I'll persuade the captain to ram the pirates. That'll be our most effective tactic. But it carries its own hazards, including damaging the screws and even holing the hull itself. So we'll also toss storage nets over the side to foul their outboard motors, and use the foam fire extinguishers to make the most accessible decks and stairways slippery. And, of course, fire flares directly at their skiffs.'

He finished off his sandwich and put aside his plate.

'Once, I was on a ship where pirates managed to attach a grappling hook to the side. We threw a fridge full of

Coca-Cola into their skiff!' Brad laughed at the recollection. 'Their skiff took in so much water they had to cut loose.'

He waved a hand around the yacht.

'The prime objective is to stop the pirates boarding the *Orchid*. Think of the hull and gunwales of this boat as castle walls. As long as they're not breached and the pirates don't reach the main deck, we're in a strong position.'

Connor glanced down at the stern to where the tender garage was. The bay doors were open and he could see the ship's engineer, a silver-bearded man by the name of Geoff, overseeing the delivery of a brand-new pair of jet skis. The tender garage was the lowest point of the yacht and appeared very vulnerable to Connor.

'What if the pirates do get aboard?' he asked.

'Then our last resort is the citadel,' replied Brad.

Connor and Ling both gave him a perplexed look.

'Safe room,' he clarified, pushing back his chair and beckoning them to follow him. They headed down the staircase to the main deck and through the galley before stopping beside a large bulkhead door.

'This leads to the crew's quarters and is our designated citadel,' explained Brad. He slapped the door with the palm of his hand. 'This bulkhead can be double-locked from the inside. It's made of steel so it's bulletproof. And down below we've got all we need to survive for several days – food, water, sanitation and, most importantly, communications equipment. If we're attacked, your first priority is to ensure the girls are inside the citadel. Then,

God forbid, if the pirates do breach our defences, along with the rest of the crew, we join them.'

'But won't we be trapped?' said Ling.

Brad nodded emphatically. 'That's the point. Trapped and safe. Once we're all inside the citadel, military forces can storm the ship with minimum risk to our lives. However, the citadel is only effective if *everyone* makes it inside.'

'What a cheery conversation!' said a blonde-haired young woman, emerging from the crew's quarters.

'Hi, Soph.' Brad grinned, offering his most charming smile. 'I was just explaining the emergency procedures to Mr Sterling's guests.'

Sophie, a young English stewardess from Southampton, gave Connor and Ling a sympathetic look. 'Don't let him freak you out,' she remarked. 'Brad can be a little *anxious* before a sailing.'

'Only because I want to keep everyone safe, including you, sweets.'

Sophie arched an eyebrow at Brad, the corner of her mouth curling into a coquettish smile, before strolling off down the corridor. Brad's eyes followed her a moment. Then he snapped back to the matter in hand.

'Well, that just about wraps up your training,' he said, clapping his palms together and rubbing them. 'All work and no play makes Jack a very dull boy. Take the afternoon off.'

'Thanks,' Connor replied, a little stunned by the sudden grant of leave.

'About time,' muttered Ling under her breath.

Brad was halfway down the corridor before he turned back to them.

'Soph's right, though. I do get a bit edgy before a trip. But failure to prepare is preparing to fail. And our "security lifeboat", so to speak, needs to be watertight before sailing.'

An elderly fisherman in a battered wooden skiff tossed a frayed net into the pale blue waters. Then he sat and waited. His cataract-clouded eyes drifted across the desolate coastline of chalk-streaked cliffs and bone-white sands until his blurred gaze reached the headland. It jutted out into the Indian Ocean like a skeletal finger. Behind his little fishing boat lay the rusting hulk of a long-abandoned cargo ship, hulled on a jagged rock. And beyond that on the horizon, like a mirage, were three more container ships. Not shipwrecked, he knew, but hijacked and held for ransom.

With slow, laborious effort, the fisherman pulled his net in, hand over hand, his ancient limbs protesting, until he was rewarded with . . . an empty net. He cursed the foreign trawlers who plundered all the fish from their waters without permission or conscience. Then he threw the net back into the sea and waited.

As the old man fished for nothing, six gleaming Toyota 4x4s raced across the desolate beach. Spitting sand from their tyres, they were weaving dangerously in between one another in a daredevil game of cat and mouse. One of the vehicles threatened to roll over, but miraculously righted itself at the last second. Another cut through the waves, sending up showers of spray. The 4x4s ground to a sudden halt beside a row of overturned skiffs on the shoreline.

Spearhead got out of the lead vehicle and started shouting orders to his men to unload. The band of pirates flung open their doors and began dragging out wooden boxes and plastic jerrycans. Out of the back of a trailer, several pirates struggled with the enormous weight of a massive outboard motor, the first of four brand-new engines.

Stumbling across the burning sand, the skinny young pirate with the buck teeth dropped one of the boxes and an assault rifle tumbled out, still in its protective packaging.

'Cool!' he said, kneeling down to retrieve the rifle. 'Oracle has got us new weapons.'

'Move aside, Bucktooth, before you get hurt,' said the pirate with sticking-out ears. Barging the lad with his elbow, he picked up the rifle, slipped it from its protective wrapper and admired the well-oiled weapon. 'AK47. Chinese manufactured. Very reliable.'

'Let me have a go, Juggs,' begged Bucktooth.

Juggs gave him a dismissive look. 'These are for real men, not boys! Here, you can have this.'

He passed Bucktooth an old revolver. The boy gazed at it in awe and grinned.

From another box, Juggs slammed a full magazine

into the assault rifle and took casual aim at the nearby cliff face.

CLACK, CLACK, CLACK . . .

'*Wooooooo!*' he shouted above the roar of gunfire. The defenceless cliff spat shards of rock and dust as the barrage of bullets ripped into it.

'CEASE FIRE!' ordered Spearhead.

The earsplitting *crack* of the AK47 echoed off the cliff then faded.

'But there are *boxes* of them,' protested Juggs, still grinning from ear to ear with the buzz of his newly acquired firepower.

'Then load the boxes on to the boats,' snapped Spearhead, snatching away the weapon.

Juggs scowled but nonetheless bent down and heaved the ammo box across the sand.

The pirates worked slowly in the blistering sun, the harsh onshore wind offering no respite from the furnace-like heat. Gradually the skiffs filled with weapons, ammunition, diesel, navigation equipment, water and food supplies.

'And what have we got here?' muttered Big Mouth to himself as he discovered a long wooden box in the back of the last 4x4. He jimmied off the lid and hefted out a brand-new rocket-propelled grenade launcher. Sifting through the paper-pulp packaging, he also uncovered several rockets. 'I think I'm in love,' he said, caressing one of the warheads.

With hands trembling from anticipation, he carefully loaded one of the rockets, shouldered the launcher and took aim at the rusted cargo ship in the bay.

'Look out for that old fisherman,' warned Bucktooth as he eyed the formidable weapon with a mix of awe and fear.

'It's *he* who should look out.' With a crooked grin, Big Mouth depressed the trigger.

The rocket *whooshed* out of the launcher and scorched over the waves. Even at this distance, the pirates could see the old fisherman's face widen in terror. He dived into the waters just before the rocket passed over his little boat and struck the cargo ship behind. There was a deep howl of twisting metal as a massive explosion ripped through the hull. The ship's fuel tanks ignited with the last of their diesel and a ball of fire engulfed the entire bow. The little fishing skiff was caught in the expanding blast, disintegrating into a shower of flaming splinters.

'Did you see *that*?' whooped Big Mouth, dancing a jig on the beach. 'These babies are tank-busters!'

The other pirates hollered and bent double with laughter as the fisherman's head bobbed back up amid the carnage of his fishing boat. He swam desperately for the shore, leaving his only means of scraping a living to float away in shattered pieces.

Spearhead stormed over to Big Mouth and shouted in his face, 'What did you do THAT for?'

Wiping tears of laughter from his eyes, the pirate held up the RPG launcher. 'Just checking its accuracy.'

Spearhead clocked Big Mouth round the back of his head with an open palm, the slap almost as loud as the grenade explosion.

'*Ow!*' complained Big Mouth, shying away from their commander. The other pirates instantly stopped laughing.

'You'll buy that old man a new boat out of your ransom share,' Spearhead ordered, 'or I'll gut you like a tuna fish.'

'Chill, Spearhead,' replied Big Mouth, waving him away. 'With the money we'll get, I'll buy that fishhead *two* boats.'

CHAPTER 30

'The white pickup truck you identified was a ringer,' said Charley.

'A *ringer*?' repeated Connor, holding up his mobile phone so that both he and Ling could see Charley's face on the screen. They huddled in a quiet area of the Seychelles International Airport while awaiting the arrival of Mr Sterling's private jet.

'A stolen vehicle, its licence plates swapped with a set from a written-off car,' Charley explained. 'There's no way we can trace the truck.'

'What about the two muggers?' asked Ling.

'We had a bit more luck with them. Amir scoured CCTV from the local area and found a grainy shot of the two guys on rollerblades. Using the Australian Criminal Intelligence Database, we've managed to identify the man with the tattoo as Todd Logan and his associate as Doug Carter.'

Two mugshots, one of a grizzled white man, the other of a bald-headed black man, filled the screen.

'They're both heavies-for-hire,' Charley's voice continued in the background. 'Linked to numerous criminal gangs, they've a list of convictions as long as their arms: robbery, drug-dealing, extortion, arson, GBH and murder. You name it, they've probably done it. Released only last month from prison, I guess they were desperate to earn a fast buck.'

Connor exchanged a stunned look with Ling. Both realized how lucky they'd been to get away so lightly in the attack.

'So where are the men now?' asked Ling.

Charley's face reappeared on Connor's phone.

'The Sydney police haven't been able to track them down yet, but as soon as I hear anything you'll be the first to know. In the meantime, I'll see what else I can dig up on them.'

'Thanks,' said Connor. 'At least we've got decent ID shots of them now.'

'All part of the service,' said Amir, nudging into the frame beside Charley. 'So how's the weather out there?'

'Oh, rainy, cold and miserable,' sighed Ling, putting on her glummest expression.

'*Really?*' said Amir, his eyes widening in undisguised delight at the thought.

Connor couldn't help but laugh. 'Of course not! It's twenty-eight degrees and glorious sunshine.'

Amir scowled. 'Well, it's the same here,' he said, 'apart from the lack of sun and warmth. Anyway, I just wanted to check that my equipment is still functioning.'

Connor waggled the sunglasses on his head. 'All looking good.'

Hearing his name being called, Connor glanced up to see Brad beckoning them to join him at the arrivals gate.

'Have to go,' Connor explained to Amir. 'Mr Sterling's jet has just landed.'

'Oh, it's a hard life for some,' said Amir in a gently mocking tone. 'Give us a shout if you need anything *technical*.'

'Stay sharp and stay safe,' added Charley, before ending the video call.

Connor slipped the phone into the pocket of his polo-shirt, the flotation cover making it too bulky for his shorts, then followed Ling across to Brad.

'OK, guys, let's look professional,' Brad said, breaking into a wide grin. 'Now the hard work really begins.'

Brad had already performed a security sweep of the airport terminal with their help and was satisfied that the location was secure. They watched through the window as the sleek Gulfstream jet taxied up to the private gate. After a minute or so, the aircraft's doors opened and a stairway unfolded. Mr Sterling emerged followed by a slender blonde woman with long tanned legs in a daringly short dress and high heels. With the poise of a professional model, she gracefully descended the steps on to the runway.

'Pick your jaw up!' hissed Ling, glowering sideways at Connor.

Connor hadn't realized he was gawping. But he wasn't alone in his admiration. As Amanda Ryder sashayed into the terminal building, every man's head turned towards her. Rather than appear jealous, Mr Sterling seemed to thrive on the attention his glamorous fiancée attracted.

As the couple approached, Mr Sterling smiled at his

welcoming party. The tautness Connor had noticed in the man's features while in Sydney had softened, as if he'd left the burden of his work behind, but the media mogul's eyes still maintained their steely intensity.

'Good to see you both again,' he said, nodding at Connor and Ling. 'Brad, everything in order?'

'Yes, sir,' replied Brad. 'And may I welcome you to the Seychelles, Ms Ryder.'

'Why, thank you,' she replied, her voice smooth as honey. She squeezed Mr Sterling's arm affectionately. 'But hopefully I won't be using that name much longer.'

In response, Mr Sterling smiled and kissed her warmly on the cheek.

A respectful distance behind the couple stood Mr Sterling's personal bodyguard, one of the few men in the terminal not to be admiring Ms Ryder. Instead he focused on his new surroundings, offering a professional nod of courtesy to Brad in the process. Dressed in a short-sleeved shirt and chinos, he looked like any other tourist. And since he was wearing shades Connor couldn't read his expression when he also gave a barely perceptible acknowledgement to him and Ling. Recalling his briefing notes, Connor knew the man's name was Dan and that he'd been Mr Sterling's close protection officer ever since the last one was fired following Emily's kidnapping.

'And when will your daughters be joining us, sir?' Brad asked Mr Sterling.

Just at that moment, the gate opened again and the girls entered, dressed in flowery summer tops and white shorts.

Brad gestured to Connor, who stepped forward to greet them. 'Hi, Emily! Welcome to –'

'I'm *Chloe*,' said the sister he was addressing. She flicked back a lock of straw-blonde hair to reveal her ear. 'I have a mole on my right earlobe; Emily doesn't, if that helps.'

'Sorry,' said Connor, unable to believe he'd made such a faux pas.

'So how was your flight?' asked Ling, swiftly moving on from Connor's mistake as Mr Sterling informed Brad of his plans for the holiday.

'Fine, although I never can sleep on planes,' replied Emily. She offered them both an awkward smile. 'Look, I want to apologize for my behaviour the first time we met.'

'Nothing to apologize for,' said Connor diplomatically.

'No, I was rude and ill-mannered.' She glanced in the direction of her father, who was being escorted by Brad towards the exit. Still she lowered her voice. 'I was angry at my father, not you. But you proved your worth in Sydney. So I hope . . . we can make a fresh start.'

'Of course,' said Connor, shaking the hand she offered. 'Forget it ever happened.'

'Thanks.' Emily tried unsuccessfully to stifle a yawn. 'Sorry, long journey.'

'Shall we make a move to the yacht then?' he suggested. 'You can rest and freshen up.'

Emily smiled and nodded.

Chloe was already skipping off towards the exit. 'Absolutely. We're missing out on valuable sunbathing time.'

Ling called after her Principal. 'You've forgotten your bag,' she said, pointing to a small wheeled carry-on case.

Chloe barely glanced over her shoulder. 'No, I think *you've* forgotten my bag.'

Ling frowned and shot Connor a questioning look. They'd been taught by their instructor Jody that a bodyguard always needed to keep their hands free so they could react quickly to a sudden threat. Carrying the shopping, bags or belongings of a Principal immediately limited a bodyguard's response time.

Connor shrugged in response. Ling was left with little other choice than to do as she was told. By now Chloe was almost at the exit and would soon be out of sight. *That* was an even more risky situation for a bodyguard. Huffing to herself, Ling snatched the bag's handle and hurried after her Principal.

CHAPTER 31

'I wouldn't recommend sunbathing under that tree,' said Connor as Chloe and Emily laid down their towels on the pristine beach.

'Why not?' said Emily, the corner of her lips curling up into a tease. 'Worried about dropbears?'

'Not this time,' Connor replied with a glance up into the canopy. 'Coconuts.'

As if to prove his point, a large brown husk fell from a nearby palm and plopped heavily into the sand. Brad had warned Connor about the danger, recounting a story of an old rock star who'd had his skull cracked open by one.

Emily and Chloe quickly retrieved their towels.

'So where *do* you suggest?' asked Chloe.

'Try this one,' said Ling, patting the trunk of a tall tree with thick waxy-green leaves. 'It's a takamaka – no danger of falling nuts here.'

Upon the instruction of Mr Sterling, Captain Locke had sailed the *Orchid* round the southern tip of Mahé Island to Anse Takamaka, a secluded beach named after the abundance of the tree species. The idyllic horseshoe bay was like a scene straight out of Robinson Crusoe, pure white sand fringed with palms and crystal-blue waves rippling along the shoreline.

Chloe repositioned her towel, lay down and stretched herself out in the sun. 'Now this is the life,' she said, taking out a glossy teen magazine, sunscreen, headphones and her smartphone from her beach bag.

Joining her sister, Emily had an equal array of light entertainment, but ignored it in favour of watching the white-tailed birds and multicoloured butterflies flitting among the lush vegetation surrounding them. The beach was utterly unspoilt by human habitation. Mr Sterling and Ms Ryder were relaxing on sunloungers brought over on the tender. Sophie and another stewardess were serving them drinks and ensuring their every need was met. The girls had decided they wanted to be further down the beach, away from the doting couple, and Mr Sterling hadn't objected as long as Connor and Ling accompanied them.

Connor and Ling put down their Go-bags and prepared for a day of sunbathing. As Ling got out her towel, she gave Connor a sly grin and whispered, 'This is going to be a breeze if all we have to worry about are coconuts!'

Looking up and down the deserted beach, Connor couldn't help but agree. There was no one who could hassle the girls, no apparent threats, just glorious sun, sand and sea. The recipe for a perfect holiday.

Connor rifled through his Go-bag for sunscreen and the

paperback book he'd bought at the airport, then he sat down and did another visual sweep of the area. The coast was utterly clear. No other boats, aside from the *Orchid* anchored beyond the bay.

'You can take first watch,' said Ling, lying back on her towel and closing her eyes.

But no sooner had Ling got comfortable than Chloe said, 'Ling, get me a drink.'

Ling sat back up, a flicker of irritation passing across her face before asking, 'What would you like?'

Chloe waved a hand in the direction of the tender. 'Chef should have put in a pitcher of fresh lemonade.'

'Ooh, that sounds good,' said Emily. 'Can I have one too?'

'Of course,' said Ling, getting to her feet. 'I'll bring the whole pitcher.' She strode over to where Sophie was talking with Brad and Dan near the moored tender.

While Ling was busy collecting the drinks, Emily turned to Connor. 'Would you mind inflating my lilo for me, please? I fancy a float in the sea.'

'Sure,' said Connor, delving into his Go-bag and retrieving the inflatable silver mattress he'd been given earlier. Putting the valve to his lips, he began the slow process of blowing it up.

Ling returned with a tray of four iced lemonades and the pitcher. Chloe necked hers in one, asked for another, then plugged in her earphones and lay face down on her towel. Once Emily had got her drink, Ling offered a glass to Connor, who was still puffing away.

'Thanks,' he gasped, taking a large gulp of lemonade, its ice-cold zest refreshing him. After a dozen more lungfuls of air, the lilo was fully inflated.

'Here you go,' said Connor.

'Great,' said Emily, taking the lilo and trotting down to the shoreline.

While Emily paddled in the shallows and her sister lay sprawled in the sun, Connor and Ling were left to their own devices. With nothing to do, Ling stretched out on her towel and sunbathed too. Seeing Emily happily floating on the water, Connor picked up his book and began to read.

After a while, Brad strolled over. 'I'm just taking Mr Sterling and Ms Ryder back to the boat. I'll return to collect the girls for lunch. All good here?'

Connor nodded. Chloe was laid out, eyes closed and humming to a song on her headphones, while Emily still lay on her lilo, bobbing gently on the waves.

'Well, don't work too hard!' warned Brad with a playful wink.

Connor heard the tender depart, then settled back into his book.

He'd only read a couple of chapters when Ling sat up and nudged him.

'Do you think Emily's all right?'

Connor looked up. Emily was flat out on her lilo, almost thirty metres from the shore. Last time he'd looked, she had only been some ten metres away.

Putting aside his book, Connor jogged down to the waterline. 'Emily,' he called.

But she didn't respond. By the looks of it she'd fallen asleep. With a growing sense of panic, Connor realized her lilo was caught in a current and she was now drifting fast out to sea.

CHAPTER 32

'EMILY!' Connor shouted again. But she still didn't wake up. Either she was too far out to hear him or *couldn't* wake up. With the six-hour time difference between the Seychelles and Sydney and the drowsy side effects of her medication, her body clock was probably out of synch.

He looked to the *Orchid* at the opposite end of the bay. The tender was tethered to its stern and he couldn't see anyone on deck. And there were, of course, no lifeguards on this deserted beach. In the few seconds Connor had taken to search for help, Emily had drifted even further out. If he didn't take immediate action, she'd soon be lost in open water.

'I'm going to bring her back,' Connor told Ling, ripping off his T-shirt and running into the sea. 'Contact Brad.'

As soon as he was deep enough, he dived beneath the waves and swam hard. Surfacing, he powered through the water, glad now for all Charley's training.

But swimming in the sea was totally different from being in an indoor pool. Although the bay was relatively calm, the gentle swell still blocked his line of sight. Emily and her silver lilo continually bobbed in and out of view and he had to keep stopping to ensure he was still heading in the right direction.

Emily was now over eighty metres out, almost beyond the tip of the headland. Connor dug deep with every ounce of strength he possessed. His legs kicking, his arms pumping, he swam not for his life, but for hers.

Then all of a sudden he was alongside her.

'Emily!' he gasped, clutching on to the lilo's handle.

But she was still dead to the world, a blissful smile on her face.

Deciding that waking her suddenly at this point could risk her drowning, Connor turned the lilo round and kicked for the shore. After a minute or so, he looked up. The beach seemed no closer.

He put his head down and kicked furiously, driving the lilo ahead of him.

Connor looked up again. They were still beyond the headland. He realized he wasn't getting anywhere. He was fighting *against* the current.

Despair crept into his mind. There was no way he could beat the pull of the ocean. His heart was already pounding like a drum and he could feel his muscles burning from the effort made just to reach Emily.

Where is Brad and the tender?

He would never rescue Emily at this rate. Then he remembered Charley reminiscing about one of her surfing trips where she'd been caught in a rip-tide. These currents, she'd explained, were rarely more than thirty metres wide and surfers often used them as an expressway into the ocean to catch waves. The way to escape a rip-tide was to simply swim parallel to the shore and, once clear, diagonally back to the beach.

Redirecting the lilo, Connor swam towards the headland. Then as soon as he judged he was clear of the rip he took a diagonal course to where Ling stood waving to him.

With a glance over at the headland, Connor saw he was at last making progress. But the going was still tough. His lungs burnt for air and, to make matters worse, in his growing exhaustion he started to lose his rhythm. His limbs grew heavy as lead, and he imagined himself sinking to the seabed like a stone.

In the distance he could hear the roar of the motorboat's engines.

Then, all of a sudden, his foot struck sand and he glanced up in surprise.

'Are you OK?' asked Ling, pulling the lilo and Emily on to the foreshore. Further up the beach, Chloe was still stretched out on her towel, headphones on, oblivious to the near tragedy. Brad was just arriving in the tender.

Connor dragged himself out of the shallows and collapsed on the warm sand. 'Barely,' he wheezed as a wave of white water rushed up the beach, engulfing the lilo and waking Emily with a start.

'Oh . . . I must have dozed off,' she said, sitting up and brushing her wet hair from her face. Seeing Connor sprawled in the sand like a beached fish, gasping for breath, she remarked, 'Have you been for a swim?'

Connor opened his mouth to reply but was too exhausted for words and just let his head flop back down.

'You need to relax more,' Emily laughed. 'This is a holiday, you know.'

CHAPTER 33

Oracle regarded his loose band of pirates through the tinted passenger window of his Land Cruiser. The men lolled in the meagre shade of a ramshackle fisherman's hut, bored and listless in the unrelenting heat. Only the young pirate Bucktooth crouched in the full glare of the sun, forced to remain on guard by the skiffs. An unnecessary duty, imposed by the other pirates as a cruel prank, since no villager or fisherman would dare approach Oracle's gang or their boats. But the boy appeared happy enough with his revolver to carry out the duty.

Picking up the slim mobile phone from the seat beside him, Oracle pressed the speed-dial number. After several distant rings, he heard a click and his investor answered. 'Yes?'

'My men are ready,' informed Oracle.

There was a crackle on the line, the signal poor at the base of the cliff, but he could just make out his investor's response. 'Have . . . supplies . . . arrived?'

'Yes,' replied Oracle. 'And Mr WiFi has tracked down the target to its current location in Victoria Harbour. We'll be there by –'

'Your information is out of date . . . The yacht is now at Anse Takamaka . . . Tomorrow . . . sail to Bel Ombre . . . after that to Praslin Island.'

Oracle's brow furrowed slightly. 'How do *you* know the yacht's itinerary?'

As Oracle listened to the reply, his upper lip curled into an astonished smirk. 'That is quite something . . . Yes, I'll keep you fully informed of our progress.'

Snapping shut the phone, Oracle lowered his passenger window. A rush of hot dry air invaded the vehicle's cool interior as Spearhead's sweating face appeared.

'Get the men boarded,' instructed Oracle.

'Yes, boss. Are we still headed for the Seychelles?'

Oracle nodded. 'At this moment, yes, but Mr WiFi will send you updates via the satellite link.'

Spearhead gave a dismissive snort and waved his hand at a buzzing fly. 'That's all well and good, but his hacked coordinates are always out by a few hours because of the security delay. Sometimes the ship is over the horizon by the time we get there.'

Oracle offered a smug grin. 'Not this time. The investor is able to supply the *real-time* location of the *Orchid*.'

Spearhead's eyes widened in his head and he grunted an incredulous laugh. 'Then this is gonna be like shooting fish in a barrel.'

'So let the game begin,' Oracle commanded, winding up his window and barring the all-pervading heat.

As the Land Cruiser sped away across the baking sand, Spearhead barked orders at his men. Idle from chewing khat all morning, the pirates rose to their feet and trudged down the beach to their boats. They threw nets over their weapons and supplies to give the pretence they were legitimate fishermen. Pushing the boats from the shoreline, the pirates clambered aboard and started their engines. The powerful outboard motors roared, churning up a flurry of white water as the small armada of pirate skiffs surged out of the bay.

CHAPTER 34

'Pirates!' shouted Chloe. 'Pirates ahoy!'

'Where?' said Connor, looking to the horizon, his pulse immediately racing. The glassy sea was a mirror to the blue sky, the line between heaven and earth lost in the distant haze. Aside from the *Orchid*, there were five other yachts anchored around the picturesque bay in Bel Ombre on the island's north-west coast. Beyond those, a few fishing boats bobbed out at sea. But Connor couldn't see any skiffs armed with RPGs powering towards them.

'Shiver me timbers, Connor, I was only joking!' said Chloe, giggling at his overreaction. 'But you never know, we might find some pirate treasure in here.'

She ducked inside a large dark hole in the cliff face. Taking a break from yesterday's sunbathing, the four of them were exploring the headland of the bay. Clambering over granite boulders and through warm barnacled rock pools, they'd managed to reach the outermost tip.

'Hold up,' cried Ling, who'd also been caught out by Chloe's pirate prank. 'It could be dangerous in there.'

'You two *really* need to lighten up,' said Chloe, her reply echoing out of the cave mouth.

Ling disappeared after her Principal, but Emily hesitated at the entrance, eyeing the dark opening with mistrust.

'Are you all right with this?' asked Connor.

'Why shouldn't I be?' she replied, but a nervous swallow betrayed her true feelings.

Connor tried to make eye contact. 'You don't have to go in –'

'Come on, Emily!' Chloe called, her voice now eerily distant. 'You have to see this.'

Taking a deep breath, Emily plunged into the darkness.

Connor kept close on her heels. Following the lilo incident the previous day, he wasn't allowing himself to become complacent on the assignment again. He had to be ready for anything, danger lying in the most innocent of activities.

The hole narrowed to a passageway that burrowed deep into the headland. At first there was just blackness, but as Connor's eyes adjusted to the lack of light, he could make out the multitude of molluscs clinging to the hard moist rock. After a dozen or so paces, the passageway opened out into a large cavern, a crack in the overhead rock letting in a feeble shaft of sunlight. The air within was as cool and damp as a tomb and he felt his skin goosebump at the sudden drop in temperature.

'Over here,' said Chloe, beckoning them to the far wall. Ling stood beside her, both their faces in shadow, as they inspected the faintly gleaming surface.

Connor followed Emily across the cavern, their feet crunching through the coarse sand and broken shells on the uneven floor.

'Check these out,' said Chloe excitedly, pointing to some symbols on the wall. Into the rock had been carved a dog, a snake, two joined hearts, a keyhole, a staring eye, a figure of a woman's body and the head of a man.

'Creepy,' said Ling.

The boom of a crashing wave rebounded and amplified inside the cavern space. Connor glanced across at Emily, who'd become strangely quiet and withdrawn. In the feeble light, he could see that she was trembling and a sheen of sweat had broken out on her forehead.

'Emily?' asked Connor. But she didn't reply.

Chloe ran her finger over the staring eye. 'I read in a guidebook that some pirate supposedly buried his treasure on this island. On his death at the gallows, he left a cryptic map to its location,' she explained. 'This must be one of the clues . . .'

Emily now appeared to be struggling for breath.

'I think it's time to make a move,' Connor suggested, taking Emily by the arm and guiding her back towards the tunnel.

'In a minute,' said Chloe, too engrossed in studying the symbols to notice her sister's distress. 'Maybe we can work out what this says . . .'

Emily let out a dog-like whimper.

Chloe turned to her sister. 'Are you all right, Em?'

Her eyes had gone white with fear and she stared in

blind panic at the cave entrance. A huge shadow slipped along the mollusc-encrusted wall, threatening in both its size and silence.

'I'll do what you say . . .' she whispered in a breath almost too quiet to hear. 'I'll do what you say . . . I'll do what you say . . .'

Connor drew Emily closer as she repeated the words like a mantra. A muscle-bound man now blocked their only exit.

'Hope I didn't scare you,' said Brad. 'But the tide's coming in and these caves are prone to flooding.'

CHAPTER 35

'Don't forget to put the kill cord round your wrist,' reminded Ling as she zipped up her life jacket.

'I do know,' snapped Chloe, straddling the jet ski. 'I have ridden these things before.'

'Sorry, just going through the safety checks,' replied Ling in a defensive tone, as she clambered aboard the other one. 'Don't want it running away from you.'

Chloe, her hair tied back in a ponytail, looked over her shoulder at her sister. 'Sure you don't want to come with us?'

'Maybe later,' replied Emily with a strained smile.

'How about you, Connor?' asked Chloe. 'You can ride with me if you want.'

Connor eyed the sleek jet ski. He was itching to have a go, but he couldn't leave his Principal. 'I'd love to, but I'll stick with Emily on the beach.'

'Your loss,' she sighed and pressed the jet ski's ignition.

Over the thrum of the engine, they heard Amanda shout out, 'Have fun!'

She waved cheerily to them, looking glamorous as ever

in a straw sunhat, white midriff blouse and sarong. Mr Sterling, his arm round her waist, raised a hand as the two of them headed to a local beach bar, where Dan had reserved a private table.

'Off go the lovebirds again,' Chloe muttered without bothering to wave back. Twisting the throttle, she sped off across the water. As Ling depressed her jet ski's starter, there was a slight splutter from the exhaust, then she raced off after her Principal.

After watching Chloe and Ling zip back and forth a couple of times, Connor suggested a stroll along the beach.

'Are you feeling any better now?' he asked Emily.

She glanced sideways at him. 'You noticed then.'

Connor nodded. 'We're briefed on things like that,' he said, not wishing to worry her about how obvious the panic attack had been.

Emily let out a heavy sigh. 'Yeah, I suppose you are. Well, after what happened last year, I get very anxious in such places. My mind becomes foggy and I kinda blank out.'

'Then why did you go in?'

Emily dug a toe into the sand. 'To try and beat my fear.'

Connor smiled, his respect for her growing at such strength of character. 'I can relate to that. I've been in a similar situation.'

Emily looked up in shock. 'Really? When?'

'Just this year,' Connor admitted. 'I can't tell you any details, but I was held captive for a number of days.'

Emily studied his face, concern now etching her brow. 'I had no idea. How are you coping?'

Connor shrugged. 'OK, I suppose. I didn't really think about it much at the time, I was concentrating on protecting my Principal.'

Emily nodded. 'I suppose that must have helped. To have someone else to focus on, I mean.' She looked off towards the horizon, a haunted look in her eyes. 'I was completely alone.'

In the background, the jet skis buzzed like hornets above the gentle wash of the waves.

'That must have been hard for you,' said Connor.

'You don't know the half of it,' she said, her voice wavering with emotion. 'The isolation was torture. I've been beside my sister all my life. I was desperate for her company, for a friend, *anyone* . . .' She turned to look at him as if to say more, but the noise from the jet-ski engines suddenly reached a whirring pitch. Then there was a huge *BANG*.

Connor spun round to see Ling tumbling head over heels through the air, her jet ski in flames. He was already running down the beach and through the waves by the time she splashed into the sea. Chloe zoomed over, picking up Connor halfway as he swam to Ling's rescue.

Ling floated lifeless in the emerald-green waters. Her jet ski was melting into a blob of plastic and black smoke. Connor leapt from the back of Chloe's craft and grabbed Ling by her life jacket.

'Ling, speak to me!'

Her eyes flickered and she gradually focused on Connor's face. 'Wow . . . that was *wild*.'

'Are you hurt?' asked Connor.

Ling gazed drowsily down at herself then at the surrounding water. 'There's . . . no blood . . . so I don't think so.'

'What happened?' demanded Connor as he helped her on to Chloe's jet ski.

'The throttle got stuck . . . then it just *exploded*.'

CHAPTER 36

'Connor, I need your protection!'

Connor immediately looked over to where Chloe was laid out on the *Orchid*'s sun deck. In a canary-yellow bikini and sunglasses, she was wagging a bottle of suntan lotion at him. Connor rose from his chair then noticed Ling, who was filling out an accident report for Brad, glance up and roll her eyes. Connor now hesitated, wondering if applying sunscreen would cross the line of appropriate behaviour with a Principal.

'Please?' insisted Chloe, lowering her sunglasses, her expression all sweet innocence. 'I can't reach my back.'

Ling tutted quietly to herself as Connor went over. He replied with a shrug of 'what else could he do?' It wasn't as if the request was unusual considering the circumstances.

'Thanks,' said Chloe, settling face down on the padded sunbed attached to the jacuzzi.

As Connor dutifully rubbed the lotion on to Chloe's back, Ling continued with the accident report. She'd been extremely fortunate to get away with only a few scrapes and bruises, the worst injury being a minor burn on the inside of her left thigh. The water had not only cushioned her fall and extinguished any flames, but her fire-retardant T-shirt and shorts had protected her from the worst of the explosion.

The remains of the offending jet ski were now with the Seychelles coastguard pending an investigation into the cause of the accident. Profusely apologetic to Ling, Geoff, the ship's engineer, was at a loss as to how it could have happened in the first place, since the jet skis were brand new. Ling herself was surprisingly relaxed about the whole affair, although she gladly accepted Brad's proposal of an afternoon off to fully recover.

'Can you do my neck too?' asked Chloe, lifting her hair so Connor could apply the lotion.

Emily emerged from the staircase and raised an eyebrow at the scene. 'Comfortable, are we, Chloe?'

'Definitely,' purred her sister.

'How are you feeling, Ling?'

'Fine, thank you,' she replied. 'The burn cream is working a treat.'

Emily strolled over to the handrail. With her back to Connor and her sister, she admired the view as the *Orchid* eased away from Bel Ombre for their next destination. Holding up her mobile phone, she took a photo of the picture-perfect bay.

As Emily tapped away on the screen, Ling glanced over in curiosity. 'Have you just posted that on a social network site?'

Emily looked over. 'Sorry, what was that?'

'I asked if you'd posted that on the internet.'

Emily nodded with a smile. 'The view's too good not to share.'

'Next time, don't.'

'Why on earth can't she?' said Chloe, raising herself on to her elbows and glaring at Ling. 'I did exactly the same back on the beach.'

Ling put down her pen. 'The problem is your phone automatically adds your location to the photos, letting people know where you are and when.'

Chloe looked at Ling as if she was dumb. 'Duh! That's the whole point.'

'It's a security breach,' insisted Ling, holding Chloe's glare.

Chloe groaned. 'Jeez, you're being paranoid. Your accident must have spooked you. Besides, I want my friends to know where I am. So, don't tell us what to do and what not to do.'

Feeling the tension rise, Connor stepped in to back Ling up. 'It's not your friends we're worried about,' he explained gently. 'It's *anyone else* who may be following your profile.'

'Like who?'

'Those muggers back in Sydney.'

'Oh, please. We're thousands of miles from there.'

'OK, I'll be more careful in future,' Emily cut in. She offered Ling an appeasing smile. 'But I really can't imagine anyone would be interested in our holiday snaps.'

CHAPTER 37

The first stars pinpricked the sky as the horizon purpled with the coming of night. In the deepening twilight, the cluster of pirate skiffs powered over the waves, their outboards purring steadily. Spearhead crouched in the bow of the lead boat, his eyes adjusting to the growing darkness. His body had long since become accustomed to the constant to and fro of the ocean's swell and he simply conserved his energy for the forthcoming attack.

As promised, Mr WiFi had forwarded the updated coordinates – the *Orchid* was now en route to Praslin Island. Spearhead honestly believed that this would be the easiest hijacking in all his four short years as a pirate. If the bounty was as large as Oracle had hinted at, then he could retire for the rest of his life, bathed in riches and beautiful women. But, despite the lure of such a lifestyle, he knew in his heart of hearts that he could never give up the pirate life. The urgent thrill of the chase was like a drug to him, almost as addictive as the power he wielded over a hijacked ship and its pathetic crew.

'Hey!' called Big Mouth from an adjacent skiff.

Spearhead directed his gaze south-east to where Big Mouth was indicating. On the distant horizon, like a gleaming jewel, was the outline of a white luxury yacht. Spearhead considered the vessel for a few moments then signalled to the other skiffs, moving his hand in a serpent-like fashion and pointing to the target. Then he signed to Big Mouth's boat to circle round and approach from the opposite direction.

They were still over three miles away so, at this stage of the attack, stealth was the preferred strategy. With his boat leading the way, the skiffs zigzagged across the waves, gradually closing in on their target from the stern to avoid the yacht's radar.

The darkness of night descended and only the silvery gleam of a half-moon lit their approach. But the yacht's owners were considerate enough to leave on their navigation lights. Like moths to a lamp, the pirates converged on the unsuspecting vessel.

As the skiffs came within ambush distance, the buzz of adrenalin rushed through Spearhead's veins. The other pirates in his boat had fallen silent, equally edgy yet exhilarated at the imminent attack.

At less than a quarter of a mile out someone on the yacht's deck spotted Big Mouth's boat. There was a cry of alarm and a searchlight was pointed in its direction. The VHF radio in Spearhead's skiff burst into life as the captain of the yacht demanded that the approaching boat identify itself. Big Mouth responded with a hail of gunfire across the yacht's bow.

But that was all good. Big Mouth was the distraction.

As the yacht's engines burst into life and tried to make an escape, Spearhead shouted to his pilot, 'GO! GO! GO!'

The mighty outboards roared and the skiff's bow rose high in the air as it ploughed through the waves. The other skiffs joined in the pursuit, swarming towards the defenceless yacht. In under a minute, the target vessel was surrounded on all sides.

However, the yacht's crew wasn't going to surrender without a fight. A flare was shot across the bow of one of the skiffs and the yacht began to fishtail erratically, in an attempt to ram any approaching pirates and make boarding impossible.

Despite the danger, Spearhead's pilot brought their skiff alongside the yacht's stern, bumping hard against the hull. Spearhead flung a grappling hook over the rail. It held fast, but the yacht suddenly veered away and the gap between the boats became treacherously wide. This was how Spearhead had earned his nickname: fearless, ruthless and admittedly a little crazy, he *spearheaded* every assault. He was the one who took the major risk of boarding first. And the rewards were greater for it.

With his AK47 slung across his back and his hands gripping the rope, Spearhead leapt for the yacht's stern. He didn't make it and his bare feet trailed in the water as he was dragged along by the speeding yacht. He tried to gain purchase on the hull, but the fibreglass was slick and icy smooth. Sea spray blinded him and his body was battered against the hull as the yacht suddenly changed direction.

Gritting his teeth, Spearhead clung on like a limpet. Then, with a Herculean effort, he hauled himself up, hand over hand, to the lower-deck level.

Vaulting the safety rail, he unslung his AK47 and prepared to take the yacht by force. A man carrying a flare suddenly appeared from behind a bulkhead. Shocked by the pirate's unexpected appearance on deck, he went to raise his hands. Spearhead slammed the butt of his rifle into the man's jaw. The sailor dropped to the ground, no longer capable of being a threat.

With the single-mindedness of a leopard stalking its prey, Spearhead prowled the main deck, searching the unfamiliar ship for the way to the bridge.

Another sailor emerged and Spearhead levelled his AK47 at him.

'Bridge?' he demanded.

The man cowered back into his cabin, pointing to a set of steps. Spearhead swiftly bounded up them and kicked open a wooden door. On the other side, the captain was shouting into the radio. 'Mayday, Mayday, Mayday! This is motor yacht *Sunriser*–'

'STOP!' snarled Spearhead, planting the barrel of his AK47 against the captain's temple.

His eyes wide with panic, the captain let the receiver drop to the floor. 'Please . . . don't kill me.'

Spearhead's maniacal grin flashed in the darkness. 'I won't. As long as you do *exactly* as I say.'

CHAPTER 38

'Sure you don't want to join us?' asked Emily.

Chloe wrinkled her nose at her sister. 'Why would I want to walk around a hot wet forest?'

Emily shrugged. 'For something different to do. Vallée de Mai is a World Heritage Site.'

'No, thanks. I'm perfectly fine.' Sipping from a freshly opened coconut, Chloe settled back on the sunlounger beside the palm-thatched bar on Anse Volbert. She closed her eyes and sighed contentedly.

The exquisite beach, an unbroken line of silky white sand fringed by lush green takamaka trees, stretched the entire length of the bay. At anchor in its crystal-clear waters, the *Orchid* held court over the other luxury sailing yachts and catamarans moored off Praslin Island. Brad had just returned the tender to the yacht, having dropped off Mr Sterling and his fiancée at an exclusive golf and spa resort on the island's north-western tip. This meant the girls had the whole day to themselves – but Emily was impatient for a change of scene.

'Don't get lost,' said Ling, waving Connor off and

grinning as she too made herself comfortable on a sunlounger.

Taking a little yellow taxi, Connor and Emily were delivered five minutes later outside the entrance to Vallée de Mai. A small group of tourists were filing past a rustic wooden ticket office that marked the start of the forest trail. Connor paid the entrance fee and he and Emily took the sand-beaten path into the eco-reserve. A tangle of green fronds enveloped them and they were soon immersed in an Eden-like setting.

'Vallée de Mai is the only place on earth where you can see the rare coco-de-mer palms,' explained Emily, reading from the pamphlet she'd been given. 'The palms produce the largest seed in the plant kingdom.'

'No kidding,' said Connor. 'Look at the size of them!'

On a wooden bench beside the trail, three massive heart-shaped nuts had been laid out. Emily tried to pick one up and almost toppled over with the weight. Laughing, Connor tried to lift it. As big as his upper torso and heavier than a medicine ball, even he struggled with the enormous seed.

'Supposedly they have aphrodisiac properties,' said Emily, referring to the pamphlet.

'Aphro-what?'

'You know . . .' said Emily, a slight flush to her cheeks, '*romantic* effects.'

'Really?' said Connor, quickly putting down the two-lobed nut.

Emily laughed and said, 'Only when eaten.'

Connor stared at the massive seed. 'What? All of it?'

They exchanged amused glances, then sniggered to one another. As a middle-aged couple strolled up behind them, they stifled their laughs and continued down the path. Trekking deeper into the emerald-tinged undergrowth, the atmosphere became almost eerie, the dappled sunlight occasionally disappearing altogether beneath the monstrous corrugated leaves of the coco-de-mer trees. Like giant umbrellas, the fan palms soared thirty metres up to a shadowy canopy where unseen creatures flitted from branch to branch.

'This place is like a real-life Jurassic Park,' breathed Connor, gazing round at the primeval forest.

The call of bulbul birds and the whistling of black parrots sounded among the trees. The air was heavy with the odour of decaying vegetation and the sweet scent of flowering orchids. At any moment, Connor expected a pack of Velociraptors to burst from the undergrowth and surround them.

As they wound their way along the path, Emily turned to him, her eyes downcast. 'You know . . . I've not met anyone quite like you before,' she admitted.

Connor glanced sideways at her, wondering where this conversation was going.

'I mean,' she quickly added, 'who could understand my *experience*.'

Connor smiled gently. 'Well, I've only got a notion of what you went through. I was a hostage for a few days. You were held for months.'

'Yeah, and it felt like years,' she said, running her fingers through the fronds of a fern. 'But it *never* had to be that way.'

'What do you mean?'

Emily looked up at the canopy where a bright green frog clung motionless to a palm leaf. 'My father wouldn't pay the ransom. He abandoned me.'

Connor tried to hide the shock on his face. 'I'm sure he . . . he was advised to get proof of life before paying anything,' he said, fumbling for a logical reason.

Emily shook her head gravely. 'My father has always been a ruthless businessman. That's why he's so successful. The kidnappers were originally asking for five million dollars. At first he plain refused. Then he bargained them down. And down.'

No wonder Mr Sterling's so rich, thought Connor, *if he can play hardball with his daughter's life at stake.*

'But isn't that just part of the normal negotiation process?'

'I suppose so, but he reduced them to five *hundred thousand* dollars in the end.' Emily looked Connor in the face, her eyes shining with tears. 'He makes more than that in a week! Just goes to show how much my father values me.'

Connor shifted awkwardly on the balls of his feet, uncertain what to say to that. He watched as another party of tourists made its way through the forest towards them. 'Look, I'm not really in a position to judge. But your father has hired me and Ling to protect you and your sister. Surely that proves he cares for you.'

Emily's gaze returned to the tree frog, which still hadn't moved. 'For my sister, at least,' she mumbled, then walked on.

Connor remained by her side as she continued to talk. 'Me and Chloe may look the same. But in truth we're yin and yang. I've no interest in business, media or socializing. That's why Chloe's always been the favourite. My father expects her to succeed him in managing his empire.'

'But your sister doesn't seem too happy with him at the moment.'

'That's because of *Amanda*,' said Emily, her tone hardening. 'We're supposed to be on holiday as a family, yet we've barely seen our father.'

Out of nowhere the hairs on Connor's neck rose. He had the distinct feeling of being watched. His alert level went up a notch from Code Yellow to Code Orange. While pretending to admire the forest, he swept his gaze over the faces of the tourists behind.

'I suppose it's understandable, in a way,' Connor said, spotting a black man in wrap-around shades and a blue baseball cap. The tourist was studying his pamphlet and purposefully not looking in their direction. 'They seem very much in love.'

'That's the problem. And it's not helped by the fact that Amanda is –' Emily appeared to struggle for the right word – 'so self-centred. She *only* shows interest in us when our father's around. It seems like an act. Chloe's feeling pushed out by our father and she's really not used to that.'

Sliding his mobile phone from his pocket, Connor

accessed the mugshot of the criminal Doug Carter on his screen. He tried to match the faces, but it was difficult since the tourist's features were mostly hidden by his cap and shades. Still, Connor's sixth sense was twitching.

'I can see how Amanda's presence could cause problems,' Connor replied, his attention now half on the man behind them. 'Tell you what, shall we go back to the beach? I spotted a cool-looking ice-cream hut. They've mango and coconut flavours.'

'Do they have coco-de-mer flavour too?'

Connor glanced at Emily, surprised, then realized she was attempting a joke. 'Well, let's find out,' he smiled.

Following the circular trail round to the entrance, Connor subtly checked behind them. The suspect man had broken away from the rest of the tourists and was keeping pace with them. Connor went to Code Red. *High alert.* Exiting the nature reserve as fast as he could, Connor hurried Emily over to the waiting taxi.

'You must be desperate for an ice cream,' she said, laughing as he opened the door for her and clambered in after. Connor was now glad he'd been wise enough to pay the driver extra to wait for them. As the taxi pulled away, he glanced through the back windscreen. The man with wrap-around shades had disappeared.

'Are you all right?' asked Emily.

'Yeah, just thought I saw someone I knew,' Connor replied, allowing his alert level to return to Code Yellow, 'but I was wrong.'

When they returned to the beach, Chloe and Ling were

surrounded by a group of lads. Ling stood chatting with one of them, keeping a cautious eye on the scene. Chloe was reclined fully back, teasing a lock of hair with a finger, while laughing with two boys perched on the end of her sunlounger. She looked over and waved excitedly as Connor and Emily approached.

'We've been invited to a beach party!'

CHAPTER 39

'How convinced are you it was him?' asked Ling, digging her toes into the soft warm sand.

She and Connor sat a little distance from the bonfire, the wood crackling and sending sparks like fireflies into the night sky. Bathed in the flickering glow of the flames, they kept a careful watch on Chloe and Emily dancing and chatting with the other guests at the beach party. Initially Mr Sterling hadn't been at all comfortable with the idea of his daughters attending. But Amanda had convinced him otherwise – either in an attempt to win favour with the girls or, as the sisters thought more likely, so she could have extra time alone with her future husband.

Connor shrugged in response to Ling's question. 'Fifty per cent. It was more a *gut feeling*.'

'You know how unlikely this is,' she said, sipping from a can of Diet Coke she'd got from the bar. 'I mean, we're thousands of miles away from Sydney, virtually on the other side of the world.'

'I realize that,' Connor replied, beginning to doubt his own eyes. 'I just wish you'd been there to ID him.'

Ling held up her hands. 'Hey, I was busy fending off the boys swarming round Chloe.'

'You weren't doing too badly yourself,' Connor remarked, nudging her with his elbow.

Ling narrowed her eyes at him. '*He* was talking to me. I was still in Code Yellow. Anyway, have you reported your sighting to Brad or the captain yet?'

'No,' Connor admitted. 'You remember what Bugsy taught us: *Once is happenstance, twice is circumstance. Three times means enemy action.* Unless I see that man again, the sighting means nothing.'

Ling pursed her lips. 'Well, Chloe seems to be getting into the full swing of the party.'

Over the bar's speakers Bob Marley's 'Could You Be Loved?' pulsed its summery lilting beat. Chloe was gyrating her hips and dancing with a lad in Bermuda shorts. Although not wanting to intrude on her fun, Connor realized they'd have to keep a close eye on her. They couldn't have their Principal disappearing with some boy along the beach. Meanwhile, Emily sat by the fire, chatting with two girls and a red-haired boy who was showing a clear interest in her. But Connor didn't judge him a threat. He was half his size and, by the looks of it, was getting nowhere with Emily.

As Connor surveyed the party, a tall lad with curly sun-bleached hair swaggered over to them.

'Hey!' he drawled.

'Hi, Dave,' Ling replied, offering a friendly yet reserved smile. Connor recognized him as the boy who'd been speaking with her earlier that afternoon.

'What you doing over here? The party's happening over *there*.' Dave wafted his arm in the general direction of the music.

'There's a better view from here,' replied Ling.

'Really?' Dave turned his head and looked for himself.

Ling rolled her eyes at Connor, the lad having no idea what she actually meant by this. From their position outside the party, the two of them occupied the best surveillance point. They could see the beach, the bonfire and the bar. Their two Principals were always under their watchful guard yet had the freedom to enjoy themselves without Connor or Ling constantly at their side. And by not being too close to the fire they kept some of their night vision, meaning people didn't suddenly materialize out of the darkness.

'Seems good to me wherever you look,' said Dave, gazing directly at Ling. 'Especially this way.'

He flumped down in the sand beside her and offered her an open-topped coconut with a straw sticking out.

'No thanks,' said Ling. Even from where Connor was sitting, he caught the sharp whiff of rum. Mr Sterling had made it absolutely clear that, as one of the ground rules for attending the party, alcohol was forbidden. He'd given the two of them specific instructions to ensure his daughters steered clear of it, holding them fully responsible if the girls returned in anything but a sober state.

'Too young to drink?' said Dave, taking a slurp and laughing. 'Me too!' He jutted his chin towards Connor. 'He your boyfriend?'

Ling glanced at Connor and smirked. 'No, I have taste.'

Dave broke into a broad grin. 'Didn't think so.' He bent forward to catch Connor's eye. 'No offence, mate.'

'None taken,' replied Connor, wondering when the lad would realize he wasn't welcome.

But Dave persisted in his attempt to hit on Ling by talking about his surfing prowess that day. Tuning out from the conversation, Connor's eyes swept the party again. Chloe was now jumping up and down to 'In The Summertime' by Shaggy. Her sister had joined her and the red-haired boy from the bonfire was dancing alongside them both.

As he observed the dancers, he caught sight of a tattooed arm in the firelight. His alert status went from Code Yellow to Code Orange. *Focused awareness*. His eyes searched among the partygoers for another glimpse. But, outside the glow of the fire, the beach was too dark to make out any individual beyond their silhouettes. The next pool of light was the bar with its glistening oil lamps.

Then Connor saw a flash of a muscled bicep with a roaring lion tattoo.

CHAPTER 40

'Ling, I think I just saw Todd,' said Connor, interrupting Dave's surf monologue.

Ling turned to him, a frown on her face. 'Todd?'

'*Yes*, Todd Logan,' Connor repeated, giving her a pointed look. 'You remember, the rollerblader.'

'So, the wave pulled me under. I thought I was gonna be *fish food . . .*' continued Dave, trying desperately to keep Ling's attention. But she ignored his ramblings as the name's full significance hit home.

'Where?' Ling demanded, her eyes sharp as she hunted the darkness.

'Over there, by the dancers.'

Ling craned her neck. 'I can't see him. Are you sure?'

'I didn't see his face,' admitted Connor, 'but I recognized his lion tattoo.'

Ling leant over to Connor and whispered, 'We can't simply extract the girls from the party just because you saw a tattoo. There's loads of guys here with tats, even Dave has one.'

Connor glanced over at her new friend, a surfboard inked on his leg with the words *Surf or Die*.

'But it's too much of a coincidence to ignore,' he insisted. 'We can't take the risk.'

'OK,' relented Ling, getting to her feet. 'Then we need to eyeball him first. Get confirmation.'

Dave looked up with a slightly forlorn expression. 'Hey, Ling. Forget Todd. Think Dave!'

'In another life,' replied Ling over her shoulder as she and Connor strode towards the main party.

Struggling to stand up, Dave slumped back in the sand with a drunken sigh and called out, 'See ya later, Ling!'

'Let's split up,' Connor suggested, 'but stay in comms.'

Ling nodded in agreement and they both inserted their covert earpieces.

'*Alpha One to Alpha Two. Comms check*,' whispered Connor.

'I'm standing right next to you, idiot!' hissed Ling. 'But I hear you loud and clear. Now you take left flank and I'll take right.'

The two of them circled round the mass of people raving on the beach. The music was pumping and in the flame-lit darkness the dancers became a tangle of bare arms and legs, faces shifting in and out of view, making it hard to identify anyone. But, as he worked his way through the party, Connor kept a visual lock on Emily and Chloe's position.

'*Have you spotted him yet?*' came Ling's voice in his ear.

'Negative,' replied Connor.

A pretty girl swayed in front of him, trying to catch his eye. He smiled at her. At any other time, he'd leap at such an opportunity, but there were more important matters at stake right now. He edged past her, heading in the direction of the bar.

Above the music he suddenly heard Chloe's voice shout, 'CONNOR!'

He spun round, his heart in his mouth at the anticipated sight of her being dragged away into the darkness. But she was just bouncing up and down, waving for him to join her in a dance. Breathing once more, Connor pointed in the direction of the toilets. Chloe gave him the thumbs up in understanding and returned to her boogying. On the opposite side of the dancers, Ling continued with her surveillance sweep. She made eye contact with him.

'*Any sign?*' she asked.

Connor shook his head.

'*Maybe you were mistaken.*'

'No, I'm sure I saw –' At that moment, Connor noticed movement behind the palm-thatched bar, a figure lurking out of sight from all the other partygoers.

'I've spotted him,' he whispered. 'Behind the bar.'

'*Are you sure?*' said Ling, altering course towards the building.

Using the palm trees for cover, Connor moved in for a definite confirmation. The man had his back to him. He couldn't be certain. He crept to within a few metres of his target. Then he saw, in the reflected glow of an oil lamp, the tattoo.

'It's Todd!' whispered Connor into his mic.

'*Watch out,*' cried Ling as the figure turned towards Connor's voice. '*He's got a machete.*'

A gleam of steel flashed in the lamplight, the vicious blade slicing through the air. Connor leapt aside as Ling ran up behind and launched into a flying side-kick. Her foot struck the man's back, sending him sprawling into the sand. Kicking away his machete, Connor grabbed his arm and twisted it into a lock. Ling seized the other arm, rotating it until the wrist threatened to snap.

'Ow! Help!' he cried, writhing on the ground in agony.

'Don't struggle or I'll break your wrist,' Ling hissed.

'What the hell is going on here?' shouted a gruff voice from behind. 'Leave my barman alone!'

As the bar manager stormed over, Connor and Ling stared at the man they had pinned to the ground. Although tattooed and dark-haired, he was *not* Todd Logan. Only now, up close, could Connor see that the tattoo wasn't a roaring lion. It was a tiger.

CHAPTER 41

'Well done, hotshot!' said Ling, her tone dripping with sarcasm, as the two of them, having made their apologies to the barman, beat a hasty retreat to the party.

'Sorry, it was dark, I couldn't see his face,' Connor replied. 'And he *did* have a machete.'

'To cut coconuts with.'

'But *you* were the one who jumped him,' argued Connor.

Ling spun on him and jabbed a finger in his chest. 'Don't blame me for your mistakes! I'm always having to pick up the slack on this mission.'

'What do you mean?'

Ling let out a derisive snort and fixed him with a withering look. 'Well, to start with, on Manly Beach you completely failed to spot that mugger's approach. And I had to stop him escaping with *your* Principal's handbag.'

'That was Jason's fault,' explained Connor. 'If he hadn't –'

'Don't bring Jason into this,' said Ling, cutting him off. 'Your reactions were slow and you know it. And what about the other day? I believe it was *me* who noticed *your*

Principal floating off on a lilo. I thought you were supposed to be a gold-winged buddyguard. Now you're seeing threats where there aren't any!'

Connor held up his hands in surrender. 'OK, you're right. I realize I've made some mistakes. That's probably why I'm being so jumpy, but I know what I s–'

'Hang on,' Ling interrupted. 'Where's Emily?'

For the second time that night, Connor felt his throat tighten in panic. He scanned the crowd for Emily's face, but everyone kept moving and twirling, the dark and firelight confusing the scene. Then he spotted the red-haired boy dancing with – 'No, it's *Chloe* that's missing,' corrected Connor.

'Are you sure?' said Ling, squinting at the remaining sister.

'Yes, that boy hasn't left Emily's side all night.'

Ling cursed. 'Chloe could be pretty much *anywhere*,' she muttered as she hunted the darkness for her Principal.

Connor didn't like the situation either. Beyond the glow of the bonfire lay a two-kilometre stretch of starlit beach. It would be virtually impossible to find her, especially near the treeline where the darkness was absolute.

They did a sweep of the party, down towards the bonfire. When this didn't produce a result, Connor checked his watch. Chloe had been missing at least five minutes, long enough to start getting concerned. He approached Emily in the crowd. She greeted him with an unexpected kiss on the cheek.

'Have you come to save me from this boy?' she whispered

in his ear, flicking her eyes towards her dancing partner. The boy frowned at Connor, clearly wondering who was moving in on 'his girl'.

'Sorry, mate,' said Connor with an apologetic smile. 'We have to go.'

Connor led Emily away by the hand, leaving the boy open-mouthed and crestfallen.

'Thanks,' said Emily. 'He was sweet, but a real bore.'

'Do you know where your sister is?' Connor asked, getting straight to the point.

Emily shrugged. 'She said she was going to the toilet.'

Connor relayed this information to Ling.

'*I've already checked. She's not there,*' came Ling's tense reply in his ear.

They regrouped at the edge of the party, Connor keeping Emily close. If her sister was missing, then he couldn't afford to let Emily out of his sight. There might be a completely innocent explanation for Chloe's disappearance. However, the longer she was gone, the less chance the outcome would be good. She could have wandered off with a boy, whose intentions may or may not be honourable. She could have gone swimming and been caught in a current, or fallen over in the darkness and hurt herself. Or maybe he *had* seen Todd, as well as his accomplice earlier that day in the forest, and the two men had snatched her. The nightmare scenarios were endless.

'What shall we do?' said Ling, a hint of desperation edging her voice.

Connor realized he had to take charge of the situation.

Definitive action was the best solution to such an emergency. 'First, we call Brad to bring the tender over,' he said, pulling out his phone. 'We can't search the beach and protect Emily at the same time.'

Once he'd spoken with Brad and explained the situation, Emily asked, 'Do you think my sister's OK?'

She eyed the darkness fearfully as if invisible hands would reach out and spirit her away too. Connor wore his most reassuring smile. 'I'm sure she is. But we can't take any risks. I'm sending you back to the *Orchid* while we look for her.'

'Hey! I thought you were leaving?'

The three of them turned to see the red-haired boy approaching, an aggrieved expression on his face.

Emily nodded. 'We are, but we have to find my sister first.'

'Well, I just saw her.' The boy pointed up the beach. 'She's in the bar with Matt.'

'*What?*' exclaimed Ling. 'I must have walked straight past her.'

The three of them hurried up to the bar, leaving Emily's admirer behind again.

'Does that mean you're staying now?' the boy called out hopefully, getting no reply.

They found Chloe perched on a stool, chin resting in the palm of her hand as she gazed into the dark eyes of the lad with Bermuda shorts. Matt had broad shoulders, a six-pack and an easy-going smile. A few years older than Chloe, he had clearly charmed her. The barman was serving up two coconuts with fancy cocktail umbrellas and straws.

'Well, panic over,' said Emily, sighing with visible relief.

'I still think it's time to go,' Ling said to Connor, nodding at the two drinks. She strode determinedly over to the bar. Breaking up the intimate twosome, Ling gave Chloe the news of their imminent departure.

Chloe's jaw dropped. 'But the party isn't over yet!'

'Brad's on his way. Besides, your father said no alcohol.'

'Oh, don't be such a killjoy,' said Chloe, waving her off and reaching for the coconut. 'You don't *have* to tell him.'

Ling pulled out the straw before Chloe could take a sip. Chloe looked mortified, her cheeks flushing with a mix of embarrassment and rage.

'*Just leave us alone,*' she hissed.

Ling stood her ground. 'No can do.'

'Look, if you're worried about my safety, don't be. Matt can protect me.'

'Sure I can,' he said, resting a hand on Chloe's knee while offering Ling a winning smile.

Ling remained unmoved by his charm. 'You don't get a hungry lion to protect a lamb.'

Matt's brow knotted in confusion. 'Say again?'

'Oh, forget it,' said Ling, losing patience with him. 'We have to go.'

Chloe glared at her, refusing to shift from her stool. After several moments of uncomfortable silence, Matt held up his hands. 'Listen, I can see I'm causing problems.' He turned to Chloe. 'I'll catch you another time.'

'But we might be sailing to another island tomorrow,' she protested.

Matt glanced uneasily at the small yet forceful Chinese girl standing beside him. 'I think it's for the best if you do go.'

Chloe fumed at Ling. 'Well, *at least* give me a chance to say goodbye.'

'Certainly,' replied Ling, turning on her heel and rejoining Connor and Emily.

She raised her eyebrows at Connor and tutted in exasperation. Connor shrugged sympathetically, although he thought Ling could have handled the situation a little more tactfully.

They waited while Chloe enveloped Matt in a hug and kissed him on both cheeks. When she finally released him, he grinned and winked at her. Chloe then made her way out of the bar.

She threw Ling a scathing look. 'Thanks for nothing, I was just starting to enjoy myself.'

'It looked like it,' replied Ling. 'But you do realize that the drink could have been spiked.'

'What? Matt's not that sort of guy.'

'How do you know?' challenged Ling.

Chloe stared at her in disbelief. 'You don't trust boys very much, do you?'

'No,' replied Ling, leading her towards the jetty. 'Especially ones I don't know.'

CHAPTER 42

'What a night!' said Ling, collapsing in one of the recliners on the *Orchid*'s foredeck. The area was secluded from the rest of the yacht and little used by the Sterling family, who preferred the more spacious and wind-sheltered living quarters towards the stern.

Lying back in the adjacent recliner, Connor gazed in awe at the galaxy of stars overhead. He'd never seen so many in his life. Unobscured by clouds or light pollution, the sky seemed dusted with glimmering diamonds.

'Well, we survived and both Principals are safe and sober,' he replied, making himself comfortable.

'Yeah, no thanks to Chloe,' muttered Ling. 'Look, I'm sorry I had a go at you earlier.'

'Not a problem. I deserved it.' Connor glanced over at Ling. 'But Chloe was only enjoying herself.'

Ling tsked. 'Well, you would take her side, wouldn't you?'

'What's that supposed to mean?'

Ling rolled her eyes. 'Boys! She has you wrapped round her little finger. *Oh, Connor, I need your protection,*' she mocked in Chloe's voice, waving a pretend bottle of suntan lotion at him.

Connor brushed off her jibe. 'Come on, you must admit you were a little heavy-handed with her tonight.'

Ling huffed. 'She shouldn't have been in the bar in the first place. But it's not just that. She's a right pain in the neck. She treats me like her personal slave. Expects me to carry her bags, get her drinks, pick up her clothes. And she never listens when I try to give her safety advice. Doesn't she understand that my job is to protect her, not *serve* her?'

Connor's eye caught a shooting star trace its way across the sky. 'You should give Chloe some slack. She's never had a bodyguard before, so probably doesn't know what we're actually supposed to do.'

'Well, Emily seems to understand. And there's no reason to be rude or bossy about it. I'm sorry but I don't find it easy to sympathize with people who have everything.'

'Don't forget their mother died in a car crash, one of them's been kidnapped and their father's too busy with work, or his fiancée, to spend any time with them. They don't exactly have an easy life.'

'Well, their life isn't exactly tough either,' countered Ling, indicating the multimillion-dollar super-yacht.

Connor thought about his own situation. His gran had always said, *Wealth is empty; it's family that fills the heart.* 'Money doesn't necessarily mean happiness.'

'Yeah, but it sure helps,' said Ling, staring hard at Connor. 'I'll tell you what tough is. I grew up as a street kid in Shanghai. It was survival of the strongest and meanest. I had nothing apart from my wits to live on. And as a *girl* I was at an immediate disadvantage. I used to live in a cardboard box down an alleyway.'

Connor stared at Ling in shock at this sudden revelation.

'The only good thing about it was the kung fu club in a nearby basement. I'd spy on their lessons through a grating in the wall, teaching myself the moves. It wasn't exactly an *easy* life. I had stomach cramps on the days I couldn't scavenge food. But the kung fu kept my mind off it. The *shifu* used to say, *It's hard to beat a person who never gives up*. I lived by that mantra every miserable day of my life on those streets.'

Connor was speechless. He'd had no clue about Ling's troubled past. *Did anyone else in Alpha team know?* At least now he understood what the colonel had meant by her 'tough' background, and it partly explained Ling's constant need to prove herself.

'So how did you ever become a buddyguard?' he asked.

'Colonel Black caught me picking his pocket.'

Connor sat up in surprise. 'You did *what*?'

Ling knitted her fingers behind her head, grinning at the memory. 'Yeah, I almost got away with it as well. But at the last second the colonel grabbed my wrist and put me in a lock. Not that it stopped me. I simply spun out of it, kicked him in the knee and ran. But he was with Steve, our combat instructor, at the time. Gee, was he fast! He cornered me in an alley. I thought I'd be beaten within an inch of my life, but, rather than punish me or turn me over to the police, the colonel *recruited* me.'

Connor was stunned. 'Why did he do that?'

Ling shrugged. 'Said he was impressed with my stealth and fighting spirit. Being streetwise, he thought I had the makings of a bodyguard.' Ling laughed. 'Anyway, the colonel arranged a passport and a visa for me and I ended up at Buddyguard HQ. The rest is history.'

She looked at Connor and narrowed her eyes thoughtfully. 'I do sometimes wonder, though, whether he *let* me pick his pocket.'

Recalling his own recruitment, the corner of Connor's mouth curled into a smile. 'Sounds like the colonel's tactics to me.'

CHAPTER 43

Connor looked at his watch. 'Time to do our final security sweep.'

'Yep, better check the princesses are safely tucked up in bed!' quipped Ling, hauling herself out of the recliner.

Connor switched on his torch, the bright beam shining off the smooth wooden deck. They headed aft along the port side of the yacht. All the crew members were in their quarters, apart from one of the deckhands, Scott, who was on official watch duty on the bridge. There was no real need for an additional security check, yet since Brad had said the more eyeballs the better, Connor thought it couldn't do any harm.

With the girls having gone to their cabins and Mr Sterling and his fiancée tucked away in their personal suite, all was quiet on board. Only the lapping of the sea against the hull and the distant beat of music from the beach intruded on the tropical night's peace. Connor could see the bonfire burning on the shore, its glow reflected in the rippling waters of the bay.

As the two of them reached the stern and headed back

up the starboard side, Connor wondered if they'd overreacted to Chloe's 'disappearance'. It wasn't as if she'd been gone long, nor had she gone far. In hindsight, they could have spent a bit more time *looking* before jumping to the wrong conclusion. It was certainly a sign of their inexperience as buddyguards, but Brad had been kind in his appraisal. He considered they'd made the right decision, saying it was better to act on a potential threat and be wrong than ignore it and find out to their cost the threat was real.

'Look! The crew's left the gangway down again,' said Ling, pointing to the steel steps leading up from the waterline. 'I thought Brad warned them about that.'

She pressed the button to retract the gangway. As they waited for it to whirr quietly back into its recess, Connor's torch caught a gleam on the deck. He looked closer. It was a damp footprint. Fresh.

He widened the arc of his beam and more footprints appeared, leading away into the darkness.

'One of the crew?' suggested Ling.

'Swimming at this time of night?' said Connor, shaking his head dubiously.

They followed the trail to the first flight of external steps. Silently ascending to the upper deck, Connor felt a growing disquiet at the thought of an intruder on board. Brad had informed them about a spate of thefts that had occurred on yachts docked at Victoria Harbour and the surrounding bays, but those boats hadn't generally been occupied at the time.

Peering round the final step, they saw no one on the

upper deck at first. Then Ling spotted a shadowy figure spying through a window into the VIP guest room.

'I think we should get Brad,' whispered Connor.

'Too late for that,' replied Ling as the intruder opened the door leading to the suite. Chloe was standing on the other side. The intruder grabbed her. She squealed.

'Quiet!' he hissed, his hand over her mouth.

Without waiting a second longer, Ling leapt up and ran full pelt at the intruder.

'Let her go!' she cried, kicking at the attacker's knee from behind.

His balance broken, he toppled backwards. Ling seized his hair in one hand and his chin in the other, then twisted his head and pushed down. But, rather than guiding the intruder to the deck, she launched him over the rail.

Where the head goes, the body follows, Connor recalled their combat instructor saying when he'd first taught them the 'head-twist' technique.

Screaming, the intruder somersaulted through the air and splashed into the sea.

'What did you do *that* for?' Chloe cried, her jaw dropping open in shock and horror.

Ling stared in bafflement at her Principal. 'He was attacking you.'

'He was my *guest*! That was Matt you just threw overboard.'

'Oh!' said Ling, putting a hand to her mouth. Connor couldn't quite tell if it was to hide her embarrassment at the mistake, or her amusement.

'Well, you know, we can't just let anyone on board,' said Ling in her own defence. 'It's a security risk.'

Chloe threw up her hands in despair. 'You are a *nightmare*!' she cried, before slamming the door in Ling's face.

CHAPTER 44

Ruth McArthur lit her second cigarette of the night. Exhaling a puff of acrid smoke, she watched it rise up to the grime-stained ceiling of the pedestrian underpass running beneath Manning Road on Sydney's University Campus. The fluorescent strip lights, naked and harsh, cast a sickly glow on to the colourful scene surrounding her. The walls, ceiling, and even the floor were infected with a profusion of graffiti and tags, as if the tunnel itself was bleeding paint. Cutting through the smog of her cigarette, the lingering fumes from aerosol cans filled Ruth's nostrils and made her slightly nauseous.

Yet as editor-in-chief of Sterling's flagship paper, *Australian Daily*, she'd experienced her fair share of war zones, drug dens and slums. So this particular location didn't spook her at all. Not that this meant she was naive. She kept a firm grip on her car keys in one hand, a tip she'd learnt from self-defence lessons. The protruding metal points made an effective improvised weapon if the situation demanded it.

The tunnel was deserted, the silence almost echoing in

on itself. In these late hours of night, the only life passing through would be the occasional tagger or graffiti artist wanting to make their mark.

Ruth glanced at her watch, beginning to wonder if her contact from the Government Department of Resources and Energy would show. Acquiring information on the Harry Gibb case had been like getting blood from a stone. No one seemed to want to pursue any other line of enquiry than death by natural causes. Case closed. But her inside contact claimed to have proof otherwise.

Stamping out her cigarette, Ruth reached into her bag for her phone. Her contact might have left a message. She thumbed in her password, but there were no missed calls and her inbox was empty. One of the strip lights flickered and buzzed overhead, dimming the passageway momentarily. She glanced up and had to stifle a scream in her throat. Where there had been just shadow now stood a man in a grey suit. Having not heard or seen his approach, it was as if the man had materialized straight out of the graffiti, leaching all colour in the process.

'Ruth McArthur?' the man said, his voice dry and somehow soulless.

'Yes,' she said, unclenching the keys in her fist. This must be her contact. 'And you are . . . James?'

The man was older than Ruth expected, yet at the same time strangely ageless. *Like a well-preserved corpse*, she thought, before shuddering away the unsettling image in her mind.

'So you want to know about Harry Gibb?' he said.

Ruth nodded.

The man glanced up and down the tunnel. 'You're not an undercover cop or federal agent, are you?'

'No, of course not.' Ruth produced her press ID.

He studied her photo and credentials. 'Press passes can easily be faked.'

Ruth appreciated the reason for her contact's wariness. The fallout from Harry Gibb's corrupt dealings was catastrophic for the current government. Many in power had been glad of the politician's death and were hoping the scandal would be buried along with him. But Ruth had caught the scent of a bigger story, a far wider and more sinister conspiracy, and she wanted to know the truth. She sensed this might be the journalistic scoop of her career.

'Well, how about I tell you what I think happened? Then you can just confirm or deny it,' she suggested.

The man neither nodded nor shook his head, so she continued, 'My theory is that Harry Gibb was murdered. Or to put it more accurately, assassinated.'

There was a barely perceptible twitch of his eyebrow. 'You have proof of this?'

'No, nothing concrete,' admitted Ruth. 'I was hoping you could provide that.'

'How did you come to this conclusion about Harry when the cops didn't?'

'I'm a journalist. I always look deeper than the police. I get the sense that something's missing in this case. For example, there was alcohol in Harry's bloodstream. Not unusual. He was a known alcoholic. But there was no bottle found at the scene. When I spoke with his secretary, she told me that he kept a silver hip flask in his desk. That was gone.'

The man nodded. 'It's true, Harry did have a hip flask. What else have you discovered?'

Ruth didn't usually give so much away during an interview with a contact, but she needed to win his trust. 'Well, his PC's hard drive was secure-wiped to a zero state. The accepted truth was that Harry did this to cover his tracks. But a malware virus, linked to his computer, infiltrated the rest of the office network. The IT technician said he'd seen nothing like it. The virus was highly advanced, targeting specific keywords and files and leaving holes throughout their system, despite multiple firewalls and anti-virus software. In his opinion, it smacked of governmental espionage. Then there's the missing physical file from the archives.'

The man took a step closer. 'You know about the missing file?'

Ruth nodded. She was *definitely* on to something. 'It took me some while to discover it. The CCTV on that day had malfunctioned. Yet a digital record showed that Harry had accessed the archive room ten minutes prior to his death. A folder entitled MINING RIGHTS, GOLDFIELDS, WA, was logged in the filing system but wasn't there when I looked. However, I did find this at the bottom of the cabinet.'

Ruth produced a slip of crumpled paper from her bag.

'It lists investment amounts and sources, although I'm

not sure how useful it is, since a number of the companies don't actually exist –'

'Have you made a copy of that?' interrupted her contact.

'No . . .' began Ruth, frowning. 'Look, it should be me asking *you* the questions. I was led to believe you had evidence relating to Harry's murder.'

A flicker of a smile registered on her contact's lean face, almost too fast and certainly too cold to pass off as a real smile. 'That I do. You're right on all counts. Harry was assassinated.'

Ruth's eyes lit up. She had her story. 'By whom?'

'One of his investors.'

'Which one? As I said, most of the ones listed here were shell companies. Unless you mean –' she held up the piece of paper and smiled slyly – 'the organization behind them?'

The man's eyes became glacial. 'What information do you have on this organization?'

Ruth suddenly felt uneasy in his presence. She tightened her grip on her car keys.

'Tell me,' said the man, seizing her arm and preventing Ruth from using her 'weapon'.

'Let me go!' demanded Ruth.

'No, not until you tell me.'

The man's fingers dug deep into her flesh, finding a nerve point and sending a spasm of pain through her.

'Not much,' Ruth admitted through teeth clenched in agony. 'There were only ghost trails from the false companies. I know it goes by the name of Equilibrium and has interests in everything from oil to water to mining. But as to what purpose I can't quite fathom. The company isn't registered on any stock exchange.'

'Who else have you told?' He tightened his grip on her arm.

'No one. I've only just discovered it for myself.'

He released her arm, the pain instantly subsiding. 'Good. Equilibrium is a dangerous organization to know.'

Ruth rubbed her arm. Her contact was clearly paranoid as well as unpredictable. 'Listen, if you're worried for your own safety, then I know people who can help protect you.'

The man laughed, hollow and cruel. 'No one is safe from Equilibrium.'

'Well then, if you've proof they're connected to Harry's murder, perhaps we can draw out this organization. Expose them.'

The man gave a long considered sigh. 'Ruth, you certainly deserve your reputation for investigative journalism.'

He reached into his jacket pocket and pulled out a fountain pen.

'I have someone you should talk to. Who can explain everything,' he said, slowly removing the top of the pen. 'Do you have a notepad? I'll write his contact number down for you.'

'Yes, of course.' Ruth scrabbled inside her handbag. She now wanted to end this meeting as quickly as possible.

Only as she was retrieving her notepad, did she notice the peculiar shape of the pen. The tip itself was a long sharp needle, far too thin for writing. In the split second that she registered this oddity, the point sank into the soft flesh of her neck. A liquid fire coursed through her veins, the agonizing shock smothering all attempts to cry out. The lurid graffiti of the tunnel swirled rapidly into blackness and she slumped to the floor, followed by the soft jangle of keys.

CHAPTER 45

'The fault lay with a distorted gasket in the fuel system,' explained Amir, his face bright on the screen of Connor's laptop.

'Well, that makes me rest easier at night!' replied Ling, who sat on the bed with Connor for the morning's video briefing with Alpha team. 'I've literally no idea what you're talking about.'

'A gasket is a mechanical seal which prevents leakage while under compression –'

'Thanks, Amir, but such detail isn't required,' Charley cut in, appearing on the screen beside him. 'The important point is that the Seychelles coastguard discovered the cause of the jet-ski explosion.'

'We saw the pictures,' said Richie, his grinning face butting in front of Amir's. 'That jet ski was totalled! Luckily it wasn't one of the sisters riding it. That could have been disastrous –'

'Hang on, *I* was on it!' exclaimed Ling, her expression indignant.

'Yeah, I know, but you're tough enough,' replied Richie.

He was suddenly yanked out of the frame and Jason's bulk appeared. 'Ignore that Irish idiot. How are you doing, Ling?'

'Fine,' she replied, clearly pleased to see him. 'To be honest, my Principal's more of a pain than the burn.'

Jason laughed. 'I'm afraid that goes with the territory of being a buddyguard. On my last assignment, I could have throttled my Principal!'

'Sorry to break up the happy reunion,' said Charley, 'but we need to focus on this jet-ski situation.'

Jason nodded. 'Stay cool, Ling,' he said, giving her the wink before slipping out of view.

'Joking aside, Ling, you were extremely lucky to have survived the explosion,' continued Charley. 'Without your protective clothing, you could have been seriously injured or even killed.'

Ling nonchalantly lay back on one of the pillows. 'All part of the job, isn't it?'

'No, it isn't,' said Charley firmly, shifting in her wheelchair. 'Or at least with the right security in place, it shouldn't be.'

Connor sensed Charley's own experience in that statement, but this wasn't the time or place to delve into her past. 'So the explosion was just an accident?' he asked.

Charley pensively bit her lower lip. 'That's one way of looking at it. Brad's report, however, stated that the *Orchid*'s engineer had checked the other jet ski and discovered a similar issue with its fuel-filler inlet. It too could have very easily exploded.'

Connor and Ling exchanged uneasy glances. Connor turned back to the laptop's webcam. 'Are you suggesting *sabotage*?'

'We can't rule that possibility out. It may just be a manufacturing defect. It does happen. But on *both* jet skis? That's why we must assume this was an attempt on the lives of the Sterling family, designed to look like an accident.'

'So, who might have done it?' asked Ling.

'Your guess is as good as ours at this time. The last person known to have touched the jet skis was the engineer, but Brad has questioned him and vouches for his integrity. That's to be seen . . .' Charley looked off-screen. 'Hang on, Colonel Black's just come in.'

Charley and Amir moved aside so the colonel could sit in front of the webcam. His jaw was set and his grey eyes hard as flint.

'I've just been speaking with Mr Sterling. Ling, you're being pulled off Operation Gemini with immediate effect.'

'Why am I taking the flak for something *she* did wrong?' said Ling, shoving her clothes into her bag with such force the seams threatened to split.

Connor stood by her cabin door, arms crossed, as Ling vented her fury on her packing.

'I mean, I was just trying to protect her. And what thanks do I get? None. I might as well walk the plank.'

'You made Matt do that,' Connor remarked.

Pausing a moment, Ling smirked. 'Yeah, I suppose I did. Well, he shouldn't have been on board anyway.' She resumed her fierce packing. 'Now the colonel won't trust me on another operation for months!'

'The colonel's not stupid. He knows the score. Don't forget, I was thrown off my first operation.'

Ling glanced up and gave a half-hearted laugh. 'I forgot about that, hotshot. Maybe I'll get to save the day too. Know any terrorists or presidents' daughters in the Seychelles?'

Connor gently shook his head. 'Look, what I'm trying to say is that it doesn't matter.'

'Not to you maybe, but I have to go back to Alpha team with my tail between my legs.'

Brad stuck his head into the cabin. 'The tender's ready.'

'Good,' said Ling as she grabbed the last of her stuff. 'I can't wait to get off this stinking ship.'

'Hey! Lightning Ling,' said Brad, clamping a hand on her shoulder and giving it a squeeze. 'For what it's worth, I think you were doing a stellar job.'

Ling looked up into Brad's craggy face. 'Then why am I being dismissed?'

'Bodyguards and their Principals can be as close as bread and butter . . . or fight like cats and dogs. Sometimes there's simply a clash of personalities. I've had such moments in my career. You just gotta roll with the punches.'

'I'll roll her with a punch,' muttered Ling, sealing up the bag and heading for the door.

Brad raised his eyebrows at Connor, then the two of them followed Ling up to the main deck.

'Aren't we risking the girls' safety by losing Ling?' asked Connor quietly.

'Both myself and the colonel voiced our concerns to Mr Sterling,' replied Brad. 'But he's adamant Ling must go. I'm not happy with it. But, since the girls won't be leaving the yacht before Ling's replacement arrives, I can't foresee any real problems. You'll just have to work double shifts!' he added with a wink.

At the top of the lowered gangway, Ling stopped. 'Well, Connor, it's been a blast.'

'Literally,' said Connor, thinking of the jet ski.

Ling laughed. 'How are you ever going to survive without me?'

Connor shrugged. 'It's only four days. And we're at sea the whole time. Besides, the colonel's sending Luciana from Bravo team to join me in the Maldives.'

'Good luck to her! She'll need it.'

'What do you mean by that? Protecting Chloe or working with me?' said Connor, feigning offence.

Ling punched him on the arm. 'You're all right, Connor. If a little jumpy.' She started down the steps to the tender. 'I'll catch you back at HQ. Just don't strain yourself putting too much suntan lotion on the girls.'

Brad started the engine. He was to drop off Ling in Baie Sainte Anne, where she would take a catamaran to the main island and catch a plane home. However, as they were about to leave, Mr Sterling appeared.

'Hold up, Brad. Change of plan.'

They all turned to him in surprise. Was Ling getting a last-minute reprieve? But Mr Sterling's expression was too grave for that hope.

CHAPTER 47

'I can't believe our father just upped and left like that!' said Chloe, perched on the edge of the jacuzzi, her legs dangling in the bubbling water.

'We haven't seen much of him anyway,' Emily muttered as she took a photo of Mahé Island receding into the distance.

Chloe glanced over the rail at the occupied sunbed in the sky lounge below. 'I just wish he'd taken Amanda with him.'

Connor sat quietly at the dining table on the sun deck. It wasn't his place to pass comment. Mr Sterling had informed his daughters that his editor-in-chief Ruth McArthur had been killed in a suspected mugging incident and that he had to interrupt his holiday to manage the fallout at the newspaper. The yacht had been rerouted via the main island to drop off Mr Sterling and his bodyguard, along with the disgraced Ling, at the airport. Captain Locke had then set a course for the Maldives, where Mr Sterling hoped to rejoin them in a week's time.

'I wouldn't worry,' said Emily, pocketing her phone.

'This boat's big enough for all of us. And she'll probably sunbathe the entire time.'

Emily screwed shut her eyes and rubbed at her temples.

'Are you all right?' asked Connor.

'Yeah, it's just a headache. I get them a lot. I think it's my medication.' Emily headed over to the stairs. 'I'm going to take a nap. See you at dinner.'

Connor offered her a sympathetic smile, but remained at the table. There was no reason to shadow her while on board. They were in coastal waters, the yacht was cruising at a sedate speed, and he and Brad had performed a security sweep prior to departing Mahé. The threat level was low.

Reaching into his polo-shirt pocket, Connor pulled out his mobile. Its orange neoprene cover was still annoyingly bulky, but the waterproofing had been a godsend when he'd dived into the sea to rescue Ling following the jet-ski explosion. Unlocking the screen, he messaged his mum and gran to let them know everything was OK, taking the opportunity before the *Orchid* entered the open ocean and they lost mobile signal altogether. Then he reached for his book and settled back into his chair.

'Come and join me,' said Chloe as she immersed herself fully in the jacuzzi.

Connor glanced over. He was more wary of her since Ling's unwarranted dismissal. 'Thank you, but no.'

Chloe sighed. 'Don't be angry with me. I realize Ling was your friend, but she was really getting on my nerves.'

'She was just doing her job,' Connor replied, not wanting to get into this discussion.

'I realize that, but I couldn't do a single thing without her intervening or passing comment. It was *suffocating*. It's my sister who needs the protection, not me.'

Connor shook his head. He recognized that Ling's manner might have been judged abrasive and heavy-handed, but the fact remained there were genuine threats to the girls' lives. 'I'm afraid you're wrong. *Both* of you are potential targets.'

'That's my sister's fault,' muttered Chloe. 'I can't have any fun because of her. Ever since she was kidnapped, I've been virtually grounded by my father. I haven't been able to go to friends' parties or down the beach or even shopping on my own. Do you know how claustrophobic that feels? This holiday is the *first* time I've been allowed any freedom in over a year.'

'Your father only wants to protect you,' responded Connor. 'That intruder last night could have been a kidnapper, an assassin or worse.'

'But it was *only* Matt,' said Chloe, dismissing the suggestion with a wave of her hand. 'The point is my father allows me no freedom at home, and puts me under so much pressure to succeed at school, that I *need* to let off some steam. Otherwise I'll go stir-crazy.'

Connor noticed tears of frustration welling up in Chloe's eyes and felt a touch of sympathy for her situation. It wasn't her choice to have twenty-four-hour security.

'Fair enough,' he relented. 'Look, when we get to the Maldives, I'll speak with Luciana and we'll work out a way to give you some freedom without compromising your safety. Anyway, Luciana's Brazilian and I've heard she likes to party.'

Chloe's face lit up. 'Thanks, you're a star. Now are you going to join me or not?'

'Best not,' replied Connor. 'I'm on duty.'

'You're *always* on duty.' She rested her chin on the side of the jacuzzi and stared at him. 'As I understand, you're now *my* buddyguard until the Maldives. So, as your Principal, I say you need to relax. That was Ling's problem; don't make it yours.'

Connor sighed. He knew he was being manipulated, but he didn't want to upset her either. An uncooperative Principal was a liability. Besides, a dip in the jacuzzi wouldn't be crossing any lines as a buddyguard. Putting down his book, he took off his polo-shirt and slipped in opposite her.

Chloe smiled. 'See, it's not so bad, is it?'

Connor returned her smile. He couldn't deny the water was wonderfully warm; the bubbles inescapably relaxing. And the setting, in the midst of a glistening ocean and crystal-blue sky, was heavenly. He leant back, resting his arms on the side.

Chloe's gaze fell upon his left shoulder where a slim, white scar line was visible. 'What happened there?'

'Knife wound,' he explained.

Her eyes widened with a mix of concern and fascination. 'Did you get that while protecting someone?'

Connor nodded. She edged round the jacuzzi for a closer look. 'Did it hurt?'

'Yes, but I didn't have much time to think about it. I was in the middle of a fight trying to escape.'

Chloe studied his face with admiration. 'You must have been really brave.'

Connor shook his head. 'I didn't have much choice in the matter.'

'So, do you like my sister at all?' she asked.

Caught completely off-guard, Connor mumbled, 'Yes, of course –' then he saw Chloe frown – 'but not that way. As buddyguards, we have to remain strictly friends with any Principal.'

'Really?' Chloe bit at her lower lip and moved closer, her arm gently resting on his. 'That must be very difficult at times, I mean, to remain *just* friends.'

As her knee brushed against his, Connor decided it was time to get out of the jacuzzi. He didn't want to have to explain himself to Charley a second time.

'The investor has sent through another update,' said Mr WiFi, presenting Oracle with his laptop.

Lifting the silver-mirrored aviator sunglasses from his nose, the pirate leader peered at the digital photo displayed on the laptop screen. A wash of turquoise-blue waters kissed the white sands of a palm-fringed bay, behind which rose a mist-shrouded peak.

'So what island is that?'

'Mahé,' replied Mr WiFi.

Oracle raised a dubious eyebrow. 'There are countless islands that look the same. How can you be so certain?'

Mr WiFi right-clicked on the image, opening up its EXIF metadata file. 'Because the photo has the exact geo-location embedded within it. Along with a time stamp indicating the precise moment it was taken – 14:32 today.'

Oracle reclined against his gold-tasselled bolster in the shaded living room and laughed. 'Oh, the benefits of modern technology and the naivety of young people. They're almost inviting us to join them!'

Reaching across to a cup on an inlaid ivory tray, he took

a sip of spiced black tea. He savoured the taste a moment before asking, 'What other information has the investor provided?'

Sitting cross-legged on the crimson rug before his boss, Mr WiFi tugged casually at his goatee. 'The *Orchid* is on a north-east bearing, headed for the Maldives. Estimated voyage time four days.'

'And where are my men now?'

Mr WiFi brought up an electronic chart of the Indian Ocean on his laptop. Zooming in, he pointed to a cluster of tiny green dots visible amid a vast swathe of blue.

'They're seventy-five nautical miles north-west of the target.'

'Then tell Spearhead to stop playing with small fry,' said Oracle, putting down his tea. 'It's time to reel in the big fish.'

Leaning against the *Orchid*'s stern rail, Connor watched Praslin Island slowly shrink towards the darkening horizon. Mahé had long since disappeared from view and soon they'd be leaving the territorial waters of the Seychelles for the open ocean. With his mobile signal down to a single bar, Connor checked in with Alpha team one last time. Charley answered in two rings.

'So how are you coping solo?' she asked.

'Fine,' replied Connor, not wanting to admit that he'd spent most of the afternoon evading Chloe's advances. With nothing else to do on board except read, relax and sunbathe, Chloe seemed to want to let off steam by flirting with him – a fact that hadn't gone unnoticed by her sister.

Not that Connor didn't appreciate such attention. Chloe was by no means unattractive. But he knew any such lapse of judgement would finish his role as a buddyguard for good and bring an end to the paid-for nursing care his mum and gran so critically needed.

'Well, Luciana's on schedule to rendezvous with you in the Maldives,' advised Charley. 'Ling's on her way back home, but before boarding she mentioned that you thought you'd spotted the two muggers on Praslin Island.'

'I thought so, but I was wrong,' admitted Connor.

'Well, there's a strong chance you may have been right.'

Connor went rigid at the news. 'How come?'

'The two suspects were pinged getting on a flight to Dubai the same day the Sterlings departed for their holiday. They were using false passports so their trail went dead after that, but Dubai is a natural stopover en route to the Seychelles.'

Connor tightened his grip on the phone. So his eyes *hadn't* deceived him that day.

'They seem a little persistent for muggers, and too well-resourced,' Charley continued. 'As heavies-for-hire, we can only assume someone has paid them to do a job on the Sterlings.'

'Who?'

'It could be any one of Mr Sterling's enemies. Amir's going through his threat report to see if there are any obvious links.'

'Well, the heavies have missed their opportunity here,' said Connor, watching Mahé retreat into the distance.

'Unless they were responsible for the jet-ski incident.'

Connor thought this over. 'I don't see how they could have got on board the yacht without being noticed. Brad's run an almost constant watch since the Sterlings' arrival.'

'Still, it's a possibility. If they're determined enough to follow you to the Seychelles, then they won't be far behind in the Maldives either. So stay alert.'

'Will do,' said Connor. 'I'll contact you as soon as we reach harbour again.'

'OK,' she replied. 'And, Connor, be careful applying that suntan lotion.'

'What?'

But Charley had already ended the call.

Connor stared at his phone, unable to believe Ling had reported that incident. Now Charley had got completely the wrong idea and, judging by the tone of her voice, wasn't too happy about it. Furious with Ling, he shoved his mobile in his top pocket and headed across the main deck to the salon. As he slid open the glass doors, he heard someone else on the phone.

'Anything could happen at sea. The girls are on their own. I understand your concern, Joey, but I can handle them.' Amanda turned round, brushing a lock of golden hair from her eyes, and she spotted Connor. 'Listen, I'd better go. Ciao.'

Flipping shut her pink diamond-studded phone, she perched herself on the edge of a leather couch, the split in her white chiffon dress revealing a shapely tanned thigh. With the setting sun streaming through the window behind her, Amanda's pose was straight out of a high-class fashion shoot.

'Can I help you, Connor?' she asked, dazzling him with her smile. 'I was just on the phone to my agent.'

For a moment, Connor was struck dumb by her beauty. 'No . . . I was simply going to check that Chloe and Emily were OK.'

'Ah, that's sweet,' she said, sauntering over and ruffling

his hair. 'But I don't think we've anything to worry about, do you?'

Connor's eyes followed her departing figure as she strolled out of the door and disappeared on deck.

'Careful, Connor. She's a real siren.'

Connor spun round to discover Brad standing at the other end of the salon, a wicked grin on his face.

'A siren?' Connor queried.

'Yeah, the femme fatales of Greek mythology. Beautiful yet dangerous creatures who'd lure unwary sailors on to the rocks with their enchanting voices and looks.' He beckoned Connor over. 'Talking of danger. Since Mr Sterling's departure with Dan, we're a man down on the watch. And with Ling gone too I definitely need you to keep an extra sharp lookout while we're at sea.'

Connor nodded. 'No problem. I can take one of the shifts if you like.'

Brad patted him on the shoulder. 'Good of you to volunteer. Since you're so keen, you can do dawn duty, four till eight tomorrow morning.'

Connor made a face.

'I know it's early, but hopefully that slot won't draw attention to your true role. So, best get your head down while you can, tiger.'

Wishing he hadn't been quite so eager, Connor headed down to his cabin on the lower deck. As he passed a door to the tender garage, he thought he heard a noise. A *clunk*. Out of curiosity, he opened the bulkhead door and peered inside. The automatic lights were already on.

'Hello? Geoff?' he called, thinking that it might be the ship's engineer.

But there was no response. On a quick inspection, he found the garage to be empty, save for the tender, the remaining jet ski and an array of diving gear. Yet Connor's sixth sense was tingling – a sensation he wasn't alone. Then he spotted the inflatable doughnut on the floor. It had come loose from its fixings. Connor put it back on its hook and returned to the bulkhead. Before shutting the door behind him, he took one last look round, but any feelings of being watched had vanished as quickly as they'd appeared.

CHAPTER 50

Spearhead stood on the prow of the skiff, looking out at the horizon. The ocean was calm, the sun high and the seam between sea and sky a faintly darker smudge in the far-off distance. There was no land in sight to gain any bearings – just a boundless expanse of glassy blue ocean stretching off in all directions.

Spearhead had received the *Orchid*'s coordinates over the sat-phone from Mr WiFi, but he still trusted his own eyes more than any GPS or radar.

'See anything yet?' Big Mouth called from his skiff.

Spearhead didn't bother replying. He'd let them know when he spotted their quarry.

'We've been floating here for *hours*,' moaned Juggs, his lanky body laid out across a wooden seat, oversized feet dangling in the water. 'If we were in the Gulf of Aden, a hundred cargo ships would have passed us by now. Easy pickings.'

'I agree,' said Big Mouth, standing up and urinating over the side. 'Why chase a dolphin when we can land a whale?'

'Oracle foresaw this bounty,' replied a pirate, snoozing beneath a red headscarf. 'When has he ever been wrong?'

Having relieved himself, Big Mouth pulled up his shorts. 'I just don't understand why we're not using the GPS.'

'Because we don't want to land right on top of our target,' Spearhead explained with irritation. 'They'd spot us in no time.'

A glint of light caught his eye. A vessel, reflecting the sun like a mirror, crested the horizon five nautical miles due east – exactly where he'd predicted. And while Spearhead could see the *Orchid*, nobody on her deck would be able to detect his tiny skiffs.

'That's our prize,' said Spearhead, pointing to the yacht in the distance. 'We attack at dawn tomorrow.'

'Why not now?' demanded Big Mouth. 'Or at dusk?'

'Because we need to hunt like the sharks – attack when least expected. When the prey is least ready to fight back.'

CHAPTER 51

Connor yawned and looked at his watch – 05:30.

Zipping up his jacket to fend off the chill sea breeze, he paced the top deck. Through the night-vision lenses of his sunglasses, the stars appeared over-bright in the sky, like theatre spotlights, and the sea shimmered as if awash with mercury.

Raising the binoculars to his eyes, he performed another sweep of the horizon. So far the only other vessels he'd sighted were a fishing trawler and the long, low profile of an oil tanker. Both had glided by in distant silence, no more than ghosts in the night.

Connor stifled another yawn. His lookout duty was progressing with painful slowness. He couldn't believe that he still had another two and a half hours to go, but at least the sun would soon be up. The faintest of glows was now visible to the east, pushing back the curtain of night.

As he completed his sweep, his eye caught a glint of something directly to the *Orchid*'s stern. Adjusting the focus on his binoculars, he zoomed in on the point near the horizon, but the roll of the yacht made it hard to keep the image steady.

Was that a boat? A wave? Or a whale breaching?

He'd spotted a small pod of humpback whales within the first ten minutes of his watch. The spray from their blowholes had looked like fountains of silver through his night-vision lenses. It was his first encounter with these magnificent creatures and he'd been spellbound by their appearance. Then the whales had dived deep and he'd lost them among the waves.

It seemed this was the case again. He scanned the ocean once more but saw nothing. Then his attention was grabbed by a flashing light on the main deck below. He leant over the rail, but couldn't detect the source.

Descending two flights of steps, he made his way to the starboard side and discovered Emily standing beside the rail.

'Morning,' he said.

She snapped her head round in surprise, but quickly recovered and greeted him with a wry smile. 'Only just,' she replied.

'Did you see a flashing light?'

Emily shook her head. 'Perhaps it was the salon as I walked through?'

Connor frowned. 'Possibly, but the beam seemed more focused than that.' He looked up and down the deck, but all was dark.

Emily stared at him, then waved a hand in front of his face. 'Can you even see? Why are you wearing sunglasses at night?'

'Oh, these.' Connor flipped them back off his head. He

wasn't sure if Amir wanted the secrets of his gear revealed, so replied, 'They're part of the standard-issue Buddyguard uniform. Sometimes I forget I'm wearing them.'

'Well, you're missing out on the sunrise,' said Emily, turning to the rail and admiring the expanding halo of red fire on the horizon.

Connor joined her. 'Is that why you're up so early?'

'Not really. I was finding it hard to sleep.' She glanced timidly at him. 'Nightmares.'

Connor nodded, but didn't press any further. He could only imagine what horrors she dreamt of following her kidnap ordeal.

The sun continued its ascent, heralding another glorious day at sea.

'I'm feeling a little peckish,' Emily announced. 'Chef usually leaves some snacks in the galley. Can I get you anything?'

Having risen so early, Connor suddenly realized that he was ravenous. 'That would be great. I'd kill for an orange juice and a piece of toast.'

'No need to go that far!' Emily laughed. 'I'll see what I can find.'

She headed inside, leaving Connor alone with the sunrise. Its first golden rays graced the ocean, streaking the tops of the waves a deep molten orange. Lulled by the view, Connor drifted into Code White, but it was only a matter of seconds before he was snapped back to full alert by a muffled shriek from the direction of the galley.

'That's our signal,' said Spearhead.

The sun had yet to make its mark in the dawn sky, so his keen eyes spotted the far-off flashing light with little problem. He raised his assault rifle in the air to alert the rest of the gang.

The pirates in the other skiffs pulled aside the nets covering their weapons. AK47s were ripped from their plastic wrappings and magazines rammed home. The harsh *click* and *clack* of rifles being primed and loaded punctured the air above the growl of outboard motors.

After several days of enforced idleness, there was an urgency to the pirates' actions, all the men eager to sink their teeth into some violence.

Big Mouth prised open the wooden box containing his RPG. Loading a rocket into the launcher, he lifted it to his lips and kissed the tip.

'Time for some action, baby,' he said, resting the mighty weapon in his lap.

Spearhead checked his AK47 one final time, ensuring the action was smooth. He didn't want any jams during the assault. He'd known of too many incidents when saltwater had corroded older weapons and left a pirate high and dry in the middle of an attack.

Twirling his finger in the air and pointing ahead, Spearhead signalled for the hijack to commence.

The powerful outboards roared and the skiffs accelerated away, charging through the waves like a pack of killer whales in pursuit of their prey.

'There's someone in there,' whispered Emily, standing outside the door to the galley.

Connor had moved like lightning on hearing her cry. He was relieved to find her unharmed. 'One of the crew?'

Emily shook her head. 'I don't think so.' Her hands were trembling. 'It happened so quickly – a flash out of the corner of my eye as I opened the door – but I definitely saw someone.'

Not wishing to raise a false alarm, Connor decided to investigate for himself.

'Stay here,' he said. Twisting the handle, he pushed open the door with his shoulder, keeping his hands free in case he needed to defend himself.

The galley was in darkness. He reached in and flicked a switch. The spotlights blinked on and a sleek white kitchen shone in the bright glare. The gleaming marble worktop was clear, save for a set of chef's knives stowed in one corner, a stainless-steel toaster, an espresso machine and a large bowl of fruit.

Connor poked his head round the door, but there was no one there.

'Perhaps you imagined it?' he said, stepping inside the spacious galley and giving it the once-over.

Emily followed a hesitant step behind him. 'I'm sure I saw something move. Do you think it might have been a . . . rat?'

Connor laughed. 'On *this* yacht? It must have high-class tastes.'

He went over and opened the stainless-steel fridge. The chef had left a tantalizing array of midnight snacks – sandwiches, fresh pineapple, cheeses and luxury chocolates. A jug of fresh orange juice had also been prepared. Connor took them out and placed them on the serving bar.

'Someone's already had a go at these,' he remarked as Emily fetched a couple of plates and glasses from an overhead cabinet.

'Must be my sister. I know she's a secret snacker. She always denies it –'

Connor held up his hand, silencing her. On the floor outside the door to the walk-in freezer lay half a sandwich. Whoever had been helping themselves to a midnight feast had been in a hurry.

His sixth sense started twitching again.

Sliding out a chef's knife from its block, Connor silently approached the walk-in freezer. Emily stood motionless, a plate in her hand. Grasping the steel handle, Connor wrenched the door open.

'Don't hurt me!' cried a pitiful voice.

Shivering in the chill air of the freezer crouched a skinny boy, his teeth chattering, his eyes wide with fear.

'Who are you?' demanded Connor, pointing the knife at him.

'Cali,' said the boy, who wore a pair of tattered shorts and a UNICEF T-shirt. He held the other half of the sandwich in one hand and an apple in the other.

'How did you get on board?'

'I from Somalia.' Cali offered a broad smile, his uneven teeth appearing pearl white against his midnight skin.

Connor narrowed his eyes and took a step closer. 'I asked you a question, now answer me.'

The smile vanished and the boy cowered away from him.

'Take it easy, Connor,' said Emily, putting down her plate and hurrying over. 'Can't you see he's terrified?'

Connor looked at the blade in his hand, then back at the trembling boy. He supposed he was quite a fearsome sight, but he had to give a show of strength to ensure Emily's protection. Connor gave the boy the once-over and having decided he wasn't an immediate physical threat, lowered the knife.

'Hi, I'm Emily.' Easing past Connor, she bent down and offered her hand to the boy. 'Don't be scared. I'm your friend.'

Cali hesitantly took it and stood up. His legs were scrawny, the bones more prominent than muscle, and his face hollow-cheeked. But he wore a ready smile.

'Thank you, Emily,' said the boy, still keeping a wary distance from Connor as she led him over to the serving bar.

'Are you hungry?' she asked.

Cali nodded, his eyes already devouring the food laid out before him. Emily passed him a fresh tuna sandwich and he bit into it ravenously, chewing fast and swallowing quickly as if worried the food would be snatched away at any second.

Connor wasn't comfortable with accepting this stowaway so readily. Although he put the knife back in its block, he kept an eagle eye on the uninvited guest and stayed close to Emily. He judged Cali to be twelve years old, no more. His hair was a tight knit of black curls. And he noticed across his raw-boned arms a patchwork of thin pale scars like scratches, only deeper. But until Connor knew more about him he had to assume the stowaway was capable of anything.

As the boy ate, Connor persisted with his questioning. 'How did you get on this yacht?'

'The gangway. It down in Mahé,' Cali replied through a mouthful of sandwich.

'Yesterday?' Connor knew Brad had kept a careful watch throughout their unscheduled stopover.

Cali shook his head. 'No, before.'

Connor frowned. 'You mean, you've been on this yacht for over a week?'

Cali bit into an apple with a loud crunch and nodded enthusiastically. 'I go to South Africa.'

'South Africa?' Emily laughed. 'But we're on our way to the Maldives.'

Cali furrowed his brow and studied the apple intensely before looking up. 'Maldives near South Africa?'

'No, a long way off,' she replied as she poured Connor an orange juice. Cali chewed his lower lip in disappointment.

'What made you think we were going to South Africa?' Connor asked.

'I saw South African flag on man cleaning deck,' he replied.

'Oh, you mean Jordan,' said Emily. 'Yes, he's from Cape Town. And he's always wearing that T-shirt. Very proud of his country.'

As Emily continued chatting with Cali, Connor sat in deep thought, barely tasting the sandwich he was eating. How come none of the crew had seen this boy? He and Brad had done a full security sweep before departing. There was no way they could have missed him.

'Where have you been hiding?' Connor interrupted.

Cali pointed beneath their feet. 'Underneath small boat.'

'*Underneath?* But we've used the tender every day.'

'No, under deck.'

Connor tried to picture the tender garage. He vaguely recalled Brad pointing out a small hatch near the locker area that led to the bilge, a sealed compartment in the lower hull where water, oil and other noxious liquids collected. Not exactly a pleasant place to hide.

'How come you speak English?' asked Emily.

Pride lit up Cali's eyes. 'My father. He a teacher.'

'So why are you trying to get to South Africa?' said Connor.

'No future in Somalia. No family.'

'But what about your father?'

The smile dropped from Cali's face. 'He dead.'

Emily put a hand to her mouth. 'Oh, that's terrible! You have no one?'

Cali's gaze fell to the floor and he shook his head sadly.

Knowing personally the heart-rending pain losing a father caused, Connor felt his resistance to the boy weaken. 'What happened?'

'Pirates attack his fishing boat –'

'But you said he was a teacher.'

Cali put aside the apple, seeming to have lost his appetite. 'He was. But there no school. Too much war. So he become fisherman, like my grandfather.'

'Why would the pirates attack a *fisherman*?' asked Connor.

'For his boat. They slit his throat. Then force me to join them. They whip me.' Cali held up his scarred arms. 'But coastguard catch us. I escape. Now I try get to South Africa for better life.'

Emily looked over at Connor, her eyes glassy with tears. 'We have to help him somehow.'

Connor studied the Somali boy sitting beside them. He

truly sympathized with the boy's plight. His life sounded horrific and in any other circumstance he would try to help. But Connor's first duty was to protect Emily and Chloe. And this boy was still an unknown quantity. 'Sorry, he's a security risk. I have to tell the captain.'

'Must you?' implored Emily.

'Yes, he bloody well must,' said Brad, entering the galley bleary-eyed with the stewardess Sophie in tow.

'The consequences of having a stowaway are grave,' said Captain Locke, eyeing Cali with as much irritation as distrust. He rubbed his bristled chin as he considered the situation.

'Can't we just drop him off in the Maldives?' suggested Connor, who stood with Brad and Emily beside the comms station.

Sophie entered the bridge with a cup of coffee. Nodding his thanks, the captain blew the steam from his first cup of the day, then took a sip. 'No. As soon as this boy boarded the *Orchid*, he became our legal responsibility. We'll have to arrange for him to be deported back to his country. And the cost in terms of time, money and legal fees is significant. Mr Sterling will *not* be pleased.'

'I don't want go back to Somalia,' said Cali, defiantly crossing his arms.

'You keep quiet,' said the captain, jabbing a finger at him. 'You've caused enough trouble as it is.' He turned to Brad. 'We'll hand him over to the authorities as soon as we dock, but in the meantime confine him to a cabin for the rest of the voyage.'

Nodding, Brad took Cali by the arm.

'Please! Can't Cali just stay on the yacht?' said Emily, appealing to the captain. 'I'll ask my father to send the *Orchid* to South Africa after the holiday.'

The captain shook his head. 'That's not how it works, Emily. If port officials discover him on board, *we* – as in myself and the rest of the crew – could face legal actions for allowing it.'

'But he's got no family,' Emily pressed. 'There's no future for him in Somalia.'

The captain held up his hand. 'I'm sorry, Emily, that's just the way it is –'

'Pardon for interrupting, Captain,' said the chief officer, 'but I'm picking up an unidentified vessel fast approaching our stern.'

Captain Locke rose from his chair and studied the radar screen. A green dot was traversing the monitor on a direct course for the *Orchid*. Then several more blips appeared, all converging rapidly on the centre. A second later, the blips were gone.

'Whoever they are, they're in our radar shadow,' said Captain Locke. 'Get me a visual confirmation.'

Brad ran outside on to the upper deck, Connor close on his heels.

The sun was now up, a burning ball in the dawn sky. They both scanned the ocean to the *Orchid*'s stern. Half a mile directly south, five skiffs loaded with men surged across the waves.

'Five minutes to contact,' said Brad, rushing back to the bridge. 'Six skiffs. Pirates, by the looks of it.'

Captain Locke put aside his coffee cup, his jaw set firm. 'If their approach is anything to go by, they mean business. Chief Officer, full speed ahead,' he commanded.

Chief Officer Fielding drove the throttle home. From deep within the bowels of the *Orchid*, a mighty rumble shook the super-yacht as the twin diesel engines were pushed to their max.

The chief officer glared at Brad. 'Who was on watch?'

'I was,' Connor replied, steadying himself as the yacht picked up speed and rode the waves.

'Then where the hell were you?'

'He was dealing with the stowaway,' defended Brad.

'You should never have given the responsibility of a watch to a *boy* –'

'This isn't the time for laying blame,' said the captain. He picked up the yacht's speaker mic. 'Calling all crew. Calling all crew. This is the captain speaking. We have a Red Alert. I repeat, a Red Alert. All hands to the bridge.'

Brad turned to Connor. 'Get Emily and Chloe to the citadel.'

Without needing to be told twice, Connor grabbed Emily by the arm and rushed her to the door.

'What about Cali?' she cried.

Connor glanced back and it was only then that he noticed a torch protruding from the back pocket of the boy's shorts. 'He's one of them! Cali signalled the pirates.'

'Me?' said Cali, his mouth falling open in shock. 'N-no, not I.'

At that moment, Geoff and the rest of the crew rushed on to the bridge.

'What's going on, Captain?' said the engineer, frowning with concern when he saw the rev counter in the red zone. 'The engines won't keep this up for long.'

'Pirates,' Captain Locke explained. He turned to one of the deckhands. 'Scott, don't let this boy out of your sight.'

Scott stared in bewilderment at Cali. 'Where did *he* come from?'

'A stowaway – *and* a suspect.'

'They're still gaining on us,' announced the chief officer, nodding towards the radar where a swarm of green blips reappeared momentarily.

Captain Locke grimaced. 'Prepare to send a distress call.'

'Come on, Emily,' Connor urged, pulling her off the bridge. 'We don't have much time.'

As he hurried her down the stairs, he caught a glimpse of the skiffs cutting like sharks' fins through the waves. He could make out the pirates, bristling with weaponry. This was the nightmare scenario they'd planned for yet prayed would never happen.

The *Orchid* slammed hard against the swell. The impact was bone-shattering. Emily lost her footing and Connor barely stopped her tumbling down the stairs.

'Keep hold of the rail,' he urged as they descended the final staircase to the lower deck.

Rushing along the corridor to Chloe's room, they could see the walls vibrating from the thrum of the engines. Connor hammered on the door. 'Chloe! Chloe! Open up!'

'What is it?' came a sleepy reply.

With no time for discretion, he threw open the door. She sat bolt upright, clutching the bedding around her. 'Sorry, but this is an emergency. Grab some clothes. We need to get you to the citadel fast.'

'Citadel?' said Chloe, staring wide-eyed and confounded at him.

'Safe room,' explained Connor. 'We're under attack from pirates. Now hurry.'

Too stunned and terrified to protest, she bundled some clothes into her arms and allowed herself to be herded into the corridor. Connor pushed the two sisters along and up the stairs. At the bulkhead to the crew's quarters, they met Amanda being escorted by Brad.

'Stay in there until I give the all-clear. Understood?' said Brad.

Amanda nodded mutely, her angelic features pale with shock. Connor ushered Chloe and Emily in after her, then turned to follow Brad.

'Where are you going?' Chloe cried, a look of abandonment on her face.

Connor hoped his nerves didn't show as he replied, 'To fight off the pirates.'

CHAPTER 57

Standing on the main deck, Connor clutched the rail, the wind whipping at his face and hair. Below him, the water rushed past like a surging torrent and the *Orchid* left a huge foamy wake in her trail. But fast as she was, the pirates doggedly closed the distance: 400 metres . . . 300 metres . . . 200 metres . . .

'Those are *powerful* engines,' remarked Brad. 'They've got to be doing over thirty knots.'

He spoke into the two-way radio. 'Captain, you need to fishtail.'

There was a crackle of static. '*We'll lose speed,*' came the reply.

Brad pressed the Transmit button. 'We won't outrun them in a straight sprint. We need to make it difficult to board.'

'*Understood.*'

A second later, the *Orchid* lurched off-course, veering hard to port. Connor gripped the rail, then was thrown against the chrome bar as she cut back towards starboard. Each switch sent a heavy wash in the pirates' direction. The skiffs rode them like bucking broncos, seawater breaking over their bows and sending spray high into the air. The pirates clung to their seats, in danger of being tossed from their craft. But, like a waterborne wolf pack, the skiffs hounded the *Orchid* on all sides. As one fell back, another took its place.

Connor's mouth became dry, a mix of adrenalin and fear. He licked his lips, but tasted only saltwater. He could feel his heart pounding and imagined this to be like the blind rush of panic a fox felt during a hunt.

A skiff came level with the *Orchid*'s port side. A pirate waved an AK47 for them to slow down.

'He's got to be joking,' said Brad, turning to Connor. 'Have you got the flares ready? Looks like we'll be needing them sooner rather than later.'

Connor nodded and primed a flare gun. The other deckhands were stationed round the boat, ready to fend off any attempt to board.

Seeing that their prey had no intention of stopping, the pirate levelled his AK47 and fired indiscriminately at the *Orchid*. Connor ducked, sheltering behind the gunwale as the deadly *zing* of bullets whizzed over their heads.

'They're trying to kill us!' cried Jordan, cowering on the deck further down.

'Warning shots,' Brad replied. 'To scare us.'

'Well, it's working!'

Taking the flare gun from Connor, Brad waited for a break in the hail of bullets, then stood up and fired back at the skiff. A red blaze zoomed through the air. The pirate dived into his boat as the flare streaked across his bow, almost knocking him into the sea. But this single attack didn't deter him. He immediately rose and retaliated with another burst of gunfire. Bullets ripped into the fibreglass hull. The *Orchid*'s crew cringed in terror behind the gunwales, their hands covering their heads.

The *Orchid* swung hard to port, forcing the attacking skiff to back off.

However, another skiff immediately came up on her starboard side. Brad and Connor rushed across. A pirate crouched in the skiff's bow; on his shoulder was the long drainpipe-like barrel of a rocket launcher. Connor flashed back to the shaky video from Alpha team's briefing and felt a chill run through him . . . This time *he* was a part of it.

Brad snatched up his radio. 'Captain, skiff to starboard. Ram them.'

'*Too risky.*'

'They have an RPG.'

The skiff had pulled level with the bridge and the pirate was taking aim.

'*I see it,*' replied the captain. '*Oh my –*'

His transmission cut off as the pirate launched the rocket. It scorched through the air, blazing a trail towards the bridge. Connor watched in wide-eyed horror as the RPG shot out of view and exploded.

CHAPTER 58

The buzzing woke Amir. He yawned and glanced at his watch – 03:30.

Why had he set his alarm so early?

As he rubbed the sleep from his eyes, the alarm continued its incessant buzzing. He reached over to switch it off and promptly fell to the floor. Dazed, Amir looked round the darkened briefing room and at his upturned chair. Of course, he wasn't in bed. He was on night duty, supposedly monitoring Operation Gemini.

The buzzing grew more urgent and Amir scrambled up to his desk. On the glowing computer screen a red alert icon was flashing. Clicking on the pulsing box, he stared at the few stark lines of text, then grabbed his phone.

'What is it, Amir?' Charley answered drowsily.

'Distress call from the *Orchid*.'

There was a moment's silence as the words sank in, then she replied, 'I'll be right down,' her voice now sharp and alert.

A short while later, Charley wheeled herself through the door, in a T-shirt and jogging bottoms.

'What information do we have?'

Amir nodded to his computer screen. 'The *Orchid* sent out a DSC distress signal at 0625 hours, Seychelles local time. It gave her position as two hundred and forty nautical miles east-north-east of Mahé.'

'Do we know the actual problem?'

Amir swallowed anxiously. 'Pirates.'

Charley looked at him. 'Seems like you've lost your bet with Ling.' She scanned the brief message on Amir's computer, then asked, 'Any communication from Connor?'

Amir shook his head. 'The distress signal was picked up by the Seychelles Maritime Rescue and Coordination Centre. Since the *Orchid*'s out of range for VHF radio and mobile phones, a satellite call is the only possible option. But there's no mention of it in this report.'

Charley picked up the phone. 'I'll contact the Seychelles coastguard for an update. In the meantime, wake Colonel Black, then see if you can get through to Connor via your SOS app.'

CHAPTER 59

The ball of fire, smoke and shrapnel flashed like a comet in the dawn sky. For a brief moment, Connor thought the captain and all on the bridge had perished. Then Captain Locke's voice burst on to the radio.

'*They missed!*' His relief was evident.

'They meant to,' replied Brad. 'But the next one won't.'

There was a pause as the captain weighed up the threat of a second RPG against the risks of ramming.

'*Prepare for collision course.*'

Connor and Brad braced themselves. The *Orchid* sheered off to starboard just as the pirate skiff was closing in. The boat's pilot, totally unprepared for such an aggressive manoeuvre, tried to veer away. But it was too late. The two vessels collided at high speed. The skiff's bow crunched against the yacht's superstructure, shattering on impact. There was a horrible screeching as the skiff scored a line down the *Orchid*'s hull. Then, like flotsam in a storm, the skiff was flipped over by the churn from the *Orchid*'s propellers, and the pirates and their weaponry were dumped in the sea.

'That'll make 'em think twice,' said Brad as they watched the capsized skiff recede into the distance.

But, like stirring up a hornets' nest, the ramming only seemed to enrage the pirates more. Powering past their stranded companions who clung to the wreckage, the four surviving skiffs swarmed towards the *Orchid*.

'Why don't they give up?' asked Jordan.

Brad gripped the rail. 'They must be desperate. Nothing to lose.'

The radio on his hip crackled into life.

'*We have a problem,*' the captain announced. '*Our speed has dropped. One of the screws must have been damaged in the ramming.*'

Brad turned to the crew. 'Everyone. Prepare to repel boarders.' He handed the empty flare gun to Connor. 'Hold the fort. I'll be back in a minute.'

Before Connor could question him, Brad disappeared inside the salon.

Connor peered over the gunwale. The skiffs were closing in on all sides as the *Orchid* lost headway. A ferocious burst of gunfire assaulted the upper deck. A window imploded and he heard a scream from one of the two stewardesses stationed in the sky lounge as lookouts. Praying neither had been hurt, Connor reloaded the flare gun, at the same time wondering what the point was. A flare was a feeble match for an AK47.

But it was all he had.

As soon as the gunfire ceased, he knelt up by the rail and took aim at the nearest skiff. The lurching of the deck made it virtually impossible to fix his target. A tall, jug-eared pirate trained his AK47 on him. But Connor squeezed his trigger first. The flare *whooshed* from the barrel. A bright-red ball of flame shot across the waves . . . and fell short.

Connor briefly saw the flare extinguish itself in the waves before diving to the deck as a hail of bullets peppered the stern gunwale.

So much for his attempt at fending off the pirates.

Brad reappeared by his side, now in possession of a stainless-steel 12-gauge pump-action shotgun. 'Time to fight fire with fire!'

Connor stared in disbelief at the fearsome weapon. 'I thought you said guns were illegal.'

Brad checked the chamber, then clicked off the safety catch. 'Only in port,' he replied with a grim smile and took aim over the gunwale.

The blast of the shotgun was deafening. Connor held his hands over his ears as Brad fired again and again. Then he dropped back down beside him.

'Did you hit anyone?' asked Connor as another strafing of bullets cut into the *Orchid*.

Brad shook his head. 'I'm trying to knock out their engines,' he explained, rapidly reloading.

On the port side, Jordan and another deckhand, Kieran, threw a storage net into the sea to entangle the outboards of an approaching skiff. But, as they were launching the net, a clatter of gunfire punctured the air. Jordan was thrown backwards. Blood splattered across the salon's glass doors.

Connor rushed to his aid. Jordan slumped to the deck, groaning, blood pouring from the bullet wound in his shoulder. Kieran ripped off his T-shirt and handed it to Connor.

'Apply pressure. I'll get the first-aid kit.'

As Kieran ran inside, Connor pressed the balled-up T-shirt against the wound. Jordan cried out.

'You'll be all right,' assured Connor, not knowing what else to say. 'I promise you, I've had worse.'

Even through the haze of pain, Jordan managed a weak smile of disbelief.

Connor's phone bleeped from inside his polo-shirt pocket. He ignored it.

Blasts like thunder echoed off the blood-smeared glass as Brad fired his shotgun in angry retaliation. But the pirates showed no sign of retreat. Bullets ripped through the air and the roar of their outboard motors buzzed like angry wasps.

'Did the net . . . stop . . . them?' asked Jordan through clenched teeth, as Kieran reappeared with the first-aid kit.

Looking to the stern, Connor spotted the net floating away on the *Orchid*'s wake.

'No,' he said, shaking his head in dismay.

Without warning, a grappling hook latched itself to the port-side rail. Connor saw the line go taut. The pirates were boarding the *Orchid*.

CHAPTER 60

Connor shouted a warning to Brad, but the repeated blasts of the shotgun had temporarily deafened him. Leaving Kieran to tend to Jordan, Connor ran to the rail. A pirate was attempting to scale the knotted rope, the bucking skiff making his progress slow, but certain.

Connor pulled the flare gun from his hip pocket. He took aim, then realized it was unloaded. He fumbled for another flare from the clip, but in his hurry he dropped them. They scattered across the deck. He frantically retrieved one. Snapping open the breach, he pushed the flare home then clicked it shut. Just as he went to take aim again, the chef rushed on to the deck, wielding a flaming bottle of vodka.

'My own special pirate cocktail!' he shouted as he launched it at the skiff below.

The bottle shattered across the bow, spreading a sea of flame along the wooden skiff. The pirates screamed and scrambled away from the blaze. In his panic the pilot veered sharply, jerking on the grappling rope and catapulting his comrade into the ocean.

Then a wave broke over the skiff, dousing the fire. The pirates, quickly recovering from the shock attack, made another approach. They powered towards the *Orchid*, leaving their fellow pirate to drown.

But the chef had plenty more bottles where that one had come from and reappeared moments later with two more Molotov cocktails.

On the starboard side, Brad fired his shotgun again. This time he hit his mark. The outboard engines of the targeted skiff sputtered and choked, smoke spewing from their exhausts. But the pilot had also been caught in the hail of buckshot. He slumped over the tiller of his outboard and sent the boat swerving off-course.

'Two down!' said Brad grimly as he sheltered behind the gunwale.

Despite their losses, the pirates refused to give up. Two of the skiffs now made simultaneous attacks on the *Orchid*'s bow. The crew up front called for help and Brad and Chef rushed to their aid. But, with everyone committed to the port and starboard attacks, no one noticed the stern assault by the third skiff.

Only Connor heard the clang of a grappling hook on the rail. He spun round to see a colossal pirate, an assault rifle strapped across his back, standing on the skiff's bow like a figurehead. The ease with which he rode the turbulent waves was unnerving. Beckoning his pilot to move closer to the *Orchid*'s stern, the pirate was preparing to make his leap.

Connor had only one shot. He couldn't afford to miss this time.

The flare rocketed the short distance and struck home. Just as he had planned, it landed beside the fuel canister for the outboard. The pilot shouted in terror and jumped over the side as a spark ignited the diesel. Showered in flaming fuel, the other pirates leapt for their lives. The skiff then exploded in a massive fireball, a plume of black smoke rising into the air like a mushroom cloud. Connor shielded his eyes from the blast. And, when he looked again, the skiff was sinking rapidly beneath the waves.

But the pirate who'd leapt from the bow still clung on to the rope. Like some monster of the deep, he hauled himself up through the rushing water towards the *Orchid*'s stern. Connor couldn't believe the man's strength, or his crazed determination.

The hook was pulled tight against the rail and Connor had no hope of wrenching it free. He raced through the salon to the galley. There, he grabbed a fire extinguisher and snatched the carving knife from the block. By the time he'd sprinted back, the pirate had reached the stern and was now clambering up the tender garage's huge bay door.

Pulling the safety pin from the extinguisher, Connor let loose a jet of white foam, turning the hull slick and oily. The pirate scrambled to make purchase with his feet and thumped hard into the fibreglass hull. Foam glistened off his rippling torso and rivulets of water ran down his smooth bullet-shaped head.

Yet still he held on.

Discarding the empty extinguisher, Connor took up the knife. The pirate snarled like a wild beast when he saw

Connor furiously sawing at his rope. With grim determination, the pirate climbed hand over hand. The rope started to fray, but Connor knew he'd never cut through in time. The pirate was already halfway up. Then the *Orchid* struck the swell hard, the pirate lost his footing again and slipped down to the waterline. Only his Herculean strength prevented him from losing all grip on the rope.

The pirate heaved himself back up as Connor continued to slice frantically at the fraying fibres. The pirate's fingers reached for the deck. The rope finally parted . . . and Connor watched the man tumble back into the foaming sea.

CHAPTER 61

'This is definitely a new breed of pirates,' said Brad as the *Orchid*'s crew recovered in the salon.

After their joint attack failed, the pirates had finally given up their pursuit and the *Orchid* had escaped, bullet-ridden but unbreached. Jordan had been moved to a guest bedroom, his wound dressed and painkillers administered. Kathy, the second stewardess, was being treated for minor cuts from the shattered window.

'I've never known so many skiffs hunting together as a pack, or seen such firepower,' Brad continued as he paced the room, his shotgun still in hand. 'Their outboards were brand new too, top of the range.'

'But how did they even find us?' asked Connor, standing near Emily and Chloe who huddled together on one of the sofas. 'It's not as if we're in the transit corridor or cruising the Somalian coast.'

'That's a fair point,' agreed Captain Locke, looking to Brad for an answer. 'We're almost as far from the mainland as we can be.'

'Why not ask *him*?' said Scott, seizing Cali by the scruff of his neck.

Cali stared back in wide-eyed alarm. 'I-I know nothing. I not pirate,' he protested.

'Of course you are,' said Scott, shaking Cali like a bag of bones. 'You signalled for them to attack. And now my friend's been shot.'

'Stop!' cried Emily, rising from the sofa. 'It's not Cali's fault.'

Scott turned on her. 'Don't you think it's a little coincidental that this Somali boy appears at the same time as the pirates?'

'He's trying to *escape* the pirates,' explained Emily. 'His father was killed by them.'

Scott rolled his eyes to the ceiling. 'And you *believe* his sob story? He must have sent them our coordinates.'

'No! No! Not true!' cried Cali, struggling in Scott's grip.

Captain Locke held up his hand to calm the situation. 'Let's hear the opinion of our security officer before jumping to conclusions.'

Brad stared hard at Cali, then answered, 'This far from Somalia, the pirates have to be operating from a mothership – unless they're on a one-way mission, which could explain their reckless determination. As regards targeting the *Orchid*, Cali may well be responsible. On the other hand, it might just be bad luck that we crossed paths with the pirates.'

'So are we safe now?' asked Amanda, who sat in a leather chair, nursing a large gin and tonic. At some point she'd managed to apply make-up, although her eyes were still glassy with shock.

Brad studied the shotgun in his hand, then glanced towards the open ocean at their stern. 'It's highly unlikely the pirates will make another attempt. But I'll feel more comfortable when we're in safe harbour.'

'And how long will that be?'

'Another forty-eight hours,' announced the captain.

'What about Jordan?' asked Sophie. 'Kieran may be a first-aider, but he's no doctor.'

'It looks worse than it is, Soph,' replied Brad. 'I've checked the wound. The bullet passed straight through. But you're right; he does need medical attention.'

'Our plan is to cas-evac Jordan as soon as we're within helicopter range,' explained the captain. 'We've retracted our distress signal, but requested medical help to be at the –'

'Sorry for interrupting, Captain,' said Chief Officer Fielding, rushing in from the bridge, 'but we've picked up a Mayday call.'

'From the pirates, I hope,' laughed Chef, who was busy behind the bar mixing up more of his speciality cocktails in case the pirates returned.

'No, a Dutch yacht,' replied the chief officer, his expression short of humour beneath his beard. 'Engine failure due to a fire. Four people on board. They're requesting urgent assistance.'

'How far are they from our current position?' asked the captain.

'They're nine nautical miles south-east.'

'Surely you can't be thinking of going to their rescue?' said Kieran. 'We have enough problems of our own.'

Captain Locke gave him a stern look. 'I'm well aware of that. But we're legally obliged to help.'

'Can't another vessel respond?' asked Amanda.

The chief officer shook his head. 'There doesn't appear to be anyone else in the vicinity.'

'Then set a course for the stranded yacht,' the captain ordered.

'But the pirates!' exclaimed Scott.

'Exactly. And, if they've picked up the distress call too, they'll be like vultures on carrion. So keep a sharp lookout.'

Connor scanned the horizon, the binoculars pulling the furthest waves into detail. Small white crests like feathers rippled on the ocean's surface, but there were no pirates in sight. The empty sea was almost as disconcerting as it was reassuring.

Connor focused on the Dutch yacht drifting a couple of nautical miles to their port bow. Roughly half the size of the *Orchid*, the sleek pearl-white boat was still an impressive sight. There was no one on deck, giving the unsettling impression of a ghost ship. Yet, with only four crew, Connor realized they'd all be below, dealing with the engine fire.

The atmosphere on the *Orchid* herself was tense. While the majority of the crew stood watch or carried out their duties on the bridge, Chloe and Emily sat in the sky lounge playing a silent and seemingly endless game of cards. Kieran kept a close guard over Cali as he tended to Jordan. And Sophie waited on Amanda in the salon, the model on her third gin and tonic as she flicked aimlessly through a pile of glossy magazines.

In the lull after the attack, Connor remembered the text message he'd received. At first he'd been surprised his phone had a signal so far out at sea. Then he saw the text had been delivered via Amir's SOS app, which allowed short bursts of satellite communication. He'd replied with a simple message:

ALL CLEAR. BUT RESPONDING TO
ANOTHER YACHT'S MAYDAY.

Brad appeared on the upper deck and joined Connor at the aft rail. His shotgun rested on his shoulder, the weapon now a permanent accessory. 'The captain's just hailed the yacht. Any sign of the pirates?'

Connor shook his head. 'Nothing.'

'They're probably still licking their wounds,' said Brad, the corner of his mouth curling into a grin.

As the *Orchid* made its final approach, Connor could make out the name on the side of the hull: *Sunriser*. A man wearing a white peaked cap and jacket appeared on the yacht's main deck and waved. Brad raised his hand in acknowledgement.

The *Orchid* decreased speed and came alongside the disabled vessel.

Captain Locke stepped from the bridge and saluted the other captain. 'Ahoy there! Captain Locke at your service.'

The Dutch captain returned his salute. The man's face was haggard, his eyes sunken and a few days of stubble coated his chin. Considering they'd come to his rescue, the Dutch captain didn't look very pleased to see them. He bowed his head. 'I'm so sorry.'

'What have you to apologize for?' said Captain Locke, his brow creasing in puzzlement. 'We're only too happy to come to your assistance.'

But the answer emerged from the yacht's dark interior: a mighty warrior of a man armed with an AK47.

Connor could scarcely believe his eyes. It was the pirate who'd tumbled from the *Orchid*'s stern.

Brad instinctively brought his shotgun down to fire.

'DON'T!' shouted the pirate, pressing the barrel of his rifle to the Dutch captain's head. 'I'll kill him.'

Brad faltered in his attack. The Dutch captain stood motionless, what little colour was left in his face draining completely away as his life hung in the balance.

'Throw your weapon over the side,' the pirate ordered Brad.

Connor could see Brad weighing up the options. His first duty was to protect the crew and passengers of the *Orchid*. But he couldn't be held responsible for the death of an innocent man either. With great reluctance, Brad tossed his only weapon into the sea.

A roar of outboard engines suddenly cut through the air as two skiffs powered out of the yacht's shadow and surrounded the *Orchid*.

'We underestimated you,' said the pirate. 'I won't do so again.'

He spun the AK47 towards Brad and blasted him in the chest.

CHAPTER 63

'That's for killing my cousin,' snarled the pirate, ceasing his burst of violence.

Brad slumped to the deck, blood pouring from multiple wounds. Connor rushed to his side, but could see the damage was catastrophic.

'C-c-citadel,' gasped Brad.

Connor tried to pick him up and drag him to safety.

'No . . .' Brad groaned, gripping Connor's hand with the last of his strength. 'Get the girls –' His eyes rolled back in his head, his body shuddered then fell deathly still.

'Brad!' cried Connor, trying to revive his friend and mentor.

Another gunshot rang out, its deafening blast making Connor cower in terror. He glanced over the rail. The Dutch captain lay at the pirate's feet, his body twitching, blood pooling round his head. In the water below, a skiff docked alongside the *Orchid*, grappling hooks and ladders latched on like claws, and pirates surged up the ropes.

This is going to be a slaughter, Connor realized with horror.

With their comrades killed in action, the pirates wanted more than just to hijack – they wanted revenge.

Having no time to mourn Brad, Connor sprinted along the far side of the yacht. The rest of the *Orchid*'s crew knew the drill and were already running for their lives.

Connor burst into the sky lounge.

'What's happening?' Chloe shrieked, their cards scattered across the table. 'We heard gunfire.'

'Brad's been shot. Pirates.'

'No . . . not again. It can't be happening,' cried Emily, collapsing to the floor at the sight of Brad's blood smeared over Connor's clothes.

'Back to the citadel,' said Connor, pulling the distraught Emily to her feet and grabbing Chloe by the wrist. He bundled them down the stairs as fast as he could.

They met Kieran and Scott dragging Jordan out of the guest bedroom. Sophie was dashing ahead with Amanda down the corridor.

'Where's everyone going?' asked Cali, running after them.

'Safe room,' cried Emily, almost tripping over her sister's heels. 'Come with us.'

They passed the staircase leading to the lower deck. Outside they could hear urgent shouts, the language strange and unintelligible to Connor's ears.

'Hurry!' urged the captain, who was waiting at the entrance to the galley. He shepherded Amanda and Sophie through the narrow doorway and towards the crew's quarters.

But, as Kieran and Scott tried to manhandle the injured Jordan through, a bottleneck formed and panic ensued.

'Not you, pirate boy!' said Scott, kicking Cali away.

The boy tumbled to the floor and was trampled underfoot. Emily tried to help him up.

'Leave him,' said Connor as he pushed her on, Emily and her sister being his sole priority.

Chloe screamed as a devilish face appeared at a nearby porthole. A gunshot went off. Like a pack of baying dogs, the pirates' whoops and cries could be heard closing in. Connor noticed the door leading to the outside deck start to open. Realizing they'd never all make it to the citadel in time, he shoved Emily and Chloe into the captain's arms and rushed back down the corridor.

'NO!' barked the captain.

But Connor was committed to the sacrifice. He launched himself into a flying kick just as a large head with jug ears poked inside. Connor's foot struck the back of the door, slamming it against the frame and crushing the pirate in the jamb. The pirate howled in pain and fury before retracting his bruised head from its vice-like grip. Connor threw his weight against the door and turned the latch lock. The pirate could be heard hammering furiously on the other side.

'Come on, Connor,' said the captain, holding the galley door open for him.

Connor could see Emily and Chloe were through and heading for the safety of the citadel. He was the only one left – aside from Cali, who was struggling back to his feet. As he ran for the galley, a burst of gunfire erupted behind him. Connor heard the lock shattering and the door being kicked open.

'*Joogso!*' shouted the pirate. '*Istaag ama waan ku tooganayaa.*'

Connor had no idea what the man was saying, but he wasn't going to stop for anyone.

'STOP! He kill us!' cried Cali, holding up his hand and getting in Connor's way.

Glancing over his shoulder, Connor saw the jug-eared pirate levelling his AK47 at him. As the pirate depressed the trigger, Connor shoved Cali aside but was too late to save himself. A bullet clipped his upper arm, spinning him round. A second bullet struck him in the chest and he tumbled down the staircase, landing in a heap at the bottom and lying there, silent and motionless.

Captain Locke sealed the bulkhead door. There was a *clunk* as the heavy-duty lock engaged. The door wouldn't be opened again for anything but rescue.

'Where's Connor?' Emily asked as the captain descended the stairs into the crew's compact living quarters. The combined kitchen-diner was cramped with nine crew and three guests. Kieran and Scott were settling the groaning Jordan in one of the tiny bunk beds, while the others huddled round the small dining table. An atmosphere of barely restrained hysteria hung in the air.

Captain Locke addressed the survivors, his expression solemn. 'Connor didn't make it.'

'What do you mean, *he didn't make it?*' said Emily, rising from the bench and clutching the table for support. 'He's still out there. So's Cali. We have to open the door.'

The captain rested a hand on her shoulder. 'No. I saw Connor get shot. He's dead.'

Emily sank back on to the bench. 'This can't be happening . . .'

She stared mutely at the cabin wall, tears welling in her

eyes in silent grief. Overwhelmed by the sudden loss, Chloe gave a grieved cry, then fell forward and buried her head in her arms.

'What about Brad?' asked Sophie in a tiny and hesitant voice.

Captain Locke sadly shook his head. Sophie collapsed into sobs, Kathy pulling her into an embrace, letting her friend weep on her shoulder.

From the stairwell, the harsh clank of metal on metal rang out. All eyes turned fearfully towards the sound.

'Don't worry,' said Captain Locke. 'They can't get through.'

'So what now?' asked Amanda, her lips thin, the make-up no longer hiding the strain. 'We're trapped.'

'We sit tight and await rescue.'

'From *who* exactly? *He* said –' she pointed to the chief officer almost as if in accusation – 'there aren't any other boats in the area.'

'NATO's navy task force,' replied the captain, trying to maintain his composure and authority while reeling inside from their desperate situation. 'Danny, send out a Mayday on the radio. See who you can contact.'

The chief officer nodded and went over to the small console in the corner of the room.

'I won't lie to you,' said the captain, leaning forward and resting his palms on the table. 'Rescue could be anything from a day to a week away. We may have to prepare for even longer. The key thing is to remain focused and positive. Chef, I want you to make a full inventory of

275

our food and water supplies. Geoff, check our power situation and what reserve batteries we have access to. Kathy and Sophie, I need you to organize the bunk rooms and a sleeping rota. Kieran, take stock of our first-aid supplies and attend to Jordan with –'

'Captain,' interrupted Danny, his tone grave. 'The radio's dead.'

Captain Locke frowned. 'Have you tried all the channels?'

The chief officer nodded. 'I even checked the battery connection.'

'Let me have a look,' said Geoff, the engineer getting up from the table to inspect. After testing a series of buttons, he opened up the front panel. He glanced over his shoulder at the captain, a dark look in his eyes. 'Somebody's sabotaged it.'

Scott punched the wall in fury. 'That little rat of a stowaway! If I ever get my hands on him again, I'll wring his scrawny neck.'

'So we're . . . cut off from rescue?' uttered Amanda, clasping her hands tightly together to stop their trembling.

'Not exactly,' said Chief Officer Fielding, managing a reassuring smile through his beard. 'I triggered the EPIRB distress beacon as I left the bridge.'

CHAPTER 65

'Shut that thing down,' ordered Spearhead, pointing to the flashing light atop the EPIRB unit.

Big Mouth rushed across the bridge to the bracket-mounted beacon and searched for the button that Mr WiFi had shown him on the laptop diagram. The emergency instructions meant nothing to him, but he found the red circle and pressed it. The light went dead.

Spearhead picked up the radio from the comms unit. Mimicking the BBC World Service presenter to whom he'd listened while learning English, he said in a gruff British accent: 'All Stations, All Stations, All Stations. This is motor yacht *Orchid*. Our position is . . .' He paused briefly, checking the GPS. 'South 2° 41' 42", East 62° 54' 19". Alongside Dutch yacht *Sunriser*. Engine fire extinguished. No further danger to crew. Cancel our EPIRB distress alert. I repeat, cancel our distress alert.'

Spearhead waited for a response. He received nothing but static.

This was good news, for it meant there were no other ships in the immediate vicinity. Any Mayday calls the

Orchid might have made by radio would have fallen on deaf ears. But he understood that the EPIRB worked differently and wasn't limited by range. Before leaving on their mission, Mr WiFi had explained that the unit transmitted a signal every fifty seconds via satellite. The yacht's identity and position would have already been received by a Maritime Rescue Coordination Centre, who'd have forwarded the data to the Seychelles or Kenyan coastguard. Once a satellite picked up an EPIRB signal, this whole process could take less than a minute.

Spearhead knew he and his men were racing against the clock. The authorities would have their position to within three nautical miles and would soon be launching a search-and-rescue operation. Either the distress alert had to be cancelled or they needed to be long gone by the time any rescue team arrived.

He broadcast the message again. Still no response. Replacing the handset, he spotted the satellite phone further along the console. This would guarantee cancellation – if he could find the right number. As he reached over for the receiver, Spearhead noticed Big Mouth plonking himself in the captain's chair and planting his feet on the control panel.

'Get off! I'm the captain round here,' Spearhead snarled, jabbing a thumb at his chest.

Big Mouth unwillingly eased himself from the leather seat as Juggs stormed on to the bridge. 'The crew have holed up in the bow.'

Spearhead spun on him in irritation. 'Well, break the door down.'

Juggs shrugged ineffectually. 'We can't. It's steel. Locked from the inside.'

Spearhead scowled. This problem would cause a serious delay. Without the *Orchid*'s captain or his crew, he couldn't sail the super-yacht – not with his knuckle-headed men, anyway. Spearhead cursed himself for shooting the Dutch captain, but his bloodlust had got the better of him. Then he remembered the equipment he'd spotted in the loading bay of the Dutch yacht.

'There's a cutting torch aboard the other boat,' he said. 'Get it.'

Spearhead turned to Big Mouth who was now randomly pressing buttons on the bridge console and watching the lights flash. 'Stop that! Take four men and search this yacht. Bring any hostages to me. If we can't cut through, we'll need an incentive to *make* them open the door.'

Connor's fingers twitched as he slowly came to. The back of his head throbbed where it had struck the bottom step. His left arm felt heavy as lead, as if he'd been punched in one spot repeatedly. And he was struggling to breathe; his chest felt compressed, his ribs bruised. But he was *alive*.

His eyes flickered open. The soft glow of the overhead spots appeared harsh and glaring to him, intensifying his pounding headache. Connor glanced down at his constricted chest. There was no blood. But there was a ragged black hole in his polo-shirt where the bullet had penetrated. How he'd survived he had no idea. The hi-tech fabric was only intended to stop rounds from a handgun, not a 7.62mm high-velocity shot from an assault rifle.

As Connor sat up, wincing with pain, there was a tinkle of glass in his breast pocket. He pulled out the remains of his smartphone, the bullet still embedded in the screen. He almost laughed in disbelief. He'd been saved not only by the pocket's double layer of bulletproof fabric but by the phone absorbing the rest of the impact. Shattered beyond repair, the neoprene case was the only thing holding it together.

Setting the now-useless phone aside, Connor inspected his arm. A thin stream of blood ran down from a gash where the first bullet had nicked him, but the fabric had been strong enough to deflect the round and protect him from more serious injury. He cautiously flexed his arm, checking he could still move it.

'*Halkan imoow.*'

Connor looked up, the fog in his head instantly clearing as his senses were brought into sharp relief by the booming voice. *The pirates.* He could hear the soft pad of their bare feet on the deck above.

Connor scrambled away from the stairs. But no one descended to look for him. Risking a glance up, Connor crept back to the foot of the staircase. A pirate was standing over Cali, speaking rapidly in his mother tongue. Cali replied. The pirate nodded, seemingly satisfied.

'*I soo raac,*' he said, striding up the stairs to the upper deck and beckoning Cali to follow.

As Connor watched Cali obediently go with the man, he clenched his fists in silent fury. This supposed stowaway had delivered the *Orchid* straight into the pirates' clutches. But at least he knew the girls and the rest of the crew were safe within the citadel. Then Connor remembered what Brad had said: *The citadel is only effective if everyone makes it inside.*

That included himself, Connor realized with dread.

Another pirate entered the upper corridor, dragging two gas canisters towards the galley. Connor pulled back from the staircase, praying he hadn't been spotted. Then he heard more feet in the corridor.

This time they were heading his way.

'I can't do this again,' said Emily, her breathing becoming shallow and rapid. Her eyes flicked round the confines of the cabin as if the walls were closing in on her. 'I-I . . . can't survive again –'

'Will you shut up!' snapped Amanda, biting at one of her perfectly manicured nails. 'You're making us all nervous. At least you've had experience of this. You know what to expect.'

'How can you say *that*?' Chloe cried, drawing her trembling sister into her arms.

Emily's eyes regained focus and fixed Amanda with a cold, empty stare. 'I'll tell you what you can expect, Amanda. Constant gnawing fear. Never knowing what tomorrow, or even the next hour, might bring. Your hopes raised, then dashed. Again and again. Until your spirit is crushed. No comfort. You'll cry your eyes dry. You certainly won't get to wash your hair –'

'Be quiet, you jinx!'

'Jinx?' questioned Chloe, frowning.

Amanda nodded. 'You have to admit your sister attracts bad luck. Taken hostage *twice* in two years.'

Chloe narrowed her eyes at Amanda. 'Funny you came on the scene about the same time,' she shot back. 'Perhaps *you're* the jinx!'

'Stop that sort of talk right now,' interrupted Captain Locke. 'We're all on edge. The key to surviving this is sticking together.' He looked from the girls to Amanda and back. There was a begrudging acknowledgement from the three of them. 'We're safe as long as we're in here. The pirates can't touch us. And rescue will be on its way.'

He glanced out of the porthole. But the horizon remained empty of hope.

'What's that noise?' asked Sophie, her eyes puffy from crying.

A harsh spitting sound, like water hitting hot oil, could be heard coming from the stairwell. Captain Locke and the chief officer exchanged an uneasy glance.

'I'll investigate,' said the captain.

Cautiously ascending the staircase, he approached the steel bulkhead. At first glance all looked secure. Then he spotted the orange drip of molten steel trickling from the door frame.

He called down for his engineer. Geoff bounded up the steps and stopped dead by his side when he saw the white-hot line worming its way millimetre by millimetre along the frame.

'That's not good,' he muttered.

'How long have we got?' asked the captain.

Geoff rubbed a hand across his haggard face and sighed. 'Five hours, maybe less.'

There was nowhere to hide in any of the bedrooms. The built-in closets were the first place the pirates would look. Connor thought about locking himself in the shower room in his cabin, but the doors were flimsy. One hard kick and the pirates would be on to him.

As he hunted for a suitable refuge, Connor spotted his Go-bag in the corner of his bedroom. He snatched it up, the liquid body-armour panel being his only defence against AK47 rounds. He just wished the bag itself wasn't luminous yellow – it made him a blindingly obvious target.

The voices of the pirates were getting closer. He could hear them ransacking the girls' bedrooms just down the corridor, laughing and shouting as they did so.

Checking the corridor was clear, Connor raced along to the tender garage. Hurriedly he opened the bulkhead door, slipped inside, and closed it behind him.

The garage was almost peaceful, the noise of the marauding pirates dampened by the door. Connor looked around in desperation for a place to hide. The locker room . . . the shower cubicle . . . the tender . . .

He supposed he could launch the tender – or even the jet ski – and make his escape. However, he doubted whether the tender or jet ski, as fast as they were, could outrun a turbo-charged skiff. And, even if he could escape, their fuel tanks would more than likely run dry before he reached help or dry land. But more importantly, as a buddyguard, the idea of leaving his Principals at the mercy of the pirates was unthinkable.

Behind him, he heard the bulkhead's lock rattle and saw the handle turning.

Panicking, Connor opened up one of the storage lockers. It was full of wetsuits. He was about to climb in and conceal himself when he noticed the small hatch in the deck. Of course, the bilge!

Connor twisted and yanked at the small recessed clasp. The hatch lifted to reveal a dark unwelcoming hole. He could hear the slop of water and caught a whiff of acrid fumes. But with no time to reconsider, Connor stuffed his bag into the black hole, then clambered in after. He pulled the hatch down over his head, clipping it into place – sealing the hatch and all light out.

Connor listened to the pirates as they tramped into the garage. The men were jabbering away, loud and fierce. Locker doors were banging open and the tender rocked noisily on its mounting as someone leapt into the cockpit. A pirate passed directly overhead, the hatch cover creaking under his weight. Connor held his breath, not only against the noxious fumes in the bilge but from the fear of being discovered.

The shower was switched on, the running water sounding like rain. One of the pirates said something and the others laughed. Then the slap of feet retreated across the deck and the voices faded away; Connor, however, didn't hear the bulkhead door being closed.

He waited a moment longer, heard no one, and let out a deep sigh of relief . . . before gagging on the foul air. A caustic mix of diesel, urine and worse assaulted his nostrils and Connor was forced to breathe through his mouth, which made it just bearable.

Water, warm and slimy, slopped around his bare knees and something firm bumped against his thigh.

Finding the absolute darkness unnerving, Connor remembered his sunglasses in the pocket of his shorts. Sliding them on, he flicked on the night-vision mode and the bilge was revealed in a pale ghostly light. Barely more than a two-by-three-metre steel box, the compartment pressed in on him like a polluted coffin. With the low ceiling forcing him to hunch over, Connor felt a sudden and overwhelming urge to escape its cloying confines. But he didn't have the option of leaving his refuge – not yet anyway. Above him, the shower water was still running and a man was singing to himself. Connor could scarcely believe it. One of the pirates was taking a *shower*!

Gazing down at the filthy bilge water surrounding him, Connor realized he'd be very much in need of one himself. But that was the least of his concerns. He was trapped in the bilge, in a yacht hundreds of miles from the nearest help; pirates were swarming all over the boat and his Principals were in real danger of being taken hostage, or worse. A crippling sense of despair washed over him as he realized he'd utterly failed in his duty as a buddyguard. And it was *his* fault that the yacht had been hijacked. If he'd just stayed on watch, he might have spotted the pirate skiffs earlier and given the *Orchid* a chance of outrunning them. Then the *Orchid* wouldn't have got the distress alert that had lured them into the trap and they wouldn't be in this mess.

Brad wouldn't be dead.

Suddenly grief welled up in Connor and he was overcome with tears. Although he'd seen an agent killed during his first assignment, he'd never witnessed a death at such close quarters, and certainly not of a friend murdered in cold blood. Connor wondered if that was how his father had died, cut down in a hail of bullets while protecting the US ambassador. Swift, brutal and agonizing.

Connor recalled the words the priest had said at his father's funeral: *Do not mourn the man who died, rather be thankful that such a man lived.*

Connor tried once more to gain comfort from this. As he wiped away his tears with the back of his hand, his feet slipped from under him and he reached out for support. His hand found a steel strut and he managed to steady himself. Glad to have avoided a dunking in the foul water, Connor looked round the bilge. He noticed a crumpled bottle of water and a litter of empty plastic wrappers on a ledge that ran the length of the compartment. This was Cali's bolt-hole, of course. Cali the stowaway: the one responsible for signalling the pirates; the one *really* to blame for their predicament.

Connor felt his despair and grief disappear beneath a rising tide of anger, bringing focus and clarity to his thoughts.

He had to keep a grip on himself if he was going to survive. *Everyone else is safe in the citadel*, he reminded himself. They had access to food, water and the radio. Rescue would be on its way.

For him, it was simply a matter of staying hidden and holding out.

CHAPTER 70

'Emergency over,' announced Amir, leaning back in his chair. 'The *Orchid*'s distress signal has been cancelled.'

'What . . . *again*?' Charley questioned, zooming over to his console.

Amir shrugged. 'The EPIRB unit's stopped transmitting.'

'Could it have just lost contact with the satellite?' Marc asked.

'No, I've checked that,' said Amir. 'There've been two satellite sweeps and no signal.'

'Then we need an official confirmation,' said Colonel Black, picking up the phone and dialling the Seychelles coastguard.

'Good morning, this is Colonel Black. You spoke with my colleague earlier regarding the motor yacht *Orchid*. What's the status on the vessel's most recent distress call?' The colonel listened intently. 'Thank you,' he said, a pensive expression on his face, and put down the phone.

'The coastguard received a satellite call from the *Orchid* confirming cancellation. The other yacht is out of danger too. So they've called off the search-and-rescue team.'

'But this is the *Orchid*'s *second* distress call,' said Charley. 'This doesn't feel right to me.'

Bugsy coughed into his fist for attention. 'It's not uncommon for an EPIRB to trigger a false alert,' he explained, chewing rapidly on a stick of gum. 'The sensor can get wet or the unit knocked from its bracket. Maybe that's what happened when they were helping the other boat.'

Charley looked to the colonel. 'Was there any mention of the casualty?'

'What casualty?' asked Ling, walking through the door with Jody and dumping her bags, the flight labels still attached.

'The *Orchid*'s been attacked by pirates,' said Jason, going over to greet her. 'One of the crew was shot during their escape.'

'WHAT?' exclaimed Ling, her eyes widening in disbelief. 'I leave Connor for one day and this is what happens. I miss out on all the action.'

'This is *not* the sort of action we want,' stated Colonel Black. He turned back to Charley. 'No, there wasn't any reference to the casualty. But, unless there's been a serious change in his condition, there'd be no real need. However, I agree, two distress calls in a morning is troubling. Bugsy, call the *Orchid*'s satellite phone and speak direct to Captain Locke. Marc, get in touch with Luciana – see if she's had any communication since her arrival in the Maldives. Amir, contact Connor. Let's obtain positive confirmation ourselves before standing down.'

The colonel addressed Ling. 'Before you left the *Orchid*, was there any indication of problems with the yacht's comms systems?'

Ling shook her head. 'Not as far as I know.'

Alpha team waited in tense silence as Bugsy dialled the satellite phone, Marc called Luciana's mobile and Amir launched his SOS app.

After his third attempt at connection, Bugsy announced, 'The line's engaged, Colonel.'

Colonel Black frowned. 'That's potentially good news. It means they're communicating at least.'

'Not with Luciana,' said Marc. 'She's heard nothing.'

'Tell her to remain on standby. Any response from Connor?'

Amir shook his head. 'I've pinged him twice. Even sent a remote activation, but the SOS app isn't responding.'

'Perhaps he forgot to charge his phone,' suggested Richie.

'You're not helping,' said Charley, giving him a hard stare. 'We should inform the Seychelles coastguard.'

Colonel Black shook his head. 'Not yet. They won't relaunch a search-and-rescue just based on our concerns. Keep trying to contact the *Orchid* every fifteen minutes. If we don't get a response within the next hour, then we raise the alert.'

Connor wondered how on earth Cali had spent a week hidden in the bilge. His eyes were already starting to sting, the skin on his legs itched and a headache was building. He'd pulled himself up on to the ledge. It was just wide enough for him to perch and keep his feet out of the water, but the steel beam was cold and hard, the rivets protruding into his backside.

Having retrieved his Go-bag, grateful that Amir had designed it to be waterproof as well as buoyant, he took stock of his limited resources. Aside from Cali's half-empty bottle of water, he had four energy bars and a packet of glucose tablets. Cali's own little larder was bare, explaining the boy's need to raid the *Orchid*'s galley. If the hijacking went on for any length of time, Connor realized he would be forced to do the same.

He rummaged through the Go-bag, careful not to drop anything, and found the med-kit. Taking out an antiseptic wipe, he cleaned the wound on his arm then covered it with a self-adhesive dressing. He took a couple of tablets to numb the pain. Then, with great difficulty on the narrow ledge, he changed his damaged polo-shirt for a new T-shirt and a long-sleeved jumper. The double layer wasn't ideal considering the bilge's airless and clammy atmosphere, but the discomfort was worth it for the increased bulletproof protection.

As he sorted through the rest of the Go-bag's contents, Connor thought about triggering the SART in the pack's side. Then he recalled the transponder had only a five-mile range and an eight-hour lifespan. If he was going to use it, he had to be sure it would be effective. The SART was now his only means of raising an alert. With his smartphone destroyed, he couldn't send an SOS message to Buddyguard HQ. And, until he could reach a radio, he was cut off from any back-up support.

The most useful item in his possession, beside the night-vision glasses, was the Dazzler torch. At least he would have light. And a defensive weapon. He switched it on, the compartment flooding with its bright beam.

His situation didn't look any more promising in the torchlight. Somehow the bilge seemed smaller and more confining. The realization he was trapped in a steel box hit home. And every minute he stayed hidden in Cali's old refuge he ran the risk of being discovered. Even if the pirates didn't yet know about this hideaway, Cali would surely tell them. Unless, by some miraculous chance, the pirates had forgotten about him in the confusion of the attack. But that wasn't a gamble Connor was willing to take.

As his beam swept the bilge, he spotted a service hatch

just above the waterline. Dropping from his perch, Connor bent down to inspect. The lock was stiff, but by throwing all his weight behind it Connor managed to open it. On the other side was another bilge compartment, bigger than his and judging by how far it went back, this one appeared to be located beneath the yacht's twin engines. Connor swung his torchbeam round, revealing a hatch in the ceiling. Perhaps there was a way to evade the pirates after all.

CHAPTER 72

'You said rescue was on its way,' cried Amanda. 'Then *where* is it?'

Her perfect blue eyes stared accusingly at Captain Locke, while the rest of the crew looked to him for leadership and reassurance. Emily and Chloe sat numb and silent at the dining table, their two plates of rice and boiled fish barely touched and now stone cold.

'I don't know. I honestly don't know,' admitted the captain, peering through the small porthole and seeing only empty ocean. 'But it can't be far off,' he added with false hope.

From the stairwell, the spitting hiss of the cutting torch grew louder with each passing minute.

'Shouldn't we arm ourselves?' said Scott.

'With what?' asked Chief Officer Fielding.

'Kitchen knives, flares, anything.'

'No,' overruled Captain Locke. 'If the pirates breach the bulkhead, fighting will be futile. It'll only result in more bloodshed.'

'Are you suggesting we simply surrender?' said Amanda.

The captain offered a resigned shrug. 'We're left with little other choice.'

The pirates' angry voices now invaded their supposedly impregnable citadel. There was a huge *clang* as the door fell to the floor, followed by an unnerving silence. Everyone's gaze turned towards the forbidding stairwell.

Chloe clutched on to her sister as the soft pad of bare feet was heard descending the stairs. The dark muzzle of an AK47 appeared first, followed by the jug-eared pirate. His eyes, bulging and bloodshot, flicked round the room, while his finger twitched nervously on the assault rifle's trigger.

'*Gacmaha madaxa saara*,' he barked, jerking the gun's barrel towards the ceiling.

Guessing the pirate's meaning, Captain Locke raised his hands obediently and the rest of the crew followed suit. Three more armed pirates descended the stairwell, quickly surrounding the hostages. One searched the crew's quarters and dragged out a groaning and pale Jordan, dumping him on the floor at their feet.

'*Dhaqaaq!*' said Juggs.

Captain Locke furrowed his brow. 'I don't understand.'

'Move,' the pirate repeated in English, gesturing with his AK47 to the stairwell.

Captain Locke looked to his crew and the girls, trying to maintain an air of calm authority. 'Do as he says. The pirates won't harm us. They need us alive for the ransom nego–'

The butt of the AK47 collided with the captain's jaw,

splitting his lip. Blood sprayed across the dining table. Emily flinched away and Chloe let out a shocked yelp.

'No speak!' said Juggs, shoving the stunned captain towards the stairwell.

'Here, for your face,' said Spearhead, offering the captain a cloth napkin from the salon's dining table. 'Sorry, my men can be overzealous at times.'

Warily accepting the napkin, the captain dabbed painfully at his swollen and bleeding lip. Then he straightened himself to his full height, which by no means could match the towering pirate. 'I'm Captain Thomas Locke, in charge of the *Orchid* and responsible for this crew and guests. And you are?'

'Spearhead,' he replied, thumping his chest with a clenched fist. 'And *I'm* now in charge.'

He took the captain's hat and placed it on his own head.

Powerless to do anything about the theft of his hat, Captain Locke said, 'You do realize a search-and-rescue team is on its way. But if you leave now you can escape punishment –'

Spearhead let out a booming laugh. 'I think you're mistaken, my friend. *No one* is looking for you.'

The pirate surveyed his hostages, who huddled on the cluster of white leather sofas under the watchful guard of his gang. The news of their hopeless situation hit them hard. Sophie began to weep. Kieran buried his face in his hands. Chloe started sobbing in her sister's arms, while Emily turned pale and started to tremble.

Spearhead frowned. 'Where's the boy?'

'Do you mean the stowaway?' Captain Locke replied, jutting his chin in Cali's direction. Cali was in the corner with an older buck-toothed lad, armed with a revolver.

'Not him, I mean the white boy,' said Spearhead.

'Connor's *dead*,' cried Chloe, daring to look the pirate in the face, her tearful eyes flashing with anger.

Unmoved by her fury, Spearhead raised an enquiring eyebrow at Cali. 'Is this true?'

Glancing over, Cali gave a single nod and pointed at Juggs. 'He shot him.'

Spearhead glared at the accused pirate. Juggs mumbled something and Spearhead snorted. 'No matter. The boy was of little value to us. Whereas you two –' he turned to Emily and Chloe, baring his bone-white teeth in a leering grin – 'are valuable property. Along with yourself, Ms Ryder.'

Spearhead's gaze raked over the model as Amanda's expression flipped from fear to shock. 'How do you know my name?' she demanded.

Laughing, Spearhead advanced menacingly towards her and the girls. 'There's a great deal I know about you, about Chloe and, of course, about *you*, Emily.'

Geoff stepped into the pirate's path. 'Leave them alone.'

Spearhead eyed the engineer with disdain. 'Oh, I've no

intention of harming them. But I can't say the same for you.'

Geoff stood his ground a brave moment longer, then reluctantly moved aside.

Amanda braced herself for the worst. The girls shrank back from the pirate as he crouched beside them.

'Don't worry, Emily,' soothed Spearhead, brushing a calloused finger along her soft cheek. '*If* your father pays up, you'll be back home in no time.'

Standing and addressing the captain, he ordered, 'Set a course for Hobyo.'

Captain Locke hesitated before replying, 'But we don't have enough fuel to reach Somalia.'

Spearhead's hand lashed out like a viper, his knuckles catching the captain hard across the jaw.

'Don't *ever* lie to me again,' snarled Spearhead as Captain Locke reeled from the blow, his split lip gushing fresh blood. 'I know for a fact this yacht has a range of four thousand nautical miles. Start the engines, NOW!'

Connor's eardrums almost burst at the sudden roar of the *Orchid*'s twin diesel engines kicking into life above him. The bilge rumbled like thunder and the stagnant water rippled with the yacht's vibrations. Covering his ears, Connor now understood why Cali hadn't ventured any further than the first compartment. His bones rattled as the propellors began to turn and the yacht got under way.

But this was good news, he realized. The chief officer had said one would need a computing degree to pilot the *Orchid*. And, with the crew secure in the citadel, Connor very much doubted that any of the pirates had the necessary skills or knowledge. Which could only mean one thing: *they'd been rescued!*

Wading through the oil-slicked water to the far end of the compartment, Connor found the hatch in the ceiling. He pushed it open and popped his head out. The engine room was glaringly bright, noisy but empty. Clambering on to the metal decking, he felt sheer relief at escaping the bilge's dark, tight confines. Even the engine room's diesel-tinged air was a joy compared to the stench of the bilge, and his throbbing headache and nausea soon began to fade.

Having been cooped up for several hours, though, his limbs were stiff and sore. He shook some life back into them, then strode over to the bulkhead door. Shouldering his Go-bag, he eased the door open and entered the service corridor.

No one was around as he made his way to the access door leading to the main stairwell and lower-deck bedrooms. He checked the girls' rooms first, discovering them both to be empty and their personal belongings ransacked and scattered all over the floor.

At the foot of the stairs Connor paused, experiencing a strong sense of unease.

Where is everyone?

His bodyguard instincts urged him to remain cautious as he climbed up to the main deck.

From the direction of the salon, he could hear music playing. A thumping party beat. Connor smiled to himself. They were *celebrating*. He almost rushed in to join them when he heard an unfamiliar voice shout above the music, the words indistinguishable but definitely not English.

He froze to the spot. He'd misread the situation. The pirates were *still* in control.

The salon door suddenly opened and Connor dived into Mr Sterling's study. A pair of pirates, jabbering away, passed right by, oblivious to him. Both of them had AK47s slung across their backs. As they entered the galley, Connor caught a glimpse of the steel door to the citadel. It lay on the floor like a discarded cardboard cut-out. Next to it were two gas canisters and a blowtorch. In an instant he knew what had happened.

His thoughts went to Emily and Chloe. *Where are they? Are they hurt? Alive even?*

Then he became aware of his own predicament. He had to get back into hiding, fast. If the pirates found him, there was no telling what they would do. And he'd be no use to anyone if he was captured.

But first he had to locate the girls. Confirm they were still alive.

As the two pirates raided the galley for party supplies, Connor crept back into the corridor and across to the door leading to the outer deck. Through the porthole, stars gleamed in the night sky. At least he'd have the cover of darkness to move about in. Once again, though, Connor wished his Go-bag wasn't bright yellow. Yet he couldn't leave it behind. He might need the protection of its liquid body-armour panel at any moment.

Out on deck, the breeze was cool and sharp, helping to focus his awareness. Keeping to the shadows, he listened out for any pirates, but heard none approaching.

The salon's floor-to-ceiling windows were obscured, both a blessing and a curse. Although he wouldn't be seen, he was forced to go to the glazed bay doors at the far end to look for the girls. With the aid of his night-vision sunglasses, Connor checked the route was clear, then headed towards the *Orchid*'s stern. As he passed the salon, the music pounding from within, the windows suddenly became transparent and he was caught like a rabbit in headlights.

On the other side, the pirates were laughing, drinking and dancing. The *Orchid*'s crew, numb with shock, had huddled on the leather sofas as if marooned. Amanda was gyrating to the music amid the pirates. But by the look on her face this wasn't out of choice. Then the windows went obscure again.

Connor dropped to the deck, praying he hadn't been spotted. The windows continued to flick between obscure and clear, a pirate inside finding the optical trick astonishing and hilarious at the same time as he repeatedly pressed the switch. By some stroke of luck, he'd been looking the other way and the darkness had concealed Connor from anyone else.

During the strobe-like flashes of the room, Connor continued to search for the girls. He saw Cali behind the bar, pouring out a steady stream of drinks for the celebrating pirates. At first Connor couldn't believe how reckless the pirates were being – getting drunk and making themselves vulnerable. Then he noticed that four of the men, positioned strategically round the room, weren't joining in with the drinking. They were keeping a watchful guard over their hostages, maintaining total control of the situation.

Eventually Connor spotted Emily and Chloe in the far corner of the room, separate from the rest of the group and overlooked by their own personal guard.

Connor despaired. *How can I, one lone boy, fight back against a gang of fully armed pirates?*

He may have trained as a bodyguard, but he wasn't a soldier like his father. He'd learnt to protect, not kill. And these were bloodthirsty men. They'd already proved their willingness to go to any lengths to achieve their aims by murdering Brad in cold blood. Who knew what they had in store for the hostages next.

With dismay, Connor turned away from the scene, realizing he didn't have a hope in hell of rescuing the girls single-handedly. Then he heard Charley's voice in his head: *Whether you think you can, or think you can't – you're probably right.*

One look at the sheer terror and despair on Emily and Chloe's faces spurred Connor to act. He was their only hope. And, although the odds were stacked against him, it was his duty to protect the girls . . . no matter what it took.

Connor stabbed at the buttons on the radio in the crew's quarters. But it remained stubbornly silent, its screen dishearteningly blank. He'd noticed the front panel had been removed, but he had replaced it, hoping that by doing so the unit would become operational again. No such luck. The only other radio he knew of was on the bridge – along with the satellite phone – and the pirates were occupying that area.

Putting down the dead receiver, Connor reassessed his options. He'd planned to get in contact with the coastguard and update them on the *Orchid*'s situation and their location. But, with the citadel's radio broken, he feared there wasn't any search-and-rescue operation in progress at all.

Connor returned to the idea of using the tender to make an escape. He could load it with extra fuel and provisions then, somehow, free Emily and Chloe and – of course, the tender! That had a VHF radio in the cockpit.

Realizing that, even if he did make contact, he might have to hold out for a while, Connor first hunted round the crew's quarters for food supplies and anything else that might prove useful. He filled his Go-bag with biscuits, dried fruit, tins of tuna fish and bottles of water. He also found a lighter, a penknife and a flare gun, complete with a spare set of flares. Then he crept back up the stairs to the main deck.

Passing through the galley, the place now littered with bottles and rubbish, Connor peeked into the main corridor. The music was still pumping loudly, but there were no pirates in sight. Then the salon's door burst open and the pirate with jug ears came staggering out. He lurched to one side, reached for the wall, missed and fell into an open cabin. Connor heard him vomiting all over the floor.

Seizing the opportunity, Connor dashed to the stairwell and down to the lower deck. He stopped short outside Chloe's room when he heard a rustling sound. A lone pirate was rifling through her belongings, pocketing any jewellery and valuables still left. While the thief was admiring a diamond ring that he'd discovered, Connor crept past towards the tender garage.

The door was still open. After a quick look inside, Connor entered, locked the door and hurried over to the tender. He clambered into the cockpit and located the radio and GPS unit. Switching them on, he was relieved to see a green light and their screens illuminate. Flipping up the safety cover on the radio, he pressed the red DSC Distress button and held it for five seconds, then waited for confirmation of a response.

Nothing registered on the screen.

Connor checked his watch as fifteen seconds went by, then thirty, without any response.

He picked up the hand-held receiver, switched the radio to Channel 16 and pressed the Transmit button.

'Mayday, Mayday, Mayday,' he said as loudly as he dared into the mic. 'This is motor yacht *Orchid*, *Orchid*, *Orchid*. Mayday *Orchid*. Our position is –' he looked at the GPS unit and saw it was still searching for a satellite connection – 'mid-Indian Ocean. We've been hijacked by pirates. We require immediate assistance. Over.'

Releasing the Transmitter button, he prayed someone, anyone, would answer. But all he got was static.

He tried again. Nothing. And again.

Connor was almost beginning to despair when he noticed he'd forgotten to switch the radio to high power. Cursing his own haste, he sent out the Mayday call once more, now at full transmission power.

The radio crackled and hissed.

Then a voice burst from the speaker: '*ORCHID . . . MANGYARING ULITIN*.'

The words echoed round the garage and Connor grabbed the radio's volume knob, twisting it virtually to zero in his panic.

'*Orchid . . . mangyaring ulitin*,' came the voice again.

Connor had no idea who the person was or what language was being spoken. It struck him that he could even be talking to one of the pirates. But that was a risk he'd have to take.

'This is Connor Reeves. I'm on board the *Orchid*. We've been hijacked by pirates. We need help urgently. Over.'

The radio squelched and spat. '*Orchid . . . maaari kong . . . bahagya marinig mo . . .*'

The signal appeared to be getting weaker.

'I don't understand,' Connor hissed desperately. 'Do you speak English? Over.'

The radio whistled amid a wash of static, the voice barely louder than a whisper.

'Hello?' persisted Connor. 'Can you hear me –'

Behind him, the bulkhead door *thunked* as the lock disengaged. Cutting the power to the radio, Connor lay flat in the bottom of the tender. The door swung open on well-oiled hinges and he heard the soft pad of bare feet enter.

'*Iska warran?*' said a man.

Connor stayed stock still, not even daring to breathe. He sensed the pirate approach the tender.

'*Iska warran?*' repeated the pirate, now less certain.

The pirate was no more than a couple of metres from him. Connor's eyes searched the bottom of the tender for a makeshift weapon. But everything was neatly stowed away. He could try to reach into his Go-bag for either the Dazzler or flare gun, but he feared any movement would alert the pirate to his presence.

After what seemed an age, the feet padded away and the bulkhead door closed.

Connor let out a long sigh of relief and lay there a moment recovering. Once convinced the pirate had gone, he sat back up and switched on the radio.

'Hello! Are you still there? This is motor yacht *Orchid*. Over.'

The radio hissed steadily but no one answered.

'I *demand* the Seychelles coastguard launch a search-and-rescue mission now,' Mr Sterling shouted, his face flushed with anger on the video-conference screen.

'I've tried, but after two false alerts they're understandably reticent to expend their resources on a wild-goose chase,' Colonel Black explained, keeping his tone even as he sat behind the mahogany desk in his office. 'Furthermore, both distress calls have been cancelled by the *Orchid* herself.'

'But *no one* can get through to them. We don't know what's happened. They could be shipwrecked or lying dead at the bottom of the sea. It's been over six hours. Surely the *Orchid* should be reported missing.'

'We're in agreement on that. I've been speaking with my military contacts to establish if there's a navy vessel in the area –'

There was a knock at the door and Charley poked her head through.

'Sorry for interrupting, but Amir's just intercepted a Mayday relay.'

'Hold on, Mr Sterling, we may have some news.'

Charley wheeled herself over and presented the colonel with a printout:

Filipino fishing boat reported Mayday call at 2014 hours local time. Message garbled. Bad signal. Transcript of call: 'Mayday . . . day . . . This is . . . Orc . . . Orchid . . . Our position is . . . require immediate assistance . . . Conn . . . eves . . . need help . . . Do you . . . speak Engl . . . Can – [END]'

'What's the news? Are my girls OK?' Mr Sterling enquired as Colonel Black read the transcript.

Charley looked up at the screen. 'There's very little information, I'm afraid, Mr Sterling. Only that the Mayday was made from the *Orchid*, apparently by Connor.'

On the monitor Mr Sterling frowned. 'Why's *he* sending the Mayday? Why not the captain or the chief officer?'

'Perhaps they can't,' Colonel Black replied, putting down the transcript. 'Just be glad it was Connor. At least we know he's alive. Which means your daughters are still under his protection.'

Mr Sterling grunted. 'What can he possibly do if they're *all* in trouble?'

'I assure you, Mr Sterling, Connor will do everything in his power to keep them safe.' The colonel glanced at Charley. 'Do we have the *Orchid*'s position?'

Charley shook her head. 'No, but the fishing boat was fifty-six nautical miles east of her last known location. As the distress call was sent by VHF radio, the *Orchid* would have been within a ten-nautical-mile range of that.'

'So what's being done to find them?' asked an irate Mr Sterling.

Charley replied, 'A French frigate, the *Victoire*, has altered course to begin the search.'

The colonel raised an eyebrow. 'I know that ship. A unit of Royal Marines was posted aboard as part of a joint operations treaty between the United Kingdom and France. I should be able to get a direct line of communication with their commander.'

'Good. I'm paying top dollar for your services so I expect results,' snapped Mr Sterling.

'We have to be realistic with respect to our chances of finding them,' said Colonel Black. 'The fact that it's night will hamper operations and it's one ship searching a large area of ocean. However, such frigates are equipped with advanced radar, sonar and infra-red detection equipment. They've also got a starting coordinate to work from. This all works in our favour.'

Mr Sterling nodded. 'Then inform me as soon as the *Orchid* is located. I want my Amanda and the girls back safe and sound.' He cut the call and the conference monitor went blank.

CHAPTER 77

As dawn approached, Connor shifted position on the narrow ledge, trying to relieve the steel rivets digging into his backside and the cold seeping into his bones. The bilge was a living hell to hide in, but at least he'd found some ear defenders in the engine room, making his bolt-hole tolerable if not comfortable.

Sitting in the darkened bilge, spooning cold tuna into his mouth, Connor didn't miss the harsh irony of his situation. *He* was now the stowaway on board a hijacked ship.

Most of the pirates were sleeping off their hangovers following the previous night's celebrations and as a result none of them had ventured down to the lower deck for the past few hours. However, acutely aware that he couldn't risk being discovered, Connor had stayed holed up below for the majority of the night.

Twice he'd made a trip to the upper decks to collect more provisions and pack the tender for a possible escape. The storage boxes under the seats were now crammed with food and water, but as yet he'd only managed to locate a couple of emergency fuel cans.

Also, he'd continued trying the radio at half-hourly intervals, repeating the Mayday call and waiting in hope for an answer. None ever came; although once he thought he'd heard some garbled transmission.

His other problem was figuring out the *Orchid*'s position. The GPS in the tender failed to connect with the satellite every time and Connor began to wonder if the yacht's hull was blocking the signal. The interference from the hull was probably also limiting the radio antenna's range, which would explain why he wasn't picking up any transmissions.

To counter this, Connor had considered opening the bay doors to the garage. However, he knew that would immediately bring the pirates running. So, using the screwdriver on his newly acquired penknife, he'd tried to remove the radio from the tender instead. But the radio was all wired in and he feared any more tampering would break his only means of communication.

Connor looked at his watch – 04:26. In one of his foraging missions, he'd come across a small compass and established that the *Orchid* was heading in an easterly direction, no doubt to Somalia. He was running out of time. If he didn't make contact soon, the *Orchid* would sail out of international waters and beyond all hope of help.

CHAPTER 78

'We've had a breakthrough,' Colonel Black announced, as Charley, Amir and the rest of Alpha team entered the briefing room. 'The *Orchid*'s EPIRB has been triggered again.'

Despite it being 3.30 a.m. in Wales, the news quickly dispelled the bleary eyes and stifled yawns.

'This *can't* be another false alert,' said Charley, speeding over to her monitor and scanning the report. 'The *Orchid* must be at full throttle! She's gone some distance since Connor's Mayday.'

'Don't worry,' said the colonel. 'The *Victoire* is already on course to intercept.'

The phone in the briefing room rang and Colonel Black picked it up. He listened intently for a moment. 'Your help is greatly appreciated, Commander.'

Placing a hand over the receiver, he addressed Alpha team. 'The Commander of 815 Squadron has arranged a live link to the operation. He's patching us through now.'

Colonel Black switched to speakerphone and Alpha team huddled round the desk to listen.

'*Victoire to Archangel. You are cleared for take-off . . .*'

The Lynx helicopter rose from the deck of the *Victoire* and banked away into the early dawn sky. The ocean was a cold steel-grey, the sun yet to grace it with its warmth. As the helicopter scudded low over the waves, the pilot and his observer scanned the horizon. Apart from a fishing trawler to the west, a large net dragging in its wake, the ocean was empty of shipping traffic. The pilot continued to head on the course dictated by the *Orchid*'s beacon.

In the cabin behind, two Royal Marine snipers perched either side, checking the sights on their long-range rifles in preparation for action. With hijacking a distinct probability, resistance was to be expected, if not wanted.

A blip sounded on the helicopter's radar.

'*Archangel to Victoire*,' said the pilot. '*Vessel located sixteen nautical miles due south.*'

Slightly adjusting course, the Lynx helicopter darted over the ocean.

'There!' said the observer, pointing straight ahead.

In the glow of first light, a yacht appeared on the horizon.

Alpha team listened in tense silence to the live relay. Static cut in and out but the words were clear enough.

'*Archangel to Victoire. Target in sight.*'

Amir smiled reassuringly at Charley. She responded with a flicker of a smile, then became tight-lipped again, her brow taut with concern.

'*Target sailing on a north-easterly bearing. Speed, fifteen knots.*'

'At least they're not sinking,' Marc commented.

'Yeah,' said Ling, 'but *who's* sailing her?'

It was a long time before the pilot spoke again and tension in the briefing room rose another notch.

'*Closing in on target . . . snipers at the ready . . .*'

'Do you think there'll be a firefight?' asked Richie, a little too eagerly.

'Shh!' said Charley, glaring at him.

'*No sign of anyone on deck . . . Hang on . . .*' Over the speaker the thud of the Lynx's rotor blades sounded like distant heavy gunfire. '*I see someone . . . port side . . . a body . . . male . . .*'

'Connor?' questioned Amir, saying out loud what was on everyone's minds.

Charley closed her eyes. 'I pray it isn't,' she whispered.

'But where's the crew?' asked Jason.

'If pirates have hijacked the *Orchid*, they'll hold all hostages below deck,' Colonel Black explained. 'Now be quiet.'

'*Archangel to Victoire,*' the pilot's voice said. '*Re-confirm target's call sign.*'

'*Victoire to Archangel.* Orchid, *I repeat,* Orchid,' replied the frigate's captain.

'*Then we have a problem. EPIRB location confirmed, but name on hull is* Sunriser, *I repeat,* Sunriser.'

Mr WiFi's grin widened as he scanned the intercepted messages from the *Victoire* to the Seychelles coastguard on his laptop screen. Oracle's idea to plant the *Orchid*'s EPIRB beacon on the other yacht and remote-trigger it had worked like a dream. All the efforts of the search-and-rescue team were focused on entirely the wrong patch of ocean.

He glanced across at Oracle, who was reclining upon his bolster, picking at a bowl of fresh dates. The morning sun streamed through a barred window, suffusing the spacious living room in a golden light.

'They took the bait,' he said.

Oracle replied with a smug smile as he popped a date into his mouth. 'Of course they did. Dumb Westerners.'

'With any luck, the *Orchid* should have a clear run.'

'When can we expect our prize?'

Mr WiFi switched to the live tracking program on his laptop. 'Around dawn tomorrow.'

Reaching for the slim mobile phone on the divan, Oracle pressed the Speed-dial button.

'Then I had better inform our investor.'

Connor peered through the glazed doors at the far end of the salon. Dusk had settled and once again he took the advantage of darkness. Several times he'd attempted to carry out surveillance during the day, but the pirates had been up on deck maintaining a constant watch for any approaching boats. This had made it impossible for him to move about the yacht without being spotted. So he'd stayed below, biding his time for the right opportunity to attempt a rescue.

The once pristine and stylish salon was now a mess in the aftermath of the pirates' party. Empty bottles and broken glass littered the floor. Red wine stained the white leather sofas, armchairs and carpet. The hostages appeared dazed, zoned out through a combination of gnawing fear and sheer exhaustion. The crew, minus the captain and the chief officer, remained under armed guard, the pirates lazily pointing their AK47s in their direction while chatting with one another.

Chloe and Emily were still sitting apart from the rest of the group. They huddled together in an armchair, Chloe dozing fitfully while Emily stared into space. Connor himself had barely slept for the past thirty-six hours, the narrow bilge ledge not exactly being comfortable. Yet, despite his frayed nerves, he'd managed to get some rest, in the knowledge that sleep deprivation would cloud his judgement and that he had to stay sharp if he was to succeed in his mission.

As he shook off his weariness, Connor wondered how he could attract the girls' attention without being noticed by the pirates. He had to communicate his plan to the twins. Connor knew his best chance of success lay in completely separating them from the rest of the group, then he'd only have to deal with one armed guard.

But neither of the girls was looking his way. Tapping on the glass would draw everyone's attention to him, so he'd have to come up with a better plan . . .

Without warning, a hand seized Connor by the shoulder and wrenched him to his feet. A gangly pirate with a hooked nose and wispy beard was glaring at him with furious astonishment.

'*I soo rac!*' he ordered, dragging him towards the doors.

Connor made a split-second decision. He could either surrender, or . . .

Flicking his hand out like a snake, he hit the pirate in the throat with a knife-hand strike. Choking, unable to breathe or cry out, his eyes bulging, the pirate staggered backwards under the blow. But he proved stronger than he looked and somehow managed to keep a grip on Connor. He swung a bony fist into Connor's gut. Connor tried to absorb the blow, but it struck hard. All the air was forced from his lungs and he doubled up in agony, slumping to his knees. The pirate slugged him in the jaw and stars exploded across Connor's vision.

However, Connor had taken punches just as hard many times before. During his years of kickboxing training, his body had become accustomed to the sudden shock of a punch or kick. His adrenalin masking the pain, he quickly got back on his feet.

Twisting himself in the man's grip, he clasped the pirate's fingers and rotated them against their joints in a jujitsu locking technique. The pirate grimaced and let go. Connor side-kicked him in the ribs with all his might. A bone *cracked*. Wheezing, the pirate collided against the access gate in the stern's handrail, the gate gave way and he tumbled over the side.

Connor rushed to the rail, but the pirate had already disappeared beneath the dark swell of the ocean, the *Orchid* powering on into the night.

Panting and in pain, Connor dropped to his knees and tried to recover his breath. But almost immediately he heard voices heading his way. Dragging himself over to the stairs, he staggered down to the lower deck and dashed for the refuge of the bilge.

'You should prepare yourself for the worst,' said Colonel Black, addressing the conference screen in his office.

Mr Sterling's expression hardened, the lines around his eyes deepening.

'All evidence indicates the *Orchid* has been hijacked by pirates.'

Mr Sterling nodded gravely, the blow heavy but inevitable. 'And what about my family?'

Colonel Black leant forward on his desk, his fingers interlaced. 'No news as yet. But it's likely they've been taken hostage.'

'What makes you believe they're still alive? The entire Dutch crew was murdered.'

'The *Sunriser* was hijacked so she could be used initially as a mothership, then, with the false Mayday, as a deception to draw the *Orchid* into their net. Finally, by planting the EPIRB, she was a decoy to keep search-and-rescue off the scent. However, once the *Sunriser* and her crew had fulfilled their purpose, they were expendable. Your family is not.

Considering the calculating nature of this hijack, I suspect the *Orchid* was *specifically* targeted.'

Mr Sterling sat up, his face filling the screen. 'By whom?'

Colonel Black held up his hands. 'Too early to tell. But this isn't standard operating procedure for Somali pirates. We'll just have to wait for them to contact us and deliver their ransom demands. Then we may find out more –'

Mr Sterling thumped his desk, causing the webcam image to flicker. 'I'm *not* going to sit here and do nothing while my Amanda, and my daughters, are at their mercy! I intend to fly out to the Seychelles tonight.'

'But, Mr Sterling, any negotiations could take weeks to –'

'Don't argue with me. I want you on site too.'

'Absolutely,' replied Colonel Black, his concern for Connor at the back of his mind. 'We'll shift operations to the Seychelles Regional Anti-Piracy Coordination Centre at once. I also have an expert ransom negotiator I can recommend.'

Mr Sterling shook his head. 'No, *I'll* be doing the negotiating.'

'But, Mr Sterling, with the greatest respect, you're emotionally involved in this.'

On-screen, Mr Sterling jabbed a finger at Colonel Black. 'I didn't get this far in business by being emotionally involved. I've brokered multibillion-dollar deals before. This is no different.'

'This is your family we're talking about. Not some company or asset.'

'Exactly. So I'm not trusting the negotiations to anyone else. I freed my daughter last time. I'll free my family this time. On my terms.'

Yes, but at what cost to your family? thought Colonel Black.

The heavy rumble of the engines eased and Connor sensed the yacht slowing down. Opening his eyes, he glanced at his watch in the darkness – 06:36. Somehow he'd managed to snatch a few hours' sleep, but still felt groggy and nauseous. His jaw ached and his stomach muscles were tender. The shock of the hijacking, the exertions of the fight and the need for constant alertness were all beginning to take their toll.

A ghostly vision of the pirate's startled face as he toppled over the stern swam before Connor's eyes. A sense of guilt at the man's fate was hanging like a heavy chain round his neck. But Connor reminded himself that he had no way of knowing that the gate would open. And, under the circumstances, was he *really* to blame? He'd been fighting for his freedom and that of the girls.

Thankfully, after escaping to the bilge, no one had come searching for him. Either the pirates didn't yet realize their comrade was missing, or they'd presumed he'd fallen overboard. Whatever the reason, Connor knew he'd had a lucky escape. But he couldn't afford to make such a mistake again.

Cautiously, he emerged from the bilge into the engine room, as ever glad to leave the suffocating coffin-like box. Making his way to the lower deck, he heard shouts coming from the stairwell. A man was barking commands and feet thumped overhead, followed by the noise of urgent activity.

Connor crept past the stairs towards his former bedroom. Ignoring the mess the pirates had made, he peeked out through a porthole. The morning sun was crawling above the horizon, a shimmering orange ball like the eye of a waking giant. To the far corner of his vision, he spied a barren coastline still shrouded in darkness. Dotting its countless inlets were the silhouettes of several large container ships. They lay motionless in the water like floating bloated bodies in a graveyard of forgotten ships. Connor swallowed hard, feeling that the noose had now tightened round their necks.

Then a huge shadow was cast over the *Orchid* as a massive tanker loomed into view. Its blue and rusting hull rose sheer from the sea to its main deck high above. From Connor's limited view of its stern, the tanker appeared endless, its hull disappearing beyond his vision.

The *Orchid* was on a direct collision course and showed no sign of stopping.

Connor braced himself. Although the yacht was going no more than a few knots, the impact was still shocking. The *Orchid* shuddered from stem to stern, there was a screeching of metal and a loud *dong* echoed through the tanker's hull. As the *Orchid* rebounded off the hull,

'Move!' ordered Spearhead, jabbing his gun at the hostages.

Captain Locke led his shell-shocked crew up the steep gangway. With as much grace as she could muster, Amanda followed close behind with Chloe and Emily in tow, the sisters clasping each other's hands for moral support. Their feet tramped up the metal steps in a slow march of despair. Far below, between the grilles, the wash of the green-blue ocean could be seen lapping against the rusting hull, no longer so inviting for a swim.

Reaching the main deck, the hostages were greeted by yet more armed men. Once aboard the pirate stronghold, the last vestiges of hope drained from the hostages' faces.

The deck itself was vast. An industrial network of walkways, pipes and machinery lined its length and breadth. The domes of several large storage tanks could be seen, upon which yellow warning signs declared: CONTENTS HIGHLY FLAMMABLE. The bow was so far away that it could have been part of another ship. At the stern, the navigation bridge towered over them like a skyscraper. Most bizarre was the sight of a pair of skinny goats tethered to the rail on the starboard side. They bleated indignantly at the new arrivals.

'Welcome to Somalia,' said a man cheerily, stepping from the disorganized ranks of pirates. Better dressed than the others, the man wore a pressed olive shirt, a cotton *ma'awis* in a black diamond pattern and a blood-red shawl slung over his shoulder. His face was smooth, his nose wide and his teeth stained green with khat leaves, but he kept his eyes hidden behind a pair of silver-mirrored aviator sunglasses.

'It wasn't our *preferred* destination,' answered Captain Locke.

The pirate laughed. 'It's good that you retain your sense of humour, Captain. I'm Oracle.'

He offered his hand in greeting. Captain Locke ignored it.

'Oh, come now, Captain. No need to be so impolite.'

Captain Locke's cheeks flushed with anger. 'You expect me to shake your hand after your men have hijacked my yacht, killed two of my crew and taken us hostage! I've an injured crew member in need of urgent medical attention. That's my immediate concern.'

Oracle waved away his grievance, barely glancing in the direction of the pale and feverish Jordan. 'With any luck, I won't need to detain you for long. Now please follow me.'

With several threatening prods from their guns, the pirates shepherded the group of hostages along the metal deck. Reaching the base of the tanker's bridge tower,

Oracle led them through a hatch and down a narrow corridor to a large open stairwell.

'Captain, my men will take you and your crew to your new quarters,' Oracle informed him. He barked an order in Somali. With a rough shove, Juggs and several other armed pirates hustled them down the steel stairs into the bowels of the tanker.

'Not you, ladies,' said Oracle, addressing Amanda, Chloe and Emily. 'You're my most *precious* cargo.'

Captain Locke glanced anxiously back at the girls, sensing this might be the last time they saw one another. Then he was gone with the others.

'This way, if you please,' said Oracle, heading up the stairs.

With Spearhead behind them, Amanda and the girls were left no other choice. They followed Oracle up two flights and down a stark white corridor to a wooden door. Outside stood a pirate on guard duty. He opened the door at their approach and Oracle strode into the cabin.

'Captain Takayama, you have guests,' said Oracle. 'Do make them feel welcome.'

A stocky Japanese man with round metal-framed spectacles rose from his chair. He blinked in surprise at the appearance of a woman and two girls on his ship, then bowed a respectful greeting.

'Well, I'll leave you to get acquainted.' Oracle smiled warmly at Emily and Chloe as if he were their long-lost uncle. 'I'll be contacting your father for the ransom. If he cooperates, you'll be home sooner than you think.'

'Good luck with that,' Emily muttered under her breath.

Oracle raised an eyebrow at her. 'Then perhaps we'll need to *persuade* him.' He motioned to Spearhead. 'Bring her with us.'

The pirate seized Emily by the arm and dragged her towards the door.

'No!' cried Chloe, clinging on to her sister's hand for dear life.

Spearhead shoved her away and she crumpled to the floor.

'*Yamae!* Stop!' cried Captain Takayama, moving to intervene.

The guard levelled his gun at him and the captain backed away, his head bowed in submission.

Spearhead hauled Emily out, slamming the door shut behind them.

As Chloe sat sobbing on the floor, Captain Takayama glanced awkwardly at Amanda, waiting for her to comfort the girl. When she didn't make a move, he helped Chloe on to a threadbare sofa. 'I'm Captain Takayama of the chemical tanker *Golden Phoenix*. My crew members are held below.' He offered her his handkerchief. 'I am very sorry that you've been captured by these thugs too.'

'No need to be,' said Chloe, wiping her eyes. 'It's not your fault.'

The captain nodded sadly, then said, 'I'll make you both some tea.'

As the captain busied himself, Amanda stared morosely

out of the porthole. 'How long have you been held here?' she asked.

Captain Takayama offered her a thin regretful smile. 'Five months and thirteen days . . . so far.'

CHAPTER 84

With the satellite phone clamped to his ear, Connor crouched beside the comms unit on the *Orchid*'s bridge, listening to the repeating ringtone.

'Come on,' he urged under his breath. 'Pick up.'

He'd finally managed to access the satellite phone, but now no one was answering.

After the hostages had been escorted off the *Orchid* at gunpoint, he'd waited for everything to quieten down before making his move. But his hopes of a deserted yacht were dashed when he discovered two pirates sprawled on the leather sofas in the salon. Fortunately, they appeared intoxicated, chewing on mouthfuls of green khat leaves and drinking the last dregs from the bar. It had been an easy matter for Connor to sneak past and up to the bridge. But he was keenly aware he wasn't alone on board, so kept his eyes and ears alert.

After three more rings, a voice answered. 'Hello?'

'Charley! It's Connor.'

'Connor?' gasped Charley. 'Where are you?'

'On the *Orchid*. Close to the Somali coast, I think.' He

glanced at the GPS unit and continued. 'Our exact location is North 5° 21' 18", East 48° 33' 30". We were attacked by pirates. Brad's dead. The girls and the crew have been taken on to a tanker. You need to organize a rescue immediately.'

There was a pause. 'You're hundreds of miles from where anyone is looking.'

'So redirect the SAR teams here.'

He could hear someone talking to Charley in the background. Her voice came on the line again. 'Connor, you're in Somali territorial waters now. Colonel Black says that means direct military intervention is out of the question.'

'So we can't be rescued?' said Connor, incredulous.

'You will be,' assured Charley. 'But we have to wait for the pirates to contact us with their ransom demands then –'

A jaunty ringtone sounded aboard the yacht, making Connor flinch. He heard a man answer.

'I have to go,' Connor whispered, replacing the receiver and dashing for the opposite door.

He slipped through just as a large pirate strode on to the bridge. Connor pressed himself against the wall of the corridor and held his breath. Continuing to jabber on his mobile, the pirate set aside his AK47 and plonked himself down in the captain's chair. He had a big nose and a wide mouth that seemed filled with too many teeth, and he talked so loudly that he was almost shouting.

Connor eyed the assault rifle and weighed up his chances of snatching the weapon before the pirate could. But he'd never fired such a gun in his life. Even if he did grab it first, by the time he'd found and released the safety catch, the pirate would easily overpower him.

The pirate swung his feet on to the console and settled back, showing no signs of leaving the comfort of the captain's chair any time soon. Connor realized he couldn't stand in the corridor all day. So, with one final regretful glance at the satellite phone, he silently edged away from the door and headed down to the main deck.

At least Charley and the rest of Alpha team knew he was alive. Where he was. And, most significantly, not held captive.

But for how long? He was on his own. No rescue was coming. While he could hold out hope of a successful ransom negotiation, the process could take months.

Connor very much doubted Emily would be able to endure another lengthy hostage experience. He also feared that he'd lose track of the girls if they were transferred across to the mainland. But most worrying was the violent and unpredictable nature of the pirates. This more than anything convinced him that he alone had to rescue the girls sooner rather than later.

Connor had already prepared himself for such a mission. He'd dressed in his darkest clothes and baseball cap, and replaced his shorts with cargo trousers. Into the pockets, he'd packed his night-vision sunglasses, the Dazzler and the flare gun. With some black gaffer tape from the storeroom, he'd covered the neon yellow of the Go-bag and emptied it of everything non-essential. He wanted to travel light and move as stealthily as possible.

It also gave him enough room to pack the last of Chef's special pirate cocktails.

As he crouched at the bottom of the tanker's gangway, he briefly contemplated waiting until dark. But that was ten hours off and anything could happen to the girls in that time.

CHAPTER 85

Connor was stunned by the sheer scale of the tanker. The deck alone had to be the size of two football stadiums. *How on earth will I locate the girls, let alone get them to safety?* he wondered.

The bridge tower seemed to be the most logical place to start searching. But that in itself was as big as a block of flats. At the very top Connor thought he saw movement – a possible pirate lookout. He'd have to be careful. At least the tangle of pipework, for loading and offloading the tanker's chemicals, provided him with good cover.

Darting from the gangway to the shelter of a mechanical pump, Connor picked his way along the deck. At one point, it seemed his ears were playing tricks on him. He could hear *bleating*.

Then he spotted a couple of goats tied to the starboard rail.

More hostages, thought Connor grimly.

He was over halfway when the sound of voices alerted him to danger. He ducked behind a cluster of oil drums. A few moments later, two pirates strode by, laughing, barely bothering to look around them. If they were on guard duty, they clearly weren't concerned about the possibility of an attack or a rescue attempt.

From his hiding place, Connor watched as they approached the goats. One of the pirates untethered a scrawny grey one and led it over to an area of open deck. With a twist of its head, he pinned the poor beast to the floor. Crouching beside it, the other pirate drew a long curved knife. With a practised hand, he slit the goat's throat and began to saw through the sinew and tendons.

Connor had to look away as the goat's pained and desperate bleats faded to a final gargled breath. When he glanced back, the deck was slick with blood. Connor flashed back to Brad's death, the security officer's corpse still lying on the *Orchid*'s deck, untouched and unmourned. If the pirates could murder Brad in cold blood and slaughter a goat with such lack of compassion, he dreaded to think how they'd treat their hostages, or him if he was caught.

While the two pirates finished butchering the goat, Connor managed to stay hidden by weaving through the maze of pipes and metalwork as he made his way to the bridge tower. With a quick check above, he sprinted across an exposed walkway and ducked through a hatch. Inside he paused for breath, the image of the bleeding goat still fresh in his mind. It impelled him to keep going.

A narrow corridor led to an open stairwell. *Up or down?* he thought.

He guessed the hostages would be held on the lower decks, secure and out of sight. Connor was about to descend when he heard Emily's voice cry from above, 'Let go! You're hurting me.'

'We know *exactly* where my family are, Clive. Send in your warship now,' demanded Mr Sterling, his hand almost strangling the phone's receiver as he spoke direct with the Australian Prime Minister. 'What do you mean *international incident*? I'll give you a domestic incident that'll end your career if you don't rescue them at once.'

Mr Sterling's face purpled as he listened to the Prime Minister's reply. 'Well, that's a fat lot of help!' He slammed down the phone. 'Bloody politicians.'

He paced the briefing room of the Seychelles Regional Anti-Piracy Coordination Centre like a caged tiger. Colonel Black sat on the opposite side of the conference table, Charley next to him. Both waited for Mr Sterling to calm down. Then the colonel said, 'What did your Prime Minister have to say?'

Mr Sterling stopped pacing and pulled out a chair. 'He'll station HMAS *Melbourne* off the coast of Somalia – twelve nautical miles out. A pointless gesture. What use is it there? Why can't my government be like the Americans and *act*? A few Navy SEALs and this would be over in no time.'

'If you're referring to the Maersk *Alabama* hijacking, that US rescue occurred in international waters,' explained the colonel. 'Unfortunately, your Prime Minister's hands are tied. The Australian Navy can't breach Somalia's territorial waters without creating a diplomatic crisis.'

'We already have a crisis!'

'Yes, but once a ship is taken it's very hard to rescue the crew and passengers without loss of life. Moreover, as soon as the pirates see the warship coming, they'll relocate the hostages. All they're interested in is the money. The lowest-risk method is to pay a ransom.'

'Fine,' relented Mr Sterling, holding up his hands. 'So why haven't the pirates contacted us yet?'

Colonel Black didn't have an answer for that one.

They sat in silence, the air-conditioning unit whirring in the background. Mr Sterling's bodyguard, Dan, poured his boss a cup of coffee then offered one to Colonel Black and Charley. Declining, Charley gazed through the glass into the centre's operations room. A live satellite surveillance feed on a monitor displayed a magnified section of the Somali coastline. In the waters beyond the port of Hobyo, several large cargo ships could be seen. Each contained hostages – more than a hundred seamen in total, from every corner of the globe, all waiting desperately for the shipping companies to pay their ransom demand. The chemical tanker in the middle, the *Golden Phoenix*, was where they presumed Mr Sterling's family and crew were being held. In her shadow, barely visible, was the white outline of the *Orchid*.

Is Connor still aboard? Charley clasped her phone in her hand, praying for another call from him. But an hour had passed and nothing. *Perhaps Connor has been captured?* Charley tried to push the dark thoughts to the back of her mind.

A mobile phone rang, breaking the tension.

Charley's heart leapt with hope until she looked at her phone's display and discovered it wasn't hers.

Mr Sterling pulled his mobile from his pocket. For a second or two, he stared at the screen. The number displayed a country code of +252. Somalia. He thumbed the Answer button, putting it on speakerphone.

A smooth, lightly accented voice spoke. 'Hello? Mr Sterling?'

'Yes,' he replied cautiously.

'My name's Mr Ali. I'm a local NGO worker in Somalia. I've heard about your family's plight. I want to help negotiate their release.'

Connor crept along the corridor. He'd followed the sound of Emily's struggle up three flights, then lost her.

Despite the overwhelming urge to run, he couldn't rush his search for Emily or her sister. A pirate could appear at any moment. There were countless cabins, storerooms, alcoves and stairways from which they could materialize; the bridge tower was like a rabbit warren. Yet the dangers of encountering a pirate were matched by the safety that all the nooks and crannies offered Connor as places to hide in.

As he approached an open door, halfway along the corridor, he heard a man speaking in English.

'No, I'm not a pirate myself,' assured the honeyed voice. 'As I said, my name is Mr Ali. I volunteered to help. I want to save your family and crew.'

Connor slipped into a storeroom opposite. Peering round the door frame, he gained a narrow view of the scene. A pot-bellied man with a receding hairline and greasy skin sat at a Formica table. Sweat patches blotted his dark green shirt that hung limp over a pair of long chino shorts, and on his feet he wore a pair of worn plastic sandals. He had a mobile phone wedged between his ear and left shoulder, while lighting up a self-rolled cigarette. Blowing out a puff of smoke, he said, 'I understand your concern. I will do my utmost to help.'

Another man sat opposite. Connor caught a glimpse of a pair of silver-mirrored sunglasses and a blood-red shawl, but most of Connor's view was blocked by the mountainous pirate who'd hijacked the *Orchid*. Beside him stood Emily, small and frail by comparison.

Connor simply wanted to dash in, snatch her and flee the ship. But he knew he'd have to bide his time for the right moment if he was to rescue both the sisters. Besides, he was intrigued by the presence of this Mr Ali and the hope he offered.

'Yes, I am on board,' said the pot-bellied man, tapping the ash from his burning cigarette on to the floor. He eyed Emily and smiled; a tooth was missing, the others were tinged a sour yellow. 'Yes, I have seen your family, and the crew. They're all in good health . . . for the time being.'

Despite Mr Ali's amiable tone, his last words smacked of a veiled threat. Mr Ali took another draw on his cigarette and casually blew smoke rings into the still air.

'The pirates are demanding one hundred million dollars.'

'*One hundred million dollars!*' exclaimed Mr Sterling, staring at his mobile phone in disbelief. 'That's an outrageous figure.'

Colonel Black and Charley exchanged astonished looks. Such a ransom was unheard of. The demand was more than half the total payout for all Somali hostages the previous year.

'It's that, or you'll never see your family again,' said Mr Ali.

'Don't threaten me,' snapped Mr Sterling.

'Please, you must understand, I'm just repeating what the pirates ask me to. I don't want your family or crew hurt any more than you do.'

'Then tell your pirates that –'

Colonel Black shot Mr Sterling a warning look. They'd discussed their negotiation strategy. A calm, level-headed approach was necessary. Somali pirates were known to be clever aggressive negotiators and quick to take advantage of any signs of weakness.

Mr Sterling took a deep breath and composed himself.

'That figure is too high. I can't possibly raise such an amount.'

'Mr Sterling, one hundred million dollars is barely ten per cent of your estimated wealth. I'm sure you can afford it.'

'*Estimated*,' repeated Mr Sterling emphatically. 'Most of my wealth is tied up in companies.'

'Then I'd advise you to start selling your companies.'

'That'll take months. I'm sure your pirates would prefer a quick resolution to this. Why don't we agree two million and be done with it?'

A weary sigh was heard over the line. 'I will ask, but time is what the pirates have in abundance.'

There was muffled noise as a hand covered the speaker at the other end. Charley thought she heard the sound of incredulous laughter. Mr Ali came back on the phone.

'They refuse your offer. It's one hundred million dollars. Nothing less.'

Mr Sterling clenched his fist. 'But what they're demanding is *five times* any previous ransom.'

'This is simply business for the pirates, Mr Sterling. You must understand: supply and demand. Fewer hijackings means less supply. Therefore the pirates demand more. And what price can you put on family? Besides, one hundred million is nothing compared to what countries like yours have stolen from Somalia.'

Mr Sterling frowned, confused by the sudden line of argument. 'What are you talking about?'

'Foreign trawlers plundering all our fish stocks. Tankers

illegally dumping toxic waste on our shores. Your newspapers must have covered the story at some point.'

'I'm sure they have. But those offences have nothing to do with me.'

'That may be true,' replied Mr Ali, 'but they have everything to do with why these men are pirates.'

Mr Sterling went to respond, but Colonel Black held up his hand to silence him. They were getting bogged down in irrelevant argument. He hurriedly wrote a message on a piece of paper and passed it across the table.

Mr Sterling read the note, then said to Mr Ali, 'Before we negotiate further, we need proof of life.'

Connor watched as Mr Ali beckoned Emily to the phone.

'Your father wants to speak with you.'

'Daddy?' said Emily, her voice fragile. 'No . . . I've not been hurt.'

As she cradled the phone, Connor could now see her face. Her eyes were sunken with exhaustion and her complexion fearfully pale.

'Yes, Chloe's fine too. Amanda is with her . . . No, the pirates haven't harmed her . . . No, you can't, I'm not with them.'

Connor could see that Emily was barely holding it together. Her hands trembled as she held the phone to her ear.

'Brad was shot dead . . . No, I don't know about the rest of the crew. They were taken below . . . Are you going to pay the pirates?'

She listened a moment. Her body visibly crumpled with the answer. Her knees giving way, she clutched at the table to steady herself.

'*Please*. Just pay. Don't leave me like you did last time. I can't face it. I'll . . .'

The pirate with silver-mirrored sunglasses stood up. He pulled a Browning handgun from his belt and pressed the barrel to Emily's temple. Connor tensed, wondering if he could cross the distance before the pirate pulled the trigger.

'D-D-Daddy, I have a gun to my head.' Emily began to sob loudly. 'Don't let them kill me . . . Just give them whatever they want. *PLEASE* –'

The pirate snatched the phone from her grasp.

'This is Oracle speaking. We're not playing games, Mr Sterling,' he said, his finger going to the trigger. 'You've got your proof of life. Now pay up, or I'll give you proof of death.'

With that he fired his gun.

The gun blast distorted the mobile phone's speaker. There was a scream then the line went dead.

'NO!' cried Mr Sterling. He jabbed at the touchscreen, bringing up the last call and redialling.

The phone rang out, its tone distant and taunting.

He looked to Colonel Black, almost pleading. 'They're not answering.'

'Negotiation is about control,' said the colonel. 'The pirates won't answer. They want to cause you as much distress as possible.'

Mr Sterling angrily shook the phone at him. 'They just shot my daughter!'

'That's highly unlikely. They'd not wish to lose their main bargaining power.'

'But you heard her *scream*.'

'Wouldn't you if a gun went off by your head?' said Charley, equally shocked by the disturbing call.

Colonel Black leant forward and met Mr Sterling's eye. 'The pirates are simply trying to intimidate you. They've clearly done their background research. They know exactly what you're worth. This suggests a highly organized gang – which means they'll have the resources for a long-term hostage situation.'

Mr Sterling slumped back in his chair and rubbed at the bridge of his nose. 'This is a nightmare. I can't believe it's happening all over again. This negotiation is nothing like the previous one. Who pretends to shoot their hostage on the first call? These pirates are worse than animals.'

'The tactics of kidnap gangs vary according to where they are and who they are,' replied the colonel. 'What works with the Corsican Mafia may backfire with an Iraqi militia or a Colombian bandit – and, in this case, Somali pirates. But one thing remains constant: mistakes can cost lives.'

Mr Sterling's eyes reddened with tears. 'My precious Amanda. She's so vulnerable. I should never have left her.'

Colonel Black studied Mr Sterling. A shadow of his former self, he was no longer the mighty media mogul – merely a father and husband-to-be, despairing for his captive family. So much for his claim of not getting emotionally involved in the deal-making. 'I think it's time to bring in a professional negotiator,' he suggested.

Mr Sterling sighed heavily. 'No, maybe I should just pay the pirates. If I sell all my shares, I might be able to raise the capital within a few weeks.'

'If you give in too easily, the pirates will simply up the asking price.'

'From a hundred million dollars?'

The colonel held up his hands. 'So far, this gang has

proved shrewd, calculating and ruthless. Not a good combination. Who knows what these men are capable of?'

'There's still Connor,' piped up Charley.

Mr Sterling gave a humourless laugh. 'What can he do? One boy against a gang of cut-throat pirates.'

The gunshot had sent Connor's adrenalin pumping. He'd almost bolted from his hiding place in an attempt to save Emily. But the pirate who called himself Oracle had fired upwards instead, blasting a hole in the ceiling.

Emily stood cowering from shock, a hand clasped to her deafened ear. 'What did you do *that* for?' she cried.

Oracle grinned at her as he passed the phone back to Mr Ali. 'To put pressure on your father to pay. That's what you want, isn't it?'

Mr Ali's mobile began to ring.

'That'll be him now.'

Mr Ali went to answer, but Oracle shook his head. 'Let him sweat a while.'

Pocketing his phone, Mr Ali laughed, his yellow teeth making a mockery of his smile. Connor realized that the man was no NGO worker. He wasn't on the ship out of the goodness of his heart. He was just one of the pirates, pretending to be an impartial negotiator.

'I expect Mr Sterling will come back with another low

offer,' said Mr Ali, rolling a second cigarette. 'What do you want me to say?'

Slipping the gun back into his belt, Oracle considered this a moment. 'Tell him we'll kill one of the crew for every offer he makes below one hundred million. That should convince him to take our demands seriously.'

This was a game changer, Connor realized. He had to free the girls before they started killing hostages. Once the pirates went down that route no one was safe from a bullet – least of all himself.

Connor heard hurried footsteps coming down the corridor. He retreated away from the door as a young lad in shorts and a grimy T-shirt rushed by and into the cabin opposite. For a second, Connor thought it was Cali. But the boy was slightly taller and older with buck teeth. A revolver, too big for him, was thrust into the back of his shorts. Connor was stunned – even the kid pirates had guns!

The lad yabbered something in Somali. Oracle and Mr Ali exchanged astonished looks.

'What's going on?' asked Emily as Mr Ali rose from his chair and headed for the door with Oracle and Spearhead.

'Nothing to worry your pretty little head about,' said Mr Ali. 'We've just found out our investor's come on board.'

Bucktooth was left behind to guard Emily. Connor realized this was his best opportunity to attempt a rescue – he could go head to head with just one pirate. Emily was perched on the chair next to the Formica table, picking numbly at a loose piece of veneer with her fingernail. Bucktooth leant against the wall, eyeing her long blonde hair and pale skin with fascination.

With the boy distracted by Emily's appearance, Connor crept across the corridor and into the cabin, planning to snatch the gun and subdue the young pirate. However, as he entered the room, Emily's eyes widened in amazement. She tried to hide her reaction, but the boy had already noticed. He spun round faster than a rattlesnake, whipping the revolver from his shorts.

Connor darted forward, slamming an open palm into Bucktooth's chest and striking the solar plexus. The boy gasped, doubling over in pain. But still he tried to point his gun at Connor and take a shot. Connor grabbed his wrist and slammed the weapon against the wall repeatedly. Bucktooth dropped the gun. Connor kicked it away then drove his forearm across the boy's throat, pinning him to the wall in a choke.

'Don't make a sound,' hissed Connor, putting a finger to his lips. 'Do you understand?'

Gagging, his eyes on stalks, the boy nodded.

Connor slowly released the pressure and stepped back.

Bucktooth took a desperate gulp of air then shouted, '*I caawi!*'

Given no choice, Connor drove an upper-cut into Bucktooth's jaw. His head rocked back, his eyes rolled in their sockets and the boy collapsed to the floor in a lifeless heap.

'Have you killed him?' whispered a stunned Emily.

Connor shook his head. He'd connected perfectly with the sweet spot on the boy's jaw, the impact causing his brain to shut down. Bucktooth would be out cold for a good few minutes. When he did regain consciousness, he'd have no memory of even being hit.

Emily ran over and wrapped her arms round Connor, sobbing. 'I thought *you* were dead.'

'Almost,' replied Connor. 'I'll explain another time.'

He dragged the unconscious Bucktooth across the corridor to the storeroom and locked him in.

'Come on, we have to find your sister,' said Connor, taking Emily's hand and heading down the corridor. 'Do you know where she is?'

Emily nodded. 'In the captain's cabin with Amanda.'

Emily directed Connor down two flights of stairs and along another corridor. Connor, taking the lead, kept a sharp eye out for pirates. But the bridge tower seemed deserted. Most of the pirates, he guessed, were either on deck or guarding the hostages below. They came to a bulkhead door with a small round window.

'In there,' said Emily.

Connor peered through the glass. He couldn't see any pirates, but his view was limited. 'Let me go first.'

Opening the door, he cautiously stepped into the room. It was full of boxes.

'This can't be right,' he said, turning to Emily.

But she was no longer with him. Behind, the bulkhead door clanged shut. Connor ran to it and yanked on the handle. It wouldn't budge.

He looked through the window and saw Emily turning the lock. Sealing him in.

'This is all your fault, Colonel Black!' snapped Mr Sterling, pointing an accusing finger at him. 'I can't believe you convinced me to hire teenagers to protect my family. How could you be so reckless? Your organization is irresponsible and ill-conceived. When this is over, I'm going to expose Buddyguard for the dangerous frauds that you are.'

Colonel Black rose from his chair, thunder in his eyes. 'You're angry and upset, Mr Sterling,' he said evenly. 'Perfectly natural reactions under the circumstances, but the blame lies squarely with the pirates.'

Mr Sterling went to reply, but Colonel Black cut him off. 'Need I remind you, you also employed an experienced crew and a ship security officer. But that didn't stop a determined and ruthless enemy. Brad's now dead. And at your insistence Ling was dismissed. Which means Connor is your daughters' last and only ring of defence. *Don't* rule him out.'

The two men held each other's stares. Charley knew Colonel Black wouldn't back down. She'd seen him deal with such tense situations before, with the client becoming hot-headed and irrational under the pressure. Clients rarely praised the security team when a mission went smoothly and nothing happened. But they were quick to attribute blame when things went wrong, even if it was their own fault for ignoring security advice in the first place.

A phone rang. All eyes went to Mr Sterling's mobile on the table.

'Is it them?' asked Charley.

Mr Sterling shook his head. 'It's my lawyer.'

He held the phone to his ear and listened, then cupped a hand over the receiver. 'He says a freelance reporter has got wind of the hijacking and wants to speak with me.'

Colonel Black grimaced. 'In this situation, the last thing we need is the media involved.'

'I *am* the media,' reminded Mr Sterling.

'Then control it. Smother the story for as long as you can.'

Returning to the phone, Mr Sterling muttered, 'My rivals are going to have a field day.'

While he spoke with his lawyer, trying to limit the damage, Charley leant close to Colonel Black and whispered, 'I'm worried about Connor. We still haven't heard from him.'

'He can handle himself,' said the colonel.

'Shouldn't we be doing more to help him?'

'What can we do? He's on his own out there.'

Colonel Black caught the sting in Charley's eyes at his apparent indifference.

'Listen, I'm just as concerned as you. But I can't let such

emotions cloud my judgement,' he explained. 'I'm sure Connor's managing the situation. When he does get in contact, inform him of HMAS *Melbourne*'s location. Find out everything you can about the pirates, the ship, the hostages' location, anything that might prove helpful in a rescue attempt.'

'I thought you said military intervention was out of the question.'

'Until all other avenues have been exhausted, it officially is.' His steel-grey eyes flicked towards Mr Sterling. 'But, if the negotiations continue to go south, a Special Forces raid might be the only option left . . . whatever the risk.'

Connor sat on the cold steel floor, staring at the locked bulkhead. He'd kicked at the handle, hammered on the lock with his torch, even thrown himself against the door. But it refused to budge. He'd searched for another way out, but the storage room had no other exits, not even a porthole.

His mind whirled in a fit of anger, shock and confusion. He still couldn't believe that Emily had locked him in the room. She hadn't done it under duress. She was alone as she calmly walked away. Then she'd met the pirate called Spearhead in the corridor and, by the looks of it, willingly surrendered to him.

Has something snapped inside Emily's head from the stress of being a hostage again? Or is her medication to blame?

During their operation briefing Charley had pointed out that Emily's anti-anxiety drugs could cause impaired thinking. That seemed the most logical explanation for her behaviour. The other was unthinkable . . . that Emily was somehow in league with the pirates.

But why? What has she to gain?

Connor tried to think if there were any clues. The *Orchid*

had been sailing far from the danger zone. There shouldn't have been any pirates for over five hundred miles. *So how had they found the yacht?*

Despite Ling's warning, he recalled Emily still posting pictures and comments on her social network site whenever they departed or arrived at a new location. *Could she have been secretly communicating with the pirates? Sending their coordinates via geo-tagging?*

Then the morning of the attack when he'd seen the flashing light, had Emily been responsible rather than Cali? Was *she* signalling the pirates? Connor tried to picture her expression when he'd found her on deck. Emily had definitely appeared surprised, even shocked . . . *or was it guilt?*

And, if she was conspiring with the pirates, then it would explain why she'd been so quick to defend Cali. *Are they working together?*

The radio in the citadel had been sabotaged. *Was that Cali's doing? Or Emily's?*

Yet none of this took away from the genuine fear in her eyes, or the heartfelt plea to her father to pay the ransom, or the relieved hug she gave Connor on her initial rescue. The pirate leader had even put a gun to her head. *If Emily is with them, why would he do that?*

There were too many questions. Too many conflicting possibilities.

The only known facts were that Emily had led him into a trap. And that *he* was now a hostage.

'I never expected to meet you in person,' said Oracle, settling into a chair opposite the investor. 'Nor did I expect you to be *white*.'

The investor stared hard at the pirate, adjusting the cuffs of his grey shirt and saying nothing.

Oracle shifted uneasily under his gaze. The cabin they sat in was hot and muggy, and the man's presence seemed to intensify the discomfort.

'Not that it's a problem, of course,' he added. 'Can I offer you some water? Your journey must have been tiring.'

The investor nodded. Oracle clicked his fingers and barked an order at Cali, who was standing obediently in the corner. Cali rushed over to an old fridge, pulled out a bottle of chilled water and handed it to the investor. The white man took a measured sip then replaced the cap. Cali backed away, not taking his eyes off him. To Cali, he was like a desert scorpion upon a rock. The rock appeared safe enough, but anyone getting too close would be struck with a lethal sting.

Oracle, a man used to being in charge, found his investor's silence unnerving.

'So, what brings you here?' he demanded. 'As I reported, we've successfully hijacked the *Orchid* and are now waiting for the ransom to be paid.'

'And it won't be long before we receive good news on that account, I can assure you,' added Mr Ali, keen to impress. 'The cracks are already beginning to show. We should close this deal within a week or so.'

He grinned broadly at the investor, awaiting his praise.

The investor didn't smile back. 'Change of plan. When the ransom is delivered, you're *not* to release his family.'

'What?' exclaimed Oracle, taking off his sunglasses and frowning. 'So what am I supposed to do with them?'

'Hand them over to Seven Sabres.'

Mr Ali's mouth fell open in shock. 'The terrorists? But they'll torture and kill them.'

'And you won't?'

'That was just an empty threat to force the price up,' explained Mr Ali. 'We're not religious extremists. We're businessmen.'

'I never make *empty* threats,' said the investor. 'What's the point?'

'But, if we double-cross Mr Sterling, my gang will get a bad reputation,' argued Oracle. 'That's not good for business. Shipping companies won't pay next time.'

The investor snorted. 'With a share of a hundred million dollars in your pockets, what do you care? And since when did pirates worry about their reputation?'

'We're not terrorists. We're simply making a living from the sea. And since other nations have stolen all our –'

'Don't justify your crimes with false moral arguments. You are pirates, blood and bone. That's why we selected you. The organization I represent wants to break Mr Sterling's heart as well as his bank balance. He's come too close to the truth too many times for our liking. We need his mind *occupied* until we've tied up all the loose ends.'

'And who exactly do you represent?' challenged Oracle.

The investor's icy stare fixed upon him. 'Such questions can get a man killed.'

Oracle felt his blood rise. His hand went to his gun. 'Are you threatening *me*?'

The investor didn't blink. 'No, it's just a fact.'

With an effort, Oracle subdued his anger and relaxed his grip on the gun. The investor had, of course, funded this hijacking and delivered a golden catch virtually into his lap. If the ransom came good, he'd become one of the richest men in Somalia overnight. *Why not play his little game?*

Oracle offered a civil smile. 'I just don't understand why you couldn't tell me this over the phone.'

'Because I needed to commend my little spy.'

The investor turned towards the door. Emily stood there, accompanied by Spearhead and Bucktooth, nursing his jaw.

'Hello, my little sparrow. You have done so well.'

CHAPTER 96

Connor searched frantically through the boxes in the storage room. There had to be something that could help him escape. But all he'd found so far were spare machinery parts, gaffer tape and other repair supplies. As he rifled through the last box, Connor heard the door behind him unlock.

'You were supposed to be dead,' said Spearhead, his bulk filling the open doorway.

The pirate had the barrel of his AK47 trained on Connor.

'Sorry to disappoint you,' said Connor, backing away, his Go-bag clasped to his chest.

Scowling, Spearhead cocked his head to one side. 'One of my men, Abdul, is missing. Was that your doing?'

Connor could only presume he meant the pirate with the hooked nose. 'He fell overboard.'

Spearhead narrowed his eyes. 'Maybe you will too.'

His finger went to the trigger. Connor braced himself for the shot, the panel of liquid body armour suddenly feeling far too small a shield. From behind its limited protection, he reached for the flare gun in his pocket.

'Stop! What do you think you're doing, Spearhead?' said a voice from the corridor.

'About to shoot a ship's rat,' replied the pirate.

Oracle appeared in the doorway and placed a hand on Spearhead's rifle, forcing the barrel to the ground. 'All in good time, my friend, all in good time.'

The pirate leader stepped into the room with Mr Ali. He looked Connor up and down. 'And they call Africa's warlords evil for recruiting child soldiers. But a *child bodyguard*? That is truly beyond belief.'

'I don't kill. I protect,' said Connor, his fingers wrapping round the handle of the hidden flare gun.

Oracle chuckled. 'Well, you're not doing a very good job then, are you?'

Connor had no answer for that. He'd been doing his level best, but had been betrayed by the very person he was protecting.

'Emily's told us everything about you,' explained Oracle, confirming Connor's worst fears. 'Quite a little James Bond, aren't we?'

At that, Connor whipped the flare gun from his pocket. But, before he could aim it, Spearhead seized his arm in a vice-like grip.

'Nice try,' he spat in Connor's face, prising the flare gun from his grasp. Then he stripped him of his Go-bag and emptied his pockets.

'And to think I was going to be merciful to you,' said Oracle, shaking his head in exaggerated disappointment.

He handed Connor a mobile phone.

'Call your people. Tell them you have only twenty-four hours to live.'

CHAPTER 97

Charley answered her phone on its first ring. 'Connor, is that you?'

'Yes –'

'Thank goodness,' she said, glancing across at Colonel Black and giving him the thumbs up. 'Listen, there's an Australian warship twelve nautical miles due east of your position. Can you tell me –'

'Charley, you have to listen to me,' interrupted Connor, his voice sounding strained. 'I've just been captured. I've been given twenty-four hours to live. Emily is . . .'

The line crackled and Connor's voice was lost.

Charley pressed the phone to her ear. 'Connor! Are you still there?'

'Hello there, Charley.'

She felt her blood run cold at the unfamiliar voice. 'Who is this?'

'We have your *buddy*-guard.' There was a snort of derision. 'I'm afraid his protection days are over. Unless Mr Sterling agrees to the ransom demand.'

The connection was cut.

Charley stared at her phone, the small hope she'd harboured for Connor ending with the call.

Mr Sterling crossed his arms and stared at Colonel Black. 'Well, we can rule out your final ring of defence!'

Charley could hold her tongue no more. 'Connor's life's at stake because he risked it trying to protect your daughters!' she exclaimed. 'Don't you understand the sacrifice he's made? That Brad has *already* paid. Are you that pig-headed and self-centred that you can't see we're doing everything in our power to bring back your family? Yet all you can do is criticize and complain. If you were the one with those pirates, I'd leave you there to rot. But it's not you. There are nine loyal crew, your fiancée, your daughters *and* Connor. You're not helping resolve this crisis. Now either work with us, or get out!'

Charley glared at Mr Sterling, daring him to argue with her. The media mogul stood open-mouthed as if he'd been slapped across the face. It was quite apparent no one had ever spoken to him like that before, let alone a teenager.

Colonel Black turned to Charley, not sure whether to be angry or proud. 'That's no way to speak to our client.'

'Quite right,' fumed Mr Sterling. 'I want her gone.'

The colonel turned on the media mogul, his eyes hard and unforgiving. 'No. Charley made a very valid if blunt point. Your attitude, Mr Sterling, is an obstacle to the success of this ransom negotiation. It could very well get them *all* killed.'

Mr Sterling swallowed hard, trying to compose himself under the colonel's ferocious glare. He lowered himself back into his chair and clasped his hands together, his expression almost contrite. 'No one speaks to me in that way, let alone a child, although I accept the stress of this situation may have been clouding my judgement.' He seemed as if about to apologize. But he didn't. Instead he focused on Colonel Black. 'So what's the plan now?'

'We continue to negotiate. Play for time. That's all we can do until I speak with your navy and establish what action –'

Mr Sterling's mobile rang. He looked at the display. 'It's them.'

With Connor's life now at stake, Colonel Black was determined to direct him.

'Offer them ten million dollars,' he instructed. 'That's half the highest ransom paid to date. They'll probably reject it, but it's a decent sum. Shows we're serious. We can work our way up to twenty million.'

'But *that* was for an oil tanker and its crew,' retorted Mr Sterling, becoming belligerent once more as he pressed the Speakerphone button. 'Mr Ali?'

'Yes. Sorry I missed your call earlier –'

'Is my daughter alive?' demanded Mr Sterling, ignoring the negotiator's hollow apology.

'Yes, she's shocked but unharmed. I can't guarantee I'll be able to stop Oracle next time, though.'

'I want to speak with Amanda and Chloe.'

'Maybe later,' said Mr Ali. 'Now, let's get down to business before anyone is seriously hurt.'

Charley gripped the arms of her chair, listening intently to the call. All she could think of was Connor and Colonel Black's words: *Mistakes can cost lives.*

Whether through arrogance, stubbornness or stupidity, Mr Sterling decided to continue the negotiations himself. He wet his lips before replying. 'I can fly in five million dollars within two days.'

Colonel Black glared at Mr Sterling, but said nothing.

On the phone they heard Mr Ali sigh. 'Mr Sterling, I thought I'd made myself abundantly clear: *one hundred million* dollars, nothing less. You should know that, if you do not pay, or are *unwilling* to, you will leave the pirates no option but to kill Connor and hand your family over to Seven Sabres.'

Mr Sterling's eyes widened in alarm. 'The terrorists?'

'That's correct, and those extremists aren't known for their hospitality to Westerners.'

'Well, ten million then.'

Mr Ali didn't reply.

'Plus the yacht. It's worth fifty million alone.'

'They already have your yacht. And what use is it to them? Mr Sterling, I advise you to think very carefully.

Oracle has vowed to kill one of the crew for every offer you make below a hundred million. He may even start with your beautiful fiancée.'

Mr Sterling went to answer back then shut his mouth.

'Are you still there? Mr Sterling?'

'Y-yes . . . I need to speak with my accountant. I'll call you back.'

CHAPTER 99

Beginner's luck. That's all it had been.

Connor was a fool to think he possessed the skills to be a bodyguard. It was luck that had saved the President's daughter's life that day. Not him. And now good fortune had turned its back on Connor. He was a captive of the pirates, the same as Chloe, Amanda and the *Orchid*'s crew. Just another hostage . . . another liability.

Connor clenched his fists in frustration and despair. He wanted to scream. To tear down the walls of the storage room that was now his prison. Why had he ever thought he could follow in his father's footsteps? What had possessed him to do the very job that had *killed* his father?

And that would now end his own life.

Failure is the key to success; each mistake teaches us something.

That's what Colonel Black had said. Well, Connor had certainly learnt the hard way not to trust his Principals. Not that such knowledge would be of any use to him now. He'd be dead within the next twenty hours – unless Mr Sterling agreed to pay the ransom. But, based on the man's previous track record, Connor doubted that would happen in his remaining lifetime. Mr Sterling was stone-hearted enough to gamble with his own daughters' fate, so from his viewpoint Connor would be expendable. No wonder Emily had turned against her father.

Colonel Black and Charley would, of course, be doing anything and everything to secure his release. But he wasn't the pirates' main prize. He was simply leverage in the negotiations. Like the crew, his life would be sacrificed simply to prove the pirates' resolve.

Connor's thoughts turned to his mum and gran. How would they cope? His mum's health was frail enough as it was. His death might even be the end of her. His gran would tough it out, like she always had through life. But he'd promised to see them both soon. And he *never* broke his promises to his gran. Connor fought back tears. He realized this would likely be the one promise that he couldn't keep.

The door swung open and Connor looked up. Cali the stowaway appeared with a tray. Behind him stood a hollow-cheeked guard, gun slung across his chest, his mouth chewing lazily on khat leaves.

Cali put the tray down at Connor's feet. There was a steaming bowl of brown mush along with a bottle of water.

'Is this my last meal?' said Connor dryly.

'Goat stew,' Cali replied, not meeting his eye. He stood. 'I thought you dead.'

'What do you care?' snapped Connor. 'I should've trusted my gut instinct on the yacht. You're a pirate and a liar. Just like Emily.'

'*Hadal ma jiro!*' barked the guard.

Cali hurried out of the room and the guard slammed the door shut.

Connor eyed the goat stew, the waft of meat thick in his nostrils. Despite his hunger, he pushed the bowl away. Having seen the animal slaughtered, Connor had no appetite for it. Tomorrow he'd likely be suffering the same fate.

Connor stirred. The exhaustion of the past few days had finally caught up with him and he'd succumbed to sleep. But it was a fitful rest, full of nightmarish visions. Goats with slit throats. Decks awash with blood. Brad's bullet-ridden corpse bloating in the sun. His own body lying next to it, quivering in a death twitch.

His nerves so on edge, Connor snapped awake as soon as he heard the lock turn. The door swung open and Cali entered.

'You not eat,' he said, looking at the untouched bowl of congealing goat stew.

'I can't stomach it,' said Connor, 'like I can't stomach you.'

Cali frowned at him. 'I come to get you.'

A cold dread seized Connor at the impending execution. Surely it couldn't be that time already. He glanced at his watch. It was only 22:17. Twenty-four hours hadn't passed. *Does that mean a deal has been struck?* Unlikely in so few hours. In all probability, the pirates were going to torture him to put more pressure on the negotiations.

Connor glanced into the corridor behind Cali. There was no guard in sight. Connor rose to his feet. This might be his last and only chance to escape. He could easily overpower Cali.

'Where's the guard?' asked Connor, preparing to pounce.

'I tell the guard a boat come. More khat for him. Now I guard you.'

Smiling, Cali stepped aside from the door, offering Connor no resistance and a way out.

Connor hesitated in his attack. He narrowed his eyes at Cali. No longer did he trust anyone. *Is this a trap? A cruel game to break my spirit?*

When Connor didn't move, Cali took a step forward and unslung a familiar rucksack. 'Your bag,' he said, his expression expectant as he offered it to Connor.

Connor cautiously took it. 'Why are you helping me?'

Cali blinked in surprise. 'You save my life.'

Connor recalled the moment he'd shoved Cali aside as the jug-eared pirate blasted the *Orchid*'s corridor with his AK47. 'You were in my way!'

Cali shrugged. 'Still save me.'

'But you're one of them.'

'I *never* pirate!' hissed Cali, bitterness in his voice.

'I don't believe you.'

'I have no choice,' said Cali, showing him his scarred arms. 'They whip me if not.'

He glanced nervously towards the open door. 'Guard be back soon. I hear bad things. They not release your friends. No one.'

'What do you mean?' exclaimed Connor. 'Not even if the ransom is paid?'

Cali shook his head. 'They hand them to Seven Sabres. White man order it.'

Seven Sabres? A white man? Connor was confused, as well as troubled, by this development.

'You're in great danger,' urged Cali. 'We go now. There are skiffs on port side. We take them. We escape.'

Connor searched the boy's eyes for any hint of deceit. But saw none. Against his better judgement, he decided he had to trust Cali with his life. After all, what other choice did he have?

Connor waited in the shadows as Cali approached the guard from the other end of the corridor. Connor recognized him as the jug-eared pirate from the yacht. He was dozing, slumped against the wall, his arms wrapped round his AK47 like a pillow. The pirate roused at Cali's approach and stood up. He muttered something. Cali smiled innocently and produced a handful of green stems. Grunting in satisfaction, Juggs snatched the fresh khat from Cali's grasp. As he picked through the leaves, searching for the smallest, greenest, most potent ones, Connor crept up behind.

His rescue plan relied on stealth, cunning and a great deal of luck. Cali was opposed to the idea, but Connor refused to leave the ship without Chloe, at the very least, under his protection.

Despite his nerves, Cali kept the pirate's attention focused on him by chatting and pointing out the choicest leaves.

Connor got within ten paces . . . then five . . . three . . . two . . . He pressed the barrel of his gun into the small of the pirate's back.

'*Gacmaha madaxa saara*,' said Connor, repeating the Somali phrase Cali had taught him.

The pirate froze, then dropped the khat and obediently raised his hands. Cali grabbed the AK47 before unlocking the door to the captain's cabin. With a prod from his gun, Connor directed the pirate inside.

A middle-aged Japanese man in a creased and dirty captain's shirt was startled from his sleep on the sofa. Switching on a table lamp, he scrambled for his glasses.

'*Nani?* What's happening?' he demanded, blinking in astonishment at the teenage boy holding the pirate at gunpoint.

Connor tossed the captain a roll of gaffer tape that he'd taken from the storage room. 'Quick. Bind him.'

Without needing to be told twice, the captain bound Juggs' wrists, torso and ankles, and lastly taped up his mouth, pinning his ears back in the process. He then rolled him on to the floor, where Juggs lay helpless as a trussed-up turkey. The pirate, wrestling against his bonds, shook with fury when he saw that he'd been duped by a boy with a flare gun.

Connor pocketed the improvised weapon. The plan had worked; luck once more on his side.

The captain frowned at Connor. 'I'm Captain Takayama. Are *you* the rescue party?' he asked dubiously.

'Sort of. I'm Connor Reeves. Chloe and Emily's buddy-guard.'

If the captain was surprised, he didn't show it. 'You certainly have courage, young man. But where's the rest of your team?'

383

'This is it,' admitted Connor. 'Where are the girls?'

The captain pointed to an adjoining door. 'One of them is in my quarters with Ms Ryder. The other was taken by the pirates to speak with her father.'

'That'll be Emily,' said Connor as he opened the door to the bedroom. He heard someone sleepily protest in the darkness. 'Chloe! Amanda! Get up. It's Connor. We have to leave.'

'Connor?' Chloe rushed out and threw her arms round him. 'I thought you were dead!'

Connor experienced a moment of déjà vu. He pulled away, wondering if this was *actually* Chloe . . . or Emily. He'd confused the twins once before and he wasn't about to make the same mistake again – not when one was a possible traitor. He studied her face hard, then ran a hand through her hair.

'What?' said Chloe, smiling at his touch.

On her earlobe Connor spotted the telltale mole. He was rescuing the right one.

Connor returned her smile. 'Nothing.'

Amanda emerged barefoot behind her. For once the supermodel wasn't a picture of unblemished beauty. Her complexion was pale, her hair a mess and her make-up smeared from crying. 'Captain Locke said the pirates shot you.'

'They did. But my phone saved me.' Chloe gave him a perplexed look and Connor added, 'It's a long story. Look, we have to go.'

Chloe remained rooted to the spot. 'What about my

sister?' she asked, her voice as fragile as glass. 'The pirates took her.'

Connor didn't know how to soften the blow. Nor did he have the time to do so. 'I suspect she's in league with the pirates. Possibly has been all along.'

Chloe's eyes glazed over with shock. 'That's insane.'

'I know,' said Connor. 'But when I tried to rescue her she tricked me and led me into a trap.'

Chloe went to argue but saw the harsh truth in Connor's eyes. She sat down on the sofa, struggling to come to terms with her sister's supposed betrayal.

'I'm sorry,' said Connor, laying a hand on her shoulder, 'but you're my priority now. And we have to get off this ship before they discover we've escaped.'

'What's the plan?' Captain Takayama asked.

Connor explained about the pirate skiffs tethered to the tanker and HMAS *Melbourne* stationed twelve nautical miles due east. 'It'll be a blind run in the dark, but Cali says the skiffs are all equipped with VHF radios, fuel and water. Once we're a few miles clear of the pirates, we'll contact the navy and hopefully they'll send help.'

'It sounds suicidal,' said Amanda. 'Why don't we wait until Maddox pays the ransom rather than risking our lives like this?'

'Because the pirates never intend to release us. Cali says we're to be handed to the terrorists – Seven Sabres.'

Amanda went deathly quiet.

Captain Takayama took the AK47 from Cali and flicked off the safety catch. 'After nearly six months of being a prisoner, it's time I was a proper captain again. I must rescue my crew . . . *and* yours. I know where they're being held. And if, as you say, there's been a fresh delivery of khat, the pirates will be distracted and off-guard.'

'Cali and I will help,' said Connor.

'No, your duty is to these ladies. Get them to safety. We'll meet on the port side. If there are any problems, just go. Don't risk your lives waiting for us.'

With a bow of respect to Connor, the captain hurried out of the cabin.

CHAPTER 102

'I have to get my shoes and belongings first,' said Amanda, returning to the bedroom.

'Just your shoes – and hurry,' urged Connor, feeling every second ticking away was another lost opportunity for escape.

The pirate Juggs continued writhing on the floor, but the captain had done his job well and the bonds held firm. He glared at Connor then at Cali, his eyes venomous and filled with hate. Connor had no doubt that if the pirate got free he'd tear them both limb from limb.

'I can't believe my sister would do such a thing,' murmured Chloe, looking to Connor to take back his words.

'I'm sorry, Chloe, but I can't deny what I saw –' Connor caught a flash of movement in the doorway. Bucktooth, a bruise purpling his jaw, had just walked in on them, stunned to see Connor free and Juggs held prisoner. Connor rushed to grab him, but this time the pirate boy got to his revolver first.

'*Joogso!*' said Bucktooth, shoving the gun into Connor's

face, his hands trembling ever so slightly as his finger wrapped round the trigger. Connor didn't know if the boy had it in him to actually kill someone, but he wasn't willing to take the risk. Retreating back into the room, Connor raised his hands. So did Chloe.

Bucktooth spoke rapidly to Cali in Somali. Cali's reply sounded to Connor as if he was pleading. He then stepped away, distancing himself from Connor. For all his protests at not being a pirate, the boy was quick to change sides when it suited. *But can I really blame him?* The boy was a survivalist. In his brutal world, he had to be.

'*Hubka dhiga!*' said Bucktooth.

'Put your weapons down,' Cali translated.

Bucktooth was taking no chances with him this time. Connor slowly withdrew the flare gun from his pocket and dropped it on the floor. The pirate boy dipped the revolver's barrel towards Connor's other pocket and gave another order. Connor obediently reached in and pulled out the slim black tube Bucktooth had spotted.

'It's just a torch,' explained Connor, holding it up for the boy to see. 'Look.'

As Bucktooth peered at it, Connor depressed the button and a glaring green laser shot out. The Dazzler blinded the pirate. Darting forward, Connor leapt on Bucktooth and sent him crashing to the floor. In panic at losing his sight, the boy thrashed wildly and Connor fought to pin him down. Cali rushed to Connor's aid, grabbing the boy's gun and wrenching it from his grasp. Connor immobilized Bucktooth with a reverse choke.

The pirate boy started to shout for help, but Connor applied pressure and the cry died in his throat as pain racked his body.

'Quick, get the tape,' Connor ordered Cali, glad to discover the stowaway was still on his side.

As Cali bound Bucktooth, the pirate boy started to sob. Connor couldn't help but feel sorry for the lad. 'Tell him the blindness is only temporary.'

Cali spoke quietly and the boy calmed down. Then Cali taped up his mouth.

Amanda peeked round the bedroom door. 'Is it safe to come out?'

'Depends upon your definition of safe,' replied Connor, rolling Bucktooth on to his front and leaving him beside the other trussed-up pirate. He picked up the flare gun and Dazzler, pocketing them. Cali armed himself with Bucktooth's revolver. 'Time to go.'

The four of them hurried from the captain's cabin, Connor taking a moment to lock the door. Then they dashed along the corridor to the main stairwell. Connor was about to lead them down, when he heard footsteps and saw the bald dome of Spearhead through the metal grilles. The pirate was coming their way.

Doubling back, they discovered another flight of stairs, reaching it just as Spearhead entered the corridor. Descending two flights to the main deck, they arrived at the external door. Connor peered through a porthole. Outside it was pitch dark, the stars pinpricking the sky. There were no guards in sight.

Connor looked back at Chloe. 'Stay close to me.'

Chloe nodded. Connor put on his night-vision sunglasses. He'd need every advantage if they were to reach the skiffs without being spotted.

CHAPTER 103

'What's with the sunglasses?' hissed Amanda.

'Night vision,' whispered Connor, checking through the porthole once more; a good thing too. In his silvery enhanced vision, he spied a pirate leaning against the rail, smoking a cigarette. He'd been partly hidden behind a stack of oil drums stockpiled to refuel the skiffs. They'd have to wait for him to move on.

A tense minute passed. Still the pirate leisurely puffed away, seemingly unconcerned at holding a lit cigarette beside containers of flammable fuel.

'We can't stay here forever,' whispered Amanda, glancing nervously over her shoulder at the cabins behind, any one of them potentially harbouring a pirate.

'I know,' said Connor, aware that Spearhead might have discovered Juggs and Bucktooth and already raised the alarm.

Footsteps rang out on the stairwell above.

They couldn't wait any longer.

'What's *hello* in Somali?' Connor asked Cali.

'*Iska warran*,' he replied, bemused.

Connor opened the bulkhead door and strode through the darkness towards the pirate.

'*Iska warran*,' he called out.

The pirate turned to him, expecting a friend. Instead he was blinded by a strobing laser. Connor rushed forward and shoulder-barged the pirate over the rail. The man let out a shocked cry then tumbled from view. Connor heard a splash and hoped he could swim. Noticing a life ring, Connor tossed it over the side just in case the man couldn't.

Connor glanced along the tanker's port side. Halfway down the deck, he spotted the figure of Captain Takayama. His crew clambered, one at a time, over the gunwale to descend a rope ladder. One of the skiffs was already full. He was too far away to be certain but Connor thought he recognized two women among the passengers, Sophie and Kathy from the *Orchid*. Which meant Captain Takayama had been true to his word – he'd freed the *Orchid*'s crew too.

Connor beckoned Chloe, Amanda and Cali out.

'Stay underneath the pipework,' he instructed. 'There may be lookouts on the bridge tower.'

With a quick check above, Connor led the dash across the exposed deck to an overhead walkway. They ducked beneath its shelter, then picked their way through the tangle of struts, pipes and metalwork. The going was slow, since only Connor could see well enough in the dark. As he helped Chloe over a pipe, there was a startled movement and strange noise. Amanda let out a scream. Cali stifled it with his hand.

'Goat,' he whispered in her ear.

Amanda, her eyes wide, nodded that she understood and Cali removed his hand. But the damage had been done: her cry had caught the attention of a pirate. Through the lattice of pipes, Connor saw someone approaching on the walkway above. He signalled to the others to stay absolutely still. The pirate stopped no more than a few metres from them, his sandaled feet visible through the metal grilles. Connor watched the pirate as he hunted for the source of the sound. His eyes passed over them, but evidently he didn't see them in the darkness. Then the pirate heard the goat bleat, a forlorn cry for its missing companion. The pirate spat at the beast, then shouted some abuse before walking away.

Further along the deck, Connor noticed Captain Takayama glance in their direction. He'd heard the pirate shouting and now hurried the last of his crew over the side before following them down the ladder himself.

'They're going to leave without us!' gasped Amanda, abandoning their hiding place.

'No! Wait!' hissed Connor.

But Amanda had already bolted. She ran out on to the deck, putting herself in full view of the pirate. Connor prayed the man wouldn't turn her way. Amanda reached the rail and was climbing over when a blaring alarm shattered the night and the tanker was suddenly ablaze with light.

CHAPTER 104

Connor grabbed Chloe's hand to make a run for it. But the pirate came charging back down the gantry. He saw Amanda and raised his AK47.

'*Joogso!*'

He shot at her, bullets peppering the deck, just as she disappeared over the side and down to the skiff below.

With their escape route cut off, Connor hurriedly led Chloe and Cali round a storage tank to the opposite side of the ship. Pirates were now rushing on to the main deck. Some started firing over the port side. Connor could hear the roar of outboards as the two skiffs powered away.

With a sinking heart, Connor realized Captain Takayama and Captain Locke had been left with no choice but to abandon them. The Japanese captain had said himself, *If there are any problems, just go.*

'What do we do now?' said Chloe, cowering in the shelter of a pump. 'We've no way to get off this ship.'

Connor glanced along the tanker's starboard side. The

gangway was still down. 'The pirates think we're on the skiffs. We need to get to the *Orchid*.'

'Do you know how to pilot it?' asked Chloe. 'I certainly don't.'

'No. But the tender's ready to launch.'

The alarm ceased. Only the crack of gunfire now punctured the night. Spearhead appeared on deck, barking commands at the pirates to pursue the hostages.

'Let's go,' said Connor.

Stepping from the cover of the storage tank, they sprinted along the deck towards the gangway. Suddenly gunfire burst around their feet. Connor pulled Chloe into his protection and dived behind a control box. Cali dropped down next to them. More bullets pinged off the metalwork.

'*Joog halkaaga!*' screamed a pirate.

'He say to stay where we are,' whispered Cali, his eyes white with fear.

'As if we have another choice,' Connor muttered, peering round the control box. Pirates were closing in from all sides. They were pinned down. Just as he'd been in his Buddyguard training exercise only a month before. But this time the bullets were real. And this time any mistake meant certain death.

As before, his next move would be crucial. He shook off any sense of tunnel vision, making certain to look everywhere for threats. In the daylight brightness of the tanker's halogen floodlights, Connor spotted a pirate positioned by the oil drums, another on the walkway overhead and two sneaking down the port side, concealed by the network of pipes. Oracle was on a gantry overlooking the main deck. Emily was with him, Mr Ali holding a gun to her head.

Over the ship's tannoy, the pirate leader announced, 'Give yourselves up, or the girl dies!'

Chloe locked eyes with Connor. 'We *have* to surrender.'

'They won't shoot her,' Connor insisted. 'Whether Emily's one of the pirates or not, she's more valuable to them alive than dead.'

'I'll give you to the count of five,' said Oracle, his fury evident in his tone.

Chloe grabbed Connor's arm. 'How can you be so sure? They killed Brad!'

Connor couldn't be sure.

'*Five* . . .'

'Emily could've been *forced* to trap you. Tortured. Anything!' cried Chloe, becoming more and more distraught.

Connor realized he was taking a huge gamble by assuming Emily was one of the pirates.

'*Four* . . .'

'The Emily you describe isn't the one I know,' continued Chloe. 'She's my twin sister. We have to save her.'

'*Three* . . .'

Chloe went to stand, but Connor pulled her back down behind the control box. 'You may be right. But we're *not* surrendering. The pirates never intend to release you.'

'*Two* . . .'

'My job is to protect you. And I'll fight to save you *both*.'

'*One!*' shouted Oracle.

Connor drew the flare gun from his pocket, took aim and fired.

The flare struck the oil drums, its sparks igniting spilt fuel and causing a massive explosion. The expanding ball of fire engulfed the nearest pirate. His flaming body plummeted like a comet over the side, the fire extinguished in the sea below.

The force of the explosion then ripped across the deck. Pirates dived for cover. The gantry above rocked on its supports, knocking Oracle and Mr Ali off their feet. Emily, thrown against the rail, struck her head and was laid out cold.

As the pirates reeled from the blast, Connor broke from behind the control box and over to the port side. He pulled Chef's Molotov cocktail from his Go-bag, found his lighter, lit the fuse and tossed it. The bottle shattered on impact, spreading a river of fire across the deck. The two pirates there fled from the flames. The pirate on the walkway didn't know which way to turn as chaos reigned around him. The Molotov's flames reached another set of oil drums.

Connor darted back to Chloe and Cali as the fuel in these now ignited with a roar.

'Run!' he shouted.

He felt his skin scorching from the heat of the blast. He tried to shield Chloe as they sprinted for the gangway, the smell of her singed hair in his nostrils.

'Connor, you crazy!' screamed Cali, running for all he was worth.

Flames seemed to lick at their heels. Thick black smoke swirled around them. They reached the top of the gangway as the blast from the drums at last subsided.

Chloe stopped, panting hard, her face smeared with sweat and smoke. 'What about my sister?'

Connor was caught in a dilemma. He couldn't leave Chloe unprotected, yet he had a duty to rescue Emily, even if she was helping the enemy. Now more than ever he wished he had Ling at his side.

Connor looked to Cali. Once more he'd have to trust the Somali boy. But this time with Chloe's life.

'Get Chloe to the tender garage. If anyone comes, hide in the bilge.'

Cali nodded. 'I guard her,' he said, holding up Bucktooth's revolver. 'With my life.'

Connor hoped Cali wouldn't have to put that claim to the test, but he admired the boy's courage. He grinned. 'We'll make a bodyguard of you yet.'

The tanker rocked with another explosion. Louder. Deeper. And more ominous. Whatever chemicals were aboard the ship, they were now igniting.

Connor rushed across the deck. With the tanker ablaze, the pirates were panicking, more concerned with abandoning the ship than stopping him. Black smoke billowed in the air, obscuring the halogen spots and turning the scene into a hellish twilight, the fires flickering orange-red.

Connor fought his way through the flames and up the stairs to the gantry. Emily still lay on the metal decking. He prayed she wasn't seriously hurt. Or worse, dead.

'Emily!' he called, running over.

She didn't respond.

Kneeling down beside her, he put his fingers to the pulse in her neck.

'You've cost me millions!'

Connor spun round. Oracle stood behind him, the tanker's flames reflecting in his silver-mirrored glasses. He aimed his gun at Connor's chest.

'A hundred million dollars, to be exact. And you'll pay for it with your life.'

Oracle pulled the trigger. The gun blast rang in Connor's ears. At the same time he felt the devastating impact of the bullet and was thrown backwards over Emily's body. He lay across her, stunned and immobile. Then he took a heaving gasp for breath. His T-shirt and top had withstood the handgun's attack. But he'd been winded badly and his chest throbbed from another blunt trauma.

Oracle cocked his head to one side when he realized Connor wasn't dead. Then he spotted the compacted lead shot that had dropped into Connor's lap.

'Bulletproof clothing?' He laughed. 'Now that is something *I* need.'

Through the haze of pain, Connor frantically reached for the Dazzler in his pocket. His flare gun was useless, having not reloaded it. He fumbled for the torch, but his body was still in shock from the bullet's impact and he dropped it.

'Well, at least I get the pleasure of killing you twice,' said Oracle, raising his gun. 'I'll shoot you in the head this time, though. Just to make sure.'

Connor's fingers found the Dazzler. Too late.

A shot rang out.

Connor recoiled, expecting to die. But it was Oracle who fell to the ground, a bullet through *his* head.

Connor blinked, disbelieving what he saw.

A white man stood on the gantry, flames like hellfire rising up behind him. He seemed completely unperturbed by the destruction and panic around him. His face was a mask, no emotion, no colour, his skin pale as ash.

The man pointed his gun at Emily. 'Does she live?'

Connor nodded, trying to shield her with his body.

The man studied Connor a moment, his gaze as pitiless and cold-blooded as a snake's.

A third explosion shook the tanker to its core and a cloud of black smoke enveloped the gantry. Connor coughed, his eyes stinging from the chemical fumes. He heard a voice, disturbingly close, whisper something about 'a little sparrow', then Emily spluttered for breath.

When the smoke cleared, the man was gone.

CHAPTER 107

Wincing from the bruising on his chest, Connor lifted the semi-conscious Emily on to his shoulders. Another detonation rumbled through the tanker. The gantry lurched sideways. Connor staggered across to the stairwell. His heart pumping, smoke clogging his lungs, he carried her down to the main deck. Only now did Connor fully appreciate his instructor Steve's fitness training.

In an emergency, you'll need such strength to get you and your Principal out of the danger zone.

Connor just hoped he could muster enough. His body had taken a serious battering over the past few days. He was running purely on adrenalin.

At the foot of the stairs, he passed the lifeless body of Mr Ali with a bullet through his head, execution-style.

A pirate raced past screaming, his back in flames as he threw himself over the side.

The tanker' main deck was now a sea of fire. The route to the gangway seemed impassable. But Connor had no option. He sprinted along the outer edge, the heat so intense that he thought his skin would melt. Acrid smoke swirled in front of his eyes and he became disorientated. He shot straight past the gangway. Backing up, he stumbled down the steps, Emily now a dead weight on his shoulders. Starved of oxygen and pushed to his limit, Connor felt that his legs might give way any moment.

Then his feet touched down on the *Orchid*'s stern.

As he rushed towards the aft stairwell, he almost tripped over a pirate lying on the deck in a pool of his own blood. The pirate looked up, his face taut with pain. Connor recognized him from the *Orchid*'s bridge, the one who'd been on the phone. The man was clasping his leg, blood seeping from a gunshot wound. He blathered something in Somali, angry and demanding, but Connor ignored him and kept going.

Hurrying down the steps, Connor entered the lower deck's corridor. He staggered the last few feet. At the door to the tender garage, he spun the lock, kicked it open and came face to face with a gun.

CHAPTER 108

'Don't shoot!' cried Connor. 'It's me!'

Cali lowered the gun. 'Sorry, I thought you Big Mouth. I shoot him once already.'

'The pirate on deck?' said Connor. 'That was *your* doing?'

Cali nodded and grinned. 'He not believe I would. But I bodyguard.'

'Good work,' said Connor, impressed that the boy had been true to his word. Connor carried Emily into the garage. 'Where's Chloe?'

'She safe,' replied Cali, running over to the bilge hatch.

Chloe emerged, damp and dishevelled. 'I can't believe you hid in there, Cali, it's revolting.' Then she saw her sister. 'Emily!'

Emily moaned in pain as Connor lowered her into the tender.

'Is she all right?' asked Chloe.

'I think it's only concussion,' replied Connor, dashing over to the garage's control panel. 'Get in quickly and put a life jacket on her.'

As Chloe climbed aboard, he slammed the green Open button with the palm of his hand and the bay doors slid apart. The monstrous noise of the blazing tanker rushed in, more storage tanks detonating like hydrogen bombs. The *Orchid* trembled in the tanker's furious shadow.

Turning a key, Connor initiated the tender's launch. He ran back and jumped into the boat with Cali. As soon as the tender left its mountings and slid into the water, he pressed the ignition and the engine kicked into life.

'Hold on tight!' he shouted, pushing the throttle forward.

The tender's engines roared and the boat took off. Behind them, the tanker burned like an open furnace. It felt as if the heat was chasing them even as they escaped.

The motorboat cut through the water, the waves fire-red in the reflected light of the inferno. Gradually the sea darkened as the tanker receded into the distance and they entered the open water of the Indian Ocean.

'You've done it!' sobbed Chloe, cradling her sister in her arms. 'You've rescued us, Connor.'

Switching on the radio, Connor picked up the receiver. 'Mayday, Mayday, Mayday. This is motorboat *Sunbeam*, *Sunbeam*, *Sunbeam*. Mayday *Sunbeam* –'

'*We hear you*, Sunbeam. *This is HMAS* Melbourne. *What's your position?*'

Connor glanced down at the GPS which, to his relief, had finally picked up a satellite signal. 'This is motorboat *Sunbeam*. Our position is –'

The radio shattered as a strafing of bullets cut across their stern.

406

'Everybody down,' cried Connor, ducking behind his seat.

He spun the wheel hard to port as more bullets whizzed overhead.

Out of the darkness, a pirate skiff surged towards them.

CHAPTER 109

Through his night-vision lenses, Connor identified Spearhead crouched in the skiff's bow, his AK47 tucked against his shoulder. He let loose another volley of shots, then broke from firing to load a new clip.

Connor leapt back into the pilot's seat. Straightening their course, he pushed the throttle into the red zone and the tender powered away. They thumped over the waves, Chloe, Emily and Cali clinging on for dear life.

The gunfire resumed and Connor veered left then right, trying to avoid the bullets.

'They catch up!' shouted Cali.

Connor glanced over his shoulder. The super-charged skiff was gaining on them rapidly.

'What now?' cried Chloe over the strained roar of the tender's engines. 'The radio's gone.'

Connor reached behind and yanked the tag that activated the Go-bag's SART. The high-powered LED beacon began to flash as the device transmitted its high-powered locating signal.

'What do you think you're doing?' exclaimed Chloe. 'Are you *trying* to make yourself a target?'

Connor didn't have much choice. If he shrugged off the backpack, he'd lose the protection of the liquid body-armour panel. But Spearhead certainly seemed to appreciate the flashing light. The tender rattled with the impact of more direct hits from 7.62mm high-velocity rounds.

Cali knelt up and began firing the revolver in retaliation. But he was being thrown around so much that Connor doubted a single bullet was on target.

After five shots, the gun clicked empty.

'No more,' Cali despaired, ducking down as Spearhead returned fire.

Spray breaking over the tender's bow, Connor steered them blindly into the night. There was nowhere for them to hide in the open ocean. All he could hope for was to outrun the pirates. But the tender's engines were already being pushed to their limit. And still it wasn't enough.

The pirate skiff relentlessly closed the gap.

'Cali, grab the flare gun in my pocket,' ordered Connor.

Crawling over the jolting deck, he pulled out the gun.

'Spare flares are in the side of my Go-bag.'

Reaching up, Cali unzipped the pocket and found the clip of flares.

'You need to aim at the rear of the skiff,' Connor explained, 'where the fuel cans are.'

Nodding, Cali loaded the flare gun.

Spearhead's skiff was now so close they could hear him shouting his vengeance. '*I KILL YOU! I KILL YOU ALL!*'

'Hold boat steady,' demanded Cali.

Connor shot him a disbelieving look. At this speed that was impossible, but he steered as straight a path as he could.

Cali closed one eye, took careful aim and fired. The flare whooshed across the waves. A bright red trail streaked through the night sky. The flare hit its target and, at the moment of impact, the skiff exploded in a massive ball of flame, obliterating the craft and all on board.

'*What* on earth did you load?' Connor exclaimed, easing back on the throttle, their pursuer now destroyed.

Cali stared in astonishment at the gun, then at the flaming wreck of the skiff.

'It just a flare,' he replied with a shrug.

Then they heard the whirr of rotor blades and a Seahawk helicopter armed with hellfire missiles thundered overhead.

CHAPTER 110

The assassin gazed out of his hotel window at the dusty, war-torn streets of Mogadishu. The building opposite, once the glamorous al-Uruba Hotel, was now a crumbling shell, pockmarked with the scars of gunfire. The bullet holes always held such fascination for the assassin. He could never understand why so many missed their target. He only ever needed one bullet.

He put on a fresh shirt, glad to be rid of all the lingering soot and reek of burnt chemicals following his escape from the flaming tanker. He held his fingers up to the light and picked at some residual grime. He hated dirt under his fingernails.

His phone rang. He answered it.

'Status report,' the caller demanded, the voice distorted by the encrypted line.

'Mission parameters were met. Mr Gibb is dead. Files wiped. *Australian Daily* editor silenced. All evidence destroyed.'

'But what about the ransom negotiations? Those came to a rather *unexpected* and premature end.'

The assassin continued to pick at his fingernails. 'Nothing to be concerned about. The hijacking accomplished what it set out to do. Mr Sterling is no longer a threat to the organization. The story is buried.'

'And the pirates?'

'Dead men tell no tales.'

'The Sterling girl lives. Is that a problem for us?'

A trace of a thin smile cut across the assassin's lips. 'My little sparrow served her purpose, so I wiped her memory of our encounter before freeing her. She knows nothing that could unbalance Equilibrium.'

The caller seemed to weigh up his answer, then said, 'We lost significant investment and risked unnecessary exposure as a result of Mr Gibb. Ensure our next investment is secure.'

'Of course.'

'And, Mr Grey, don't leave any loose ends.'

'I never do.'

'Nice suntan,' smirked Jason as Connor entered Buddy-guard's briefing room with Charley.

Where his fire-retardant clothing hadn't protected him, Connor had suffered first-degree burns escaping the blazing tanker. The skin on his face, arms and hands was still red and sore a week later, but healing well. 'Very funny. I must have used the wrong oil,' he replied.

Jason laughed. 'Welcome back, Connor. Sorry for the dropbear prank. I honestly didn't think you'd fall for it.'

After the turmoil of the past few weeks, Connor had forgotten all about that incident. 'Don't worry, I'll get you back one day,' he grinned.

Ling walked over. At first Connor thought she might hug him. Instead she bumped fists with him.

'I can't believe you blew up a tanker!' she exclaimed. 'Why am I never there for all the action?'

'I wish you had been,' replied Connor. 'I could've seriously done with your help.'

'I doubt that,' said Marc. 'I heard the fire was seen over twenty miles out at sea!'

Connor gave a sheepish grin. 'I needed a distraction to rescue the girls.'

'Some distraction!' Marc replied, holding up his hand and high-fiving him.

'So who's picking up the bill?' asked Amir, patting his friend gently on the shoulder.

Charley produced a letter headed with the official logo of Sempaku Shipping. 'Connor will be glad to learn the shipping company's insurance covers that little firework display.'

Amir frowned. 'I meant for all the gear I loaned Connor and he managed to destroy.'

'Hey, it wasn't my fault your smartphones aren't bulletproof,' pleaded Connor.

Amir sighed in exasperation. 'You're making a habit of getting shot. Perhaps we should just wrap you in a bulletproof bag?'

'Good idea,' said Richie. 'Then you could cover his ugly head!'

'Make sure Richie's bag is double-layered,' shot back Connor. 'Seriously though, Amir, your tech kit was a lifesaver. I couldn't have succeeded without it.'

'Connor's right,' said Colonel Black, striding into the briefing room. 'The success of an operation doesn't rely on a single bodyguard. It's the work of a whole team. Without the SART in his Go-bag, Connor and his Principals would have been recaptured by the pirates and most likely dead.'

'Well, I'm sure glad I stayed in wet and windy Wales then,' said Amir.

As Alpha team took their seats for the debrief, Connor asked, 'Have you had any news about Emily?'

The colonel nodded. 'I just received the report. It appears her somewhat *unusual* behaviour was the result of brainwashing, carried out during her captivity last year. The perpetrators of that kidnapping and this hijack must be linked – possibly as a way to extort money from Mr Sterling, or to gain control over him or his media companies, or both. But all this is speculation.'

'Has Emily been able to shed any light on it?' asked Charley.

The colonel shook his head. 'Even though we have proof of her communications from the photos she posted on her social network site, she doesn't remember anything about contacting the pirates. Nor does she recall locking Connor up. The knock to her head may have caused amnesia. But the doctor thinks she may never have been fully conscious of her actions in the first place.'

'How can that be?' asked Ling.

'Her captor could have programmed subliminal suggestions into her mind, hypnotism being the most likely method.'

'That's freaky,' muttered Richie. 'I hope nobody ever plays with my brain like that.'

'No chance,' said Ling. 'They'd have to find it first!'

Colonel Black silenced her with a stern look. 'The good news is that Emily is on the mend. Her doctor says she's responding well to treatment.'

'So who do you think is behind all this?' asked Jason.

'It has to be an international crime syndicate. There are several possibilities, but no firm leads.'

'What about the man I saw on the tanker?' asked Connor. 'Cali said he was the one ordering the handover to Seven Sabres.'

The colonel sighed. 'Your description of him was pretty vague. There's been no trace of him. We can only assume he died in the blaze.'

Connor wasn't so sure. The man struck him as a snake who could slip any net.

'Anyway, the Australian Federal Police are investigating the hijacking, so it's out of our hands now,' announced the colonel. 'But Mr Sterling is deeply grateful to us for rescuing his family, and the crew, *especially* without the need to pay a ransom.' Colonel Black raised an eyebrow and gave a wry smile. 'As a gesture of his appreciation, he's invited Alpha team to a private party to celebrate his marriage to Ms Ryder and his daughters' safe return.'

'Where's the party?' asked Ling eagerly. 'Not on a yacht, I hope.'

'Sydney. And we're flying first class all the way.'

CHAPTER 112

Mr Sterling had hired an entire island for the party.

Named after its shape rather than its marine life, Shark Island was a unique location for a celebration. Located at the eastern end of Sydney Harbour, it boasted spectacular views of the harbour bridge, opera house and Rose Bay. Connor couldn't think of a more ideal setting for a party brimming with famous film stars, musicians, supermodels and high-level politicians. Nor could a location be more secure. Being encircled by water, no one could approach the island undetected. And Mr Sterling hadn't spared any expense on security measures. Besides the high-profile close protection team patrolling the island, Connor's trained eye had spotted numerous covert bodyguards mingling among the guests.

'Is that who I think it is?' said Ling, nodding towards a suave, dark-haired man in a tailored suit.

Jason nodded. 'But he looks a lot shorter than he does in the movies.'

'I don't know where to look,' sighed Marc as his eyes bounced between all the fashion models sashaying past.

'Don't trip over your tongue, Marc,' said Charley, sipping from a glass of sparkling fruit juice.

Chloe and Emily walked towards them, dressed respectively in coral-pink and straw-yellow summer frocks.

'How are you enjoying the party?' asked Chloe.

'It's amazing. Never seen so many famous people,' Connor replied. 'Thanks for inviting us.'

'It's the least we could do.' Chloe turned to Ling with a repentant expression. 'I hope you can forgive our little disagreement. I realize now you were just doing your job.'

'Live and learn, eh?' said Ling coolly.

'We almost *didn't* live,' said Emily. 'That's why we're so grateful to Connor.'

The two sisters exchanged a glance, nodded at some unsaid agreement, then leant forward and kissed him on either cheek. Connor felt himself blush at the unexpected affection and noticed Charley glance over then quickly look away. He hoped he wouldn't be in trouble again.

'Hey, I supplied the equipment!' piped up Amir.

The girls laughed and kissed him too. Amir was momentarily lost for words.

Connor studied Emily's face. It seemed like a shadow had been lifted. 'You're looking well.'

'Thank you, I feel much better,' she replied, smiling freely. 'My head was so clouded before, always getting migraines. I thought it was the medication I was on. But that clearly wasn't the case. Now it's like sunshine has broken through. I can think . . . my own thoughts.'

Connor returned her smile. 'I'm glad you've found yourself again.'

He heard his name being called and turned to see a slim African boy among the partygoers. His white silk shirt looked a size too big for him, but he was no longer skin and bones. 'Cali! What are you doing here?'

Cali greeted him with a beaming smile. 'Mr Sterling arrange a visa for me.'

'I thought you wanted to go to South Africa.'

'Yes! Maybe on holiday. I live in Oz now,' he replied proudly.

The party went on all afternoon, taking full advantage of the glorious summer sunshine.

Connor and Ling were reunited with the *Orchid*'s crew, Captain Locke even greeting Connor with a salute. The crew members were relaxed and carefree, a world away from the trauma of the hijacking. But Connor noticed they all bore their scars, Jordan's being the most obvious, although he was more than happy to show a glamorous model his 'war wounds'. The rest of the crew's scars weren't so visible, just the occasional nervous twitch at the sound of a cork popping or Sophie's sad gaze as she looked across the water at the harbour bridge, no doubt thinking of Brad.

As dusk approached, Mr Sterling and Amanda – his new wife outdoing all the models in an ivory chiffon slit-gown – eventually broke from their socializing to thank Connor and the others in Alpha team.

'I always had faith in you, Connor,' said Mr Sterling,

warmly shaking his hand and beaming a silvery smile. 'Never once doubted that you'd deliver the goods and bring my Amanda and daughters safely home.'

'Thank you, sir,' replied Connor, although he caught the incredulous look on Charley's face.

Amanda graced him with a kiss, her heady perfume enveloping him as she leant into his cheek.

'You're one brave boy,' she said, ruffling his hair. 'If we have a son, I hope he grows up to be like you.'

She laid a protective hand over her belly, Mr Sterling beside her beaming with pride. Chloe and Emily exchanged surprised looks.

'You're *pregnant*?' asked Chloe.

Amanda nodded. 'Twelve weeks.'

'Congratulations,' said Emily. 'That's wonderful news.'

As word spread and guests clustered round to toast the new baby, Chloe leant close to Connor's ear.

'Fancy taking a trip in our speedboat?' she whispered, pointing at a sleek red boat moored at the end of the island's jetty.

'Shouldn't we ask your father first?' said Connor.

Chloe glanced at the crowd of well-wishers and shook her head. 'No, he's busy celebrating. And he won't mind.'

'But what about security?' asked Connor.

'Hey, I have you!' she said, taking his hand. 'And Ling can come too.'

'Now that sounds like my sort of fun,' said Ling, setting aside her glass of fresh lemonade.

'Emily, are you going to join us?' asked Connor.

'Sure. Why not?' she replied, clearly still trying to take in the news of their pregnant stepmother.

Chloe led the way down to the jetty.

'Want to drive, Ling? It's way faster than a jet ski.'

Ling grinned. 'Definitely. As long as this one doesn't explode!'

Jumping in, Ling settled into the pilot's seat, pressed the ignition and took them out into the harbour. She headed in the direction of the bridge, where the sun was beginning to dip through its arch.

'I can't believe Amanda's having a baby,' exclaimed Chloe. 'It's the first I knew about it.'

Emily glanced at Connor, then smiled at her sister. 'Do you know what? I'd actually quite like a brother.'

'Hey, let's see how fast *this* baby goes,' said Ling, driving the throttle forward.

The speedboat surged across the harbour, cutting through the water like an arrow. As they zoomed past another boat, Connor did a double take. The boat was being piloted by a bald-headed black man. And in the stern, removing his scuba gear and wetsuit, was a white man with a lion tattoo on his arm.

Todd Logan and *Doug Carter*.

The two men watched the Sterlings' speedboat pass by with an unsettling intensity.

Connor's sixth sense went into overdrive. He hunted round the boat.

'What's the matter?' said Emily. 'What are you looking for?'

Connor didn't really know until he glanced over the side and found it. On the speedboat's hull, just below the waterline, was a small black box with a transmitter. It could only be one thing.

'Bomb on board!' cried Connor.

The girls stared at him in shock and horror. But Ling reacted with a bodyguard's instinct. She threw the speedboat's throttle to its max, grabbed Chloe and dived over the side. Connor was a split second behind with Emily in his arms. They hit the water hard, plunging beneath the surface.

A moment later, the speedboat exploded.

Connor was sparring with Ling in the Buddyguard gymnasium when Charley entered and announced, 'Good news! Todd Logan and Doug Carter have been caught.'

Momentarily distracted by the news, Connor almost got his head knocked off by a roundhouse kick from Ling. He countered with a front-kick, then backed away to a safe distance. Amir rang the bell, pausing the boxing-ring timer at one minute and twenty-two seconds remaining. Connor wiped the sweat from his brow, while Ling took a slug from her water bottle.

'Where did they find them?' he asked, handing his towel back to Amir.

'It took a while, but the police tracked them down to a guesthouse near Broken Hill in the Australian Outback,' Charley replied. 'They've confessed to planting the bomb. Just as you thought, Connor, Todd had attached the device after the security teams had completed their sweep.'

'Have they said *why* they did it?' asked Ling.

'For the money. It was just another job as far as they were concerned.'

'So who hired them?' asked Connor.

Charley brought up a photo on her smartphone of a tanned middle-aged man with auburn hair. 'Mr Joseph Ward.'

'Mr Sterling's business rival!' gasped Amir. 'The one he exposed for corporate fraud.'

'The very same,' replied Charley. 'Ward blamed Mr Sterling for destroying his life and family. And he was determined to take his revenge on Mr Sterling's family. Eye for an eye, tooth for a tooth.'

'But isn't he still in jail?' said Ling.

'Yes. And guess where the two ex-cons both served their last sentences? Long Bay Prison. The same prison Ward is being held in.'

Amir frowned. 'But how did Ward pay them? When I was compiling Operation Gemini's threat report, the papers said all his assets had been seized by the courts.'

'As you know, Mr Sterling has *many* enemies. Not that it surprises me,' said Charley, raising an eyebrow. 'The disgraced politician Harry Gibb funded the criminal operation.'

'But he died of a suspected heart attack,' said Connor.

Charley nodded. 'Gibb had wanted revenge, for having his illegal dealings exposed by Mr Sterling's newspapers. However, he didn't have the necessary criminal contacts – whereas Ward did. Ward's now been charged with *multiple* counts of attempted murder, Todd and Doug having also admitted to sabotaging the jet skis.'

Connor and Ling exchanged astonished looks.

'Sorry, Connor,' said Ling, holding up her gloved hands in apology. 'Those dudes *were* in the Seychelles.'

'Does this mean Ward was also responsible for the hijacking?' asked Connor.

Charley shrugged. 'He denies knowing anything about that. The Australian Federal Police are investigating further, but we may never know the truth. I tell you one thing, though: Chloe and Emily were just innocent victims in this tangle of revenge against their father.'

'Those poor girls,' said Amir, touching his cheek where they'd both kissed him.

'They didn't do too badly,' said Ling. 'They had Connor protecting them.'

Connor grinned – that was the closest he'd get to a compliment from Ling. He allowed himself a moment to enjoy the feeling. But already Ling had raised her gloves into a fighting stance.

'Come on, hotshot. The round's not over yet.'

Amir rang the bell and restarted the timer. Connor needed to be on his guard – Ling *always* won her fights. But if his recent assignment had taught him one thing, it was that Charley's motto was true: *If you think you can, or think you can't, you're probably right*. So this time he was determined Ling wouldn't be the victor . . .

RANSOM

ACKNOWLEDGEMENTS

This is my tenth novel. And I can tell you the writing process doesn't get any easier. In fact, I believe it becomes harder. The bar to entertain, surprise and thrill the reader is set higher each time. That's why I continue to rely on so many people to ensure I deliver the best story I can. So I'd like to thank the following who have supported me from start to finish:

My long-suffering wife, Sarah, who has to manage the ebbs and flows of elation and despair that I experience when writing. My two wonderful sons, Zach and Leo, you are a constant inspiration for me. My mum and dad who diligently help to proofread all my drafts. Sue and Simon for helping with the boys and keeping our garden looking lovely. Steve and Sam for taking the boys swimming; and Karen and Rob for being such wonderful friends.

Charlie Viney, my agent, who has my best interests at heart all the time. Clemmie Gaisman and Nicky Kennedy at ILA. Pippa Le Quesne for her insightful advice.

My team of loyal Puffin editors: Alex Antscherl, Shannon Cullen, Wendy Shakespeare and Helen Gray.

A special thanks must go to Abdilahi Nur and his mother for checking the Somali translation. *Mahadsanid*.

Trevor Wilson and Shelley Lee at Authors Abroad for all their diligent work in organizing my book tours around the world.

And all my good friends for their encouragement and support, including but not exclusive to Geoff and Lucy, Matt, Charlie, Jackie and Russell, the members of the HGC (Dan, Siggy, Larry, Dean, Giles), my cousin Laura and the Dyson clan (especially my god-daughter Lulu!).

Stay safe.
Chris

Any fans can keep in touch with me and the progress of the Bodyguard series on my Facebook page, or via the website at *www.bodyguard-books.com*

BE READY FOR

BODYGUARD
AMBUSH

COMING
MAY
2015

HUNTER.
KILLER.
SURVIVOR.

Connor's **MISSION**:
to protect a foreign ambassador's
family on safari in Africa.

Considered the **PERFECT** assignment, the holiday turns
to hell when their convoy is ambushed by gunmen.

FLEEING through the bush, Connor and his assigned
family become the prey in a **SHOOT-TO-KILL** hunt
across the African plains.

As they fight for their **SURVIVAL**, Connor realizes
the gunmen are the least of their problems.

For no amount of **BODYGUARD TRAINING**
can prepare him for the wilds of Africa and one prowling
hungry leopard . . .

YOUNG SAMURAI

BLACK-BELT NINJAS & BLOCKBUSTER ACTION

 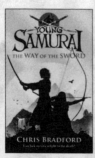  

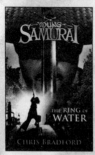   

www.youngsamurai.com

WANT MORE ACTION? MORE ADVENTURE? MORE ADRENALIN?

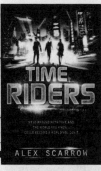

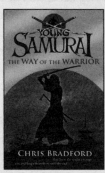

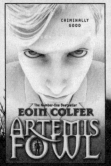

GET INTO PUFFIN'S ADVENTURE BOOKS FOR BOYS

It all started with a Scarecrow

Puffin is over seventy years old.
Sounds ancient, doesn't it? But Puffin has never been
so lively. We're always on the lookout for the next big
idea, which is how it began all those years ago.

Penguin Books was a big idea from the mind of
a man called Allen Lane, who in 1935 invented
the quality paperback and changed the world.
**And from great Penguins, great Puffins grew,
changing the face of children's books forever.**

The first four Puffin Picture Books were hatched in 1940 and the
first Puffin story book featured a man with broomstick arms called
Worzel Gummidge. In 1967 Kaye Webb, Puffin Editor, started the
Puffin Club, promising to **'make children into readers'**.
She kept that promise and over 200,000 children became devoted
Puffineers through their quarterly instalments of *Puffin Post*.

Many years from now, we hope you'll look back and
remember Puffin with a smile. **No matter what your age
or what you're into, there's a Puffin for everyone.**
The possibilities are endless, but one thing is for sure:
whether it's a picture book or a paperback, a sticker book
or a hardback, **if it's got that little Puffin
on it – it's bound to be good.**